For Ka[i]
Enjoy the Adventure.

THE ALCHEMIST'S MAP

JASON LEE WILLIS

For Kattina,
Enjoy the adventure!

[signature]

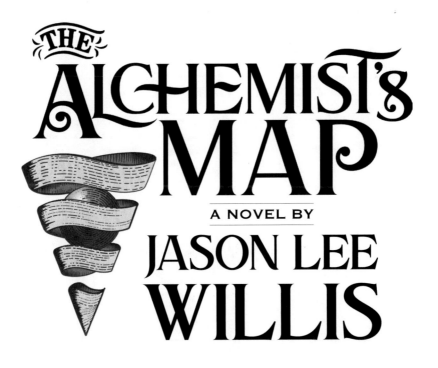

THE ALCHEMIST'S MAP

A NOVEL BY
JASON LEE WILLIS

FOX POINTE PUBLISHING

This book is a work of fiction. Names, characters, places, and incidents are products of the author's imagination or are used fictitiously. Any resemblance to actual events or locales or persons, living or dead, is entirely coincidental.

Between 1831 and 1839, Joseph Nicollet mapped regions of Georgia and the upper Mississippi watershed. The Alchemist's Map is a fictitious account of these expeditions.

During his scientific travels, Nicollet studied the cultures of the Sioux and Chippewa. Please note that, to remain true to the era, the historic nomenclature for these cultures are used in this novel. Please refer to the index for an overview of indigenous names and terms.

Copyright © 2021 by Jason Lee Willis

All rights reserved. Published in the United States by Fox Pointe Publishing, LLP. No part of this book may be reproduced in any form or by any electronic or mechanical means, including information storage and retrieval systems, without permission in writing from the publisher.

www.foxpointepublishing.com/author-jason-lee-willis

Library of Congress Cataloging-in-Publication Data
Willis, Jason Lee, author.
Farr, Chelsea, editor.
Hudson, Becca, designer.
The Alchemist's Map / Jason Lee Willis. – First edition.
Summary: An astronomer follows clues left in an ancient map to find the Philosopher's Stone and ends up becoming an oppositional force to Manifest Destiny in mid-19th century America.
ISBN (hardcover) 978-1-952567-36-0 / (softcover) 978-1-952567-37-7
[1. Historical Fantasy – Fiction. 2. Native American – Fiction. 3. Mythology – Fiction. 4. Action & Adventure – Fiction.]
Library of Congress Control Number: 2021900989

Printed and bound in the United States of America by Lakeside Press Inc.
First printing February 2021

For my Uncle Dave, teacher and storyteller,
who took the cousins for walks along the Minnesota River Valley,
pointing out ancient rock formations
and places where Bigfoot often hid.

To him, I dedicate this work of fantasy, science, and history.

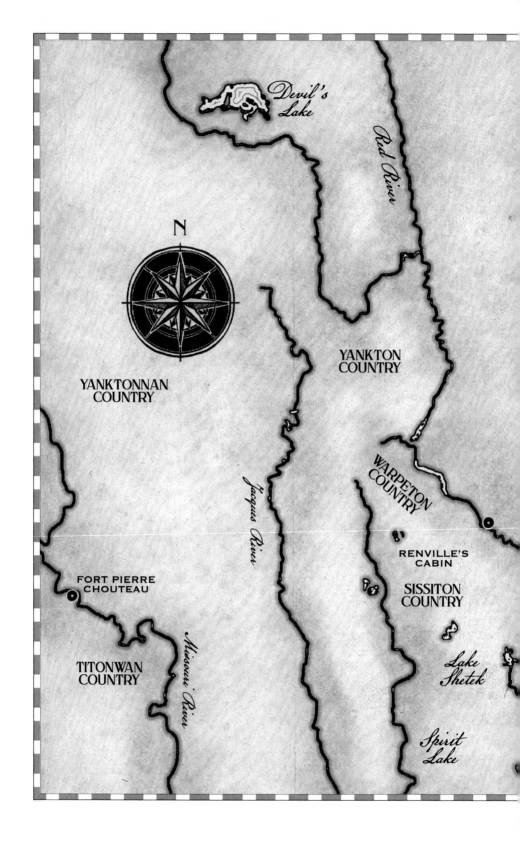

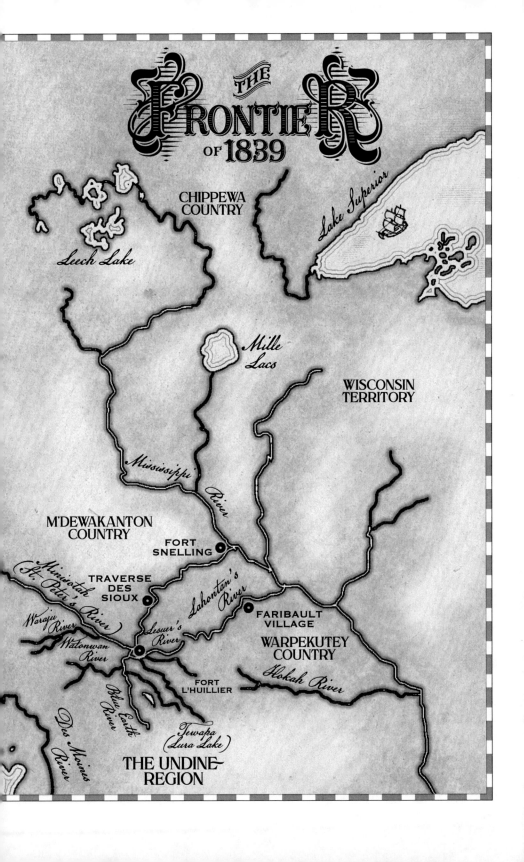

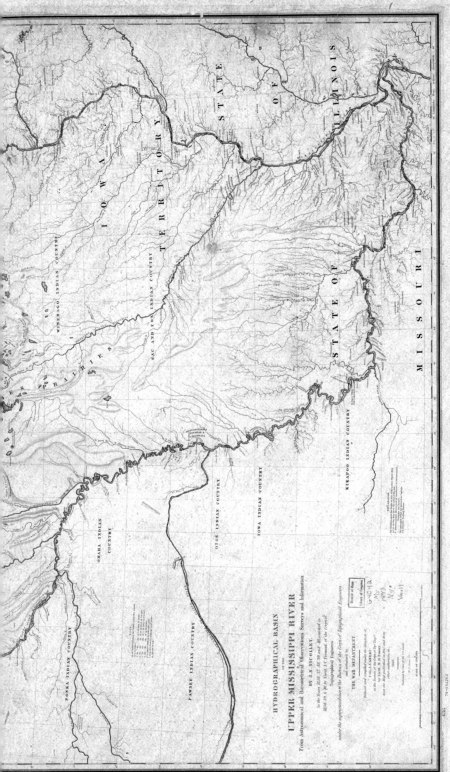

Nicollet, J.N. (Joseph Nicolas). *Map of the Hydrographical Basin of the Upper Mississippi.* Published by order of the U.S. Senate, 1843.

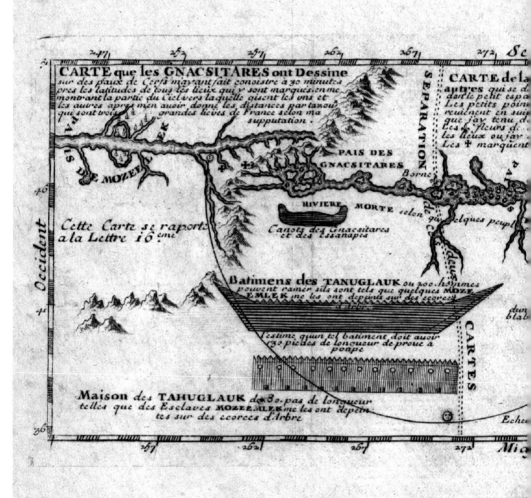

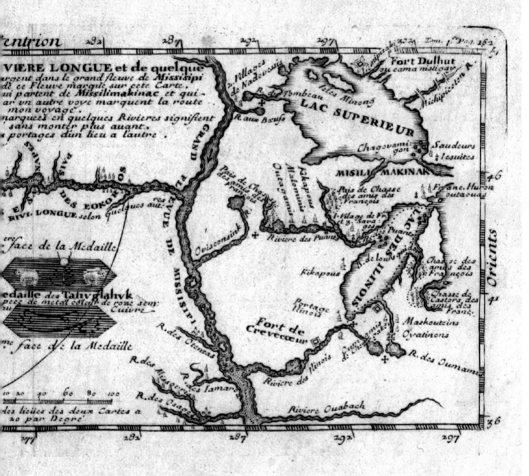

Lahontan, Baron de. *Carte de la riviere Longue*. La Haye, Netherlands, 1703

TABLE OF CONTENTS

Maps				*viii-xi*
Prologue	*Paris, France*	1830		1
Chapter 1	*Paris, France*	1830		6
Chapter 2	*Le Havre, France*	1830		15
Chapter 3	*Paris, France*	1830		18
Chapter 4	*Paris, France*	1830		25
Chapter 5	*Paris, France*	1830		30
Chapter 6	*Rouen, France*	1830		38
Chapter 7	*Murthly Castle, Scotland*	1830		47
Chapter 8	*Paris, France*	1830		53
Chapter 9	*New York*	1831		62
Chapter 10	*District of Columbia*	1831		72
Chapter 11	*Paris, France*	1831		79
Chapter 12	*District of Columbia*	1831		82
Chapter 13	*District of Columbia*	1831		86
Chapter 14	*Santee River*	1833		93
Chapter 15	*Santee Hills*	1833		100
Chapter 16	*St. Louis*	1835		107
Chapter 17	*St. Louis*	1835		115
Chapter 18	*St. Louis*	1835		120
Chapter 19	*St. Louis*	1835		125
Chapter 20	*Florissant Valley*	1835		131
Chapter 21	*Pelican Island*	1835		138
Chapter 22	*St. Louis*	1836		144
Chapter 23	*Fort Snelling*	1836		149
Chapter 24	*Fort Snelling*	1836		160
Chapter 25	*Fort Snelling*	1836		163

Chapter 26	*Anoka*	1836	169
Chapter 27	*Crow Wing River*	1836	176
Chapter 28	*Crow Wing River*	1836	186
Chapter 29	*Lake Manito*	1836	188
Chapter 30	*Lake Manito*	1836	196
Chapter 31	*Lake Manito*	1836	200
Chapter 32	*Leech Lake*	1836	203
Chapter 33	*Leech Lake*	1836	206
Chapter 34	*Lake Itasca*	1836	213
Chapter 35	*Fort Snelling*	1836	219
Chapter 36	*Madeline Island*	1837	226
Chapter 37	*Namekagon River*	1837	233
Chapter 38	*Albany, NY*	1838	238
Chapter 39	*Mitu'tahakto's*	1838	243
Chapter 40	*St. Louis*	1838	246
Chapter 41	*Fort Snelling*	1838	250
Chapter 42	*Swan Lake*	1838	255
Chapter 43	*Pipestone*	1838	265
Chapter 44	*Pipestone*	1838	272
Chapter 45	*Grand Oasis*	1838	277
Chapter 46	*The Coteau des Prairies*	1838	282
Chapter 47	*Lake Poinsett*	1838	286
Chapter 48	*Two Lakes*	1838	289
Chapter 49	*Lac Qui Parle*	1838	295
Chapter 50	*Murthly Castle, Scotland*	1838	300
Chapter 51	*The Haunted Valley*	1838	303
Chapter 52	*Blue Earth River*	1838	309
Chapter 53	*Fort L'Huillier*	1838	313
Chapter 54	*Fort L'Huillier*	1838	320
Chapter 55	*Albany, New York*	1838	324
Chapter 56	*Faribault Village*	1838	327
Chapter 57	*The Haunted Valley*	1838	335
Chapter 58	*The Haunted Valley*	1838	338
Chapter 59	*Lura Lake*	1838	344
Chapter 60	*Lura Lake*	1838	353
Chapter 61	*Detroit*	1839	359

Chapter 62	Fort Pierre	1839	363
Chapter 63	Standing Rock	1839	367
Chapter 64	Devil's Lake	1839	371
Chapter 65	Devil's Lake	1839	376
Chapter 66	Fort Snelling	1839	380
Chapter 67	Georgetown	1839	386
Chapter 68	Rome	1841	391
Chapter 69	District of Columbia	1841	395
Chapter 70	District of Columbia	1841	401
Chapter 71	Cambridge	1842	405
Chapter 72	District of Columbia	1843	410
Chapter 73	Platte River	1843	415
Chapter 74	Boston	1843	418
Chapter 75	Baltimore	1843	421
Chapter 76	Baltimore	1843	425
Chapter 77	Baltimore	1843	430
Chapter 78	Cambridge	1844	435
Chapter 79	Rome	1846	438
Chapter 80	Detroit	1846	443
Chapter 81	Detroit	1846	452
Chapter 82	Detroit	1846	454
Chapter 83	Detroit	1846	457
Chapter 84	Charleston	1850	461
Chapter 85	Fort Sumter	1850	464
Chapter 86	Murthly Castle, Scotland	1851	468
Chapter 87	Santee Hills	1851	470
Chapter 88	Santee Hills	1851	473
Chapter 89	Santee Hills	1851	477
Chapter 90	Santee Hills	1851	479
Epilogue	Lake Manito	1852	484

Author's Note	490
Acknowledgments	492
Cast of Characters	494
Indigenous Names and Terms	501
Discussion Questions	505
About the Author	510

PROLOGUE

PARIS, FRANCE
1830

So the rumors about the map are true.

Lady Margaret Drummond smiled as she stood outside the door of the Paris Observatory. She waited for her tall footman to raise the parasol to shield her from the afternoon sun. She didn't have to wait long; Whitmore might have been a brute, but his strong hands were deft with the delicate lever on the parasol.

Once in the shadow, Lady Drummond looked for the carriage, but it was no longer parked at the end of the newly paved walkway. Instead, a dozen French soldiers stood at the front gate. "Whitmore, where is our carriage?"

"The driver was forced to move it around the block, Milady. It is parked over there," Whitmore said and pointed.

A strong metal fence surrounded the entire observatory complex, isolating it from the city and Lady Drummond from her carriage.

"I am an old woman! Who had the audacity to force us to move the carriage?" Lady Drummond snapped.

"I apologize, Milady, but King Charles is coming to the observatory tonight."

"King Charles is coming *here*?" Lady Drummond asked.

"It would seem so, Milady. Shortly after you entered the observatory, soldiers came to secure the entire block. It took quite a bit of explanation for them to not chase me off. Apparently, King Charles has questions about Halley's Comet and wanted Professor Nicollet to explain it to him."

Lady Drummond's eyebrow rose at the thought. *The signature of Professor Nicollet is suddenly worth even more.* "What did you say to them?"

"I told them you were meeting with Professor Nicollet to discuss matters of astronomy, and that we would be returning to our hotel within the hour."

Lady Drummond glanced down at the cylindrical case she held in her hands. "Good. I'm surprised King Charles is still residing in Paris, considering the political turmoil he is facing."

Near the side gate where the carriage now waited, she saw a pair of soldiers standing in the shade of a young oak.

"Did your meeting with Professor Nicollet go well, Milady?" Whitmore asked as they walked.

"It did," Lady Drummond found herself smiling after a moment of reflection. "Nicollet is an excitable fellow who seems incapable of giving a succinct answer, but he provided all the verification I need to fetch a higher price."

THE ALCHEMIST'S MAP

"With your permission, Milady, when we return to the hotel, I'd like to pay a visit to this antiquities dealer, Monsieur Beranger."

"I'd rather deal with Beranger myself."

"Of course, Milady, but I'd like to investigate the Fontaine de L'Elephant neighborhood and watch over his shop for a while. I won't speak with the man. I just want to make sure you'll be safe."

Safe? How much does Whitmore know about this map? The sooner it is out of my life, the better. "Yes, I suppose once we return to the hotel, you could investigate matters for me."

The two soldiers opened the gate for them as they passed to the street, and before Whitmore could even put away the parasol, the carriage door flew open.

"What took you so long?" The saucy question came from Lady Drummond's teenage niece, Susan, who had waited in the carriage with the driver and a small fortune in new dresses and shoes.

Remember, you're selling it for the family. "Professor Nicollet was thorough in his examination of the map, as well as his certificate of authenticity."

"Which means you'll get more money for it?" Susan asked, extending a hand to help her aunt into the carriage.

"Money that will be used to sustain the estate, not to fill your closets," Lady Drummond amended.

At Whitmore's insistence, they drove through Paris with the curtains drawn until they returned to the relative safety of their hotel.

Le Pavillion de la Reine hotel had all the finest amenities a wealthy tourist such as Lady Drummond might want. It was situated in the Marais, on one of Paris's loveliest squares. It had private dining and a spacious lobby for its aristocratic guests, yet was located near some of the best shopping districts, which appealed to Susan. The duplex suite on the top floor, which Lady Drummond had chosen, had beautiful décor, an elegant bathroom, four-poster beds—and a state-of-the-art safe.

Susan reached for the doorknob and found it locked. "Do you have the key, Aunt Maggie?"

Whitmore set the packages on the floor and handed the key to Susan. "Lady Drummond, could I get the address of Beranger's shop?"

"Of course," she said, and handed him the map canister so she could open her purse. Along with the papers from Professor Nicollet, she found the letters she'd exchanged with Beranger and other antiquity dealers, both in France and England.

"Gerard Beranger
Fontaine de L'Éléphant
117 Rue de la Contrescarpe"

"Thank you, Lady Drummond. I will call on you when I return."

"Thank you, Whitmore."

Susan carried the shopping bags into the suite while Lady Drummond clutched the canister. Once all the bags were inside, she bolted the door.

If what Nicollet said is true, this map was the oldest item in my brother's collection.

"What do you want me to do with your new shoes?" Susan asked from the pile of bags.

"Just put them on the table. I'll come look at them in just a bit." Lady Drummond walked to the other room.

"Do you want help with the safe?" Susan called out loudly.

"I'll just be a moment."

"Are you sure?"

"I know what I'm doing," Lady Drummond answered sharply.

She didn't.

With the balcony curtains closed, it took her three attempts at the dial to unlock the safe, but then the big hinges creaked loudly.

THE ALCHEMIST'S MAP

Lady Drummond sat on the rug in front of the open safe, her back to the doorway. She set the map and her purse at her side. Now open, the three-foot-tall floor safe revealed its pathetic contents: two jewelry boxes and a fat wallet of money.

I have no choice but to sell this map after my brother squandered our family fortune. What good does it do us if our castle crumbles around us from disrepair?

Thinking of her selfish niece, she suddenly became aware that the rustling of shopping bags had stopped.

Then she heard a soft whimper.

Turning, Lady Drummond saw a man wearing a gentleman's outfit and polished shoes, standing with a gloved hand over Susan's mouth and the other hand holding a double-edged knife at her niece's throat.

If she hadn't already been sitting on the floor, Lady Drummond might have fainted.

The man removed the knife from Susan's throat for a moment, holding it out and up as a sign of parlay. The gesture revealed that two of his fingers had been removed, leaving him with a delicate grasp on the hilt.

A thief.

Lady Drummond watched as the three-fingered man pointed to the metal cylinder in front of her.

"Open it," he said, softly but firmly.

She complied, and from the soft velvet interior of the tube, a yellowed map emerged, wrapped in wax paper. All of Nicollet's verifications and assessments now came to nothing.

"Good. Now put it back in the cylinder and roll it over to me," the man instructed.

This is my family's fortune. How do I let this thief just walk away with it?

Lady Drummond nodded, and the map vanished back into the

tube, which she sealed and set on the floor.

Without Whitmore to protect them, she knew it fell on her to not only protect Susan but the entire House of Drummond.

Even though her hands shook, Lady Drummond managed a coordinated roll and the tube traveled over the rug and onto the bare floor, stopping just a few feet from where the three-fingered man stood.

As he glanced down at the cylinder, Lady Drummond slipped her hand into her purse. Just under the papers from Nicollet, she had a small pistol for just such an occasion.

Her hand found the cold curve of the grip, but as she looked back up to aim, the knife flew from the man's hand directly toward her face.

The world exploded with blinding pain and she saw the floor rush up to crash against her cheek. Her body began to twitch and move like a marionette upon unseen strings.

The dull crunch of breaking bones and a soft thud came right before she heard footsteps coming closer.

CHAPTER ONE

PARIS, FRANCE
1830

The cave wall turned and beyond a bend, pale light illuminated the rocky path. With each cautious step and tentative reach, the source of the light became obvious.

A woman trapped in ice.

Joseph Nicollet studied her face on the other side of the opaque sheet of ice, which stood floor to ceiling at the end of the cave. Her placid face and closed eyes gave the impression of sleep instead of death, and her white gown moved in the gentle currents of the water suspending her.

Her eyes opened.

Nicollet gasped and stepped away from the sheet of ice, then, just as quickly, rushed forward to place his palms upon the frigid surface.

"Where did you go?" she asked him.

It's not her, Nicollet told himself. *She did not have blue eyes.*

Her hair flowed in the water and the light made it vary from shades of light blonde to deep burgundy. Her face held the prime of youth, white and without blemish. "Why didn't you look for me?"

"I did look for you," Nicollet answered, the ice melting under his palms. In its reflection, he saw himself as a vibrant young man in plain garb—trousers, suspenders, a white shirt. "I've found you."

"No," she said, "You have forgotten me. But it's not too late. Come and find me, Nicky."

Her form withdrew from the ice until she was only a light in the darkness.

Nicollet reached down to the floor of the cave, picked up a heavy stone, and smashed it against the ice.

He struck it again.

And again.

Finally, it broke through the ice, but a torrent of water swept him away and back down into the darkness of the cave.

Joseph Nicollet awoke to the sound of ticking. His tired eyes slowly focused on the far wall of his living room where the chorus of periodic clicks echoed. Still clothed in his dinner jacket, he reached into the pocket of his vest and found his father's watch.

Almost two o'clock in the morning, Nicollet noted. *Why can't I sleep?*

A few lamps had gone out, but his house remained well-lit, casting a glow on the remnants of the evening's celebration. He sat on one end of the couch with a beautiful young woman leaning against him, while an

THE ALCHEMIST'S MAP

equally handsome young man slept on the other end. He slid out gently, resting the woman's blonde head on the tall arm of the couch.

Because of the alcohol still in his system, it took a few moments for him to find his balance, but he held a steady course to the far wall behind the piano where twelve clocks hung. One by one, he compared each clock against his pocket watch until he found the Bavarian cuckoo clock to be the mistimed culprit.

In the glass of his sixteenth-century Italian wall clock, Nicollet caught his own reflection. At forty-seven, he still had a youthful face and dark curly hair, even though his career was far from healthy. Around his neck, he wore the Lalande medal, although it might as well have been a professional noose. Instead of a panel of peers, the medal had been given by the government of King Charles, and despite dozens of friends who helped celebrate the accomplishment, he could see in their eyes it further tarnished his waning reputation. He took it off and tossed it aside.

Leaning against the piano where his violin now rested, Nicollet watched the second hands spin around the clocks until a symphony of chimes brought the top of the hour.

"What time is it?"

Back on the couch, Juliana Leeves stirred without opening her eyes. Her brother Charlie remained unconscious.

"It's late," Nicollet said to her, and as he walked back toward the couch, his toe hit a bottle, spinning it wildly across the floor.

Juliana opened her eyes. "Are you mad at me?"

"Of course not," he said, pulling the blanket up to her shoulders. She gently kissed his hand and he stroked her blonde hair. "Tomorrow is a new day. Go back to sleep."

My world is changing too quickly.

Nicollet gathered wine glasses, smiling at the memories of each holder. Tonight, while he and John Herschel played music, Juliana

Leeves and Margaret Herschel danced for a crowd of scientists, intellectuals, and philosophers.

I can't leave such a mess for Cosette, Nicollet decided, knowing his hired maid would be arriving at the break of dawn to cook his breakfast.

The door to the kitchen remained closed, keeping the hedonistic spill from ruining the kitchen. With his hands full of wine glasses, Nicollet leaned his back against the door to push it open.

"A fine party."

The voice startled him, and a stray wineglass fell to the floor and broke into a hundred pieces.

A bearded Frenchman sat at the small kitchen table with notebooks and documents spread over it.

"Shouldn't you be home with Rosine?" Nicollet asked, carefully setting the rest of the wine glasses on the counter.

The forty-year-old man sitting at his table was his friend, Jean-François Champollion, the curator of the Louvre Museum, who'd just returned from Egypt with crates of antiquities and an unseemly beard that reached to the middle of his chest. "Absence makes the heart grow fonder. We all can't be wildly in love like you and Juliana."

This is going to hurt more than I thought. "Juliana is returning to England to marry Edward Sabine," Nicollet said before turning his attention to the shards of glass on the floor.

"Say it isn't so!" Champollion said. "She certainly has a thing for aging astronomers. But, but... Juliana adores you."

"She adores attention," Nicollet said, allowing himself a little bitterness. "The two of us have a mutual infatuation with science. I shall miss her company, though."

"So it will be Charlie?"

Nicollet laughed heartily. "No, sweet Charlie will also be returning to England with his sister. Between my tarnished reputation and the

THE ALCHEMIST'S MAP

tensions in Paris, Mr. Leeves thought it best they return home. They offered me a cottage for the summer."

"You should accept," Champollion said a bit too eagerly.

Nicollet stopped tidying to study his friend. "I hardly noticed you tonight. What are you doing at my kitchen table?"

"Planning a new revolution," Champollion said, raising his thick eyebrows playfully.

Honesty wrapped in sarcasm?

While Nicollet's career in astronomy had been built with what remained of the Ancien Régime—noblemen, clergymen, and members of royalty, Jean-François Champollion's career gained international renown during the reign of Napoléon, and even afterwards, when he deciphered the famed Rosetta Stone, unlocking the Egyptian hieroglyphic language for the first time in millennia.

Although friends, Champollion remained a symbol of science freed from the shackles of the Church while Nicollet was an enigma—a devout Catholic scientist.

"Alas, I have nothing to offer your cause other than fine wine," Nicollet remained cordial. "And it seems as if even the wine is now gone."

"I've heard rumors of your financial difficulties," Champollion said, gathering up the papers. "With the death of Laplace, your career is falling faster than a shooting star. But you are a man of true talent. You'll land on your feet. Do you remember how that plagiarism scandal almost ruined me? You will soon recover, but you might want to recover in England."

Is that a threat or a warning?

Champollion quickly gathered up his paperwork and shoved it all in a satchel. "I will leave you to your domestic duties and show myself out."

"If I left for England, I would miss all of our conversations about the occult world," Nicollet said. He followed his guest out of the kitchen and back into the main room. "There are few scientists with such wild tales of spooks and specters."

"The world is full of mystery," Champollion said as he passed by Juliana Leeves. "There is magic out there still to be discovered."

That is what Humboldt said, too. Nicollet followed him out onto the dark steps facing the silent streets of the Savoy district, nestled a few blocks from the Seine River.

Champollion looked up to the night sky. "So where is your comet?"

"It won't be visible for another five years," Nicollet said of Halley's Comet, upon which his wobbling reputation still stood. "But it is out there."

Champollion nodded and began walking.

"Do the Egyptians write of comets?" Nicollet's question caused Champollion to stop. "I've found accounts from Chinese historians that seem to align with the timing of Halley's Comet."

"I'm sure accounts will be found," Champollion said, standing near the big elm in Nicollet's small front yard. "The Egyptians used stars for aligning the pyramids. The ancients understood astronomy better than crusty Irish astronomers like Edward Sabine."

"Yes, in fact, I'd like to speak with you about Mesopotamia. What do you know about Phoenician astronomy?" *Did I rush the question? I should have waited for another time.*

"Well, Phoenician culture advanced during the same time period as Egyptian culture, so there are quite a few—"

Nicollet heard it also.

Snoring in the darkness.

It came from the deep shadows of the elm tree's trunk, nearer Champollion.

In a flash, Champollion had a pistol drawn, and with three quick steps, he vanished into the shadows.

THE ALCHEMIST'S MAP

A groan followed a hard kick.

"Who are you?" Champollion asked. "What are you doing here?"

"Please, sir. I am unarmed," a young man's voice answered in a panic.

"Nicollet, fetch a light," Champollion ordered.

Nicollet spun back around, running back inside to grab the lamp on the stairway post leading to the second floor. When he stepped back outside, Champollion pulled the stranger to the steps with his left hand while pointing the pistol in his face with his right.

"Who are you?" Champollion asked the young man, who appeared no older than fourteen.

"Louis Sejan."

"Who sent you to spy on this house?"

"I'm not spying," Sejan said. "I was sent to deliver a message to Professor Nicollet."

Oh dear. "I am Nicollet."

"I was sent by Father Simmons," Sejan said.

"Just what I thought," Champollion said. "A spy of the Catholic Church."

"I'm not a spy. I'm the son of the organist at St. Sulpice. Father Simmons sent me to collect Professor Nicollet, but when I arrived, there were so many people that I decided to wait until everyone left, but... then I fell asleep."

"I don't believe him," Champollion said. "He was sent here to keep track of those at your party. Empty your pockets!"

The boy had no weapons, no writing utensils, yet did have a folded letter, which Champollion held up to Nicollet's lamp. "Who is Lady Drummond?"

Again? What did I get involved in? The ghost of the murdered noblewoman already haunted him. "She contacted me a few months ago about matters of astronomy, and three days ago, she visited my office at the observatory to have me inspect an astronomical item."

"She was murdered?" Champollion added after looking at the letter again.

"Yes, the police came and asked me questions about her, and they told me she was killed during a robbery. Luckily, I was entertaining King Charles and Cardinal Croÿ-Solre."

"So who is this Father Simmons?" Champollion asked.

"I have no idea," Nicollet said to Champollion. He then turned to the boy, extending a hand to help the lad off the ground. "I take mass at St. Sulpice, so I'm familiar with your father, but who is this Father Simmons?"

The terrified boy kept darting his eyes at Champollion. "Yesterday was the first time I've ever met him. I saw him speak with Bishop De Quélen and then he left. I swear I wasn't spying."

"You should hurry home," Nicollet said to the boy. "Tell your father that you delivered the letter and that I will give it my full attention."

The boy ran down the walkway and vanished beyond the yard wall.

"A murder investigation?" Champollion asked. "Your streak of bad luck continues. For your sake, I'd avoid meeting with any Catholic officials in the near future, even those at St. Sulpice."

My sake? Dear François, what awful plans are you and your friends hatching? Nicollet tried to focus on the common ground he shared with his radical friend. "I'd like to speak with you about the map Lady Drummond showed me. It was quite curious."

"Curious enough for an old lady to be murdered? When life allows it, stop by and visit me at the Louvre."

When life allows?

Champollion nodded earnestly before glancing over his shoulder. "I think I'm still a little drunk. If you could point me in the direction of my museum, I'd be in your debt."

Nicollet pointed in the direction of the Seine and watched his friend vanish into the darkness.

CHAPTER TWO

LE HAVRE, FRANCE

1830

One hundred miles away in the port city of Le Havre, Jacques Palissy clamored for his pistol after three loud knocks on the door woke him.

The young man walked through his living room and glanced at the clock hanging on the wall. One o'clock. *A knock this late at night means trouble.*

On the large kitchen table, he saw two dozen letters still spread out on the table and rushed over to scoop them all up and shove them in a nearby satchel. He cocked the pistol and approached the door from the side.

"Who is it?" he asked, feeling vulnerable in only his breeches.

"Open the door, Palissy," a man answered in French yet with a strange accent.

The Russian.

It had been a month since Palissy had last seen him, and his hand shook as it reached for the chain, bolt, and door lock. Even when he opened the door a few inches, he kept the pistol ready.

Three fingers gripped the outer doorknob and opened it the rest of the way, revealing the cold eyes of Krasdan Krai, who held something other than a weapon in his other hand.

Krai stepped into the small apartment, closed the door, and locked himself in with Palissy.

"Is that what I think it is?" Palissy asked, hoping the information he'd given the Russian was about to be rewarded with promotion and not murder.

"Come see for yourself," Krai said as he walked over to the table. From the metal cylinder, he carefully extracted the wax paper, which he gently unrolled to reveal an ornate map.

An honest to goodness treasure map, Palissy thought. *The letters from England were true.*

"There is a change of plans," Krai said as he studied the lands drawn on the map.

Hearing this, Palissy felt himself squeezing the pistol grip tighter, ready to defend himself against the assassin.

"Your services at La Poste are no longer needed," Krai straightened his back, glanced at the pistol, and then into Palissy's eyes. "I'm going to need you to bring this map to America for me."

Relief, confusion, and despair flooded over him when he realized Krai had not come to murder him. "What about you?"

Krai's dark eyes studied him without a fleck of emotion. "We can trust you, can't we?"

THE ALCHEMIST'S MAP

"Of course you can," Palissy said, "but..."

"Our benefactor will find you a new career in America. If you want to remain a postman, pick a city. He's a powerful man, and when you hand this over to him, he'll give you a deserving reward."

"You're staying in France?"

"The influence of the Drummond family has waned recently," Krai assessed. "But there will be investigations into Lady Drummond's death, and our benefactor will not want any loose ends."

Palissy looked down at the ornate case holding a stolen map to an uncertain prize.

Yes, I'll go to America, he thought, *and then vanish before this psychopath decides I am also a loose end.*

CHAPTER THREE

PARIS, FRANCE

1830

The French Revolution of 1830, later known as the July Revolution, took place over three sweltering days in late July when members of the Ancien Régime were vacationing and the workers in the city were miserable. The explosion of violence had been festering for six years from an even older wound. King Charles of the House of Bourbon had inherited his throne from his brother and had immediately begun pandering to the Catholic Church and supporters of the Ancien Régime. When King Charles suspended the freedom of the press, fifty journalists had signed a collective protest and sparked a second revolution.

During the first day of riots, the Garde Royale patrolled the streets during the day, but by night, cries against the aristocrats and ministers

THE ALCHEMIST'S MAP

and calls for the guillotine filled the streets. After failed negotiations, the riot turned into a revolution by the second day.

Four thousand barricades were erected in the Parisian streets, keeping any military support from rushing in to crush the riots. The tri-colored flag soon flew throughout the city as the last bastions of the Ancien Régime were swept away. By midmorning, the Swiss Guards ran from their posts at the Louvre. Next, the Palace of Justice on the Île de la Cité fell to the crowds, followed by the Archbishop's Palace. Across the Seine, both the Hôtel de Ville and Tuileries Palace fell by midafternoon.

Several blocks from the fighting, Gerard Beranger prepared to defend his shop against looters, liberals, and aristocrats alike.

Anyone who steps through my doors tonight deserves death, he decided.

For the mob, Beranger carried a fowling gun, a hunting rifle used to take down birds. One pull of the trigger could wound a dozen men. While the rioters had swept through the district looking for chairs, desks, and tables to create barricades in the streets to prevent the military sweeping, Beranger had created his own barricade at the entrance to his shop.

Now, a dozen full whiskey barrels, imported from Tennessee, formed a wall across the large shop window and entrance door, something he could reasonably patrol by himself.

He peered through the gaps between the barrels for a glimpse out into the streets. Although there had been a lot of shooting, shouting, and destruction, all that remained now was a mess of debris in the streets. Everyone who had not joined the riot had hunkered down, remembering the bloodbaths of the previous revolution. Reinforcements from the military did not concern him. He didn't even give too much thought to the liberal mob trying to take control of the government. Beranger was mostly worried about his enemies.

They will come under cover of darkness.

His shop faced the street of a shopping district, but the back of his shop had access to a canal, where goods, both legal and illegal, could be brought in from the four corners of the world.

While the most transparent funds came from imported alcohol, he also sold more exotic wares. A small staircase led to his modest three-room apartment above the shop, where he guarded his more expensive products.

His barricade made it almost impossible to see the staircase, and if a large crowd did come seeking access to the alcohol, he would offer it to them rather than die for a few beverages. Upstairs, however, was a veritable apothecary shop of internationally sourced drugs.

Laudanum, opium, exotic tobaccos, powders, pastes, and even poisons from sellers across the seven seas had become the backbone of his business. It was a collection that had taken twenty years to acquire, hence the need for the fowling gun.

The back door had also been barricaded from the inside, but the door could still be opened a few inches before crates and beams prevented it from opening further. Beranger looked through his slivered window to the canal.

At one end, a small bridge led to the Seine, and at the other end, the massive statue of an elephant stood as a testament to previous failures, both the Bastille and the era of Napoléon. The pattern of gunfire intensified in the direction of the elephant.

The mob is moving north. Have they taken the city in only two days? If the revolution had rolled past his district already, it would still be days before order could be restored. *The real danger will come tonight.*

Beranger sat on a stool normally used over at the cash register but now placed in the middle of the room. At his perch, he placed the fowling gun across his lap and yawned, waiting.

THE ALCHEMIST'S MAP

Over the next few hours, several noises caused him to ready his rifle, but most looters kept hunting, looking for easier prey. While he sat in the darkness of his shop, the outside lights—moon, stars, fires, torches—made it easy to see when someone passed by. Sneaking up was also impossible, what with debris and glass littering the streets on both sides of his shop.

A week earlier, Beranger would have given a friendly wave to a passerby, but tonight, he would greet them with lead shot.

A horsefly bit his right shoulder, and as he swatted at it, he almost dropped his gun from his lap. "Dirty bastard," Beranger muttered, and his left hand, stretching over his shoulder to the fleshy area above his scapula, found a bit of blood—and a feathery dart.

What the hell?

Beranger stood to turn around and face the direction the dart had come from—the barricaded staircase—but as soon as his feet touched the floor, his legs gave way and he collapsed onto the ground.

His hands gripped the fowling rifle tightly, sensing imminent danger. He turned the rifle toward the stairs and then heard a slight puff of air.

A second dart hit him in the belly, without the same sting.

Numb, he thought as the rifle slid from his fingers. *Everything is numb.*

From the staircase, he finally saw a bit of movement, and a moment later, a few crates toppled and fell down the stairs to the space where he normally made transactions with customers.

The rooftop, Beranger realized too late. *I did not secure the rooftop.*

More crates came tumbling down the staircase as the stranger's foot easily cleared away an obstacle more visual than effective. In his hands, he held a four-foot stick.

Not a stick. A dart gun.

"Gerard Beranger. It is time we talk plainly."

I know that voice. The strange accent.

It was so dark inside of the shop that even when the man stood over him, he still could not see the face.

"Plant," Beranger gasped. *Jean Plant. He came in a week ago looking to order an exotic vodka. Horilka! Why is he here?*

"You remember me? Perhaps I should pick aliases harder to remember. You are probably realizing that I have not returned for the horilka. The numbing sensation you are feeling is a toxin from the kokoi frog. The people of the Embera tribe in Panama prick the skin of the kokoi frog to poison their dart for hunting. I hope you are not feeling too much pain. I bear you no ill will. The two of us are just errand boys, after all."

Outside the door, shadows crossed by the barrel barricade, followed by a loud gunshot.

Save me from this madman, Beranger called out to the mob, but no sound came out.

"I should get to the point. The clock is ticking." He squatted beside him, using the dart gun as a cane. In his other hand, the one with missing fingers, he held a small vial. "One dart might have left you sick for a few days, but two darts will certainly seep into your heart and more likely than not kill you, unless you take this... ah, what is the word..."

Antidote.

"Well, whatever the word, I'll give this to you if you can just answer a few of my questions... honestly. Now, since my last visit, I've been doing a bit of investigating into who you are and how you operate, so let's get right to the point. Who wanted the Alchemist's Map? Who was your buyer?"

The Alchemist's Map? The Drummond map. Al Marakk!

Beranger tried to voice a name, but his throat no longer obeyed his command.

THE ALCHEMIST'S MAP

"I'm a fool for putting a second dart in you, but you had a rifle. I guess I lost my nerve."

The three-fingered man pulled Beranger off the floor, propping him against the counter in a sitting position.

Just give me the antidote and I'll tell you whatever you want!

"Can you still nod and shake your head?"

Beranger nodded.

"Good. Let's get to the point. If Lady Drummond had managed to reach your shop and sell you her priceless family heirloom, she would have certainly had a wealthy buyer. Was the buyer French?"

Beranger hesitated.

"Let me rephrase. Does the buyer currently live in France?"

He shook his head.

"Excellent. Does the buyer currently live in England, Scotland, or Nova Scotia?"

Again, Beranger shook his head.

"Does the buyer currently live in the United States of America?"

A nod.

"Wonderful. Our masters probably even know each other. I'm not sure how many states there are now, and in your delicate condition, time is of the essence, so I won't just rattle down a list of places. Does your master belong to the Order of Eos?"

With a nod, Beranger found himself looking at a small glass vial, which Plant held an inch from his nose.

"Did you send Lady Drummond to Professor Nicollet or did she do that on her own accord? Err...that's not a yes or no answer, is it? Professor Nicollet authenticated the age and subject of the map. Did you send her to him?"

Head shake. *I have no idea who this Nicollet fellow is. Just give me the antidote and I'll tell you everything about the Drummonds, my crazy American cousins, and that damned map. I'll even tell you the truth about the star. Just let me live.*

"So was the old gal just greedy?"

Most likely trying to drive up the price, which is how she got herself killed. She was going to try to negotiate with me. She's killed us both. Beranger nodded.

"Even after I left Professor Nicollet as a prime suspect, he avoided being put in custody. He seems to be either lucky or protected. Does Professor Nicollet have any connections to the Order of Eos? Freemasons? The Carbonari? The Periphery? The Illuminati?"

Five successive shrugs left the three-fingered man chuckling. "You've earned this, Monsieur Beranger. Drink up."

The vial of antidote touched his bottom lip and the few ounces of precious liquid drained onto his tongue, numbing it even more.

His throat constricted.

Breathing grew more difficult.

Not an antidote.

Kokoi toxin.

CHAPTER FOUR

PARIS, FRANCE
1830

Nicollet couldn't believe he was doing something so foolish. In his hand, he held an elegantly curved flintlock pistol with a polished brass hilt and artistic etchings along the plate of the firing mechanism. He cocked the hammer so it would be ready to fire.

Cosette Lavoisier sat across from him at the table, her arms crossed.

"In case something happens while I am gone," Nicollet insisted and slid the pistol across the table to her.

"This isn't my first riot," Cosette shrugged. "I don't know what the revolution was like in the country, but it was hell on earth here in the city. Savages."

"We are both survivors, you and I, but the mob wouldn't bother chasing after a little fellow like me. You should have the pistol."

"What would I do if there is more than one intruder?" she asked. "If I kill one of their friends, I'll be unarmed and matters will be even worse."

"Fire it in the air and run. The noise will certainly startle them," he countered and stood up, walking over to give her a peck on her cheek.

"You should take it with you."

I'd probably shoot myself in the foot. "I could never harm another human being. You know this. Besides, I'll need my hands free."

"Be careful, you gentle fool," Cosette added as Nicollet reached the door. "You don't have to do this."

"I've been hiding inside for three days now. I could use some fresh air."

"Then take this locket. It has an engraving of Napoléon on it, and it will protect you in case any of the revolutionaries grab you. Get back before the sun comes up. The police will most likely ride in at dawn."

Nicollet pulled out his father's watch. "Half an hour. I'll be back by five-thirty."

Dear Lord, what am I doing?

Once outside, Nicollet realized all of the street lamps were unlit or destroyed, and the stars were blanketed in smoke or cloud, leaving him at the mercy of his memory.

Creeping out of his alley, Nicollet looked both ways down the silent Rue de Savoie. To his left was the familiar path to the Paris Observatory, which he had taken for the better part of two decades. To his right, there were two important stops he needed to make.

Now is the safest time to do this, Nicollet convinced himself and then gingerly began to tiptoe along the edges of darkness. For three days, Nicollet had sat in his darkened house, listening to the chants and destruction happening in his beloved city. While the modest Savoy District was spared from complete destruction, the rioters brought fire to specific

THE ALCHEMIST'S MAP

targets throughout the city and a generation of disgruntled youth joined the revolutionaries until even the young grew tired and slept.

The streets were narrow and the walls were tall, and hundreds of windows looked down at him at all times. Debris littered the streets, having been tossed down during the cheering and chanting, but when the shooting began, everyone closed the windows and barricaded themselves inside.

The rioting had been loudest across the river, so Nicollet risked a quick peek. On the far bank, he could see dozens of armed citizens sitting along the outer gates of the Louvre, where more tri-colored flags of the revolution hung.

If Champollion wasn't a leader of the revolution, he at least made sure his museum was protected during the riot. Clever man.

Five harrowing blocks later, Nicollet stood at the corner of Rue Palatine looking up at the majestic Church of St. Sulpice.

Nicollet's church home was a strange mixture of old and new. Even the exterior had mismatched towers. Inside, along with beautiful sculptures, decorated domes, and awe-inspiring tapestries, the Gnomon of Saint-Sulpice married science and religion together. With an inlaid line of brass on the floor, a towering obelisk modeled on Egyptian art, and a transept window along the southern wall, the equinoxes could be accurately measured to determine the date for Easter.

As much as he wanted to earnestly pray for those caught up in the violence, he also wanted to pray for himself, and at the gnomon, he hoped he could see the new path God set before him.

But even more than that, he wanted to solve the mystery of Father Simmons and Lady Drummond's map.

Nicollet took a bold step across the street and immediately heard a gunshot come from the direction of the seminary.

Was that directed at me? Nicollet wondered and hunched down, continuing across the street.

A bullet ricocheted off the stairs in front of the church.

Okay, it was a warning shot.

"Go back where you came from or next time we won't miss!"

I'm a friend of the Church, Nicollet wanted to shout, but he turned tail and ran back toward the narrow street he'd just come from. *Paris has gone mad*, he decided, having almost been killed by seminarians.

He started back home and turned into his alley when he suddenly remembered he had a second stop to make—the most important stop.

He turned back around and found the Rue de Condé, and even though the streets were narrow and tall, he found the big walnut tree behind the ten-foot wall.

It only took a few moments to collect enough debris on the streets for him to stand upon and reach the metal bars along the top.

"Cluck, cluck, cluck," Nicollet called out loudly and then scaled the wall. He dropped over and into the darkness.

"What's it like out there?" A man's voice called out softly.

Nicollet clutched his chest before answering. "Strangely quiet, although I was almost killed by seminarians at St. Sulpice a few minutes ago."

A grunt. "How many eggs do you need?"

"A half-dozen should suffice. Cosette Lavoisier sent me but said that I could not use the front door."

"If you had waited, I have a basket I would have lowered over the wall."

"Oh," Nicollet chuckled. "All I knew was the password, my apologies."

"You may as well leave through the side door. If people see you hopping back over my wall, it might start a trend."

"Thank you. I haven't eaten for two days. These riots caught me ill-prepared."

THE ALCHEMIST'S MAP

"What rock have you been hiding under?"

The stranger led Nicollet through his dimly lit storage room and showed him out the kitchen door, which was promptly locked behind him.

With the six eggs wrapped in cloth, he briskly walked back home.

Finally, he stepped back into his alley and found the rear door to his apartment. He knocked with the heel of his foot but Cosette did not answer the door. With his left hand, he held the eggs against his chest so he could open the door.

Stepping back into his kitchen, he found things mostly as he'd left them. The cooking utensils were ready, the stove was lit, and all the ingredients for his omelet were ready except for the eggs, which he dropped on the floor.

Sitting at his table was a man holding his flintlock pistol.

CHAPTER FIVE

PARIS, FRANCE
1830

I'm going to die on an empty stomach.
In the cradle of his left arm, Nicollet still held three of the six eggs. "On the assumption that I might live to fight another day, pardon me while I tend to my eggs."

With his left toe fixed to the floor, he took one long step with his right foot toward the table, setting the cloth and eggs on the edge. Once deposited, he returned to his little island on the kitchen floor, stooped down to scoop up the cracked eggs, and then repeated his extended step, setting the egg goop onto his breakfast plate.

Leaning back to where he'd stopped, Nicollet sighed and calmly said, "Now, what has become of Cosette? She was going to prepare an omelet."

THE ALCHEMIST'S MAP

The man sitting at the table had a slender face that had been freshly shaved. His gray hair was full, despite being at least fifty. A small scar hid in his right eyebrow, leaving a little gap where no hair grew—the only flaw on an otherwise manicured façade. He dressed in dull colors but the fabric was expensive and pristine.

"May I sit?" Nicollet asked. "Seeing you with my gun has made me a little nervous."

"No, but imagine how I felt when the same gun was pointed in my face."

"Where is Cosette?"

The pistol clunked onto the table as the man set it down and slid it to the middle. "She is far safer now than you are. There are men coming to torture and kill you."

"Oh, dear. I didn't realize I'd made such enemies." *The pistol is closer to me than it is to him. If I lunged for it...*

The man chuckled. "Enemies? It seems there is a good reason for you to have such a fine pistol. Who would have motive to kill such a noble little fellow such as yourself?"

He is trying to elicit information. Is he an ally? "I have no idea who would stoop to such measures or why. How do you know someone is coming to kill me when all of Paris is up in arms?"

"A single death during a riot would almost go unnoticed. Running around during a riot is foolish, but it is more foolish to remain here any longer."

Who is this man? Nicollet wondered.

With his feet still firmly planted, he leaned slightly to one side to note the long wool coat draped over the back of the man's chair. "Foolish to remain here? Tell me, Mr. Wool Jacket, who would be so foolish as to want to kill me?"

"Mr. Wool Jacket," the man laughed. "For now, call me Signore

Giacca. Lana Giacca. There's your first clue."

Friendly yet mysterious, and Italian. He spun my phrase into an Italian name. "As you wish, Mr. Giacca."

"Most gracious of you. Now, as to your earlier question, they are unfortunately the same men who have been trying to kill me most of my life; you just don't know their names. Yet you have quite a few enemies with motive, don't you? First, there was that very public feud with François Arago over some celestial matter that gave me a headache."

"Arago? The man is a liar and fabricates data to advance his career. Of course I called in a few favors to sabotage his publications—the man was going to tarnish the reputation of the observatory."

"Arago is a member of the Carbonari," Giacca said with disdain. "The Carbonari have been carefully plotting this revolt for months, along with the help of Masonic lodges, and other covert organizations of a more nefarious nature. If Arago wasn't so busy with more important matters, you'd probably be dead in an alley somewhere. Don't you remember what happened in the last Revolution?"

I remember all too well. "Arago would never send someone to kill me. We worked together for years—it would be beneath him."

"Perhaps you are right about Arago not being a killer, but it wasn't beneath him to sabotage your career. While you didn't see the writing on the wall, he stole away all of your supporters from the Ancien Régime with threats and coercion, even Humboldt and Laplace, which is why Arago was given the position you'd been groomed to receive. Where did that lead? You borrowed money from your liberal friend and invested it in stocks which were doomed to fail."

Doomed to fail? "Killing me will not help my friends regain their money."

"No, but the same men who lost their fortunes during the

THE ALCHEMIST'S MAP

financial crash have now overthrown the Bourbon Dynasty and will be in positions of power. Your life in Paris is over."

The eyebrow. Giacca seems very familiar. How do I recognize him? "Who is coming to kill me?"

"A short time ago, an English noblewoman came to you with a map—"

"This is about the map!" Nicollet let out a long sigh. "Why would... the police came and spoke to me about it. I even spoke with private investigators hired by the Drummond family. Everyone knows I have an alibi. King Charles himself can verify my alibi."

"Everyone knows you have an alibi, including the man who murdered Lady Drummond, but now everyone knows you've seen the map and the secrets it holds, which has put your life in danger."

"For a silly map?" Nicollet asked, blinking his tired eyes repeatedly.

"I've followed your career, so I knew about your impressive academic abilities. Isn't it rumored that you can look at a book once and recall every word on every page? You saw the map, which means you *are* the map. If someone was willing to pay a fortune for the map, you have value. If another party was willing to murder to acquire the map, you are in danger."

This is ridiculous. "The map isn't real. It's fable. Lady Drummond might as well have had a map to Atlantis, or El Dorado, or the Fountain of Youth."

"Lady Drummond is very dead, and the men who killed her are very real, and they know who you are. Now, go pack up a chest because we are leaving in ten minutes."

"Leaving? You're abducting me?"

"Nicky, I'm *saving* you."

Only two people called me Nicky. My mother and... "Who are you?"

"You don't remember me? Then I need you to trust me anyway. I've spent my life investigating legends, lore, and secret societies. There are now two powerful factions that know the name Jean-Nicolas Nicollet, and I am not about to let you become a victim to your ignorance. Now, go pack. We don't have much time."

Nicollet took a few steps, right past the pistol on the table. "Where are you taking me?"

"Someplace safe, at least for the rest of the summer."

The rest of the summer?

Giacca rose and followed Nicollet a few paces behind.

How am I supposed to pack enough clothes to last me a few weeks? Nicollet looked to the front door, which had been barricaded from the inside with tables and chairs. He also looked to the window, which would only allow him to run from the frying pan of an abduction and into the fire of a revolution. He walked up the stairs to his bedroom and study.

With Giacca standing in the hallway with his arms crossed, Nicollet yanked a large chest from his closet and found his favorite outfits and a few bowties. Next, he tossed an assortment of toiletries into the chest along with a robe and sleeping garments.

"A single chest?" Nicollet complained again. "Could you help me carry it into the study for a moment?"

Giacca obliged, and Nicollet realized the man had to be four or five inches taller than six foot. *I am indeed a gnome.*

In the study, Nicollet took a moment to make some key decisions. "Ego," he said while waiting. "This is punishment for having a big ego. When I received that cursed letter from Lady Drummond, she caught my attention with flattery. As soon as she called me 'a foremost expert in all astronomical matters,' I walked right into this fiasco."

"Can we talk about it later, Professor Nicollet?"

THE ALCHEMIST'S MAP

"Very well, but tell me, do I know you? You know me, and you also have a familiar look."

"I'm repaying a favor. We can talk about our shared history once we are out of Paris. Now hurry up, we don't have much time."

Nicollet walked over to the shelf of his private library and retrieved his sextant from the shelf. The metallic device, built of brass knobs, swivels, and angled bars, was used to compare the angles of stars against the horizon in order to navigate. Although an antique, it was functional and precious to him. His dead mentor, Pierre-Simon Laplace, had given it to him as a gift.

Arago coerced Laplace into stealing the Observatory from me? How did my life tumble off its axis so quickly? It would seem the Drummond map is only the final nail in the coffin.

Next, he found the barometer. Unlike the sextant, it was a state-of-the-art instrument given to him by a living mentor, Alexander von Humboldt. The German scientist gave him the instrument before leaving for Berlin with a new mentee, Louis Agassiz, a Swiss geologist.

How have I lost both Juliana and Alexander? Both wanted love I could not offer.

"Are those instruments really necessary?" Giacca asked impatiently.

"Yes," Nicollet insisted. "They are keys to a new field of science. I will use both astronomy and meteorology to create maps indicating elevation. It's my chance to restart my career. Plus, they hold sentimental value for me, and what is life without sentiment?"

Nicollet placed the sextant and the barometer into the chest, which had filled quicker than he'd hoped. Nicollet turned to his shelf of books and hastily grabbed *Archidoxis Magica* by Philippus Aureolus Theophrastus Bombastus von Hohenheim. He set the big leather-bound book into one of the two remaining cavities in the chest.

Giacca eyed it with a raised eyebrow. "Something about Lady Drummond's map caught your attention, Professor Nicollet?"

"Yes. Mr. Giacca, especially after the police came and spoke with me. I must admit to having a restless mind. I have trouble sleeping, and puzzles distract me. You were right about my memory, and even though I can still picture the map, I don't understand most of it."

"Even the wisest of men have struggled to solve the riddles found on that map," Giacca said.

Nicollet ignored the platitude and returned to his shelf to find a few more books with connections to the Drummond map. He found *Astronomy in the Islamic World*, as well as *Constellations and their Meanings*, which he tossed into the final space of the chest.

"Curiosity killed the cat," Giacca said. "I am glad we found you when we did. Your enemies believe you are ignorant. That should give us the advantage for our grand endeavor."

"What endeavor?"

"I'll explain it on the way," Giacca said as he picked up one end of the chest.

Nicollet took the other end of the chest and the two of them walked down the stairs, through his quiet living room, and back into the kitchen.

He jumped when he saw five men standing in his kitchen, but Giacca seemed to expect them, setting down his end of the chest to ask, "How are things?"

One of them answered, "We escorted Mlle. Lavoisier back to her home and left her with money and a plausible explanation for your departure. She seemed quite amiable."

Oh, thank goodness.

THE ALCHEMIST'S MAP

Another stranger added, "We've also found a route out of the city—and a carriage."

"Excellent," Mr. Giacca said to his team of men. "Load up Professor Nicollet's belongings and put them on that carriage. I want out of this city as soon as possible."

Nicollet glanced at the six eggs on the table. *You would have made a good omelet, mes amies.*

Hours later, Professor Nicollet was safely out of the city, King Charles and his son had abdicated the throne, and Krasdan Krai stood over a plate of cracked eggs.

Some of the yoke had dribbled out and dried on the plate, but most remained still inside of the egg. He opened the eggs into a pan, and in minutes, had the eggs cooked and scrambled.

Consider yourself lucky, Professor Nicollet, Krai thought. It would have been convenient to kill both Beranger and Nicollet during the riots. *It's doubtful he understood it.*

With a full stomach, Krai sighed and then proceeded to start a fire in the kitchen.

Perhaps now I can go back to America and finish the work of my lady, Columbia, Krai hoped.

CHAPTER SIX

ROUEN, FRANCE

1830

During the Reign of Terror in the first French Revolution, nearly seventeen thousand people were guillotined along with Marie Antoinette. Forty thousand prisoners were also executed by les enragés, or "the enraged ones." Within ten years, the Catholic Church withered from a dominant position to near extinction. Catholic leaders were killed, priests and nuns were thrown out of parishes, religious holidays were removed, and the classic seven-day week was turned into a ten-day week to remove the emphasis on Sundays. Even Pope Pius VI and his military forces were defeated by Napoléon, who brought him back to France to eventually die as his prisoner. Although the Papacy and the Catholic Church were restored following the defeat of Napoléon, the

THE ALCHEMIST'S MAP

once powerful Society of Jesus, known more commonly as the "Jesuits," barely survived the anti-clerical purge.

Earlier in the month, Cardinal Gustave Maximilien Juste de Croÿ-Solre had retreated from the city of Paris to his home in Rouen, Château de l'Ermitage. Far from the revolutionaries in Paris, the mansion was easily secured while all of France waited to see what would happen during the French Revolution of 1830. Along with several political figures and a scientist who'd recently given the Cardinal and King Charles a tour of the heavens, the estate also hosted a servant of the Catholic church.

Now, standing at one of the many windows of the mansion, Conrad Simmons gazed out onto the manicured lawns, wondering what Nicollet would decide. "I wouldn't have brought Nicollet here if I didn't think he was the right man for the job," Simmons said to Father Blanco Lupo, a fellow man of aliases that lived in the shadows of society.

Father Lupo sat at the cardinal's desk as if holding court. "Can we trust this watchmaker's son?"

I can trust Nicollet, but can I trust you and your people? "He is the right man at the right time," Simmons insisted. "What else is there to discuss?"

"He does not belong to either of us."

"This isn't the first time we've hired an independent agent to do an investigation," Simmons pressed. "Nicollet is a fervent believer *and* a scientist, a dying breed these days."

"The only reason we're having this conversation is the previous 'independent agent' we sent to investigate the same legend either betrayed us or failed miserably."

"If Le Sueur failed, why are our enemies killing each other over the Drummond map? They continue the race while we stand still."

"Nicollet is already compromised," Lupo asserted. "The Order of Eos knows he has seen the map, thanks to Lady Drummond, and whoever killed her will also know he's seen it. Speaking of, do we know who killed her yet?"

"Not yet," Simmons admitted. "We monitored his house for this past month hoping the killer would step into the trap. Gerard Beranger was killed during the riots, however."

"Beranger?" Lupo asked.

"The buyer—he had connections to the Order of Eos…in America."

"I want to know who killed Lady Drummond; I already know all I want to know about the Order of Eos. Perhaps you should have left Nicollet dangling as bait rather than bringing him here."

"Don't you understand? Whether this is truth or a hoax, we are still in a race. Nicollet is the only man who can unravel this mystery before our enemies figure it out, or worse, find it."

It.

Simmons had infiltrated enough secret societies to know the rumors about *it*. From the Templars to the Order of Eos, the legend pervaded both literature and folk tales. Even a secret branch of the Church, the Periphery, actively searched for it. As an intelligence agent for the ailing Pope Pius VIII, Simmons knew all about the political aspirations of modern organizations like the Carbonari, Illuminati, and Freemasons, but he also knew their occult secrets.

Like Nicollet, curiosity drove him to test the theory.

Father Lupo finished mulling over the idea. "So what is your plan?"

"Professor Nicollet is about to evolve, and not by choice. With the recent revolution, his finances ruined, and being passed over at the observatory, Nicollet will be a man looking for greener pastures—in America, a vast, unmapped region just waiting for a scientist to explore it. Conveniently, Nicollet has even learned a new map-making technique: barometric science, which can determine elevation, a helpful tool when mapping watersheds."

THE ALCHEMIST'S MAP

"The Order of Eos knows he has seen the map. And the thief will have the Drummond map. If Nicollet leaves France to map America, won't that doom him to failure?" Father Lupo asked.

"Ah, but no one fully understands the old map."

"And you believe Nicollet does?"

Simmons nodded. "Yes. He's seen it, and we know what our enemies are looking for: a watershed, a place where rivers flow in all directions. Baron Lahontan confirmed its existence, and later, Pierre-Charles Le Sueur went with his team of miners."

"And if Le Sueur already claimed the treasure?"

"Then why do our enemies still look for it in the frontiers of America? Lady Drummond was murdered for a reason. This is what I do, Father Lupo. I've spent my life infiltrating these secret societies. The race continues, and I don't want to come in last place."

Father Lupo shook his head slowly. "If Nicollet is everything you claim, and he finds this… treasure, then what? You and I are allies, but the Periphery and the Catholic Church might have different views on the treasure. Do we want the treasure to be found? Ask yourself that question, Mr. Simmons."

"Better than it falling into the hands of our enemies."

Lupo scoffed with a slight smile. "If it even exists."

Lupo is softening, Simmons realized and waited.

"I would want Nicollet supervised. I'd want a Periphery agent, ideally a Jesuit, somehow embedded in his expedition."

"Of course, your agents have already provided his Holiness with valuable information about what's happening on the frontier, which is why I wanted to work with you on this mission."

Father Lupo nodded. "Well, we can hammer out the little details later. Let's meet the man."

Simmons walked past the desk to the large double doors. When he opened them, he saw Cardinal Croÿ-Solre standing in the lobby with Nicollet.

The Cardinal is probably quite curious about what's going on today, but let him focus on matters of statecraft while we chase after legends and lore.

"Professor Nicollet, please come in," Simmons said. Nicollet nervously brushed off his red vest and affirmed his buttons, and with a quick step, followed Simmons into the lion's den. "I would like you to meet Father Blanco Lupo, a dear friend from Rome."

Nicollet walked up to the edge of the desk and vigorously shook Father Lupo's hand. "It is a pleasure to finally meet you, Father White Wolf. Mr. Giacca has told me so little about you. Should I also adopt a pseudonym? I could be…Star Man!"

The little fellow is agitated. I hope he does not ruin this.

"Mr. Giacca?" Father Lupo asked as both men sat down.

"A little inside joke," Simmons explained. "Before we were reacquainted with one another, he dubbed me 'Lana Giacca,' or 'Mr. Wool Jacket.'"

Lupo laughed. "It is a good alias. Before we discuss business, I'd like to thank you for being a hero of the Faith. Your bravery as a young man helped preserve the Catholic Church during the dark days. If not for your family's sacrifice, Mr. Simmons would not be sitting with us today."

The scar on his eyebrow suddenly itched, and Simmons felt his fingers touching an old wound.

Three decades earlier, the rabble from the French Revolution reached Nicollet's home in Savoy. Simmons and four other seminarians were in the city of Chambéry when the mob stormed the church, killing the priests and teachers. Simmons and the others managed to escape while the rioters decided what to do with them, but blood was in the air, and they followed them to the village of Cluses.

THE ALCHEMIST'S MAP

A sharp rock had hit Simmons in the brow, almost blinding him. Because of the wound and the terror of being hunted, he did not remember much of the Nicollet house where they'd been given shelter. He remembered the kindness of the mother, the concern of the father, and the wonder of the children who watched them huddled together in fear.

And he remembered young Nicky, of course.

In the middle of the night, under the cover of darkness, Nicky led the five seminarians up a narrow goat path that led into the Alps. Several days later, through fifty miles of rugged mountain terrain, Nicky brought them to safety at Fribourg, Switzerland. The young boy shook their hands before he bounded back down the goat path to a home that no longer existed.

Conrad Simmons told himself to remember the boy—Joseph "Nicky" Nicollet, the son of François and Marie. From time to time over the past thirty years, he had checked on the boy who'd saved his life, and when the secret societies he'd been spying on suddenly began to speak of the astronomer, Simmons found a way to repay the favor—by saving his life.

"Mr. Simmons has told me all about your harrowing ordeal and encounter with the Drummond map, so let me be plain: we'd like to hire you to investigate a legend."

"What sort of legend?" Nicollet asked.

"Don't be coy. Mr. Simmons has told me about your academic talents, and that if you've seen the map, then you can still picture all of the details."

"Seeing and understanding are two different things," Nicollet added.

"Yes, and I'm sure the map had all sorts of strange occult puzzles that meant nothing to you. In the past, we've hired men with vast occult and paranormal training to unlock the meaning, but all for naught.

This time, we'd like to hire a scientist."

"A bankrupt scientist with a tarnished reputation," Nicollet chuckled.

God continues to give me signs. Now if I can only convince Nicollet of it. "And one who has recently learned barometric science from Alexander von Humboldt," Simmons said.

Nicollet nodded but then added, "Perhaps *he* should be sitting in this chair."

"From what Mr. Simmons has told me, you are a devout man of God, which is why your rising star has suddenly fallen. Let me show you specifically what we'd like from you," Father Lupo said, and then reached for the two maps.

He first unrolled Baron Lahontan's map. "In the 1680s, a Frenchman by the name of Baron Lahontan journeyed into the American frontier. As you can see, the features of the Great Lakes are clearly identified, but he had a poor understanding of the newly discovered Mississippi River and the rest of his map's details are simply befuddling."

"Rivière Longue," Nicollet noted. "The Long River."

"Yes, a tributary of the Mississippi River, according to Lahontan, which led him to the—"

"River of Death," Nicollet finished. "How cryptic."

"And what do you see here, Professor Nicollet?"

"It is a watershed—a geographic divide that sends water flowing in different directions, the headwaters of a river."

"According to the story, Baron Lahontan went to this place, where he met with remote Indian tribes who guarded a mysterious treasure," Father Lupo said, "which leads us to Pierre-Charles Le Sueur."

Father Lupo unrolled another map. "As you can see, this map was made a decade later by an associate of Le Sueur, who traveled into the unknown to mine copper."

THE ALCHEMIST'S MAP

"Copper?" Nicollet recoiled.

"A worthless endeavor, yes. Although the details of the Mississippi River are more refined on this map, you can see that the pattern is similar—a tributary of the Mississippi that leads to a watershed, and at this watershed—"

"A mine."

"Yes, 'Fort L'Huillier,' it was called, in honor of the Farmer-General of the time who funded Le Sueur's foolish endeavor and was purportedly an alchemist."

Nicollet nodded in understanding. "And you believe that Lady Drummond's map matches Le Sueur's mine and Lahontan's mysterious treasure?"

"America is a vast continent," Simmons began. "We are only beginning to understand what lies west of the Mississippi. We want you to find this watershed."

"And the treasure? Why were men willing to kill Lady Drummond? What will I find when I reach the end of the rainbow?"

Simmons decided to give him the sane challenge first. "Don't fret over the treasure. We're offering you the support of the Jesuit universities in both Washington, D.C. and St. Louis. We will support a mapping expedition that will establish you as America's finest cartographer. Find the true location of Fort L'Huillier."

Simple enough, Simmons thought as he leaned back in his chair. Nicollet looked at the two maps for a moment and then suddenly stood up, extending his hand to Father Lupo.

"As much as my mother would have wanted me to accept this covert mission on behalf of the Church, I must politely decline your offer. I am but a humble professor, and come September, I have classes to teach at the naval academy in Brest. I am too old to be running around the world."

You fool, Simmons wanted to shout. *You have no life left to go back to.*

Nicollet turned and warmly shook Simmons' hand also. "Will you be offering me a ride back to Paris, or must I see to it myself?"

CHAPTER SEVEN
MURTHLY CASTLE, SCOTLAND
1830

The pounding in William Drummond Stewart's head did not just come from the jug of Drambuie whiskey he'd consumed the previous night but from the knocking at the front door.

Don't they know to leave me alone? Stewart thought and groaned. *I'll have to speak to my brother about the damn servants.*

The knocking continued.

"Wake Duncan with thy knocking," Stewart muttered Shakespeare, causing stirring beside him.

Stewart kicked under the sheets, searching for the right pair of legs. He nudged them softly. "Christina, get dressed and answer the door."

Christina Battersby woke with a gasp and then slid off the side of the big bed. Sunlight came from the top of the velvet curtains, indicating it was late in the morning, if not already noon. Stewart watched with a smirk as the curvy servant walked around the canopy bed in the nude to retrieve her clothes that had been ripped off the previous night.

She looked back at the bed, shaking her head in disbelief which was betrayed by her wry, wicked smile.

With her simple clothes back on, she opened the bedroom door, flooding the chamber with even more light, allowing Stewart to see the clock on the wall.

It is almost noon.

He reached out a hand and found a hairy chest, which he shoved hard. "Get up, you're late."

The figure moved. "What?"

"You're late, Eliot. You were going to speak to my brother up at the big house about the constable's position in Perth."

"Oh, shit!" Eliot McKinlay sat up in bed, tossed the sheets aside, and jumped naked from the bed, searching for his clothes the same way Christina had done.

McKinlay hopped on one foot as he slid his trousers back on. He slipped into his boots, and then snatched up his shirt and overcoat.

"Thanks again, Captain Billy," McKinlay said, and then glanced back at him with his crooked, dimpled grin. "For everything."

Then McKinlay vanished out the door, still dressing himself.

I guess he got what he was looking for, Stewart thought, but the hangover kept him from enjoying any of the decadent moments from the previous night.

He heard Christina in the entryway speaking to whatever idiot had been knocking on the door, but he could not hear what was being said.

A few moments later, he heard the stairs creak as Christina returned. "Who was that?"

THE ALCHEMIST'S MAP

"He said he's an investigator."

Open locks, whoever knocks. Sergeant Cairns has already returned from France?

Despite the nausea and throbbing head pain, Stewart sat up. "Help me get dressed."

"Of course, Lord Stewart," she said and picked up the only clothes remaining on the floor, extending her arm with his briefs in her hand. One by one, she handed him all the items of his formal attire.

"Your cute friend left quickly," Christina said.

"Yes, he was late for an appointment with my brother up at the castle."

"He was very charming. Is he married?"

"He is, actually, but we knew each other from our time in the Waterloo campaign. Men who fight and die together have a strong bond."

"Yes, I seem to remember some of it from last night," Christina said with a grin. Of all the women in and around Perthshire, Christina had the most liberal mind. Despite her position in life as a servant, she understood him better than anyone else, especially his appetites. "Should I be jealous?"

"Ah, he's just a ship passing in the night. You will always have a part in my life. Now, let us go see what Sergeant Cairns has learned."

Sergeant Lewis Cairns went over the whole report while Christina prepared lunch for the two men conversing at the kitchen table. Cairns was a man in his mid-forties, still fit and serious. In the Napoleonic Wars, he'd been a veteran platoon sergeant who had privately given a young Lieutenant Stewart sage bits of advice.

Now, he gave Stewart a dry account of the murder of his Aunt

Maggie and his cousin, Susan. Cairns' investigation ended up getting slowed by the simmering revolution and the death of Beranger.

"So it was not the buyer who killed her? The Beranger fellow?"

"Beranger was poisoned even though he didn't have the map," Cairns recapped. "The killer either did it out of spite or because Beranger knew too much."

Why didn't she listen to me? The Al Marakk Map was my uncle's most prized possession. This is my fault for not warning her better.

"Is it possible that her footman, Whitmore, killed her and fabricated the whole thing?"

"I thoroughly interrogated him, as you requested, and I left no doubt—just a few reminders he'll bear the rest of his life."

"Good, so what did you mean Beranger knew too much?"

"I went through Beranger's shop with a fine tooth comb, and I have a few leads regarding Beranger's client."

"I already have a good idea who would have wanted it. When I helped her sort through my uncle's vast library, I found a few family trees and correspondence. Apparently, there were two rival families seeking the same goal."

"The map?"

"A treasure, actually," Stewart rolled his eyes and shrugged. "Tell me more about the killer."

"A fairly sophisticated assassin, I'd assume. The man who hired him must come from either wealth or power, with a network of spies able to intercept the mail from either Lady Drummond or Beranger."

"But no leads yet? What about this Nicollet fellow?"

Cairns shook his head. "Tight alibi. No motives. Just a man in the wrong place at the wrong time. Your aunt used him to try to drive up the price, and if I didn't know better, it almost cost Nicollet his life."

"How so?"

THE ALCHEMIST'S MAP

"His house burned down a day after Beranger was killed. Your nemesis wants all knowledge of this map wiped from the earth, I'd guess."

"It does seem that way. I appreciate everything you've done for me. How much do I owe you, Lewis?"

"For the Hero of Hougoumont? Nothing. I owe you everything, Captain Stewart."

"Please, Lewis. You were there for weeks. Right after a bloody revolution!"

Christina returned with two plates of steaming food. "For the Hero of Hougoumont."

Cairns grinned at the chemistry shown between the two. "Has he told you about it?"

"I've seen a few of his scars, so I knew he fought in a war, but no."

"Hougoumont was the turning point of the entire war. It was a small farm with a rock wall, and the young lieutenant and our sharpshooters fortified that spot as the entire French army tried to sweep through to cut off an escape route. But it was a trap within a trap. Tell her, William."

Stewart sighed but Christina held her hands on her wide hips, waiting for an answer. "My men were told to hold the gate, so we held the gate, despite how many Frenchmen poured through. By the end, we didn't even need the gate, the bodies were piled so high. The little house held, the position held, and Napoleon fell... all because I held that gate to the last man. A lot of friends died that day."

Cairns reveled in the memory. "We were down to just a dozen men, trapped in a stone house. The French sent this monster of a man to chop down that farmhouse door with an ax, and when he poured through, Stewart dodged three swings from that big ax before he took the monster's head clean off his shoulders."

"Fucking French," Stewart shook his head.

"As your master said, we won the fight, won the day, won the battle, and won the war," Cairns praised. "While he might be the black sheep of the family, you treat this man like he's the King of England."

"I already do," Christina replied, back at the stove.

"Let us be serious, Lewis. I must give you something in return for your help."

"Nonsense. You needed help, and I was more than willing to give it."

Despite all of his flaws, Stewart had learned the meaning of loyalty during the Napoleonic Wars, and he knew what had to happen next. "How about following me to America?"

"Excuse me?"

Christina also echoed, "Excuse me?"

"My Aunt Maggie needs to be avenged and the only way to find her killer is to go where the map leads…and wait."

"So where does this map lead?" Cairns asked.

"There are several maps and several accounts, which is why they don't know where to go. But I've seen the map in my Uncle William's library, and whoever stole the map will draw attention searching for it, and then I'll add another head to my wall."

CHAPTER EIGHT

PARIS, FRANCE

1830

Professor Nicollet hurried across the Cour Napoléon, allowing himself a quick glance at the Arc de Triomphe, just to confirm it remained following the July Revolution. As he neared the main entrance to the Palais du Louvre, he pulled his father's pocket watch out of his pocket.

I'm late.

He jogged up the stone steps, across the landing, and into the front doors of the oldest part of the Louvre.

"We are closing in five minutes," a man at the doorway said.

"Yes, my apologies, I am here to meet with Monsieur Champollion. Here is a letter he sent to me in Brest. Could you direct me to the

Egyptian History exhibit?"

The Rosetta Stone, an ancient Egyptian stele with three versions of a royal decree, was discovered in 1799 by the French forces of Napoléon. For thousands of years, ancient Egyptian scripts were a dead language that no living man could read, until Jean-François Champollion cracked the code and unlocked thousands of years of Egyptian history.

Although Champollion was only a boy when the Rosetta Stone was discovered, he cracked the code at the age of thirty-four and became an international celebrity, which allowed him to return to Egypt, bringing back relics and artifacts from the Valley of the Kings to the Louvre.

After the turmoil of the July Revolution ended, Champollion found himself promoted to chair of Egyptian History and Archeology and curator of the Louvre's Egyptian exhibit, which is where Nicollet found his friend and peer.

Nicollet spun himself in a circle as he walked by the Sphinx in the middle of the room and almost didn't see Champollion hidden by crates and boxes, who called out loudly, "You're late."

"It was much easier when all I had to do was walk across the bridge," Nicollet said. "Give my apologies to Rosine."

"Ah, you know how it is. She is used to me being away. It is Zora you should apologize to."

"How is your precious daughter?"

"She cries when I try to kiss her with this beard. What do you think? Should I keep it or shave it?"

"You look like a Bedouin," Nicollet said. "I've never been able to grow a beard.

Champollion laughed loudly. "I suppose I keep it to remind my peers that I've actually been to Egypt. Perhaps it is time I should shave it."

Plot a course, Nicollet reminded himself. "I've heard you have the

THE ALCHEMIST'S MAP

mummy of Ramesses the Great in here?"

"Mummy, no. But we did find the tomb of old Ozymandias."

"It must be fascinating to unearth relics from the old world." *Ironic, but you are steering him in the right direction.* "It is like opening the Book of Exodus and seeing it come to life before your very eyes."

"Yes, but I do not think you'd like what I have learned. The dates written upon the tablets include dynasties that predate your Book of Genesis. My only regret is that I wasn't able to go to Egypt before it had been looted and plundered so badly. Imagine what I could have discovered if I'd found her a virgin, pristine."

Virgin and pristine—like the American frontier. "Someone told me you carved your own name onto a line of pharaohs. Does that mean a thousand years from now you'll be considered a pharaoh of Egypt?" Nicollet said, and regretted his need to counter-punch.

"I don't think I'll be welcomed back to Egypt, especially after the plundering I myself have done." Champollion stood up from where he crouched and stretched his back. "Before we waste any time, I just want you to know that I will not be able to give you a loan, so if you've come to borrow money, the answer is no."

Is that how all my friends see me? A desperate beggar? "I'm not here for money. I have a minor position proctoring exams in Brest until I can find steady employment. I'm here to ask you a few professional questions."

"Yes, so you alluded in your letter. Well, let's see it. Let's see this ancient language you need decoded."

Remember what Father Simmons said. Don't show him too much. Nicollet reached for his leather satchel and set it down on one of the crates. Inside, he found his leather-bound notebook where he kept his drawings. Past the drawn images of the Drummond map, he found the phrases he'd seen upon it.

Reveal it slowly, or he will laugh at you and throw you out of his museum. "Here is a strange phrase. I believe it might be Arabic."

Nicollet knew what it said from the astronomical identifiers he'd seen on the Drummond map. While human languages changed or died, the language of astronomy had stayed the same since the dawn of mankind.

"Yes, it is close to Arabian. It appears to be Phoenician."

"Can you decipher it?"

"Yes. Phoenician was considered the father of modern languages until recently. It developed side-by-side with the Egyptian hieroglyphics and shared traits with Hebrew, which is why it doesn't have any vowels."

"What does it say?"

Champollion stared intently and then smiled, throwing a skeptical look at Nicollet. "Are you teasing me?"

"No, what does it say?"

"'Animal groin?'"

Nicollet steered, "Or... 'loin of the bear?'"

Champollion looked back down, this time laughing at himself. "Yes, now I see it. 'Loin of the Beast.' The lack of vowels produces an imperfect translation. Where did you see this phrase?"

Lie to him. "A history professor in Brest showed me his collection of old astronomical maps. It was a star map that showed Ursa Major, which would most likely make the translation 'loin of the bear.' It is a reference to one of the seven stars in the asterism. The star is now known as Merak, the lower of the two pole stars used by navigators to find the North Star."

"Lower star...groin. Now I understand it. Merak, eh?"

"I thought it might be Arabian because they were some of the finest astronomers and scientists in the day. Our modern word 'Merak' is based on the old Arabian 'Al Marakk,' but you believe this is Phoenician?"

THE ALCHEMIST'S MAP

"Those symbols were written down by Ursa Major? I'm fairly certain."

He's interested. Now keep him going. "The Phoenicians were a sea-faring civilization on the Mediterranean. Is that why their language was so influential?"

Champollion accepted the theory with a nod. "It was the original language of commerce. Technologically, the Phoenicians were far more advanced than other cultures, which allowed them to sail wherever there was money to be made. If you wanted to trade with them, you'd learn their language, which is why linguists credit Phoenician with being the father of languages."

"What time period did they exist?"

"At their height, 1,000 B.C. Eventually, Alexander the Great defeated them when he destroyed Tyre, but the zenith of their culture occurred long before that. Again, they weren't conquerors... just sailors."

"How... far... did they sail? What was the range of their empire?"

Champollion tilted his head like a confused puppy.

Go ahead. Let's see how hard he laughs at you. "Could the Phoenicians have reached North America?"

"Before Christopher Columbus?" Champollion shook his head. "No one knew America existed."

"Ah, but Plato described the lost continent of Atlantis being beyond the Pillars of Hercules, which is how the Atlantic Ocean received its name. If the Greeks believed there to be a continent beyond the Straits of Gibraltar, why couldn't the Phoenicians believe the same thing? Don't the Welsh, Norse, Irish, and Scots tell stories about finding America prior to Columbus? Perhaps there is truth in their stories."

"Are you saying you looked at a Phoenician star map that described the American continent?"

I wish I'd never seen it. "I also thought it was a hoax, but the

Phoenician text seems to indicate it was made almost three thousand years ago, does it not?"

"Phoenician, unlike Egyptian Hieroglyphics, is not a lost language. Right now, I could write ancient Hebrew upon the map, but that does not mean it is an old map, does it? Only an old language."

"Oh, I am not defending the notion. I'm just trying to understand what I saw," Nicollet said and began flipping through the notebook in a way only he understood. The Drummond map was parceled into a hundred pieces on the pages of the notebook, and only his mind knew where they belonged.

Nicollet suspected upon first glance what the Drummond map had shown. Now he needed to have Champollion say it. "There were some strange symbols drawn on the map as well, which made me think of you."

"For what reason?"

"At first, I thought it was a reference to Egypt. The river could have been the Nile River and the symbols were the great pyramids. But there are strange markings on the pyramids."

Play dumb. Feed his ego.

"Let me see that," Champollion said, and before Nicollet knew, he'd taken the notebook away. "These aren't pyramids. They are the four elements of alchemy: fire, air, water, and earth."

"Please, can I have that back," Nicollet said and lunged for it, only to have Champollion turn a shoulder and walk away with it.

He leaned in closer with some pages, his brow wrinkled; with other pages, he cracked a wry grin. "What in the world is all of this gibberish?"

"I was hoping you could tell me."

"You've been pranked. Do you want to know what this is all about? This single symbol right here explains it all: An outer circle, with a circle inside of a square inside of a triangle. Do you know what this refers to?

THE ALCHEMIST'S MAP

It is the symbol for the Philosopher's Stone."

He confirmed it—now make him put it all together. "The what?"

"A good Catholic boy like you never learned about the Philosopher's Stone? It was science before there was science; alchemy before chemistry. I suppose you went to school after Antoine Lavoisier separated science from the occult, though. Prior to modern chemistry, alchemy focused on the study of the elements, and the Philosopher's Stone was the quest to understand how elements worked."

"So was it a literal rock or a symbolic quest?"

"At one time, both. The actual Philosopher's Stone could transform objects and elements as an alkahest."

"It would transform lead into gold," Nicollet added, still playing dumb.

"See, you have heard of it," Champollion turned his attention back to the pages of the notebook. "Wait! I remember you talking about trouble right before the latest revolution. An English noblewoman was murdered. Did she show you this?"

"Please, forget I ever said anything about it. Forget I even came here today. For your sake."

"How intriguing. She was murdered for a treasure map? A map to the location of the Philosopher's Stone?"

"Can I have this back for a moment?" Nicollet took the notebook away from his old friend and flipped to the image that had brought him back to Paris. He kept his finger there, and then flipped back to the basic alchemy elements. "So the upside down pyramid with a line through it is—"

"The water symbol."

"Does it have a name?"

"Yes, I believe an alchemist named Paracelsus dubbed them 'Gnome' for earth, 'Salamander' for fire, 'Sylph' for air, and 'Undine' for water."

"Undine," Nicollet repeated thoughtfully, having already read Paracelsus himself. He just wanted Champollion to confirm his theory.

On the Drummond map, four rivers on a foreign continent came together in a single spot—a scientific impossibility. At the place where the four rivers came together, the artist had also drawn a symbol of two pyramids touching point-to-point, divided by three lines.

"Is this also the symbol of the Undine?" Nicollet asked.

"Yes and no. The top half of the symbol is the Undine, but as a whole, the two pyramids with the three lines are the symbol for copper."

"Copper?" Nicollet said, reflecting on what Father Simmons had said about Pierre-Charles Le Sueur mining copper at Fort L'Huillier. "I thought you said the Philosopher's Stone turned objects into gold."

"Solid copper transforms into powder known as vitriol," Champollion began.

Say it, and I'll go. Say it, and I'll know I'm not imagining all of this.

"During his studies of alchemy, Paracelsus dug into its history, past the works of Rosenkreutz or Flamel, to the Arabian scientists like Geber and Avicenna, and all the way back to Ancient Egypt, which explains the sacred geometry shown in the basic elements."

And Solomon. Don't forget King Solomon, Nicollet thought of his own theory. *If Solomon wanted to sail, he would have hired Phoenician sailors.*

Champollion continued, "Back then, the universal solvent was known as 'Azoth,' or 'Ormus,' but during his study of chemical transformation, and his quest to find the stone itself, Paracelsus not only coined the four elemental names, but he also invented a new word—'vitriol.'"

"Copper residue."

"Yes, but here is the strangest part of the word in alchemy lore. 'Vitriol' is an acronym for a Latin phrase, a manifesto of sorts. 'Visita Interiora Terrae Rectificando Invenies Occultum Lapidem.'"

He said it. Nicollet's heart fluttered. *I can't believe he said it.*

"Occultum Lapidem?"

THE ALCHEMIST'S MAP

"The phrase translates as, 'Visit the interior of the Earth; by rectification thou shalt find the hidden stone.' Lady Drummond obviously had an old treasure map, one that leads to the Philosopher's Stone."

"So X marks the spot?" Nicollet asked about the symbol drawn over the place where the rivers came together.

"I guess if you're looking for the Philosopher's Stone, you'd look for vitriol and then begin to dig."

Nicollet slammed the book shut and slipped it back into his bag. "I'm sorry for wasting so much of your time. This is very embarrassing. Please, for the friendship you bear me, do not tell anyone that I came to you with these crazy drawings. Paris already mocks me."

"I won't say a word," Champollion promised as Nicollet began to leave. "You should come to my house soon and have supper. Rosine and I would love to have you."

I have another destination in mind, Nicollet thought, and found himself walking out of the exhibit room. "Remember, don't speak a word of the map or Lady Drummond. A crazy person murdered her, after all."

"Where are you going?" Champollion called out.

"America," Nicollet answered, *or as the Phoenicians called it, "Merak." If I follow the North Star, the Loin of the Beast will guide the way.* "I'm going to see if there is still a little magic out there in the world."

CHAPTER NINE
NEW YORK
1831

With the colonization of the American continent, the fur trade industry had become a global market. The New World sparked the imagination of consumers in Europe, and pelts, especially those of the beaver, became a prized commodity. European nations such as England, France, and Holland competed to control and expand trading influence via trading posts, where Native American tribes violently competed for control of rivers. As the American colonies grew and the eastern rivers failed to keep up with demand, dozens of Native American tribes were displaced, stacking up in the territories of Wisconsin, Iowa, and Illinois for fear of entering into the territory of the still powerful Oceti Sakowin alliance, known by their enemies as the "Sioux."

THE ALCHEMIST'S MAP

After three centuries of aggressive plunder, once-powerful nations such as France and the Iroquois League lost their territory to new nations—the United States and the Anishinaabe, with the Ojibwe (Chippewa) controlling the region surrounding Lake Superior. Capitalizing on the sustained demand for felt hats, the American Fur Company, led by America's first multi-millionaire, John Jacob Astor, monopolized control of the region and market.

Astor, a German immigrant who once worked in his father's butcher shop, expanded his operation into the Upper Mississippi watershed while also expanding sales into new markets such as China. His standing as one of America's most powerful men secure, Astor sold his company to Ramsay Crooks and, with the profits, began investing in New York City real estate. He also became a prominent Freemason, serving as Master of Holland Lodge #8.

Hank Sibley held Astor's letter of invitation as he stood staring up at the façade of the Holland Lodge.

When summoned by the king, you better damn well come running with hat in hand. Do whatever these bastards want.

Even with his black tie and finest jacket, Sibley still felt like a boy. At his father's insistence, he had cut his black hair short and shaved off his beard, leaving a mustache to avoid looking like a schoolboy. Unlike his peers, who spent time at colleges, Sibley just returned from the frontier. At twenty-one, he was energetic and fit.

This will be my second step in becoming a great man, Sibley decided as he walked through the front doors of the lodge. *Today, my life changes.*

"Henry Hastings Sibley," he told the clerk, a man of similar age. "I have a three-thirty meeting with Mr. Astor."

The clerk looked down, almost surprised to find the name on the schedule, and arranged for him to be escorted to the waiting room, where he waited for another hour.

As the time for the meeting approached, another man with a slender hooked nose entered the lobby and sat down across from him. Trying not to stare, Sibley stole glances to identify his rival.

Who the hell is Mr. Chicken Beak? My competition for a promotion? Well, the job is mine.

Astor's office door opened, and Sibley found himself leaning forward to stand.

"Mr. Astor will see you now, Mr. Delhut."

The narrow man shot through the doorway, slamming it behind him, causing Sibley to confirm the time. He stood and approached the lobby secretary. "Are the meetings running ahead or behind schedule? *I was supposed to meet with Mr. Astor at three-thirty.*

"Yes, a joint meeting with Mr. Delhut. I'm sure they will call for you when they need you."

During the next few minutes, Sibley could hear raised voices from inside the room, which only heightened his anxiety.

When the door opened, Mr. Delhut finished his sentence and then abruptly stopped, turning back to the door. Mr. Astor, a portly man with a square face, sat behind the desk. At the door, a mousy man with an apologetic face ushered Sibley into the room.

"Mr. Astor, this is Hank Sibley, the young clerk from Mackinac Island. Hank, this is Mr. Astor, I'm Malcolm Gunn, his personal assistant, and I believe you already know Solomon Delhut."

Shit. I have no clue. Sibley found himself joining the men around the large desk. "Actually, I do not know if we've—"

Delhut interrupted, "I'm a friend of his father. I don't remember if we've been properly introduced before. Solomon Delhut," he introduced himself and gripped Sibley's hand like a vice.

The two Solomons. Son of a bitch, yes, I remember mother joking

THE ALCHEMIST'S MAP

about it once. Solomon Sibley. Solomon Delhut. Off to a bad start, Hank. Get it together.

Astor began, "Hank, I know you've been patiently building a career for yourself as a clerk in the American Fur Company, as well as joining the local Masonic Lodge, but we're going to have to change the pace of things due to—"

"Someone stole from me," Delhut bristled bitterly, stealing the smile from Astor's face. "What good is a network of secret societies if you can't discover any secrets."

Astor shifted nervously, and for the first time, Sibley realized who had called the meeting—Delhut. A strange silence fell over the room.

"If anything was stolen during my time at Mackinaw, I can assure you—" All three men scoffed, prompting Sibley to cut his losses mid sentence. *So what the hell was stolen?*

The silence continued.

"Tell him about the promotion then," Delhut said.

Astor put a smile back on his face. "There are big changes happening in the Wisconsin Territory. With a little nudge, the United States government is strengthening its presence at the rededicated Fort Snelling, at the confluence of the Mississippi and St. Peter Rivers. It will hopefully be a strong enough presence to stabilize the tensions between the feuding Chippewa and Sioux nations."

"Think of it as a parent standing between two fighting siblings," Gunn added.

I thought things were peaceful between the Chippewa and Sioux. What are they talking about?

"Along with this new financial investment, the American Fur Company is also investing in the territory with a permanent, cut-stone outpost, one that we would like you to manage upon completion."

Dammit all. Farther west than Mackinaw? "Managing an outpost?

It would be an honor."

"Mr. Crooks will speak to you about the details of the operation," Gunn said. "By the time the building complex is completed, you will be familiar with the operations in the region."

"But that is not why I'm here today, is it?" Sibley asked.

Astor said, "As you already heard, Mr. Delhut recently had something—if you don't own it, is it really stolen?"

Delhut's eyes tightened. "They murdered a member of my extended family."

"I thought he died in the riots," Astor countered.

"Have I come to the wrong man?" Delhut asked. "Are you going to provide the fealty that was promised?"

Astor grimaced. "Mr. Delhut had something very precious stolen from him, and he has come to me for information and assistance, which is why we'd like you to be our trusted friend at Fort Snelling."

A fucking spy.

"Do you want to explain what Hank will be... monitoring?" Astor asked.

"I would have preferred an older man, one with a track record of trustworthiness," Delhut said, studying Sibley with venom in his eyes. "Do you vouch for him, Astor?"

"Mr. Gunn and I gleaned Hank from a list of impeccable candidates, most of whom are Freemasons. So yes, we believe Hank is our man."

"Then you tell him," Delhut said.

Astor obliged, "Before it was stolen from him, Solomon was attempting to purchase a rare and very old map. While we have not yet learned the identity of the thief, the details on the map will most likely lead him to the headwaters of the Mississippi River.

"The thief will not be alone, and will certainly need a support

THE ALCHEMIST'S MAP

team—more likely than not, a team of laborers. Our thief will need extractors for the operation, so remember the person you meet may have considerable financial and political power backing him."

It sounds like a treasure map. The lost gold of Captain Kidd? Sibley kept his thoughts to himself and listened to Astor.

"As manager of the Fort Snelling outpost, you will have dozens of fur traders, both licensed and unlicensed, at your door, along with countless bands of Indians. It will be your duty to know the business of every man who steps foot in the upper Mississippi watershed. Is that understood?"

What the hell? "I understand. Am I to obtain this stolen map?"

Delhut answered. "If you want to advance in this world, you are not to ask any questions, but only be our eyes and ears in the West. Yours is a defensive position. I have others who can do my bidding. If you see anything suspicious, you need to let us know."

"Speaking of suspicious activity," Astor interrupted, "Mr. Gunn has a few leads that Hank might want to keep an eye on."

"Spill the beans, Malcolm," Delhut said. "Tell me who might have my map."

Gunn looked down at his notepad. "First, there is an interesting development in Washington D.C. A young Colonel Abert in the U.S. Corps of Engineers is trying to reshape a Corps of Topographical Engineers under the War Department."

"Easily blocked by our friends in Congress, and it is very unlikely our thief would be so…public," Astor assessed. "What else?"

"There have been two curious arrivals in St. Louis. First, a German prince and apprentice of Alexander von Humboldt, Maximilian of Wied-Neuwied, has announced his intentions to explore the Missouri River."

"The Missouri? Not the Mississippi?" Delhut said, shaking his head. "Not according to the Lahontan Map."

"Maximilian has brought a painter with him, Karl Bodmer," Gunn finished.

"If he'd brought a geologist with him, I might be interested," Delhut said.

Astor nodded, "What else, Gunn?"

"The last one falls into the category of small world coincidence. Sir William Stewart, a Scottish hero in the Battle of Waterloo, has arrived in St. Louis, also looking for transportation into the wilderness."

"So?" Delhut snarled again.

"Sir William *Drummond* Stewart. His aunt was Lady Margaret Drummond, which makes his uncle the late Lord William Drummond, former owner of—"

"The Al Marakk Map," Delhut muttered. "Did he kill his own aunt to obtain it?"

Gunn seemed pleased with himself, his favorite suspect apparent in his expression. "Captain Billy, as he was known by his men, is a man of low character, which, despite his pedigree, kept him from joining any of the societies his uncle once belonged to. Shunned by his family, it *is* possible Billy killed his aunt to obtain the family's ancestral treasure; however, he did have an alibi at the time of Lady Drummond's death, and he leaves Murthly Estate after many rumors and scandals. He's in St. Louis now, looking for 'Mountain Men willing to go on an adventure.'"

Delhut turned to Sibley. "What do you think?"

"He has motive, means, ambition, and cunning," Sibley assessed. "I would say he is certainly a man to watch."

"Speaking of Lady Drummond," Gunn continued. "There has been a very curious development from France. Professor Jean-Nicolas Nicollet, one of the last people to see Lady Drummond alive, has abandoned his scientific career in France to begin anew in America, marketing himself as a cartographer."

THE ALCHEMIST'S MAP

"Nicollet again?" Delhut asked. "My investigator said he had an alibi and no motive."

"He's the astronomer, isn't he?" Astor clarified. "The one Lady Drummond went to about the map?"

"Yes, and against my better judgment, dismissed in the crime. What connections does he have, Gunn?"

"None. He is a devout Catholic, but has avoided assistance from the Catholic Church. The scientific community respects him, but shuns him for his celebrity and lavish lifestyle. He was a childhood savant whose flame has burnt out."

"And now the astronomer has become a cartographer—after seeing the Drummond map."

Astor dismissively shook his head, "And also a student of Alexander von Humboldt. The West is more than just beaver pelts to scientists—it is a chance to make a name for oneself."

Gunn shrugged. "In any case, you can rest easy knowing that he is currently in Washington, D.C., having exhausted his funds for travel, but I thought you needed to know."

Delhut turned back to Sibley. "Now do you understand why we need a gatekeeper? You will watch over the frontier for any of these known threats, as well as any unknown ones."

"I look forward to my duties, but—"*Why did you add 'but?' Fool, why did you stop short?*

"But what?" Delhut said.

"If we maintain control of the territory, why do we sit back and wait for the inevitable to happen, waiting for Abert, Maximilian, Stewart, or Nicollet to steal from us again? You said earlier that whoever killed Lady Drummond will most likely hire his own agent to do his bidding. Why don't we hire our own Nicollet? A scientist and explorer able to find whatever we're looking for before the others show up."

Delhut's mouth tightened.

"We've already tried," Astor said. "Over the past few decades, we've sent our finest to the headwaters of the Mississippi looking for Delhut's treasure, which means one of two things."

"Either I've spent my life on a wild goose chase," Delhut answered. "Or the information given to me by my ancestors is wrong, which is why I needed that map."

"Then I will watch over your territory for any threats," Sibley affirmed, *and hopefully learn what the hell these men are looking for.*

Hours up the Hudson River, another servant put to rest his questions about the map. Unlike Hank Sibley, Jacques Palissy no longer cared about the mystery of the map, for along with an address, he had paperwork making him the new postmaster of Albany, New York.

Slipping the metal tube under his arm, Palissy knocked on the stately door of the large farm house.

A tall Englishman, looking slightly agitated, stood at the door.

"Greetings, Mr. Fanshaw," Palissy began his introductions, which did little to change the stern expression of Fanshaw until the name of their shared benefactor was spoken.

"Of course, of course," George Fanshaw said, opening the door wide. "Come in, Mr. Palissy."

Even though the farm was built in the rugged hills outside the city of Albany, the interior held all the amenities of a London home.

"Hospitality is not necessary," Palissy added. "I was instructed only to deliver this letter and the map."

After years of intercepting mail at La Poste, Palissy had no problems opening and then resealing the correspondence to Mr. Fanshaw. The letter congratulated Mr. Fanshaw on his appointment

THE ALCHEMIST'S MAP

as the official United State Geologist and his commission to explore the Upper Mississippi.

Surely, they know my skills as a snoop and spy, even among friends.

The contents of the cylinder had been thoroughly inspected, as well. Instead of the ornate Alchemist's Map, which had been his companion on the Atlantic crossing, it held a cheap copy, drawn upon thin paper so as to overlay it on another map of the Upper Mississippi River.

"Then you're dismissed," Fanshaw said, closing the door on his face.

You are an errand boy also, Palissy decided as he walked back down the road into town. Rural New York seemed an unnamed beast just a few yards from the road. Palissy could not imagine the wild hell west of the Great Lakes where Fanshaw had just been sent.

CHAPTER TEN

DISTRICT OF COLUMBIA
1831

The White House was originally known as the "President's Palace." When Thomas Jefferson took office, he claimed that the house was "big enough for two emperors, one pope, and the Grand Lama."

The President's Palace became referenced as the "White House" after the War of 1812, when British forces almost burned it to the foundations in 1814. Rebuilt and expanded, the exterior was whitewashed to protect it from the elements.

By the time Andrew Jackson took up residence, a north and south portico had been built, allowing Joseph Nicollet to walk right up to the front door.

I am older than the house of America's president, Nicollet observed as he joined others in line in front of him. *How strange.*

THE ALCHEMIST'S MAP

Dressed in a borrowed suit jacket, Nicollet nervously produced his invitation to the evening festivities and was then led to the North Portico, where he waited by the stairs as he'd been told.

Freshened with a spritz of Caswell No. 6 cologne, also borrowed, Nicollet studied the architectural choices involving the newly remodeled building. The sound of a rustling dress caught his ear, and when he turned, he saw the beautiful young woman who had invited him. "Bonsoir, Mademoiselle Eastin."

"Please, Professor Nicollet, I told you before to call me 'Mary Ann.' Are you ready to make the gentlemen of Washington D.C. green with envy?"

So much for being discreet. Nicollet bowed low, causing her to giggle. "I will certainly do my part."

"Mmm, is that lavender?"

"It is. I promised rigorous dancing, and I wanted to remain fresh for the entire evening.

She received his extended hand. "How has your first spring in America treated you?"

"I have been given numerous promises that Maryland will be lovely in May."

"Yes, it does eventually thaw out around here. What are the springs in Paris like?"

"Rainy and quite gloomy."

"Ah, then Washington should feel like home already," she smiled flirtatiously. "I must be honest with you, Professor Nicollet—"

"Please, if I am to call you 'Mary Ann,' then you must call me 'Joseph.'"

"'Joseph,'" she repeated. "What happened to 'Jean-Nicolas?'"

"Excusez-moi, I am an American now, and 'Joseph' suits me better. It is the name my father gave me. My mother preferred 'Jean-Nicholas,' or 'Nicky.'"

Even though she was almost half his age, Nicollet noticed how easily the young woman warmed to him. "Just so you know, Uncle Jackson has decided to attend the party, so everyone will be watching us."

"The president," Nicollet said, suddenly feeling light-headed. "Merci bien."

"Yes, Uncle Jackson seems determined that I find a fiancée soon, to avoid any future scandals. So why is it that a handsome man such as yourself has remained single for so long?"

An icy face appeared in his mind. Nicollet rolled his eyes and looked down, "I am simply unlucky in love."

"I heard a rumor that the talented Juliana Sabine once made a trip to Paris in a desperate attempt to win your affections, only for you to spurn her."

"No, no. It was the other way around. Juliana found a nobler man in the end."

"Ah, I see. Well, if I were back in Tennessee, I'm sure I would have three children by now, but here in Washington, under the spotlight of politics, love is a little fickle. How did your experiments in the garden turn out?"

"Merci beaucoup, Ferdinand Hassler and I are still overwhelmed with the data we collected."

"How could I turn down the requests of such a sweet old man like Ferdinand? Besides, the two of you will make Washington the center of the West."

Entering the East Room, a crowd of a hundred or more people was flitting about like a host of sparrows, though each with their own agenda. Nicollet could feel the eyes of the crowd upon him as they all tried to figure out who the stranger was on the arm of the most eligible lady in the capital. "What do you think of Washington so far?"

"Everything is so fresh and new. The trees are young and orderly,

THE ALCHEMIST'S MAP

the streets are straight and flawless, and even the residences are built symmetrically."

"What are your impressions of the White House? How does it compare?"

"Magnifique," Nicollet held back from being too superfluous. "Are there grander residences in Paris? Certainly, but there the taint of the past seems to hang upon all of the buildings. Everything here is much more… open. I was actually surprised by how accessible the White House was. In Paris, there would have been gates and guards surrounding it."

"Yes, well, Uncle Jackson is not called 'The People's President' for no reason," Mary Ann explained, slowing upon entering the fray to allow the crowd to come to them. "My sympathies about what is happening to your country, but America is the land of opportunity."

Yes, Ferdinand Hassler helped me get in the front door of the White House, now it is time to get my funding.

A few weeks earlier, he and the Swiss-American scientist decided to make the White House garden the center of all measurements in America, which was not only practical but also caught the attention of those in the White House, especially Miss Eastin, who'd heard of Nicollet and the coming comet.

Now, Mary Ann identified faces for the important names he'd learned while his presence made her many suitors jealous.

"Joel," Mary Ann guided him to a tall, slim man with thin black hair on his head and striking sideburns along the sides of his stern face, "this is Joseph Nicollet of France; he is a fellow man of science, and much like yourself, a bachelor for far too long."

"Joel Poinsett," the tall man vigorously shook Nicollet's hand.

"A man of science? What is your field?" Nicollet asked.

"Botany, isn't it?" Mary Ann interjected. "We received your Christmas plants. They were beautiful."

"La flor de Noche Buena," Poinsett added.

"We call it the 'Poinsettia.' Besides being a brilliant scientist, Joel is one of Uncle Jackson's most trusted advisors," Mary Ann said. "He is far more internationally savvy than all of the men in this room combined."

"You flatter me, Mademoiselle Eastin, but my scientific prowess is amateur at best, when compared to the illustrious astronomer, Jean-Nicolas Nicollet."

"He prefers 'Joseph' now that he is American."

Poinsett added, "I hear you have been working with Ferdinand Hassler."

Nicollet was taken aback. "Oui."

"Don't worry, Professor Nicollet. I'm not secretly spying on you. I have friends on the steering committee responsible for funding projects. I came across your name on a bill trying to establish a Hydrographic Office separate from either the supervision of the Army or Navy."

"Yes, Mr. Hassler is patiently waiting to find out the fate of the bill."

"Patiently? Hah, perhaps we are talking about a different cantankerous old man," Poinsett laughed. "Why your sudden interest in hydrology? Lose interest in astronomy?"

"Of course not, not with Halley's Comet almost upon us. If Ferdinand's Hydrographic Office is funded, I can follow my heart's desire to explore and map rivers, like my mentor Humboldt once did."

"Mapping rivers? What a surprise. I'll see what I can do to help Hassler's bill, but if you really want to make a name for yourself, you must become friends with that man over there."

Poinsett fixed his eyes on a fierce fellow at a distant table. "That man is Thomas Hart Benton, the senator from Missouri. It used to be the Chouteau family who held the keys to the West, but Senator Benton has them now. He can help fund you."

THE ALCHEMIST'S MAP

Nicollet already knew the name of Thomas Hart Benton. *Already a thorn in my side.*

Mary Ann also seemed to cool at the mention of Benton. She whispered in Nicollet's other ear. "Senator Benton is originally from Tennessee and used to be Uncle Jackson's most trusted friend, but in the War of 1812, they quarreled openly, and things have never been the same. I would not trust that man."

Poinsett whispered even lower. "There is a saying that Senator Benton never quarrels, but when he does fight, a funeral follows."

"Would you like to meet him?" Mary Ann asked softly.

"Could he fund an expedition?"

Eastin and Poinsett both nodded.

"Proceed."

Mary Ann took him by the arm and led Nicollet through the crowded floor.

"Be careful with Senator Benton," Mary Ann said. "It is said he shot a rival attorney through the throat. The man challenged Senator Benton's honesty."

"Humboldt was right about America being a wild place. Terrifiant!"

"Benton is a proponent of Manifest Destiny, which is why Joel said he now holds the keys to the West. I believe you will find him receptive to your plans to utilize your new mapping techniques."

"I hope he is more receptive to it than Hassler's proposals. I will forever be in your debt, Mademoiselle Eastin."

"And from the jealous looks I've been getting, I shall be in your debt also."

Before they could get any closer to Benton, however, Nicollet felt a strong hand on his arm. "Excuse me," a man said.

Someone has come to challenge me for the arm of Mary Ann, but when he turned, he could tell immediately that the man had come for him and not a dance with Miss Easton.

The sinister man said, "Professor Nicollet, I've been looking for you. I will bring him back shortly, Miss Easton."

Nicollet wasn't so certain.

CHAPTER ELEVEN
PARIS, FRANCE
1831

In the deep recesses of the Louvre Museum in France, the night was almost over.

Jean-François Champollion felt his head spin and knees buckle as he tumbled sidewise over a wooden crate holding the bust of Pharaoh Akhenaten.

Oh, I should have eaten more before I accepted the drink.

The crate lessened the fall, and he balanced himself to a sitting position on the crate. One of the surprises of his tour of the Valley of the Kings had been the discovery of the tomb of Akhenaten, a heretical pharaoh despised by his predecessors after a religious revolution away from classic polytheism toward monotheism.

Either the creator of God, Champollion reflected numbly, *or a disciple of Moses.*

Champollion looked back over to the uncorked bottle of wine and the two glasses set on the edge of his workbench. One glass remained almost as full as it had been when poured—the other, his, barely had a drop remaining.

Fifty thousand francs—the news had been worth celebrating, and as a show of gratitude, Champollion had gulped the wine down and slammed the empty glass on the table, much to the amusement of the courier, Jean Plant.

When dawn comes, I must go home and tell Rosine that we will be rich, and Zora will get a chance to visit America.

As Champollion pushed himself back onto his feet, he felt a sharp pain in his forehead, a symptom antithetical to a bit of drunkenness. He stopped himself from taking another step, but then his balance spun wildly out of control. His arms did little to stop him from falling and he crashed hard on the cold floor, striking his head.

The dull pain in his cheek did not trouble him as much as seeing his limbs begin to twitch and shake beyond his control. The pain in his sinus cavity expanded and his stomach, which still held the contents of the glass of wine, had tightened.

Poison?

The smooth-talking stranger, a courier from America, had come to him with promises of a financial windfall with a single trip to America for two months during the summer. The deal would not only line his pockets for the rest of his life, but it would also expand his reputation in America as the ultimate authority on the Rosetta Stone and Egyptian Culture.

Who would want to kill me?

A strange comfort came over him, along with a full seizure, that he

THE ALCHEMIST'S MAP

and Akhenaten had both been poisoned. For Akhenaten, it had been his long-time military commander, Horemheb, who poisoned him. For Champollion, his friend, Jean-Nicolas Nicollet, had brought on his demise.

I should have kept my mouth shut. Nicollet tried to warn me. Why did I have to say something in public about the map?

He tried to think of the men who'd laughed with him at the bar, but the muscle spasms took control of his body, and then released for a moment.

I'm only forty-one. My daughter is just a child. I'm too young to die.

Then another spasm, worse than the previous, stole his concentration for almost a full thirty seconds.

Catching his breath, Champollion clawed at the crate as if trying to will himself back onto his feet, but even his hands no longer obeyed. He remembered his hands once carving his name onto the Pillar of Karnak.

Thus dies Pharaoh Jean-François Champollion, master of ancient languages.

CHAPTER TWELVE
DISTRICT OF COLUMBIA
1831

"Qui êtes-vous? What do you want with me?" Nicollet stared at the angry ogre, hoping not to quiver in fear.

The man in front of him would have looked the part of a butcher, including a blood splattered apron and a massive cleaver in his hands. Instead, he wore all black, making him look like the grim reaper, albeit without his sickle. The emotionless man had the face of a bulldog and square shoulders to match. With a strong hand, he'd grabbed hold of Nicollet's lapels and practically dragged him out of the dining hall until both men stood outside beside the tall pillars.

"Je ne comprends pas, Monsieur?"

"Father," the man said, sweeping his thick mane of black hair away

THE ALCHEMIST'S MAP

from his face. "Father Pierre-Jean De Smet. And you have become a real burr in my saddle."

"Excusez-moi?" Nicollet asked, almost convinced the priest was about to murder him. There were people nearby, but none of them would be able to intervene in time if this De Smet man wanted to kill him.

Mon Dieu, is this the man who killed Lady Drummond?

"I know who you are, Professor Nicollet, for it is I who sent for you."

"You? I came to America of my own accord."

"Did you? While I've never been to Cluses in Savoy, I have visited Paris, but my favorite place to lay down my weary head is at the Chateau de l'Ermitage in Rouen. Are you familiar with this place?"

"Yes."

"I know you are familiar with it, because I wrote to my superiors requesting help. While I have been working closely with various Indian nations for several years now, I need a man with a specific skill set if I am to do my job properly."

"Do your job properly? What is that exactly?"

"To protect the weakest members of Christ's flock," De Smet said, his chest almost even with Nicollet's nose. "Presently, I tend to the countless tribes of refugee Indians that have been displaced by the expansion of European immigrants. As shepherd, I battle wolves in all sorts of sizes and shapes, including the ones who come in the darkest hour at the break of dawn."

Don't reveal anything. "As admirable as that all sounds, I believe you are under false impressions. I came to America of my own accord, with my last franc. I am here on no other mission than to acquire a sponsor for a scientific expedition that will allow me to utilize barometric measurements to advance the field of cartography."

"Do you have any idea who Father Lupo is? Or who Conrad Simmons personally reports to? You are either a man of great cunning or a great fool. Nevertheless, here you are. I see it as a sign of God, the true master of your destiny."

Nicollet looked around, trying to see who else had stepped outside. Inside he could still hear the music, where Mary Ann Eastin waited. "Who are you to know the will of God?"

"Excuse me?" De Smet recoiled. "I don't have time to set you straight. I'm taking a ship across the Atlantic to explain what is happening out on the frontier. Until I return, you are to take up residence at the White Marsh in Maryland, where the Jesuits will tend to your needs until I return. Then you and I will properly finish this investigation… together."

"What is happening on the frontier?" Nicollet ignored the order and continued his own investigation.

"Fear. Anticipation. A war is brewing and I have only begun to understand why. Because of your foolishness, I've been summoned to present an update to men like Simmons and Lupo. If I were you, I'd keep my head down for the next few years… if you value it. White Marsh is a safe haven, and nearby, you'll find Jesuit colleges such as Georgetown, where you can teach and study astronomy. I need you to understand that if you are not our agent, then you are an enemy, so go to White Marsh and wait."

Wait? It'll be months, if not years, before De Smet returns, and time is of the essence. "No, this is what is going to happen. I am going to go right back into that ballroom, find Mademoiselle Eastin, and continue to play the part of the pathetic, penniless Parisian."

De Smet's bulldog face scowled.

Nicollet did not fear the threats of De Smet. "And hopefully, none of our enemies saw you foolishly steal me away. Because as long as they see me as a pathetic, penniless Parisian, and not a pawn of the powerful Catholic Church, I am invisible to our enemies."

THE ALCHEMIST'S MAP

And now, to put his tail between his legs. "You have no need to question my loyalties or my methods, which is why your powerful friends came to me in the first place. So, no, Father De Smet, I will not wait for you at White Marsh. You can look for me at the headwaters of the Rivière Morte."

De Smet fumed, "The frontier will chew you up and spit you out as a juicy ball of phlegm. Your bones will wither and rot before I can even return to find them."

And now, march back into the party. Nicollet did not look back, but as he neared the doorway, De Smet called out, "Wa-ha-na-tan."

Nicollet stopped in his tracks and spun back around, his tails flapping like the wings of a bird landing. "Is that supposed to mean something to me?"

"Wahanantan. He is an elderly Sioux chief, and the last of a generation that lived the last time Halley's Comet crossed the skies," De Smet said, standing on the edge of the darkness.

Halley's Comet? What does that have to do with anything?

De Smet finished his point. "If God wills that a man such as yourself do his bidding, then seek Chief Wahanantan. Perhaps *you* will have better luck finding him."

Nicollet nodded and turned back to the party, where he saw Mary Ann Eastin making a beeline for him.

"Where have you been? There is someone other than Benton you need to meet. He is looking for map makers."

CHAPTER THIRTEEN

DISTRICT OF COLUMBIA

1831

John James Abert, like many of the men in the room, wore a military uniform. From what Nicollet could tell, he wore the rank of colonel, although determining the branch of military proved more elusive. A man in his mid-forties, the tightfitting uniform no longer flattered him, which Nicollet took as a sign he was more bureaucrat than soldier now.

"Colonel Abert, this is my handsome friend, Professor Nicollet, the astronomer," Mary Ann Eastin began. "It sounds like the two of you are long overdue for a meeting. I'll let you gentlemen speak about matters of… great importance… and I'll return in a few minutes to rescue one of you from the other." She flitted away and was immediately swept up by another man hoping to have her ear.

THE ALCHEMIST'S MAP

"Bonjour, Major Abert," Nicollet said, extending his hand, which Abert gripped uncomfortably hard.

"Hello, Professor Nicollet."

"Yes, I was hoping we could talk for a few minutes."

"Of course, have a seat."

"I did not expect to meet you here tonight."

Abert scoffed at the lie.

Oh, dear. "Did you happen to have a chance to review my qualifications? I've conducted a few experiments with Ferdinand Hassler, and he told me about your interests in mapping."

"Your qualifications are quite impressive, Professor Nicollet. As a member of several scientific communities, I know you are spoken of quite highly. In fact, I'm glad to have met you here tonight. Tell me about your idea of using a barometer for map making."

He is interested. "It really isn't an idea I invented but one that I borrowed from a mentor of mine, Alexander von Humboldt."

"Well, it's a good thing for you that von Humboldt didn't apply for the job then," Abert bluntly joked.

Nicollet took a few minutes to explain how barometric pressure readings could be used to create a map that showed elevation instead of just mapping based on the two dimensions of longitude and latitude. When he finished, he felt certain he'd done enough to secure his funding.

But Abert did not seem impressed.

"I must be honest with you, Professor Nicollet. Given your age, I honestly do not think you are the right man for the job. I am looking for soldier-scientists, men who have a military background and can defend themselves in hostile Indian Territory."

"Indians do not frighten me, sir. On the contrary, they make the assignment into the Dakota Territory even more interesting to me.

87

Over the last few months, I've read all about the Indian tribes out on the frontier."

"Really? What do you know about the frontier?"

"Government policies and population growth have caused a dozen Indian tribes to stack up along the shores of the Mississippi River. The Chippewa, Menomonie, Winnebago, Fox, Sacs, Pottawatomi, Iowa, and Illinois Indians all sided with the English during the War of 1812, only to ultimately be defeated by the United States Army. A generation prior to that, these same tribes sided with the French, only to lose to the American colonists and the English. I think I understand why they are hostile. All these tribes that had once existed as far east as the Hudson are now stacked up against the Mississippi, standing in the way of progress."

"Progress, yes, Manifest Destiny. Do you know why they were so foolish as to listen to the English and enter into a war against the United States?"

"They were desperate."

Abert chuckled. "Fighting us was the lesser of two evils."

"I'm not sure I follow."

"There is a tribe that lives on the other side of the Mississippi River called the 'Oceti Sakowin,' or the 'Seven Council Fires.' Until recently, their kingdom stretched several hundred miles from the Great Lakes all the way to the Black Hills near the Rocky Mountains. All those tribes you just rattled off affectionately refer to this nation as 'the serpents,' or the 'Sioux,' as your French predecessors called them. Lewis and Clark called them the most 'warlike' and the 'vilest miscreants of the savage races.' Have you read the recent news about the Black Hawk War in Illinois and Iowa?"

"Black Hawk is the leader of the Fox and Sac tribes," Nicollet answered, having read about it in the papers.

THE ALCHEMIST'S MAP

"Yes, it has been a brutal, bloody fight down to almost the last man. Black Hawk would rather face our bullets than migrate further west. What does that tell you about the Sioux, Mr. Nicollet?"

Wahanantan, the last great Sioux Chief. "It tells me that the United States government might want to rethink its policy toward the native population." The words came tumbling out faster than Nicollet could stop them. *Well, that should end this conversation.*

At this, J.J. Abert laughed aloud. "You've only read about the Noble Savage in your books, haven't you?"

Nicollet nodded in defeat, knowing he debated when he should have been flattering.

"I'm afraid you are a victim of poor timing," Abert said with an eye roll. "Are you familiar with George Fanshaw?"

"The English geologist?"

"Yes. Unfortunately for you, I recently hired him to produce a map of the mineral resources of the Louisiana Purchase and to produce a map of the elevated country between the Missouri and Red River watersheds. He has already departed for the Upper Mississippi."

With a stolen map? Or is this mere coincidence? Nicollet's heart sank. "I am sure he will do a quality job."

"My department is in its infancy, Professor Nicollet. If I am to get more funding, I will need men like Hassler and Fanshaw to meet early success before the government purses open up for much-needed expansion."

"Oui, I've seen some of these maps."

"You have?" Abert acted surprised. "Tell me what I have purchased with my investment."

"Mr. Fanshaw is a reputable geologist. Who am I to question his work?"

"But?" Abert pressed.

"I am sure the good old guide's information was meant well."

"But?"

Nicollet sighed in polite resignation. "I believe my predecessors made a monstrous blunder in describing the mouth and watersheds of some of these rivers."

That was bold.

Abert weighed his claim. "Well, in the days to come, the United States Military will need accurate maps before sending men into Indian Country. The accuracy of the watershed could be a matter of life and death to these commanders, and knowing elevation is paramount. That is why I would like to hire you to train some of my officers in your barometric techniques."

The wind left Nicollet's sails. *A teaching position? No, I need to personally investigate these rivers.* "Excusez-moi, but I was under the impression that you were looking for a man to lead an expedition."

"That is correct, Professor Nicollet. But I simply do not believe you are the right man to lead his expedition."

"May I ask why?"

Abert clenched his teeth for a moment. "A colleague wrote to me about my idea of hiring you. He felt your Catholicism would prejudice any discoveries you might make in fields other than barometrics."

A colleague, Nicollet repeated to himself. *Could it be the murdering thief?* "I can assure you, Colonel Abert, that my dedication to scientific pursuits is not blinded by any belief that I have. I might believe in the guiding hand of Providence, but I am a man of science, rest assured."

"I respect your abilities, which is why I want you to train my officers. America is founded upon the separation of church and state. How do I know you will limit your studies to matters of geography?"

Nicollet nodded, taking it all in stride. "I have indeed passed the middle years of my life; I do believe that there is a hand behind the

THE ALCHEMIST'S MAP

design of nature and the acts of Providence seen in life. Yes, I am not the most robust man, but I assure you that having grown up in the foothills of the Alps, I am made of mettle far stronger than it may seem. I have grit!"

"So you will not accept the job to train my officers?"

"You need me to lead this expedition, Colonel Abert. Science is not made like bread: not with an oven and a recipe and a knead of the wrists. A man in the field needs to know not only techniques but must be able to adjust his method to many circumstances. You want a man with the experience to develop new strategies for unexpected situations."

Just then, Mary Ann Eastin swept over to their table and sat down across from the two men. "Joseph, you need to come back and save me from these bad dancers."

"You see, Colonel Abert. Why hire an amateur when you can have a master?"

Nicollet stood and extended his right hand to Mary Ann and bowed slightly to her. She giggled and took his hand.

Nicollet turned back to Abert, who was clearly amused with his timely remark. "Perhaps time will show you that I am a man of science. If it makes you feel better, a priest at St. Mary's College questioned my dedication to Catholicism because of my close friendship with Humboldt."

Nicollet winked at Abert and walked off with the most eligible maiden in America.

"So did you get the job?" Mary Ann Eastin asked.

"Not yet, but I think I am getting closer. All I need to do is prove myself to him."

"I have an idea," Mary Ann announced.

"Please do tell."

"You have something none of these other men have."

"It's certainly not money…"

"Not that, no," she chuckled. "You are a celebrity. America is built by lumberjacks who want to be aristocrats, and with the coming of Halley's Comet, everyone wants a piece of your sophistication. Wherever you go, you will be received as an esteemed guest. Just announce your intentions… and go."

"I am afraid I currently do not have funds to travel where I want to go."

"Could you afford to travel to Georgia?"

"Georgia? I don't want to go to Georgia."

"Yes, you do. I apologize for forgetting that our controversies are lost on strangers to our shores. Do you see Mr. Poinsett? The two men he is talking to are politicians from Georgia and South Carolina. South Carolina is upset about tariffs placed upon them, and Georgia is trying to claim as much land as possible from the Cherokee after the Indian Removal Act. Joel is probably trying to negotiate peace between the two rival states. If you were to show up in Georgia, there would be a bidding war for you."

Cherokee? I want to visit the Sioux. "A bidding war?"

"Throw caution to the wind, Joseph. Go to Georgia."

CHAPTER FOURTEEN

SANTEE RIVER

1833

Johnny Frémont rode up to the scientific camp on the finest horse from the plantation stables. It had taken more time than expected to find the Pied Piper of Savoy, and the heat of the South Carolina sun pounded down upon his layers of civility, threatening to strip away all of the lies that covered him.

Seeing the group of scientists in the distance, Frémont reached down to his canteen and took a sip of water, then used his handkerchief to dab away at the sweat that collected along his brow below his hat.

Use your assets, he'd been told earlier that morning. And what fine assets they were.

Approaching the Santee River, Frémont held his horse at the edge of the water to observe the band of scientists and also take measure of his own appearance. At twenty, he barely needed to shave, but having done so, his skin glistened in his reflection in the river, accenting his notorious dimples. Despite the ride, his dark hair still behaved itself, parted down the middle but swept back.

Use my assets.

"Professor Nicollet!" Frémont announced loudly enough so that all the men gathered on the southern side of the river could hear him. "Good afternoon!"

Against a backdrop of dogwood trees, the entire expedition took note, with some waving back and others continuing right on with their tasks. A young man with a notebook in one hand and the knobs of a tripod in another recorded the measurements while a local surgeon waved two white flags at the mouth of a small creek.

A few yards away at the shoreline of the Santee River, two local chemists searched for fossils and rocks to add to Nicollet's collection of specimens gathered during his expedition through the Great Smoky Mountains.

Sitting in the drooping arms of a massive southern live oak tree, a local science teacher instructed a new recruit on the science behind the Humboldtian principles of the barometer.

Where is Professor Nicollet?

Frémont gently spurred his borrowed horse forward into the current of the Santee River to get a better look.

They all know I've come to take him away. Most of these men don't even know me yet know what I am.

"Professor Nicollet?"

A hand emerged from the tall grass and Frémont steered toward it. From his position atop the horse, he found Professor Nicollet lying on his back, face up to the sun, with a hat placed over his head.

THE ALCHEMIST'S MAP

"Has the Mountain Goat of Currahee been bested by the South Carolina sun?"

Nicollet quickly lifted his hat, squinting. "Ah, the young mathematician, Johnny. Enchanté."

"It is a pleasure to see you again, Professor Nicollet. When I heard you'd entered South Carolina during your tour of the south, I had to come and see you again, and invite you to stay at Santee Hills, one of the finest plantations in the state, for an early Christmas party."

"A Christmas party? Merci beaucoup. My legs are still strong, but I can't catch my breath. The humidity near the ocean had made it even more difficult to breathe. I think a Christmas party is just the antidote to this exhaustion."

Without invitation, Johnny Frémont jumped off his horse to lay down in the grass beside Nicollet. "Did you ever find Dugas?"

"Unfortunately, yes. He wandered off to relieve himself in private and got lost. For all his sophistication, he doesn't have any common sense out in nature."

These other men might be acclaimed scientists but they are all great fools. "So you are following the watershed from Currahee all the way down to the Atlantic. Is that why you've come this far?"

"You've hit the nail on the head, Johnny. I have learned a great deal about mapping as well as choosing traveling companions during this trip. I am also beginning to worry my ambitions might exceed my ability."

"Nonsense. As a college dropout, it took me the better part of a month to understand what you were doing with the data from your barometer, but now that I understand the math, it is pure genius, Professor Nicollet."

"Stolen knowledge from an actual genius."

"I have a hard time picturing Alexander von Humboldt climbing

95

up Currahee or Look Out Mountain. Nor can I picture any of these other men lasting a few more weeks."

"What are you suggesting, Johnny?" Nicollet asked, opening his eyes.

"I heard that you were once the apprentice of Pierre-Simon Laplace, the legendary astronomer, and that he helped guide your career. Let me be your apprentice."

If the other rumors are true about Nicollet, this might work.

"Who says I am looking for an apprentice?" Nicollet coldly answered.

"I'm not blind, Professor Nicollet. I understand why you are mapping Cherokee country."

"You do? For such a young man, you must possess great wisdom to understand me so well."

"I saw you cry when we visited New Echota. None of the other scientists felt the pain and loss of the Cherokee people the way you mourned what was being done to them. I realized then you were neither a dispassionate scientist nor were you a crook taking advantage of an opportunity. You see the Cherokee as your fellow man, don't you?"

"I do, Johnny. I didn't realize you had seen my reaction."

"It made me realize you've given much thought to the state of the Indian in America. When I saw how you viewed them, it became obvious that mapping the south was an exercise. You mean to go west, don't you?"

"West? I could barely survive Nashville."

"I've dreamed of going west since I was a boy. I want to see the frontier and meet the wild Indian tribes like the Sioux and the Chippewa. I want to make a name for myself in a land where no one knows who I am."

"A name for yourself? Aren't you proud of the name Frémont?"

The sins of the father... "Isn't that why you've come to America, though? To make a new name for yourself? Everyone who can read knows the name of the famous astronomer Nicollet, but we've also heard rumors about why you left Paris. Rumors hang over my head also."

Nicollet grew silent for a few moments.

"I'm more than just a mathematics teacher. I'm also a novice linguist."

"You are?"

"There is the local Santee tribe, no more than a hundred souls tucked along the river, who speak a unique variation of Siouan. Apparently, they are a distant cousin to the Sioux on the Great Plains. As an apprentice, I could translate for you."

"Even if I were looking to take on an apprentice, and even if I were planning on going west, I could never afford to pay you. I can barely afford to take care of myself, Johnny. I am nearly destitute. I've spent months in the South trying to make a name for myself so that I can secure patronage to fund my studies. All I've received so far is charity."

"Oh," Frémont said, disappointed. "I just assumed you were a wealthy aristocrat traveling the world. I didn't mean to beg you for a job." Lying on his back in the grass, Frémont suddenly felt like a cheap whore as Nicollet, once again, gave him no indications that the rumors of his sexual preference were true. In disgust, Frémont stood back up and brushed off his pants.

Nicollet shielded his eyes as he looked up at him. "If I were to hire an apprentice, you'd be my first hire."

Don't say that. You have no idea what kind of man I am. "You don't mean it."

"Yes, I do. You're a skilled mathematician, and you seem at home on a mountain peak or beside a river. I too have dreams of seeing the frontier and meeting the wild Indian tribes before the greed of the white man steals everything from them. I'm looking for magic out there in the frontier. Why have you returned to the expedition? I thought you'd acquired employment."

"Yes, I now work for Mr. Poinsett."

"Joel Poinsett?"

"Do you know him?"

"Yes, I met him last year at a party in Washington, D.C. How do you know Mr. Poinsett?"

"I've known Joel since I was a boy. He only recently married, and without any children of his own, he's taken down-on-their-luck boys like me and helped them find their way in life. He helped me attain a position at the local college, before I was expelled for… an intimate relationship with the president's daughter. It was a rumor, of course, but with my name, everyone believed it."

Nicollet sat up in the grass. "Poinsett sent you all the way out here to invite me to a Christmas party. Why would he do that?"

"Honestly, I think the two of you might have a lot in common."

"What exactly would we have in common?" Nicollet asked.

Frémont laughed, seeing that Nicollet took offense at his playful innuendo. "He is a world traveler and scientist. If anything, you must see his greenhouse. He has botanical specimens from all over the world. He's a remarkable man."

"Are you suggesting I flash my dimples and bat my eyes and the man will hand over money?" Nicollet asked.

"Poinsett is a discreet man, a private man, a gentleman through-and-through. In that way, he reminds me a lot of you. He's always focused on his work, too. He was a congressman and, more recently, the Minister to Mexico. Joel knows everybody. Will you come to the party?"

"How could I refuse such an offer?"

"Wonderful. Would you like to see some of the ancient burial mounds of the Santee? It's a bit off the main road, but local experts believe the mounds predate European contact."

"If what you say is true about the Santee being cousins of the Sioux,

THE ALCHEMIST'S MAP

I'd rather see this burial mound than attend a party. Lead the way, young pathfinder."

Pathfinder, Frémont reflected as he helped Nicollet begin to pack. *I better hope I can find that burial mound from here, or Nicollet will think I'm a fool.*

CHAPTER FIFTEEN

SANTEE HILLS
1833

"He's in the greenhouse," Johnny Frémont said over the noise of the party. "He wants to speak with you...alone. Do you want me to come with you?"

"I'll be fine," Nicollet said. *If I can handle Alexander von Humboldt, I can certainly manage Joel Poinsett.*

Upon arriving from their thirty-mile trip to Santee Hills, both men had been immediately welcomed and given rooms, but not by Poinsett.

When they had arrived at the plantation, Frémont had a private conversation with his mentor, who'd stayed in the greenhouse rather than attend his own party.

The mansion was then filled with more than a dozen other guests,

THE ALCHEMIST'S MAP

and by the time Christmas music began to play, hundreds filled the ballroom.

Outside the party, the wind and the rain beat against the plantation, making Nicollet notice how the swell of heat and music rivaled nature herself. Yet in the protection of the little greenhouse, the environment was controlled, producing perfection unmatched elsewhere in the world. The glass and green frame kept the air humid and warm.

On the ride from the Santee River, Frémont fully briefed Nicollet prior to arriving at the Poinsett plantation, so it came as no surprise to see hundreds of green and red plants filling the greenhouse.

A remarkable man, Nicollet reflected.

Across the length of the greenhouse, Joel Poinsett carefully pruned his prized possession: the Poinsettia.

"Flor de Noche Buena," Poinsett said without even turning. "As with the Franciscan friars in Mexico, the local Baptist preachers have quickly adopted the plant into their Christmas traditions, which means on the morrow, my inventory of plants will all but disappear. Left alone to nature, the plant would end up looking like a weed, but with a little patience, I will hopefully produce another crop of masterpieces by next Christmas."

"Your skill with a scalpel is almost as impressive as your skill as a mentor. Young Mr. Frémont said you'd like to speak with me."

Joel Poinsett hovered over a microscope to study sap residue on a slide. "Yes, are you enjoying your tour of the South, Professor Nicollet?"

"Of all the states I've visited in America so far, South Carolina is certainly the most accepting of the French. And until this evening, the weather has been delicious."

"You must remember that the French liberated South Carolina from the English in the Revolutionary War. Young Mr. Frémont's father was French."

"Bien sûr. With a name like Poinsett, I would assume you are French also."

Poinsett seemed to tense for a moment but only to hastily change slides on the microscope. "I am an American, Professor Nicollet, born on American soil. But yes, the French are indeed popular here in Charleston. My wife and I are pleased that you found time to visit us, now that political tensions have eased."

American politics are still a mystery. "Oui, things are improved. The talk of secession over tariffs and taxes was breaking my heart. I am glad to see the war ships beginning to leave Charleston Harbor again. I saw war rip apart my country twice in my lifetime; I do not wish to see it destroy such a beautiful country as America."

"Peace can be fickle. I've been hearing tales of the 'Pied Piper of Savoy' leading the youth of the South over hill and vale with his barometer instead of a pipe."

Nicollet chuckled at the metaphor. "Is that how I am seen?"

"All of Dixie is ablaze with stories of the French explorer. I was told you were nicknamed the French Mountain Goat after your studies of Currahee Mountain."

Frémont's doing, to be sure. "No," Nicollet blushed and shook his head. "I broke my ribs after tripping on my own tripod and falling out of a window. All things considered, I am glad to have southern hospitality to nurse me back to health and good spirits. Thank Heaven for the protection that has followed me everywhere. I have suffered much but not from men, whom I found good to me."

"You are welcome to stay at the mansion as long as you like," Poinsett continued speaking without looking at Nicollet.

What does he want? "You are too kind."

Poinsett remained focused on his work for several moments before pushing away from his microscope. He glanced at Nicollet, and then

THE ALCHEMIST'S MAP

focused on his plants. "Botany is a vastly different field of study than astronomy. I have heard you are quite reputable in the field of astronomy, that you've done studies on a comet that flies by the earth once in a lifetime."

"I stand upon the backs of greater men," Nicollet shrugged. "It is Halley's Comet you speak of, and I have only polished theories already put to paper."

"I understand," Poinsett looked up from the green leaves of his plant. "Theories can bounce around for centuries until the right man unlocks their meaning. How many supposedly great men have made scientific claims, only to be disproven by a better man? I hear you have combined your astronomy skills with meteorology skills to create a new sort of map."

"You know about the map?"

"I am an international diplomat. I have cultivated hundreds of relationships in Washington and abroad, and they all like to whisper. The world is about to become much smaller, thanks to science and maps. How are yours different?"

"Topographical maps show elevation as well as longitude and latitude. With a baseline comparison of a known elevation, I can take readings of barometric pressures at a certain location and compare that to my barometric readings to determine height, factoring in the effects of weather upon the readings. I've found considerable success in mapping the territory of the Cherokee.

"When your man Frémont found me, I was charting the descent of the Santee River back to the ocean. America is like a great Christmas present waiting to be opened by a child. We know the general size and shape, but what lies within? That is the great mystery."

"The great mystery..." Poinsett repeated the phrase as if tasting it. "The great mystery is which of the Indian tribes will try to kill you first."

The words chilled Nicollet, but he brushed them off. "The world is made up of all sorts of people. Indians are no different."

"They are barbarians, sir. I have fought the savages, including most recently in the Seminole Wars. Now those same savages are once again causing problems, like a pest limiting the growth of a plant. Humanity simply needs a little pruning to become what it was meant to be. So yes, I do find your topographic maps quite intriguing. How did you find the Cherokee during your trip to Georgia? How did the Noble Savage strike you?"

"The Cherokee were poor, but so too are many when their land is taken from them either by force or by politics."

"Their time has come and gone, and now greater people will show them a new theory. Soon, they will be removed west of the Mississippi."

How can I ask him for money after all he's said? Nicollet took a moment to gather his thoughts. "I hear you're working on a national museum from the inheritance of the late chemist James Smithson."

"You're familiar with Smithson?" Poinsett asked.

"I am. He was a bachelor like us, married to science," Nicollet teased.

"Alas, I have found Mary, but it is doubtful I will have children. My legacy will have to be the works I leave behind, like Smithson's museum. It will be the nation's attic, dedicated to men of science who are helping to shape a new world out of an old weed. You are a man of science, aren't you, Professor Nicollet?"

"Je suis désolé, but I must get to the heart of the matter. I am seeking funding for a scientific expedition, and—"

"You would like me to help fund it?"

"Oui."

"Have you tried the offices of the U.S. Corps of Topographical Engineers? Colonel Abert?"

Nicollet bit his lip. Before he could answer, the door burst open and

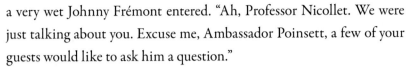

THE ALCHEMIST'S MAP

a very wet Johnny Frémont entered. "Ah, Professor Nicollet. We were just talking about you. Excuse me, Ambassador Poinsett, a few of your guests would like to ask him a question."

Frémont had Nicollet by the arm and didn't seem to wait for permission.

Just as the two of them reached the doorway, Poinsett called out. "One moment, Johnny. After careful consideration, I've decided that the time has come for you to leave the nest. I've arranged a new teaching position for you, one where you might have a chance to learn a trade and also go on a great adventure."

Is Poinsett jealous? Have I ensnared the affections of his young protégé?

"Where will I be teaching?" Frémont asked, his hand still on the handle of the exterior door.

"Now that the nullification crisis has ended and the Charleston harbor no longer needs to be secured, you will serve on the USS Natchez under Commander Shubrick."

A math teacher on a warship?

"Thank you, Sir," Frémont said. "I won't forget the kindness you've shown me."

"Professor Nicollet," Poinsett added. "Go back to Washington. Show Colonel Abert the work you've been doing here in the south. Perhaps it will change his mind. The wheels of government move slowly. Give it time."

"Thank you, Ambassador Poinsett. I will consider your advice."

Once outside, between the stillness of the greenhouse and the joy of the party, Frémont stopped. "Perhaps it is a good thing he said no. With Joel, there are always strings attached."

"You knew he was going to reject my request?"

Frémont nodded. "Earlier, I asked if I could join you on your

Mississippi River expedition. Now I'm to serve on the USS Natchez. With the harbor now open, I will not go back to Washington like a beggar. Take a ship around the gulf and go to St. Louis. Someone will hire you."

CHAPTER SIXTEEN

ST. LOUIS
1835

St. Louis, known as the Gateway of the West, is older than any other city in North America by hundreds of years. Established at the confluence of the Mississippi and Missouri River, it controls the fourth largest river system in the world. The modern American city also contains the ruins of Cahokia, which exceeded London in population hundreds of years before Columbus arrived on the continent.

For generations, the city belonged to the French territory of La Louisiane, named after the French king Louis IX. French fur traders Pierre Laclède and Auguste Chouteau established the city in 1764, but following the Seven Years' War, the ownership of the city and territory shifted from France, to Spain, back to France, and eventually to the

United States as part of the Louisiana Purchase.

In the 1830s, the uniquely French city witnessed an influx of international immigrants as steamships and paddle boats traveled up the Mississippi from New Orleans and down the Ohio River from Tennessee. One of these new immigrants to the city was Joseph Nicollet, who finally arrived in 1835 following a cholera outbreak that left him stranded in New Orleans for a time.

At least the stars have waited for me to make a good impression, Nicollet thought as he rested in his simple hotel room.

His steamer trunk still held his sextant and barometer, but a cheap telescope he'd purchased in the French Quarter had done the trick—announcing the arrival of a world-renowned astronomer to a city starved for attention, just as Halley's Comet neared Earth.

Two weeks earlier, after securing a cheap room for a six-month lease, he had hauled the telescope down to the docks near dusk and had pretended to take measurements of a cosmos barely visible through the worthless instrument.

Two days later, the Jesuit associates of Father De Smet knocked at his door, begging him to tour their college campus. By the end of the tour, they offered Nicollet a paid teaching position, which he nearly accepted due to his extreme poverty.

A few days after visiting St. Louis College, another stranger knocked on his door, one Pierre Chouteau, Jr. The grandson of the city's founder, Chouteau took it upon himself to meet the traveling celebrity and show him around the town. He even invited him to a party that Saturday. In exchange for a promise to give the family a private viewing of Halley's Comet, Chouteau gifted a set of family texts chronicling the influence of the French on America.

With his fiddle silent, his belly empty, and his clothes a bit ragged, the idleness of his particular kind of poverty allowed him to spend

THE ALCHEMIST'S MAP

hours reading about the history of the Mississippi River Valley and the Great Lakes.

When another knock came at the door, he held *The Annals* by André Joseph Pénicaut in his hands.

Opening the door, he came face to face with a towering fellow with straight ebony hair that swept over his left eye.

"Professor Nicollet?" the man asked in perfect English, revealing a chipped tooth. His steely eyes studied him impassively, allowing Nicollet to note the giant's dark complexion which revealed his heritage, even if Nicollet could not place the specific tribe.

"Yes," Nicollet said, taking in every little detail about the handsome figure in front of him. Although the stranger wore deerskin clothes, they were in no way barbaric—a crafted collar, cuffs, frills down the seam of the arms, and small little ornamental buttons. Some sort of leather talisman hung around his neck, and a pistol was shoved into the man's belt. Just like the Cherokee, the man had a smooth face, without beard or mustache, but the eyes were fair instead of brown.

A Métis. He is a half-breed.

"I've been asked to bring you down to the docks to speak with Captain Billy."

"Captain Billy?" Nicollet chuckled. "And what is your name, my friend?"

The Métis quickly reached down, drew his pistol, and leveled it at Nicollet's face. "No questions. Grab your jacket and come quietly."

He doesn't want to kill me, so what does he want?

Nicollet did as commanded, grabbing his jacket and closing the door to his room behind them.

"We will go out the backdoor to the alley," the large Métis said, still with no malevolent attitude beyond the bradishment of a deadly weapon.

Soon, Nicollet found himself in a small carriage, side-by-side with his captor, who had nodded to a waiting driver as they'd climbed in.

Captain Billy? Is this all a prank?

All along the St. Louis Levee, crude buildings and warehouses created a wooden wall where everything from buffalo pelts to kegs of alcohol waited to be distributed. A dozen steamships parked, some loading, others unloading. Even at night, bells, steam engines, and shouts of working men filled the night.

Would anyone pay me any mind if I shouted for help?

The somber Métis brought him to a small steamship about twenty feet long, much shorter than a passenger steamship.

My abductor has money. If he wanted me dead, I'd be dead. Whoever this is, he wants to talk. Has the buyer finally come to collect me?

Once aboard the steamship, the Métis tossed over the ropes, kicked the vessel away from the docks, and turned the ship upstream.

If necessary, I could jump overboard and swim to shore and hide in the woods until morning.

A face lit up at the prow of the ship, illuminated by a cigar. It was the face of a European man with a prominent mustache and dark hair. He wore a felt hat with a large feather on one side.

"Do you know me, Professor Nicollet?"

"Yes, I believe I do," Nicollet said. *You are Captain Billy.* "I recently saw you from a distance at the Chouteau mansion."

"Yes, all of St. Louis has had the opportunity to be introduced to the illustrious astronomer, including many of your enemies."

"Enemies? Why would I have enemies?"

"That is one of the reasons we're taking this little cruise—to determine if I am one of your enemies. Senator Benton doesn't like you. Now he's far away in Washington, but still finds a way to block your passage.

THE ALCHEMIST'S MAP

The Chouteau family knows you, but aside from a bit of curiosity, they won't help you either. What do they know about you? What secrets have been whispered to the powerful of St. Louis?"

The dark river soon took away all witnesses, leaving the sound of the boiler, the turn of the paddles, and their passage through the water as the only sounds. Nicollet found himself shivering, unsure if it was the cold or the terror.

Nicollet asked, "How could I be your enemy when I don't even know you?"

"Ah, yes. I like the anonymity of America. Here, on this river, I am Billy Stewart."

An English name?

"Is that why you have come to America, Joseph? To make a new name for yourself? To be a different person than you once were?"

"I suppose that does have a certain appeal. America is an alkahest for change for migrant Europeans. What role did you once play in Europe?"

"The spoiled second son of a nobleman."

Sir Billy?

"Back in Europe, my father simply bought a captaincy for me and as a young man, I was ordering older men, sending some of them to their deaths as we held the gate against the forces of Napoleon. None of it was earned, however. The opportunity was purchased. Here, on the frontier, respect is earned.

"I now have friends like mountain man Jim Bridger, guide Kit Carson, and trapper Thomas Fitzpatrick because I have earned their respect through hard work and deeds. Do you think Antoine followed me all the way down here because he is my slave or servant? No. He has watched you for the past several days because I am his friend."

"What a dull chase I must have given him," Nicollet said, trying to think of all the places he'd been.

"On the contrary, you should have heard Antoine speak of the Basilica of St. Louis. Growing up in the wood and wild of Canada, he'd never seen a church before. Tell me, Professor Nicollet, what does a man of science such as yourself do so often in a church?"

"I confess my sins, both minor and egregious, and look to God for guidance as I seek his path for me here in the new world."

"You sound like a priest."

"Merci beaucoup. As a boy, all I wanted to do was become a priest, but there were few paths that led to priesthood during those years."

"Why haven't you married? Everything I've heard claims you are more chaste than most priests."

"I have taken a bride." *I'd probably be surrounded by grandchildren rather than books if that path hadn't been taken away from me.* "Science is my mistress."

"Then it would seem you've been having issues in your relationship."

"I certainly didn't expect she'd lead me to a dark river with Billy and Antoine. What do you want, Sir William?"

"After spending two years exploring the west with Mr. Clément, I had planned to return to Cuba and refill my depleted coffers. Then, from across the seas, the good Lord delivered you into my grasp. What do I want? I want what is inside your head."

"All you needed to do was ask. We could have had drinks."

"Yes, but so few men are honest, and the truth can be so very... loud. Many Native American tribes torture their prisoners over flame. The tribes of America are filled with beautiful people, but they can also become very violent. I once saw Antoine gut an elk in less than ten minutes. It was horrifying to see what he could do with that knife of his. I couldn't share a tent with him for two days afterwards."

"Let's hope it doesn't come to that," Nicollet said. "What do you want to know?"

THE ALCHEMIST'S MAP

"Why have you come to St. Louis?"

"I'd like to study the upper Mississippi River."

"Bah!"

"Excusez moi?"

"I said, 'Bah!' And spare me your fucking French phrases! I'll cut off a finger just for spite. The Mississippi River is a dead end. Dozens of explorers have gone there. She is a flirtatious whore with nothing special between her legs. Countless explorers have taken their turns with her. What makes you think you're any different than them? Your Humboldtian technique?"

Nicollet felt his jaw drop. Stewart had done his homework but had also revealed that there was no longer a race to the headwaters.

"Antoine! I am about to ask Professor Nicollet an important question. Have we traveled far enough from the city yet?"

The giant Métis, Antoine Clément, looked back, then at Nicollet, and nodded and flashed a smile, showing his chipped front tooth.

"Why do you want to go to the headwaters specifically?" Stewart asked.

He already knows the answer, so I will give him more truth than he wants.

"When I was a young man—still a boy, really—there came a desperate pounding on our door in the middle of the night. Being a young fool, I rushed to the door and flung it open, and there stood five Jesuit priests who had managed to escape death from the mob during the early days of the French Revolution. While my father wanted to be rid of them, my mother welcomed them into our house, gave them food and water, and then did something which would ultimately prove to be foolish.

"'Come with me, Nicky,' she said, and after feeding them, my mother sent me with the Jesuit priests to a trail leading out of Cluses and into the Alps. She tasked me with leading these heroes of the faith to safety, a journey that would take almost two weeks of my life.

"When I returned, I found my house occupied by men of the revolution. They weren't the same men who'd raped, tortured, and murdered my mother, but they knew what had happened to her because they told me. They'd buried her in the backyard along the stone fence. Revolutionaries decided the Jesuits needed to be killed, and they tortured my mother to find out where they had gone. She died with her secrets, choosing to save her son and the Jesuits I led to safety. So go ahead, Mr. Stewart. Threaten me with violence. Cut my flesh or burn it, but while you hurt me, I will be thinking of my mother."

"And I will be thinking of my aunt," Stewart said as his finger played with the curl at the end of his mustache. "If you'd like to avoid answering the question while trying to create an emotive bond between yourself and your captor, then let me share a story also. I hated my Uncle William, after whom I'm named. Growing up, my mother always talked about her strange Drummond relatives, especially her siblings. William was a strange man. Since he was wealthy, friends of the family called him eclectic. He wrote poetry as a profession and spent the family's wealth on his library of everything old and odd. My aunt Margaret suffered from the same peculiar mind as Uncle William, which is why, after obtaining some of his strange artifacts from his library, she went to visit the illustrious Professor Jean-Nicolas Nicollet of Paris. Now tell me... who do you work for?"

CHAPTER SEVENTEEN

ST. LOUIS
1835

Clément's big knife slid back and forth across a whetstone as Nicollet tried to focus on the telling of his story to Stewart. He looked over at the Mètis in the prow of the boat. *That man would kill me without a moment's hesitation.*

Nicollet managed to withhold the specific details about the map while also revealing a theory he'd conjured.

"The Longue River?" William Drummond Stewart repeated after hearing the story.

"Yes. Finding it unlocks the puzzle. Lahontan and Le Sueur implied that the copper mine was built off of a tributary of the Mississippi River, but in the 1680s, the Mississippi River system was uncharted, with only a few landmarks, such as Lake Pepin."

"Which is why it is like searching for a needle in a haystack?" Stewart asked.

"Before you can begin to search, you have to find the right haystack."

"So the church wanted you to find the right haystack?"

"Yes, the location of Fort L'Huillier. I was told not to concern myself with acquiring the treasure."

"And what is this treasure they seek?"

"The map did not clearly answer," Nicollet answered honestly, even if he had been able to deduce its subject. "The obvious value of the map was its age, which I assessed to be hundreds of years old." *If not older.* "The mysteries written upon it also relate to occult lore. So anyone with an obsession for alchemy or grail lore would see it as a penultimate collector's item."

"And its actual value?"

"Before I tell you that, there are things I'd like you to answer for me. I've openly told you what I know about Lady Drummond's map, but trust is a two-way street, William. If you and I are to trust each other, there are a few questions I need answered also."

"Such as?"

"I am in a race against forces I do not understand. Someone wanted to buy the map from your aunt. Someone killed her to obtain it. Who am I competing against? Who are my enemies?"

Stewart's face was long and thin, with cold, empty eyes that sorted through the pieces of the puzzle. "Most of the men belong to masonic organizations, such as the Freemasons, which only serves as a vetting organization for men of true power, like my Uncle William."

"Freemasons?"

"Surely a Frenchman knows about secret societies, else your kings would still rule the kingdom."

THE ALCHEMIST'S MAP

"Of course, but why would Freemasons have an interest in the Alchemist's Map?"

"Modern freemasons don't. Even to men who decorate their lives with arcane symbolism, the Alchemist's Map would seem foolish, but the older organization that created Freemasonry understands it, which is why they are two steps ahead of you."

"How do you know this?"

"My Uncle William, of course. I am competing against my own family, in a way. When I was young, I would sneak into his room or library. I wanted to follow in his footsteps to become a Freemason, and then, to join the Order of Eos."

"The Order of Eos?"

"That is the answer you seek. I don't know if they were the ones who wanted to buy the map or the ones who killed her for it, but the Order of Eos is behind some very strange things."

Eos, the ancient goddess. "What is the Order of Eos?"

"As you've probably figured out, their name refers to the dawn."

"As a reference to the east?"

"Or a reference to the beginning, but not as a devout Catholic would see it—they seek to understand the prima materia that formed our universe. They are a religious order of sorts, with connections that weave through Freemasonry, Templar Knights, Cathars, and the Gnostics of old. It is one of the oldest religions, even if it is unknown by most."

"An ancient religion? A friend of mine once told me that the art of alchemy goes back to the pyramids of ancient Egypt," Nicollet said, feeling a wave of depression splash against the rocks of his soul, despite the waning but still very present threat from Stewart and Clément. *The newspapers said Champollion died from a sudden stroke, but I worry he spoke openly about what he saw.*

Stewart shrugged. "I don't understand what they want, any more than I understand what the map will reveal. As it turns out, I was not worthy of such secret knowledge."

"Not worthy?"

"My poor character, I was told. I suppose I was a bit of a sneak, which is the only reason I know as much as I do. Lurking around my uncle's library taught me enough, but it seems my sexual appetites prevented me from being trusted with the Drummond family secrets. Love one of the stable boys, and they all look away. Get a servant girl pregnant, and they all but cut you out of the family."

Nicollet looked long at Stewart and then glanced at Clément playing with his knife at the prow of the boat.

"Antoine and I will soon be parting ways. As a Métis, he understands what it is like not to belong, but I assured him I will return as soon as I can afford it. If the Order of Eos has already been to Minnesota and departed, the treasure must be up another western tributary of the Mississippi.

"Since I have resolved not to kill you, come with me to Cuba for the winter; I depart at the end of the year. Next spring, we shall go on an adventure together."

And trade Humboldt for Stewart? I think not. "Cuba is the wrong direction, unfortunately. My destination is still north." *I was asked to investigate the truth of the legend... not to acquire the stone.*

"So be it," Stewart said with a shrug. "You can be bait. When they kill you, I will know where to hunt."

The abduction ended a few hours after it began, and when the small steamer returned to the levee, Nicollet stepped onto the dock, knowing he'd dodged death.

"So what now, Professor Nicollet?" Stewart said as he helped Nicollet off the boat and onto the dock.

"For almost five years, I've carried the burden of the Alchemist's

THE ALCHEMIST'S MAP

Map with me and there are many secrets I'd like to share. I thank you for believing me and I'd like to trust you as well. If you'd like to know what men seek with this map, I will share my knowledge with you, but not under threat, and not until I know I can trust you."

"What can I do to prove my trust?"

"Meet me tomorrow morning at 9:00 at the corner of Maryland and Newstead Avenue."

"For what reason?"

"To determine how badly you want to know the truth."

CHAPTER EIGHTEEN
ST. LOUIS
1835

Lord William Drummond Stewart tried to sleep in the musty old bed but only tossed and turned. He'd grown used to the lumps and the smell of the bed, and the foul air of the hotel room. Tonight, he struggled to sleep because he was alone.

Oh, how I hate you, Joseph Nicollet.

Out on the streets of St. Louis, he heard Saturday night begin to come alive: drunken brawls, giggling whores, and loudmouth braggarts filled the streets while he suffered in the third floor of a pathetic hotel room.

To hell with this hermitage, Stewart thought, throwing the blankets aside. *Tonight, Captain Billy is going to play.*

The streetlights provided enough light for him to find the kerosene

THE ALCHEMIST'S MAP

lamp, which soon illuminated the modest room, purposefully poor except for a table stacked with texts meant to torture him day and night like a cilice.

Even the wardrobe was pathetic, filled with little vests, little jackets, and little pants, but Stewart found a loose fitting white shirt and an oversized pair of trousers that rode up his ankles. *I'll have to let my charm do all the work.*

Stewart walked over to the little mirror, thinning out the tips of his mustache and sweeping his thinning black hair to one side.

I don't even know you anymore, Stewart said to his reflection.

It has been twenty days since he found Nicollet waiting at the corner of Maryland and Newstead Avenues, standing with his arms crossed in the shadows of the Cathedral Basilica of St. Louis. After hearing the proposition, he'd told Nicollet to "get fucked" loudly enough that a dozen churchgoers gasped as they walked toward the front door.

He and Clément then waited outside for mass to end before deriding Nicollet for such a suggestion.

"Even if I did believe in Heaven and Hell," Stewart complained later that Sunday, "my hypocrisy would immediately damn me just for walking into that place."

"Churches were built for sinners, not saints," Nicollet countered. "For me to tell you the truth about the Alchemist's Map, I must first determine whose side *you* are on."

Nicollet went on like that for the next few days, and like a chaste whore, kept giving him teases of lore with conditions, flirting with the largest theories without giving it all away. Christina Battersby had once denied him for weeks on end, only to end up as the mother of his bastard child, George. Stewart assumed Nicollet was simply a harder nut to crack.

By the end of the week, though, Stewart agreed to simply step inside the Cathedral—on a Friday.

Nicollet only intended on showing Clément and Stewart around the wondrously new cathedral, but a stern nun and a rude young priest brought a ferocious defense from Nicollet, who championed Stewart's honor as if his own. By the time the squabble ended, Nicollet sat with Stewart and Clément in the plush offices of Bishop Joseph Rosati.

"An Act of Contrition, perhaps?" Nicollet offered to the Bishop.

"I'm not even a Catholic!" Stewart voiced, thinking he'd found an exit from the frenzy of the vicious mongoose that defended him.

"Well, we shall soon remedy that," Nicollet declared and Clément's smile revealed his broken tooth.

The Act of Contrition turned into a fortnight of silence, poverty, and Nicollet's favorite act—chastity.

Nicollet swapped hotels with Stewart, leaving him his books and dank room while Nicollet took Stewart's multi-room suite across the river. Yet, even in the lap of luxury, Nicollet remained restless, stealing Clément for visits to the local Potawatomi reservation on the edge of town, where Nicollet could learn the ways of the Mississippi River Chippewa from their displaced Anishinaabe cousins from Michigan.

Now, Stewart approached the door, ready to break his vows.

What good is confession if you have nothing to confess?

While he could have sated his lusts with a night in Clément's company, Stewart realized his present weakness was not sexual but social—he missed his conversations with the little scientist.

Stewart adjusted his shirt buttons, leaving a bit of dark chest hair exposed at the opening. He rummaged through Nicollet's belongings until he found enough to buy a drink. He grabbed two personal items: the Knight Companion Grand Cross Star for his bravery at Hougoumont, and his trusty boot dagger, which he'd owned even longer. One could start a conversation; the other could end it.

THE ALCHEMIST'S MAP

Time for Captain Billy to play.

The devilish grin on his face vanished when he saw a man standing in the hotel hallway.

The young man shifted back toward the stairs as if ready to run. His brown hair was greasy and matted and his prominent chin quivered.

"What do you want?" Stewart asked.

"Joseph Nicollet?" the man asked with a slight Cajun accent. He wore a soiled plaid shirt and suspenders.

"What of it?" Stewart huffed.

The Cajun reached behind his back and produced a flintlock pistol. His palm swept over the firing mechanism and the barrel leveled at Stewart's face. "The Russian sends his regards."

Just then, another hotel-room door opened, and a fat older woman in a draping nightgown became a witness to the assassination attempt.

The Cajun's fingers tightened around the pistol.

So this is how I die? Stewart wondered a moment before the hammer fell, sparking the flint, which ignited the gunpowder in a flash of flame. The discharge erupted from the barrel in thunder and lightning, and its force caught Stewart in the forehead, blinding him and knocking him off balance.

The fat woman screamed.

Strange, how can I hear her without a brain?

The residue in his eyes vanished with a few blinks, leaving him staring at the baffled Cajun assassin.

Is half my head missing? Is that why he gawks?

Stewart reached to his boot, and when he came up with the knife, the Cajun bolted for the stairs.

Stewart ran after, still in a crouch, but his quarry spun so quickly he ran into the fat woman, knocking both of them over.

Having killed in both war and the wild, Stewart let his knife do the work, sinking the blade into the man's kidney several times before pulling him off the screaming woman.

"Go get help," Stewart said to the woman as he grabbed the crawling Cajun by the suspenders and rolled him over, blade to his throat.

The young man was dying, though, and worried more about that than his mission.

"Oh God, oh God, I'm dying. I'm dying."

"Who sent you?" Stewart demanded.

"The Russian. He didn't give me his name."

"Who the hell are you?"

"Melwin," he gasped through the pain. "Melwin Devereux. I'm sorry, sir. I'm sorry. The Russian... he... he gave me so much money and promised even more if—"

While the Cajun writhed in pain, Stewart used his left hand to inspect the bloody crater in his own skull.

Impossible.

His fingers found tissue that was neither flesh nor brain matter— firing paper. Instead of blood, his fingertips came back black with residue.

It's... it's... a miracle?

"Listen, Melwin. Don't die with a guilty conscience. Tell me more about this Russian fellow. What did he look like? Where did you meet him?"

"I'm sorry, sir. It wasn't personal. Oh, it hurts. It hurts so much."

I should just slit his throat and end his suffering. But at the stairs, the fat woman brought back a half-dozen men who'd all very likely want to hear from the assassin before trusting that Stewart had acted in self-defense.

"The Hand of Providence," Nicollet had told him. "Repent, convert, and the Hand of Providence will guide you as it guides me."

Now I really need a drink.

CHAPTER NINETEEN
ST. LOUIS
1835

Halley's Comet is a short-period comet visible from earth about every seventy-five years. It is named after Edmond Halley, who built upon the work of scientists like Isaac Newton to determine the gravitational effects of the sun and planets on the course of the comet. During the winter of 1758, the comet arrived just as Halley predicted.

Astronomers could not only predict the return of the comet, but they could also go back in history to recognize its previous appearances.

Seventy-five years after Halley, the eyes of St. Louis watched as Nicollet's future hung in the balance. His fingertips held the little screw removed from Brigitte Chouteau's prized sewing machine, and by lantern light, he threaded the replacement screw into the hole. With three turns, the screw pulled the metal bar back into place.

Below the telescope, Nicollet lay on the cold ground and looked at the collection of legs belonging to the wealthy Chouteau family, politicians, clergy, scientists, artists, river barons, and the elites of St. Louis. Even in the presence of King Charles, he had not been so nervous.

A hush fell over the crowd as Nicollet crawled out from under the telescope. "Our repairs should hold."

After a round of applause, Nicollet restored the telescope settings for observing the coming comet. A missing screw had rendered the telescope useless for anything besides gazing at the moon.

One by one, the elites of St. Louis came to peek up at the heavens for a closer view of the new star above. Even Sir William Drummond Stewart waited his turn, and when finished, stood beside his new friend.

"The screw must have fallen out between here and the Potawatomi camp," Stewart said with a shrug.

Nicollet shook his head. "If any of them had found a screw, they would have come running into town to tell us."

Following the violent end of Stewart's hermitage, the suddenly silent Scotsman had joined Nicollet on a trip to the reservation. When the new telescope arrived, Nicollet insisted on "testing" it at the reservation prior to a public exhibition at the Chouteau mansion.

The aristocracy of St. Louis gasped and giggled like little children; the Potawatomi Indians acted as if Stewart and Nicollet had descended from the heavens with the telescope.

One by one, Nicollet took potential financial sponsors behind the eye of the telescope for a viewing of the comet.

"Do you know who that man was?" Stewart asked from beside the telescope.

THE ALCHEMIST'S MAP

"Which man?"

"The squatty man with his son. Just a few moments ago."

"The Englishman?"

"Yes, that was the geologist George Fanshaw."

Colonel Abert's man. "Why didn't he say something?"

"He's a person of interest," Stewart whispered.

Nicollet closed his agape mouth. "Is he?"

"Since he arrived in St. Louis, I've had Clément spying on him, and when he arrived at this party, I watched him closely. The more I think of it, the less convinced I am that my nemesis is employed by the government. I'd like to know who holds Fanshaw's purse strings."

"It is not a secret in Washington," Nicollet shared. "Colonel Abert of the United States Topographical Engineers. We competed for the same expedition funds."

"With Fanshaw?"

"Somehow, yes. He is a geologist, an expert in rocks; how could he possibly understand the complicated nature of cartography?" Nicollet asked as he helped another guest locate the comet. "If he is your man, will you and Antoine be following him to Georgia?"

Stewart looked away, knowing Nicollet referenced vengeance and murder. "No, I spoke with a member of Fanshaw's expedition, a painter named Catlin, who verified the worthless nature of the expedition. A puppet but not a puppet master. Fanshaw goes to Georgia to supervise the allotment of the newly acquired Cherokee lands."

At this, Nicollet took his eyes from the stars. "Acquired? Or stolen?" he asked, no longer shielding his exasperation. "He has been employed by a flock of vampires, William, as ruthless and unscrupulous as the same land speculators that have stolen the homes of countless Indian nations. Or perhaps I am mistaken. These Georgia gentlemen are not brigands: society determines their wealth demands our respect. Voilà!

But when the sun goes down and the stars and moon appear, they are vampires, I tell you."

"Vampires?" a deep baritone voice asked from the crowd, followed by a few chuckles. Nicollet turned to see a thick-chested man wearing an expensive jacket. Over the past few weeks, Stewart helped him navigate the aristocracy of St. Louis, including the recent arrival of Senator Thomas Hart Benton for the holiday. His young daughter, Jessie, stood at his side.

"Senator Benton," Nicollet acknowledged from his place next to the telescope. "I am pleased that you've come to the viewing. Mademoiselle Benton, you have the opportunity to see Halley's Comet twice in your lifetime, unlike the old men gathered around you. We must wait for a moment for a cloud to pass."

Senator Benton scowled while he waited. "Perhaps these wealthy vampires have turned into *bats* and pulled the clouds over our eyes, much like your earlier hoax."

Nicollet felt the knife sink into his belly and twist. The corrosion of his career had not stopped upon leaving Paris. "I was upset earlier when I called those men vampires. My apologies, Senator Benton." *Now I know who has been blocking my efforts to acquire funding. But which benefactor does he serve? Or is he himself the villain we seek?*

"Spare your apologies, Professor Nicollet. I've read all about your pseudoscience."

"What is that supposed to mean?" Nicollet feigned, already knowing what the senator was so brazenly alluding to.

"Come now, Professor. No need to be coy with us. Your former colleague François Arago recognized your work. Or was it really the work of your friend Hershel?"

"I don't understand," Nicollet said, forcing them to speak the rumors in public.

THE ALCHEMIST'S MAP

"Mr. Griggs," Senator Benton called out. "Tell everyone what the newspapers in New York are discussing."

A man from Benton's entourage glanced at Nicollet and smirked. "A short time ago, the *New York Sun* ran an article about how John Herschel observed bat-like creatures on the Moon from his observatory at the Cape of Good Hope."

"Impossible," Nicollet laughed. "John would never say such a thing."

"That is exactly what his wife told the press. She explained to the world that her husband never observed such things, but that the creator of the hoax was undoubtedly a scientist of some esteem who knew the workmanship of such astronomical observances."

"Are you suggesting that *I* am behind such a hoax?"

"No, Professor," Senator Benton took back leading the affront from Mr. Griggs. "*We* are not suggesting anything. It is the world-renowned astronomer François Arago, at a meeting of the Academy of Sciences, that named you the originator of the hoax. He claimed that no one else in America had the technical knowledge and that only Joseph Nicollet could have perpetrated such a convincing yarn."

This man wants to ruin me tonight. "I am surprised Arago would admit I had enough knowledge to perpetrate such a hoax. Even a world away, he is threatened by my shadow. Alas, I have been on the lower Mississippi these many months and would be unable to create such a fable."

The crowd chuckled, the cloud passed, and soon the dour Senator Benton and his lovely daughter went back inside the mansion.

"Senator Benton is friends with quite a few vampires," Stewart quipped.

Yet does he mock me for political reasons or personal ones?

"Professor Nicollet," a tall Jesuit priest said, walking to the front of the line from the rear entrance of the mansion. "My name is Father

Vandevelde. I am a teacher at St. Louis College."

"Don't worry, Father," Stewart said. "We're taking good care of your telescope. We'll bring it back to the college first thing tomorrow morning."

"No, I am not here for that. You see, I am a friend of Father De Smet."

De Smet? Has he returned from Europe then? Nicollet could see Stewart did not understand the reference. "Father De Smet is a friend, even though we did not see eye-to-eye at the time. If you are a friend of Father De Smet, Father Vandevelde, then you will understand why I cannot accept help or sponsorship from the Catholic Church."

"Yes, I understand, but there is a new matter. A complication that I feel you must be made aware of. There is someone looking for you."

Am I in danger again? I suppose it was only a matter of time. "Ah, yes. I am only standing here in front of you by the grace of God."

"I don't think you understand. The Indian who is looking for you showed up yesterday at the Potawatomi camp demanding to see the Star Man."

CHAPTER TWENTY
FLORISSANT VALLEY
1835

A glaze of ice covered most of Missouri. The storm came on the heels of two months of warmer-than-normal weather, turning a grey landscape into a scene of both terror and wonder.

It looks like the glassworks shop on Rue De La Boétie, Nicollet observed, feeling a keen bout of nostalgia for Paris.

The wheels of the wagon beneath him sounded like a grindstone as the ice crunched between wood and frozen gravel.

From time to time, a tree would groan, the ice would crackle, and the silence of the morning trek would briefly be upended by the shattered symphony of splintering wood as another child of summer succumbed to winter's grasp.

Beside him, Antoine Clément looked as wide-eyed as Virgil guiding Dante through the ninth level of hell. His gloved hands held the reins of the wagon, but his eyes were anywhere but on the slow road ahead of them.

"The poor Potawatomi," Nicollet said halfway to the reservation. "The residents of St. Louis suffered through the storm under the protection of roofed and walled homes, but they had to endure the storm out in the open."

"Don't pity them too much," Clément said. "These are the same people who forced my people north into Canada. I was taken prisoner by the Chippewa for two years until my father traded pelts to get me back."

From under his blanketed hood, Sir William Drummond Stewart added his thoughts. "Yes, save your pity. The Anishinaabe nation made war all the way from Nova Scotia to the Mississippi River, leaving behind a dozen of their tribes, like the Potawatomi in Michigan and the Chippewa in the north. They defeated every enemy in their way with the help of your French forefathers."

"So where were they going?" Nicollet asked coyly.

Stewart remained silent, and Clément shrugged, leaving Nicollet alone with his theories.

"Let's have it, Nicollet," Stewart said bitterly after a few minutes. "I've bent to your requests again and again. Your God spared my life so I could be on this miserable road with you today. Tell me this theory you hold."

Having been to the Potawatomi camp several times, Nicollet knew he was too far away to stall the salty Scotsman. "Ask yourself, why does the Catholic Church care?"

Neither Clément nor Stewart answered.

"A century ago, the discovery of Fort L'Huillier might have mattered

THE ALCHEMIST'S MAP

as a land claim, but now, it is irrelevant since the land has passed to the United States of America. The Philosopher's Stone? No. If the staff of Moses had been brought to a secret land, then I could understand their interest, but why did the early Jesuits fix all their means and attention on following both the Order of Eos *and* the Anishinaabe?"

"What do you mean they followed the Anishinaabe?" Stewart asked.

"What do you think those books were for?"

"To help me sleep?"

If only they could do the same for me. "The Jesuit Order methodically followed the migration of the Chippewa from their ancestral home near Nova Scotia all the way to the headwaters of the Mississippi River. The Church does not benefit by finding a lost fort. Nor does it benefit by finding some magic rock. What does the Church gain or lose in this quest?"

"So? What's the answer?"

"That's what has been perplexing me for so long. It is the unanswered question."

"Are you serious?" Stewart snapped. "You better have a better answer than that."

"Fine, I do have a theory, but it is wrapped in speculation and conjecture." Nicollet looked over to the blanket-wrapped Stewart and knew he risked losing a vital ally. "Sevens. Providence seems to be giving me clues about Sevens. The Anishinaabe are guided by a prophecy described as 'Seven Fires' and their mortal enemies, the Sioux, are a people who identify themselves as the 'Oceti Sakowin,' or the 'Seven Council Fires.' The Al Marakk Map used stars to identify the mysterious place where water flows in all directions, with Marakk, or 'Merak' as the biggest clue. You see? Seven."

"I don't know what 'Merak' means, Nicollet."

"Sure, you do," Nicollet said cryptically. "It is one of the seven stars in the asterism known commonly as the 'Big Dipper.'"

"Hmm. My Uncle William had an obsession with astrology, especially the North Star, which he lovingly referred to as 'Our Lady, Star of the Sea.'"

"The Big Dipper, specifically the stars Merak and Dubhe, point the way to Polaris. The lore behind these stars is vast." *Oh Champollion, my friend, I still have so many questions for you.*

"You're still holding back, Nicollet. So the Sioux, Chippewa, and even the Order of Eos all have their symbolic sevens... what of the Church?"

"I had hoped to advance your religious training beyond the tenets of Christ before I discussed this, but how familiar are you with *The Revelation of St. John*?"

"The End Times?" Stewart scoffed. "So it *was* you who concocted the story about vampire bats on the moon?"

"Of course not! I'm simply trying to understand what a man like Father Simmons expects. I did not say I subscribed to these theories, did I?"

"No."

Nicollet nodded, satisfied. "In *The Revelation of St. John*, there are many symbolic sevens. There are seven archangels, seven seals, seven trumpets, seven bowls of wrath, and..."

This time, even the silent Clément snapped his head away from the road to coax Nicollet into an answer.

"And an obscure passage about a seven-headed water serpent."

"A manito?" Clément asked. "The Mishi-Ginebig?"

"Providence, I tell you," Nicollet concluded. "Through my research and travels, I've learned most Native American tribes still dread a water serpent, the same way St. John used the serpent as a symbol for ultimate evil."

THE ALCHEMIST'S MAP

"So we're on a quest to find the Devil?" Stewart pursed his lips. "I'd rather find a magical rock."

"Yes, I'm sure that is what Pierre-Charles Le Sueur thought also."

"Le Sueur? The copper miner?"

"Why did he travel so far into the unknown with a professional mining crew? The Order of Eos would like to believe it was to find the Philosopher's Stone. But what would the Church expect?"

"Just tell us."

"Oh, I don't really have that part of the answer yet. The passage baffles me, so I ask the two of you."

"A monster," Clément insisted.

"A body?" Stewart offered. "Perhaps of some lost patriarch. Noah's Ark? The Ark of the Covenant? Who can figure religious zealots?"

"I certainly haven't been able," Nicollet admitted, "but it seems as if the three of us fight for their interests, even if we don't know the full truth yet."

The crunch and crackle of ice continued, and Nicollet watched as Stewart's breath continued to emerge from the blanket in white puffs of agitation.

Andrew Jackson's Indian Removal Act had forced the Potawatomi on a four-hundred-mile migration from Michigan to the western shore of the Mississippi, where they made camp along the confluence of the Missouri and Mississippi Rivers. The flood plains along the river had been left unsettled, allowing the once-mighty nation to find another temporary home.

"See?" Stewart said as he allowed the blanket to drop from his shoulders. "The Potawatomi might survive us all."

Columns of smoke drifted through the barren cottonwood trees growing along the southern bank of the Missouri. Children ran through the camp, playing on the slippery ground while the elderly piled up broken branches in front of their shelters.

Once the children recognized the visitors covered in coats and blankets, they crowded around the wagon gleefully. Nicollet hopped into the back end and began to hand out crates of food and supplies, only enough to last a week for a camp this size.

After the trio stepped out of the wagon, a few Potawatomi elders led them through the village and down to the shore. Thanks to Clément's tutelage, Nicollet understood much of what they spoke, but he allowed Stewart and Clément to translate.

The visitor Father Vandevelde had told them about waited for them across the river on Pelican Island, leaving the three men no choice but to make the perilous trek across the river.

With a dip of the paddle, Nicollet's canoe veered toward the icy shore. At first, the nose of the canoe broke the thinnest ice along the flowing Missouri River, but ten yards from the shore, the canoe halted. Flipping his paddle, Nicollet and the others had to perforate the ice, then break off chunks at a time, until finally his paddle could no longer puncture the ice, which meant it would be strong enough to stand upon.

Rushing this tedious process meant almost certain death. If his foot broke through to the icy waters, even if it was only knee deep, he risked dying before a fire could warm and dry him.

After hauling his canoe up onto the ice, Nicollet caught his breath and looked into the distant groves of trees where a single line of smoke rose into the grey sky.

Just a few miles south, a large cloud of smoke marked the edge of civilization.

"Just as Father Vandevelde described," Stewart observed. "Our prophet will be the one carrying some sort of beaded wampum belts on his shoulders. And a peace pipe?"

"How does this prophet know me?" Nicollet asked as they secured

THE ALCHEMIST'S MAP

the canoe away from the flowing water.

"He doesn't know you," Clément answered, having gone alone the previous day to verify the presence of the stranger. "He went to the Memegwesi Clan and demanded information."

"The Memegwesi Clan?"

"The Water Spirit Clan," Clément translated. "The tribe's clergymen. The Potawatomi are terrified of this stranger, which is why they sent for you. He's isolated on the island because the people fear him," Clément continued as they walked into the woods along the shore of the island.

"What did the old men call him? Hiawatha?"

Stewart smirked. "They think the prophet is either a god or sent by a god."

"He so frightened the elders that half of them threw down the crucifixes they wore around their necks, lest they offend him," Clément said. "Father Vandevelde was not pleased."

The tall cottonwoods released cold drops of water along with chunks of melting ice that fell from the upper branches.

"The Potawatomi children told him they had been visited by 'a man from the stars,'" Clément added.

"Ridiculous," Nicollet said, suddenly understanding.

"Yes, your ability to blacken the moon and summon stars has impressed the Potawatomi, and now this prophet wants to meet you," Clément finished.

"Am I in danger?" Nicollet asked Stewart.

"Besides bringing Antoine, I also brought a pistol and knife," Stewart answered. "We'll keep you safe."

Instead of finding an old witch doctor beside a fire, Nicollet spotted a young man skinning a squirrel. With bloody hands, he stood up and smiled.

CHAPTER TWENTY-ONE

PELICAN ISLAND
1835

"One of you must be 'the man from the stars,'" the young man greeted them with Nicollet's native tongue.

"I am Nicollet," the Frenchman replied

The young man walked over slowly, and once he stood in front of Nicollet, he sized him up and then took a deep breath.

"You smell like flowers," he said with a slight grin.

Caswell No. 6. "You speak French?" Nicollet asked, surprised by the fluency of the young man. "Do you also speak English? The uncertain nature of this visit has my friends on edge."

"Of course," the young man said in English. "My people have had dealings with Europeans since they climbed upon the back of the Great

THE ALCHEMIST'S MAP

Turtle. My English is much better since I only get to use French when I travel to Canada."

The Great Turtle, Nicollet pondered. *A symbol for the whole of North America, while the Chippewa's prophecy seeks a literal turtle-shaped island.*

"Have you just come from Canada? If so, you've traveled a very long way," Stewart said. "What brings you to the Florissant Valley?"

"Yes, I have traveled a long way, seeking the fulfillment of the prophecy of the Serpent Star. I've traveled to the villages of the Anishinaabe, the Meskwaki, and the Oceti Sakowin in advance of the omen, only to find it here—at my ancestral home."

"Cahokia," Stewart's grumpy expression instantly turned to the wonder of a child. "Cahokia is ancient history."

"I have returned because the ancient prophecies say a star will appear to signal the arrival of the Wishwee. Both the children and the elders told me you knew all about this star."

"I do," Nicollet said.

"My grandfather said that in the days of his grandfather, the same star appeared, signaling the coming of another Wishwee."

The appearance of 1682—when both Le Sueur and Lahontan worked in the Great Lakes region. "I am sorry, I do not know the word 'Wishwee.'"

"'Wishwee' is an old word. It is a word for a hero who will come to fight an ancient evil. The star that you summoned has made two appearances in recent memory, and I have come seeking Wishwee."

Nicollet felt flush. "Surely you don't think I am this Wishwee."

The young man wiped off his bloody hands and ran the skinned squirrel through with a stick, grinning as he worked. It was obvious he was very much a man and not a god, but he also did not look like any of the Potawatomi either.

After sitting beside the small fire, Nicollet took a moment to study the young man. If not for his long hair and deerskin clothing, the young man could easily have transformed himself into a dockworker back in St. Louis. He had almost sandy blonde hair and greyish blue eyes.

Once the young man leaned away from the fire, Nicollet asked, "What is your name?"

"I am Sha-Koo-Zoo-Shetek," the young man said proudly.

"Are you from the Mandan tribe?" Stewart interrupted.

"Those Who Go Underground?" Shetek grinned widely as if Stewart had said something funny. "My people are much older than the Pheasant People far upstream from here. My people are now spread all across the lands you call America. We are the Glusta—the Great Peacemakers."

"Is that why you have come to Florissant?" Clément asked. "To seek the Anishinaabe from Muskegon River? A peaceful people?"

The young man's eyes tightened critically. "The Anishinaabe have not always been peaceful, have they? In fact, the last time the Serpent Star arrived, the Anishinaabe violently stole peace from the land."

"How long ago was that?" Nicollet asked.

Shetek tilted his head as if studying Nicollet. "It happened when my grandfather was just a boy. I could speak to you about moons, but you White Men keep track of time by the sun, don't you? If I was to guess, I'd say it was about seventy years ago."

Nicollet couldn't help but smile. *This young man is a scientist, an investigator. Society honors him with respect yet he wanders penniless. We are brothers.* "What happened in 1758? What does it have to do with the present?"

"Something of great value was stolen, and if the Wishwee has come, then I must find it and return it to him. I began the journey south months ago, but only after seeking the truth. At a village on the

THE ALCHEMIST'S MAP

Wisconsin River, the converted Menomonie threw stones at me, rejecting the old ways, and chasing me from their village as a witch. Only by the grace of the local authorities did I survive certain death. But I learned where the Potawatomi had been sent."

"Why do you seek the Potawatomi?" Stewart asked.

"Because they were witnesses to a crime."

"What crime did they witness?" Nicollet asked.

"The theft I spoke of. This wampum belt was made shortly after the Serpent Star appeared in my grandfather's grandfather's time, when a curse fell upon the land. In my grandfather's time, the Serpent Star appeared again, and the Chippewa brought discord. I came to speak with the Potawatomi to discover if the rumors about their cousins, the Chippewa, were true. I have been charged with fixing a problem before all of mankind will suffer. Perhaps that is why you have been sent."

"Me?" Nicollet asked, glancing over at Stewart, whose eyes could not have grown any wider.

Shetek paused, then finally asked carefully chosen words. "Why do they call you 'the man from the stars?'"

"I study the stars. After showing the Potawatomi both an eclipse and a comet, they feel I am some sort of holy man that will restore health to their people."

"Are you?"

"Heavens, no. I'm just Joseph Nicollet the astronomer. I might bring them food and vaccines, but in truth, my purpose here is very selfish. I seek to rebuild my good name by creating a map using barometric data to indicate elevation," Nicollet explained. "What about you? The people whisper that you are an immortal. They whisper that you have come to punish them with disease for leaving the ways of their elders."

"No. In the days of my grandfather's grandfather, an ancient evil was released upon the land. For years now, evil and death have spread over these lands and will continue to spread unless what has been lost is returned. I am only here to find what was lost—what was stolen."

"I still don't understand what it is you seek," Nicollet pressed, knowing the comet came in 1682 and 1758.

"The Key of Death. It does not look sinister," Shetek explained. "In fact, it only appears to be a large stone," Shetek held his hands apart as if holding a small watermelon. "It is smooth and white, like an egg. But, if you were to touch this stone, it would burn your hands. Left alone, this stone transforms any substance around it."

"An alkahest," Nicollet allowed the words to spill from his mouth in front of the others. *He's talking about the Philosopher's Stone.* "Does your wampum belt tell you about visitors during your grandfather's grandfather's time?"*Pierre-Charles Le Sueur, for instance?*

"It speaks of how an evil spirit that slept in the earth woke."

Or was dug up? Nicollet could not help but think of Pierre-Charles Le Sueur's legendary mining expedition in 1700, eighteen years after the arrival of Halley's Comet.

"The elders of my people believed the appearance of the Serpent Star meant that the fulfillment of prophecy had come, but in hindsight, it was a curse. Now the French are gone, the Fox are gone, and the Oceti Sakowin and Anishinaabe will bear the brunt of the curse—if the Key of Death is not found. Now that the Serpent Star has returned again, I must wander these lands to discover what happened or else disease and pestilence will continue to plague us all."

They were all silent for a moment as they pondered Shetek's quest. "The Potawatomi told me you survive only on the charity of others, that you have no wealth or belongings. I could give you money for that pipe you carry. When I travel into the land of the Anishinaabe, it would show the people that I am their friend," Nicollet offered.

"There isn't enough money in all of St. Louis to give me a fair price

THE ALCHEMIST'S MAP

for this pipe," Shetek mused. "This pipe is priceless. It has been handed down from father to son for countless generations. Those who hold to the old ways respect the pipe and allow me admission into their villages while on my quest. I cannot sell this pipe."

Nicollet nodded. "And you believe the Anishinaabe have taken the stone—this 'Key of Death,' as you call it?"

"Yes, I believe the Anishinaabe should know where the stone is located, but they fear I will take it from them. They might not even know what it is. Perhaps the Chippewa gave it to their French allies and it is no longer in the lands to the north. Perhaps you were sent to help me find what has been lost."

"How would I find it?"

"When the Dakota guarded it, it was kept at a place they called 'Spirit Island.' When the Anishinaabe searched for it, they said it would be located 'on an island shaped like a turtle, where the food grew upon water.' In both legends, the place is guarded by a water spirit, so it will take a great warrior-prophet to find it in the vast North, if it is even there."

"What am I supposed to do if I do find it?" Nicollet asked.

Shetek gave him an answer he did not expect to hear.

CHAPTER TWENTY-TWO

ST. LOUIS
1836

It is a bold plan, Stewart reminded himself. *One that will catch all our enemies off guard.*

His luggage was transferred from the wagon and onto the large paddle boat departing for New Orleans, where he would then travel to Cuba. Fortunately, the weather had quickly warmed, allowing the Mississippi River to open for him to depart on schedule, without a dime to his name.

Neither Nicollet nor Clément were with him as he departed, and he knew it might be years before he saw them again, if ever.

I am alone, he thought, but a smirk still hid below his dark moustache.

THE ALCHEMIST'S MAP

"Your bags are loaded, Lord Stewart," a boy from the carriage said. *Lord Stewart? This will be hard on the young chap.* "Well done," Stewart praised, but instead of coin or bill, he just shook the young man's outstretched hand and patted him on the shoulder as he walked toward the plank.

A few days earlier, Stewart had taken the last of his money, counted it out, and then stuffed it into the pockets of Nicollet's vest.

"Take it," Stewart had insisted. "You've earned it. I only wish I could give you more."

"Any more and I'd draw far too much attention. I shall wear incompetence and poverty upon my chest like a coat of arms," Nicollet said, tucking away the money. "Did you give enough to Antoine?"

"Antoine does not need money to survive in the wilderness. He only struggles when I bring him to civilization. It's probably good he is not going with me to Cuba."

"I wish he was staying with me."

"Incompetence and poverty," Stewart repeated. "That's your plan."

"I will miss him, though. And his help with the language of the Anishinaabe has been invaluable."

"It is too bad we'll never see Antoine again."

"It is," Nicollet smiled warmly.

Now, days later, Stewart quickly inspected his cabin, took off his jacket, and then walked down to the dining room to watch the city of St. Louis disappear.

"Would you like a refreshment, Lord Stewart?" a cabin boy asked.

"Scotch whiskey," Stewart said. *Lest I shed a tear.*

He looked at the white table mat, remembering how Nicollet had taken a sheet of paper and set it on his kitchen table after they returned from the strange visit with Shetek.

"So you agree with me that it is a sign from God?" Stewart had asked as Nicollet gathered up his ink instruments.

"Yes, but that does not mean we have to act like zealous fools. Let's review all of the facts we've been given before we make any plans. First, according to Shetek, we are looking for an island, be it Turtle Island or Spirit Island."

"Food growing on water," Clément had added from the window by the sink. "That certainly means wild rice fields—the Wisconsin Territory."

"Thank you, Antoine," Nicollet said, writing down the second clue. "The oldest source we have, the Alchemist's Map, gave me specific clues about longitude and latitude."

"How did you determine that?" Stewart asked.

"It is quite complicated, actually. Ancient sailors used stars for navigation, but it was rudimentary. While Polaris, the North Star, is a fixed point, the other stars move in the skies from season to season, and from hemisphere to hemisphere. At a specific time of year, certain constellations will rise and fall at a specific location on the horizon. The Alchemist's Map seemed to be using the modern longitude of the forty-fourth parallel."

"And where is that?" Stewart asked.

"For a sailor, you'd first run into the American continent at Nova Scotia, but then you'd have thousands of miles of possible locations along a line that would eventually end up at the Pacific."

"So where does it cross the Mississippi?"

"Near the headwaters," Nicollet winked. "West of the Wisconsin Territory."

"What else do we know?"

"The Alchemist's Map also showed a place where the water flows in all directions toward a central point, which of course, is impossible. Nowhere on the globe do we see rivers flowing toward one spot,

THE ALCHEMIST'S MAP

or they'd become a lake. Yet the Lahontan map described a divide—a watershed. That is our clue."

"Don't forget copper," Clément said.

"Ah yes, all three maps were consistent about that fact, weren't they? We must find a place where copper is exposed to the elements, most likely near a cliff."

"And we're back to seeking an island," Stewart said.

"Shetek described a large egg."

"Clearly the Philosopher's Stone," Stewart finished. "Shetek also mentioned an evil spirit that woke from the earth. Remember your theory about the seven-headed beast?"

A most extreme theory. "Copper exposed to air becomes vitriol, a natural process with an unnatural appearance. The Alchemist Map shows it labeled with the symbol of the Undine, the water spirit. However, even with all of these clues, we have two major problems."

"The killer knows you've seen the map," Stewart said. "And that I have become your ally."

"Yes, which means if I do manage to acquire either private or public patronage, I will either be watched or killed."

"Hasn't that been a risk all along? It hasn't stopped you yet."

"But it will," Nicollet said grimly. "If I do manage to find a way north, I will have to search while simultaneously leading a campaign of misinformation. But here is the bigger problem: even if we find Fort L'Huillier, it does not mean we'll find the stone. It could be anywhere, according to Shetek."

A quick knock came at the door, and Stewart and Clément armed themselves before Nicollet warily answered it. The hallway was empty, but a wrapped package rested on the ground. When Nicollet opened it, the three men stared at Shetek's wampum belt.

"What does this mean?" Nicollet asked, rushing to the window for a glimpse of the wandering shaman.

"There's your God at work again." Stewart then suggested a plan he'd later regret. "Antoine can speak French, English, Cree, Sioux, and Chippewa, but to most white men, he's just a big Métis, only worthy of day labor."

"Your point?" Nicollet asked.

Stewart had then reached into his jacket, retrieved his wallet, and began counting out how much money he had left.

It was a plan that left him broke, alone, and heading to Cuba quite drunk.

CHAPTER TWENTY-THREE
FORT SNELLING
1836

Fort Snelling is a military complex built at a place known as "Bdote," where the Mississippi and Minnesota Rivers come together. It sits on a high bluff overlooking the confluence, giving it a strategic and very visible position in the valley. The stone walls and towers protect barracks, officer housing, blacksmith shops, and a small hospital. From its perch, the facility can view river passage from three of four directions.

Its construction left the river valley stripped of all trees and bushes so neither friend nor enemy could sneak up on the fort unseen. Immediately upon being built, it became the most important outpost in the territory, and served as neutral ground between the Chippewa nation to the northeast and the Sioux nation to the southwest.

Because of this, Major Lawrence Tolliver, the fort commander, even built a council house just west of the fort where he could mediate in the affairs of the two nations. Tolliver was dubbed "No-Sugar-in-Your-Mouth" by the local Sioux chieftain, Little Crow, because of Tolliver's honest dealings with them.

The American Fur Company also built a new stone complex, albeit on the other side of the river, where its agents brought pelts to Hank Sibley, who would prepare the shipments for departure. With rapids just a few miles north of the fort, it was also the deepest water for paddle boats to routinely bring supplies and return with pelts.

Did the ship anchor a mile away? What is it doing here so early? Tolliver wondered. Knowing there would be new arrivals on the approaching ship, he began dressing in his full uniform. At forty-two, he was still lean. Although his rank gave him privilege, he still found plenty of physical labor to keep himself in shape. He checked the mirror to make sure he'd shaved away all of the gray whiskers that grew from his chin.

Time to catch a thief, he told himself in the mirror. Content his appearance would make a satisfactory impression, he marched out of his bedroom.

"Good morning, Lawrence," his wife, Elizabeth, greeted him from the table, where his house slave, Harriet, tended breakfast duties. Although slavery was made illegal in the North with the Missouri Compromise of 1820, the institution remained in place, ignored by the United States government and practiced by its own officers and politicians. "It looks like it will be a busy day. Come and eat."

Outside of the glass window of the commander's house, he saw the shoulders of Captain Daniel Lyons already waiting.

Always in the shadows. "I must forgo breakfast to ensure order on the docks, but have Harriet prepare a hearty supper for any guests we might be entertaining." He turned for the door quickly, wanting to avoid any protests from his wife.

THE ALCHEMIST'S MAP

Out on the wooden walkway, Captain Daniel Lyons waited. An ambitious young man, Lyons had a crooked grin and a shock of hair that always seemed to be falling down over his eyes. He, too, was a lean man from several years of service on the frontier, and his cheeks were scarred from a previous battle with smallpox.

"A big steamship is coming up the river," Lyons said. "Most likely out of St. Louis. It fired off a canon and blew its horn, just like you instructed."

"Yes, I heard. I want a squad of men watching the unloading of the docks. Men who will actually watch and not just stand there."

"Crowd control?"

"Theft control. I have given these steamboat captains orders to never again show up in the evening or else half of our provisions go from the ships right into the hands of thieves. Get me someone to watch the Indians also."

"Do you want confrontations? Arrests?"

Always eager, this one. "Eyes. I want to know whom I can trust and whom I can't. I just want men to watch. I want you to have a squad help with the unloading."

"Understood. I'll have Lieutenant Colton observe the docks with his squad, and have Brunia watch the Natives."

Yes, Colton is a perfect sneak. He'd love to sell out one of his friends in exchange for a promotion. "Brunia?"

"The big fellow that showed up from the Selkirk Colony this past winter. None of the Indians trust him, so he'll be honest with me."

But will you be honest with me? Tolliver wondered.

Brunia felt like a fool, but he did as he was told.

I am a spy with nowhere to hide.

A steep ramp led down from the western gate of Fort Snelling near the top of the bluff two hundred yards down to the docks. A few of the fur traders built simple log homes along the shore, but all of the permanent structures were back atop the bluff. He leaned against one of these shacks, crossed his arms and pulled down his floppy felt hat.

I am so conspicuous. I could have spied while helping to unload the ship.

But Captain Lyons told him to stand off at a distance and watch, so he watched.

When Brunia arrived, the men were still working on securing the heavy planks between the docks and the ship, but now, people and goods flowed from the big ship.

First, Major Tolliver welcomed a fresh platoon of young soldiers to their station, and a few moments later, salutes were replaced with handshakes as a group of veteran soldiers left for home or other stations. Once the military affairs concluded, affairs of commerce followed.

Old Bets, a toothless Sioux woman, steered the ferry from across the river, where the yellow stone houses of Hank Sibley and Jean-Baptiste Faribault stood apart from the small village of traders. From all directions, men and women came out of the landscape. Even with Lieutenant Colton standing guard on the docks, it came as no surprise that theft was still a valid concern.

A few slaves and a dozen Indian boys appeared to help unload the provisions from the ship. If Brunia was to endear himself to the white officers, he needed to keep a close eye on these laborers as well as the onlookers.

One was Taopi, a young Sioux man who served as a scout and guide for Tolliver's expeditions. Of all the Sioux camped on the open field west of the fort, and those who came from nearby Kaposia, Taopi seemed to hate Brunia the most. Apparently, as a young boy, Taopi had almost been killed by a Chippewa hatchet that crushed his face, and Brunia

THE ALCHEMIST'S MAP

felt as if Taopi somehow held him personally responsible. Like himself, Taopi leaned against a building, watching.

A young Sioux boy became a prime suspect when he tripped carrying a case, and then in his efforts to put things right, slipped something in his pocket.

Is this what I have become?

Brunia barely knew the boy, *something with Cloud in his name,* but watched, almost impressed, as the same trick worked again and again. By the time the men from the AFC arrived, the boy had his pockets stuffed.

Following young Hank Sibley onto the dock were a half-dozen furry-faced voyageurs. Brunia knew their type well, men who fended for themselves at all costs. It surprised him to see one of them, a trader and cook, suddenly run into the Sioux boy.

Ah... A black market. The boy steals valuables for the corrupt cook. Big Moe Maxwell, an ironic name for a short, hairy troll.

Sibley and Tolliver soon stood side-by-side, the ruling monarchs at Fort Snelling, but truly only puppets for even more powerful men.

Finally, behind a dozen travelers of all types, Brunia saw a bright red vest beneath a tweed jacket.

Welcome to Fort Snelling, Professor Nicollet.

"Let me help you with your trunk," Big Moe Maxwell said to the funny little man in the red vest.

"Thank you, kind sir."

He called me "sir." If that don't beat all. "Call me 'Big Moe.'"

"And you can call me 'Joseph.'"

"Surely, a distinguished gentleman such as yourself has more titles than just 'Joseph.'"

Moe lifted the chest with a padlock on it on one end. A moment later, the Sioux boy, Stands on Clouds, grabbed the other handle and they lifted it off of the platform together.

"Excusez-moi? A title?" Joseph asked. "Well, I am an ambassador of science, I suppose."

"An ambassador? From what country?"

"France, and long before that, Savoy."

"A French ambassador. Which way will I be hauling your belongings?"

"I don't rightly know," the Ambassador said.

"Are you a guest of the American Fur Company or Major Tolliver up at the big fort?"

The ambassador looked around the river valley. "I suppose I should acquaint myself with the manager of the American Fur Company outpost. He certainly will be familiar with Pierre Chouteau of St. Louis."

"Ah, you know the big boss. When I was younger, I traded pelts, but now, I help Mr. Sibley at the house."

"Then bring me to Mr. Sibley, if you would."

"That's young Sibley up the road there, standing with Major Tolliver, but he lives over on that side," Maxwell said, pointing at a half-dozen limestone buildings across the river, including the newly built two-story home for the newly appointed AFC regional manager.

"Bien, I should probably stay with my belongings, lest they be misplaced. I'll come with you and meet Mr. Sibley later."

He is hiding something valuable in that chest. If only it weren't locked.

The Ambassador had few belongings for a man of his position, which meant he most likely did not plan to stay long. Maxwell and Stands on Clouds loaded the locked chest and bags onto the ferry along with the

THE ALCHEMIST'S MAP

guest, who stood nervously in the middle of the barge. Old Bets, the toothless Sioux woman who'd lived here long before the fort was built, used a long pole to push the wooden ferry back across the flowing water.

"You should have seen it back in April," Maxwell said of the water. "The flood came halfway up those big cottonwoods. Thought it was going to swallow Mr. Sibley's fine new house. Have you come to celebrate America's Independence Day?"

"Ah, it will be July 4th in a couple of days. It will be my fourth Fourth celebration since coming to your fine country."

"Major Tolliver will fire off all the cannons, terrifying all the Indians. It will clear out the whole dirty lot." Maxwell grinned his maw of rotten teeth, disturbing the ambassador greatly.

Soon, Old Bets had brought them across the river where several panicked traders showed up, trying to sell their wares before the big paddle boat returned downstream.

"Who is that standing on the porch?" the Ambassador asked.

Maxwell saw the beautiful, sad young woman at Sibley's house. "She's the granddaughter of a local Indian chief who gave her to Mr. Sibley as a sign of good faith. Honestly, I think she just wanted to live in a house rather than a teepee."

"Is she the granddaughter of Chief Wahanantan?"

"Who? No, the chief's name was Chasing Hawk. She is the niece of Little Crow, the chief of the local band of Sioux."

"What is her name?"

"Red Blanket Woman," Maxwell said. "These Indians use a red blanket as a sign they're going to war. Maybe she's a warning instead of a sign of good faith."

"Her grandfather just gave her away?"

"These people are savages, Mr. Ambassador," Maxwell said as he and Stands on Clouds lifted the heavy chest and began carrying it up the lawn to where Red Blanket Woman stood, quietly judging him with her somber face. "So why would an ambassador come all the way out here to Fort Snelling?"

The ambassador laughed heartily, "I was speaking figuratively, Mr. Maxwell. I am not an ambassador in any official capacity."

A secret identity, a secret chest of treasure, and a secret purpose— Mr. Sibley will reward me well for this information.

Maxwell dumped the ambassador's belongings onto the front porch to let young Red Blanket Woman take care of the guest and quickly returned to Old Bets' ferry to cross back over.

Back at the landing, he spotted Sibley still talking to Major Tolliver.

Maxwell stood at a distance until Sibley finally called to him. "Maxwell, who was that man in the red vest? The prissy-looking fellow."

"A French Ambassador, he said."

"Why didn't you direct him to me?" Tolliver asked, insulted.

"He said he wanted the AFC. He said he wanted to unpack. He said he would meet Sibley later."

Tolliver glared at young Sibley, who said, "The hell if I know what this is about. No one told me a goddamn thing about a French Ambassador. Are you certain he wanted to see me and not Major Tolliver?"

"He said what he said," Maxwell insisted.

Tolliver still seemed annoyed. "You should go see to your guest, Hank. I'll bring Elizabeth by this evening to give our ambassador a proper greeting."

Elizabeth Tolliver wore her finest gown for the occasion, a rich red silk affair only a few seasons out of fashion. "How do I look, Harriet? Fine enough to dance with a French ambassador?"

Harriet nodded. "You look beautiful, Mrs. Tolliver."

"Go help Mary get dressed, and when you are finished, pick

THE ALCHEMIST'S MAP

something nice for yourself. We'll be accompanying Dr. Emerson to meet the ambassador. We want to give this man a proper greeting tonight."

"Yes, ma'am."

"Oh, and one more thing. Prepare a bed for the ambassador in our guest room. I'll not have a distinguished guest staying in a pelt shed."

"Yes, ma'am," Harriet said and hustled off.

While Lawrence poured over paperwork, correspondence, and newspapers, Elizabeth Tolliver nervously paced in the living room, excited to meet the ambassador. When Lawrence sighed at her constant pacing, she exited the back door and stood on the half-moon battery overlooking the river valley.

Finally, Lawrence rose from his table, and with their daughter, Mary, and their slave, Harriett, along with Dr. Emerson and his slave, Dred, the six of them descended the landing and crossed the river to meet the new ambassador.

The Sibley house was illuminated, and fiddle music could be heard even from the landing, bringing a smile to Elizabeth's face.

Lawrence knocked so loudly on the door that it shook.

Foul Big Moe Maxwell opened the door to reveal Hank Sibley dancing with Red Blanket Woman while the ambassador played his fiddle. Once the ambassador noticed them, the music stopped.

"Mr. Sibley, we've come to meet the French Ambassador and offer him quarters at Fort Snelling."

"Have you?" Sibley said, letting go of Red Blanket Woman's hand. "Let me introduce you, then. Professor Nicollet, this is Major Lawrence Tolliver, his wife, Elizabeth—"

He is short but very handsome. Those eyes. Those dimpled cheeks.

Sibley continued, "their daughter, Mary, and Dr. Emerson, the fort's surgeon."

Elizabeth shot through the doorway and right up to the guest. "It is a pleasure to meet you, Ambassador Nicollet."

Sibley chuckled, and Nicollet took her gloved hand and kissed it gently. "The pleasure is all mine, Mrs. Tolliver, but there has been a misunderstanding of sorts. I am not an ambassador."

It was all explained in a few minutes, and Red Blanket Woman served a small supper as Nicollet explained how his career path had taken him from Paris to Washington D.C., the South, New Orleans, St. Louis, and finally to Fort Snelling.

While he is not an ambassador, he is a gentleman, and he is still very handsome, Elizabeth told herself as supper was finishing.

Once Nicollet again picked up his fiddle and began to play, her husband leaned closer and whispered into her ear, "Find out what he is doing here."

Then I shall be a dutiful wife and dance with the handsome Nicollet.

A hundred twenty-five miles away, an old Chippewa woman sat in the middle of her canoe as it emerged from a dense patch of reeds. Her daughter and granddaughter were finally quiet after arguing about veering away from the main channel of the Crow Wing River.

Although the day was quickly fading, her memory had been right: the little tributary opened up to a vast bay of lilies, and beyond, a long body of water she'd never been allowed to visit.

Lake Manito.

"What is this place?" her granddaughter asked.

"It is a sacred place," the old woman explained. "A haunted place, they say, which is why the rice fields are untouched."

The old woman could remember the star with a tail from her childhood, as well as the blood that followed.

THE ALCHEMIST'S MAP

"We shouldn't be here," the middle-aged woman said, dragging her paddle in the water. The canoe veered back toward the shore.

The old woman's brother had told her long ago about Lake Manito and what he and her father were going to do. The star with the tail was the sign of the Horned Serpent, her brother had said, and they had no other choice than to try.

The *twang* of an arrow pierced the still air moments before it impaled her granddaughter's shoulder. A war cry filled the air and she heard the sound of someone crashing through the vegetation along the bank of the creek.

Impossible. The Sioux left a generation ago.

But it was a Sioux war hammer that came crashing down on her head.

CHAPTER TWENTY-FOUR

FORT SNELLING
1836

"Do you hear that?" Nicollet asked. He was sitting in the middle of the grassy parade ground beside Dred Scott, Dr. Emerson's slave, finishing his daily barometric readings. Both men sat under a starry sky.

Scott looked around the military complex that surrounded them. Soon, cooks would begin banging in the kitchen, a harbinger of another busy day. "All I hear are a few insects, Professor Nicollet."

Nicollet suddenly doubted his own senses. Since arriving at Fort Snelling, he'd only managed a full night's sleep once, despite the comforts given to him. The pressures of Stewart's covert plan overwhelmed his nerves. "It was a strange shushing noise."

"Perhaps we're breathing too loudly," Scott joked.

THE ALCHEMIST'S MAP

Nicollet slipped his pocket watch out and held it in the light of Scott's candle to confirm the hour. Shrugging it off, he went back to his sextant to take the next measurement.

No more than a minute went by before he heard it again. "You certainly heard *that*."

"It came from over there," Scott said, pointing a finger in the direction of the western gatehouse.

"I can't concentrate with all of this noise," Nicollet mused. "Let's go investigate."

For Scott, it was just the beginning of his day, but for Nicollet, it was the very end, a nocturnal routine he'd established two weeks earlier.

Once the misunderstanding about being a French ambassador was settled, Nicollet partially confessed his purpose of showing up unexpectedly at Fort Snelling. He explained honestly how he was pioneering a new cartography technique he'd learned from his friends in Europe, and how he was wanting to beat American scientists to the punch. After Nicollet mentioned Beltrami, Cass, Pike, and Schoolcraft, Major Tolliver straightened his back a bit and insisted on hosting Nicollet for the summer, with a promise to send Nicollet north with a patrol expedition at the end of August.

Now, as he arrived at the gatehouse, Nicollet felt a strange chill crawling down his spine. When he reached the gate, he found Corporal Davey Faribault and Sergeant Jim Taopi staring out into the darkness. Faribault, whose father was a local merchant, jumped when Nicollet and Scott approached.

"They're leaving, Professor Nicollet," Faribault declared and pointed through his observation window.

Nicollet stepped closer to the window, glancing at the mangled cheek of Sergeant Taopi, the somber Indian scout. Of all the men at Fort Snelling, Taopi frightened Nicollet the most.

Adjusting his position, Nicollet saw a buffalo hide slide off the poles of the last teepee where, for the past month, a village of more than a hundred Sioux men, women, and children had camped, farmed, and fished in harmony with the Americans. Now, the last of them slipped away into the wooded ravine of the river.

"Where are they going?" Nicollet asked.

"West," Taopi declared in a rasp.

"Is this tradition?"

"Yes, but not the tradition you think," Taopi said. "The tradition is war."

CHAPTER TWENTY-FIVE

FORT SNELLING

1836

I hate that man, Major Tolliver thought to himself. *He mocks me and undermines my position here at the fort. We are on the brink of bloody war, and it is most likely his fault.*

"Sir?" Captain Lyons asked, but Tolliver had already forgotten the question.

Hank Sibley sat in the corner chair, his arms crossed, clearly upset. At the edge of the desk, Corporal Faribault served as clerk, quickly writing down everything that transpired.

Sergeant Taopi and the giant from Canada, Brunia, stood to the side of his desk, both having given him updates on the positions of the Sioux and the Chippewa, respectively. Both nations had withdrawn a hundred miles from the traditional border at the Anoka of the Rum River.

According to Brunia, Chief Flat Mouth of the Chippewa was gathering all the chieftains to wage full-scale war against the Sioux for the recent murders of two Chippewa women, as well as other wrongs he laid at Tolliver's feet.

According to Taopi, the Mdewakanton and Warpekutey bands had withdrawn to the territory of their western brothers, the Sisseton and Warpeton, in order to prepare for a coming Chippewa assault. Luckily, Chief Wahanantan of the plains Sioux remained hundreds of miles away with the remaining three bands of the Seven Council Fires.

If it came to war, a few hundred Americans in a stone fort could not outlast either nation—he'd be cut off for months and would have to witness his wife starve or be butchered by whichever tribe felt most wronged.

"What are your orders, sir?" Lyons repeated.

He wants to distinguish himself? Let him be a hero. "Go get Professor Nicollet."

"Professor Nicollet?"

"Go get him," Tolliver snapped. Lyons pivoted and marched off under orders. "The two of you are dismissed."

Taopi and Brunia both left his office, leaving just Faribault and Sibley.

"This will devastate the market," Sibley said after a few moments. "If the Chippewa and Sioux are preparing for war, they are not trading furs to my agents, who depend on them. You'll have hundreds of penniless agents showing up on your door in a few weeks."

"Good, I might need men to man the walls," Tolliver quipped.

"Which side poses the greater threat?" Sibley pressed.

"I hope neither side would be foolish enough to engage us directly here at the fort, but if they begin to kill your traders or take hostages, it will escalate quickly. If we fail to maintain neutrality, we could be swept away by either side."

"But which side should we fear?"

"In the short term, the Chippewa. They are in a frenzy about these murdered women, and it will motivate them initially. Plus, we have the mapmaker stoking fear with his lies. What is he thinking, Sibley?"

"Damned if I know, but I have a proposal that may help: I will publically marry Red Blanket Woman."

"Your servant girl?"

"She's a woman, I can promise you, but a public marriage would serve two purposes. First, it would let the Chippewa know that we see the Sioux as an ally, giving Chief Flat Mouth something to worry about. If he begins to slaughter camps of Sioux, it would be an insult to the powerful AFC. Secondly, it would bond us to Chief Little Crow through Chasing Hawk."

Chasing Hawk was her grandfather. "She's Little Crow's niece, isn't she?"

Sibley nodded. "With all of the northern Sioux withdrawing, they've left us like a sail flapping in the wind, but a public marriage to her would give him cause to defend her. If the Chippewa threaten the fort, they threaten Chasing Hawk's granddaughter. It could force a public alliance."

"You'd be willing to take her as a wife?"

"For a while," Sibley shrugged. "I can always set her aside later, if needed. It wouldn't be a Christian marriage."

A shrewd man, making him a strong ally and a fearful enemy. I hope he understands my plan instead of seeing it as a threat. Tolliver nodded, pleasing Sibley.

A moment later, Captain Lyons returned with the key to his plan, Professor Nicollet.

"Have a seat, professor. I'm sure you've been apprised of the situation developing out there, which has certainly foiled your plans a bit. Do you know what this is?" Tolliver asked, pointing at Leech Lake on the government-issued *Allen and Schoolcraft Map of 1834*.

"Yes, it is a poorly-conceived map."

Ah, you've taken the bait, you arrogant little man. Just as I anticipated. "Yes, you've made that abundantly clear to me already. Are you familiar with the men who made it?"

"Allen and Schoolcraft? I only know that they have preceded me with their own expeditions, and from what I can tell, they have left me with quite a bit of work to do."

"Henry Schoolcraft is an arrogant bastard, and after the past few weeks, I can honestly say I hate the man, albeit for different reasons than you might. When he heard your public intentions to map the west, he pulled a few strings to send George Fanshaw ahead of you, thanks to his Freemason friends back east."

Tolliver paused for a moment to address Sibley. "This is not a slight on Masonic organizations."

Sibley shrugged. "I understand and agree. Schoolcraft, Cass, Crooks, Astor, my father, they are all thick as thieves, but Schoolcraft—he is a self-righteous prick."

"Good," Tolliver continued, turning back to the Schoolcraft map. Pointing to the island along the southern shore of Lake Superior, he said, "This is Lapointe on Madeline Island, where Henry Schoolcraft acts as an Indian Agent in a similar fashion to what I do here at Fort Snelling. Unfortunately, since he only has to deal with the Chippewa, he is lying to them about the Sioux and my actions down here at Fort Snelling. He is creating a very volatile situation in the territory, which strengthens his position against me and also thwarts your efforts to map the territory."

Sibley interrupted, "If we fail, he gains."

THE ALCHEMIST'S MAP

Nicollet nodded and followed Tolliver's finger back to Leech Lake. "Right now, at a place called Onigum, Chief Flat Mouth of the Leech Lake Chippewa is gathering all the chieftains together to address the recent murders of Chippewa women by a Sioux."

"How do they know it was a Sioux?" Nicollet asked.

"A young woman managed to escape with an arrow in her shoulder to tell her father and brothers, who then went to Flat Mouth for vengeance. Thanks to the guidance of Schoolcraft, the Chippewa around Lake Superior are rallying to the call. Unfortunately, I have a good friend, Reverend Boutwell, who went to Leech Lake this past spring with his wife to minister to the Chippewa. Schoolcraft has put the dear Reverend and his wife in great danger."

Sibley added, "Don't forget, Mrs. Boutwell is the daughter of Ramsay Crooks, the owner of the American Fur Company. A foolish gamble from Schoolcraft, I'd say."

Time for your quest, Squire Lyons. "I've decided to send a small force of men, under the leadership of Captain Lyons, to go up the Mississippi River and then to Leech Lake, to rescue Reverend and Mrs. Boutwell before war erupts. Where is it you wanted to go before all of this chaos developed?"

Nicollet pointed to a spot west of Leech Lake. "Do you see this silly little line that looks like a snake drawn onto the map? Somehow, this bizarre geographic anomaly is the headwaters of the Mississippi, and this little dot, labeled Lake Itasca, is the wellspring."

"Then, Professor Nicollet, I have a proposal. What would you say if I allowed you to accompany Captain Lyons on this expedition with the promise that he'll bring you to the headwaters of the Mississippi after securing the Reverend? It would allow men to forget the name 'Schoolcraft' and appreciate the good name 'Nicollet.'"

Nicollet looked over at wide-eyed Corporal Faribault, then to

Captain Lyons, and then turned to Sibley to gauge his reaction, before finally turning back to Tolliver. "What do you say, Professor Nicollet? Interested?"

CHAPTER TWENTY-SIX

ANOKA

1836

"Anoka" is a word that shares meaning in both the Sioux and Ojibwa language. Whether "a-no-ka-tan-han" or "on-o-kay," the word references how two rivers come together. Located thirty miles northwest of Fort Snelling, it is a distinct landmark where the Mississippi River meets the Rum River flowing out of Mille Lacs.

In 1825, the Treaty of Prairie du Chien was signed by local tribes to try to negotiate peace between the Sioux Nation and the tribes pressing westward into their traditional territory. During the previous century, the Eastern Sioux, the Dakota, lost their ancestral lands in northern Minnesota to the Chippewa after a century of war, and the Anoka came to serve as a clear visual marker for the otherwise-invisible lines drawn by war.

For Brunia, it also marked the edge of safety. From behind the brush on a little island, he could see the southern shore of the Mississippi River as well as the smaller Rum River.

"I'm sorry if I kept you up," Nicollet whispered, but not to Brunia, who slept on the edge of the camp as a sentry. Nicollet spoke to Captain Lyons, the serious officer sitting a few feet away. "I suppose the two of us should get some sleep before dawn greets us both."

Tolliver had chosen the cagey Lyons to lead the expedition because of his years of experience in the Big Woods. Although still a young man, the Dakota Territory had made Daniel Lyons tough and wary. He'd also survived the smallpox, which was why he kept a long, patchy beard to cover most of his facial blotches. He looked around now, searching for signs of movement in the waning darkness. "If there is going to be an ambush, it will be here... and now."

Lyons' fingers nervously moved on the rifle he held, prompting Brunia to reach for his own rifle.

A spy among spies, Brunia mused to himself. *Remain Brunia the Brute, or even better, Brunia the Mute.*

Even though Brunia had been on countless islands, in numerous rivers, through various territories, the shores of Anoka were no less terrifying in the light of dawn than they were in the middle of the day.

The United States flag conspicuously rose ten feet from the island, making it obvious who was camped there, but Brunia also knew either side of the conflict was capable of overwhelming them, of slitting their throats and taking their scalps. Across the river on the east shore, a trading cabin remained empty. It would have been more comfortable, Brunia knew, but the island provided better defenses for their party.

Even as he kept an eye out for signs of either the Chippewa or the Sioux, he kept a closer eye on the men in the expedition to discover their loyalties. Nicollet spent weeks at Fort Snelling before the rescue mission

THE ALCHEMIST'S MAP

was ordered, allowing correspondence to catch up to him. The world knew where Nicollet had gone.

In another two hours, Lyons would wake the men, and while they struck camp, Nicollet would sneak a short nap before they continued north. When Lyons slept remained a mystery.

In the little tent beside Brunia, Lieutenant Edgar Colton blissfully snored. With one word, the stocky man from Wisconsin could wake from his slumber and shoot a brave approaching from either shore straight through the eye. Despite his youth and cherub cheeks, Colton was a feared killer that had collected a dozen Fox and Sauk scalps after being rescued by the Sioux on the other side of the Wisconsin River. For four days after his rescue, his war party had hunted down fleeing members of Chief Black Hawk's war party, bringing an end to the Black Hawk War.

Between Colton and the next tent, Sergeant Jim Taopi slept in the open, his gruesome wounds exposed for the diminishing stars to see. As a boy, Taopi had been left for dead after receiving a blow to the face from a Chippewa ax and having his scalp removed at its roots. But the ten-year-old boy survived, walking six miles upstream to find shelter with fur traders at Mendota. Now twenty-six, Taopi wore extravagant hats to cover his bare head, but nothing could hide the mass of twisted bone that was the side of his face.

Major Tolliver was wise to send these feared killers with us, Brunia decided under his light blanket.

In the tent beside Taopi, Davey Faribault slept. Brunia found that Faribault was highly educated, very organized, and could neatly pack an entire camp into a canoe in only a few minutes. *And he belongs to Major Tolliver.*

One of several sons of Jean-Baptiste Faribault, Davey enlisted to serve the officers at Fort Snelling, and on the expedition, diligently served the commands of Captain Lyons, although he always seemed to be watching, especially the comings and goings of Nicollet.

Yet with all these carefully planned details, one detail confused and worried Brunia: Big Moe Maxwell. The dirty, toothless fur trader from Green Bay apparently had come to Fort Snelling two summers earlier after wearing out his welcome in Wisconsin. A thief, Maxwell was hired by Hank Sibley to get the best price possible from Indians bringing in pelts. In the preparations for the expedition, Sibley had insisted on sending Maxwell along as Nicollet's personal escort.

This foul man puts us all in danger, Brunia decided as the wiry old codger mumbled in his sleep.

When something rustled on the edge of the camp, Brunia almost jumped, having been lost deep in thought. Nicollet's nap ended before it began and he sat back up beside Captain Lyons.

"I couldn't sleep," Nicollet said from the fallen tree beside the hairy captain.

"What has you bothered?"

"Insomnia frequently plagues me, especially out here on the river. Little thoughts fester in my mind. I was looking at my collection of maps, and I cannot figure out the proper name for this river. Schoolcraft called it by the Chippewa name, 'Missiawgaiegon,' but that translates as 'Grand Lake River,' not 'Rum River.'"

"'Grand Lake' is Mille Lacs," Lyons explained. "The Rum River flows south until it reaches there—that's why the Chippewa call it that. Perhaps on our return, I could take you there."

"That would be wonderful," Nicollet said.

Taopi cleared his throat. "The Mdewakanton are the 'Dwellers of Spirit Lake.' 'Mille Lacs' is the name given to it by my French forefathers, but my Mdewakanton mother calls it 'Wakpa Wakan,' which

THE ALCHEMIST'S MAP

means 'Spirit River.' This is a sacred place for us, stolen by the Chippewa through treachery and deceit."

A sacred place? Brunia tried not to roll his eyes.

Hearing the gravelly rumble of Taopi, the other men began to stir.

Nicollet pressed Taopi for information. "Why was the place called 'Spirit Lake?' Father Hennepin wrote that it means 'Waters of the Great Spirit.' Is that the Sioux view of God?"

"The Dakota believe Spirit Lake is the center of the earth, and during a great flood, a whirlpool pulled them out of the waters and placed them on the shores of Spirit Lake," Taopi said, speaking more words than Brunia had heard from him in the last two months.

"Why are your people also called 'Santee, Guardians of the Frontier?'" Nicollet asked.

"We simply were protecting our land, our families, and our sacred places," Taopi continued.

"That's not what I heard," Lieutenant Edgar Colton said from where he had been sleeping. "We captured a Fox warrior, and since he murdered a woman and three children in Iowa, we took our time torturing the fellow. In the middle of it all, we asked him why Chief Black Hawk and his people didn't just surrender, and he said something crazy about finding a sacred treasure that once belonged to the Sioux."

"A treasure?" Nicollet scoffed.

"Crazy, isn't it, Professor Nicollet?" Colton continued. "So don't let Taopi fool you. The Sioux had some sort of treasure."

"You're a halfwit, Colton," Captain Lyons added. "The Sioux have nothing more valuable than buffalo hides. I suppose you believe a giant Canadian named Bunyan also formed the Great Lakes with his footprints."

"Of course not," Colton sulked.

Nicollet pressed. "Taopi, why were the Chippewa so persistent in invading the lands of the Sioux? Did they seek Spirit Lake also?"

Nicollet barely knows these men yet reveals his mind, Brunia observed. *How can such a brilliant man be so foolish at the same time?*

Taopi answered, "The Chippewa believe Spirit Lake to be the location of their fabled Turtle Island, but that is another lie. In fact—"

Captain Lyons raised a hand, stopping Jim Taopi mid-sentence. With a snap, Lieutenant Colton had his rifle raised and aimed upstream at the Mississippi. In seconds, the rest of the camp, with the exception of Nicollet, was armed and ready.

Instead of a war party, a single birch-bark canoe came toward them in the morning mist. Lyons looked everywhere but the canoe, sensing a trap. Not a branch moved or a twig snapped along the banks. "Hold your fire," he said to Colton.

The man in the canoe was distinctly Chippewa, with porcupine quills and a fox tail making him seem another foot taller than he was.

As he gracefully navigated the current, his clothing jingled melodically from all the regalia sewn onto his painted deerskin clothing. Instead of the black face of vengeance, the man's face was painted white with a blue crescent covering his mouth as well as on his chest, where ten pounds of white shells hung upon a thick cord.

A ten-year-old boy sat in the front of the canoe, standing suddenly to point to their location on the island.

"We'll talk to these fools and find out why the two of them are all alone in the wilderness," Lyons said, and his men relaxed. "Brunia, go speak to him."

With Maxwell at his side, Brunia sloshed out into the current to catch the canoe. The boy recoiled a bit when presented with Maxwell's toothless grin.

"What do you want?" Brunia asked in the Anishinaabe language.

"I have come seeking the one sent by the Great Spirit," the Midé´

THE ALCHEMIST'S MAP

priest declared boldly, then pointed to the stars. "The stars announced his arrival, and I have been looking for the one with a strange light in his eyes."

"What does he want, Brunia?" Captain Lyons called out.

Brunia hesitated, knowing the stranger would only draw more attention. "He's... come for Professor Nicollet."

CHAPTER TWENTY-SEVEN

CROW WING RIVER
1836

In 1758, Halley's Comet appeared over North America, bringing wonder and terror to all who looked upon the cosmic intruder. For Chief Black Horse of the Mdewakanton Dakota, it pushed him to pick up the hatchet again and reclaim what had been lost when he was a boy. For Chief Wiyipisiw of the Wijigan Clan of Chippewa, it was a sign to finish the Seven Fires migration his ancestors began long ago in the land of the East.

Nearly a decade after the decisive Battle of Kathio in 1750 where the Sioux lost their sacred home along the shores of Mille Lacs, Chief Black Horse began a campaign to regain their sacred places. While he temporarily reclaimed his home and killed Chief Wiyipisiw in battle,

THE ALCHEMIST'S MAP

the other force fell into a devastating trap.

Near the confluence of the Crow Wing River and the Mississippi, dozens of Chippewa warriors hid themselves in nooks and crannies of a towering cliff above the Mississippi. As the flotilla of Sioux canoes passed, they emerged from their hiding places, slaughtering the main force, ending the war and preserving the territory they'd claimed a generation earlier.

After a century of war between the depleted Sioux and surging Chippewa, the Battle of Crow Wing ended open hostility, and the four eastern tribes—the Mdewakanton, Warpekutey, Warpeton, and Sisseton all settled on the edge of the grasslands. Yet malcontents within the Sioux nation refused to surrender their sacred fight, only to be cast out and labeled 'Tizaptanons' by their own people. When Halley's Comet again returned in 1835, Ohanzee of the Tizaptanons left his home on the edge of the prairie to return to the sacred lands of his ancestors, murdering two Chippewa women who crossed his path.

If I were to kill any of the men, that would be the one I would kill, Ohanzee thought to himself as he looked down at the Chippewa Midé' with the Americans. The man with the porcupine quills in his hair stood only fifty yards away on the shore opposite of the cliff face. With only a knife to defend himself, Ohanzee's desire to spill blood would have to wait.

Lying parallel to the ground with three pine branches sheltering him from the midday sun, Ohanzee knew he had to stay hidden in the little notch of the cliff face until darkness came.

Have the American soldiers come hunting for me? Ohanzee wondered, but none of them seemed too interested in tracking or hunting.

He wanted to sneak into their little camp and plunge a knife into the Midé' before anyone knew better, and he drifted in and out of consciousness thinking of murdering the Chippewa priest.

It had already been more than a month since Ohanzee came across the women gathering food along the shores of Lake Manito. Before he knew what he was doing, he had sprung on them like a mountain lion. The mother, however, did not give up without a fight. As she had tried to wrestle the hatchet away, the youngest girl took off running through the reeds.

Eventually, the mother succumbed to the three wounds he gave her, and with a fourth and final thrust, her surprisingly strong arms let go of him.

But the youngest woman had vanished like a raven in the wind, the reeds hiding her course of escape. Ohanzee spent half an hour searching for her like some rabid wolf, but the large field of wild rice hid her from his blade.

Why does this place darken my thought? Ohanzee reflected from his hiding place along the cliff face. *It was only meant to be a religious pilgrimage. I did not want to start a war.*

His pilgrimage to the ancestral home of Chief Black Horse confirmed what he had been taught: a lake with a turtle-shaped island in the middle of its water, a place where food grew upon the waters. *The true Spirit Lake.*

Hearing a commotion below, Ohanzee risked a glimpse into the river valley. The nine men had camped near the confluence of the Crow Wing and Mississippi Rivers. With an American flag planted in the middle of the camp, the men set up opposite from the cliff on a sandy bank. From what Ohanzee could see, there were five soldiers, an American shaman, and three Chippewa—a large guide and the Midé' with his son.

Shortly after noon, with the merciless sun reaching through the pine branches that sheltered him, Ohanzee heard more commotion from the river below. This time, a war party of almost forty birch bark canoes came down the Crow Wing. Quickly surrounded, the band of

THE ALCHEMIST'S MAP

Americans stood holding their guns as the Bear Clan warriors from Mille Lacs stopped to investigate and then passed right below the man they were hunting.

If any of the four Dakota tribes caught him, the torture would even be worse. Yes, he was also Dakota, but he belonged to the Tizaptanons, a band of religious outcasts hiding in the shadows. At best, he was a thorn in their side. Now, however, they were being threatened with war because of him.

Would my people protect a murderer?

While he debated his future, the Americans continued to linger at their camp, effectively trapping Ohanzee on the cliff face. Once darkness came, he could either slip away or wait out the night, hoping the party would continue their trek north in the morning.

Shortly after supper, just as the sun was setting, the American holy man slipped into one of the canoes by himself and crossed to the shore below Ohanzee. Knowing his position was blanketed with shadows, Ohanzee watched the man stop at the base of the cliff and wave back at the men on the other shore. After pulling the canoe up onto a rock, the American holy man spent a few moments studying the rocks at the base of the cliff. Then he strapped several metal objects to his body and carefully walked along the edge of the cliff until he disappeared from sight.

From what Ohanzee could see, none of the metallic objects were weapons, but he couldn't be sure. If the holy man climbed around the side of the cliff, he would easily be able to look down upon his position.

Once again, Ohanzee had no choice. Any noise he made departing from his position would be attributed to the holy man's ascent. Wanting to avoid conflict, Ohanzee snuck away to the opposite side of the cliff.

Reaching the pines, he took a few quick steps toward the top of the ridge before stopping. *There is a canoe below.*

Temptation stopped him in his tracks. Under the protection of darkness, Ohanzee would be able to travel ten to twenty miles by the following morning. With a stolen canoe, he could find himself safely back home in a matter of days.

Without the canoe, the net of the Chippewa would continue to tighten. He had dodged too many traps earlier in the day not to see the guiding hand of Great Inyan. After glancing over his shoulder, he steadily descended the ridge toward the shore.

The campfire on the opposite shore blinded the men from seeing his passage in the dim light. Twice, rocks shifted beneath his weight, causing him to freeze in his tracks. Standing on the edge of the water, it took every bit of nerve to approach the canoe.

Lifted onto a flat rock, the canoe waited in the open. If he waited any longer, the light from the flames would cast shadows on the cliff face, making him easier to see. *I must go now.*

Ohanzee carefully crept across the boulders half submerged in the river until he reached the canoe. He looked down to see a canoe stuffed with all sorts of goods. Tin pans. Cups. A kettle. Flints. Bags of sugar. Bags of tobacco. Wrapped slabs of smoked bacon. Cans of coffee. Bottles of brandy. A half-dozen carefully folded blankets. Boxes of beads and trinkets.

Thank you, Inyan, for providing me with such a bounty.

But Inyan's favor took an unexpected turn when Ohanzee looked up to see the American holy man standing a few feet from the canoe. The metallic equipment strapped to the holy man was gone, leaving him with empty hands.

Ohanzee pulled his knife, but the stranger immediately held out his empty hands to stop him. Attacking was foolish. If the holy man shouted, or if he managed to grab ahold of the knife like the old woman had done, his companions just fifty yards across the river would come to his rescue.

THE ALCHEMIST'S MAP

Both of them froze with indecision.

Then, with both hands raised and extended, the wide-eyed American took a cautious step backwards and gestured at the canoe.

He is trading the canoe for his life, Ohanzee thought, taking a step forward, but then he realized that in order to climb into the canoe, he would have to put away the knife.

Instead of fixating on the drawn knife, the man looked into the canoe at a dark green box. The frightened man collected his resolve, which made matters worse for Ohanzee. A foolish move could end in disaster.

The man reached into his vest, which caused Ohanzee to take a step forward. Attacking the holy man would mean leaping the canoe, which promised an uncertain landing on the other side.

Instead of drawing a weapon, though, the small American drew a shiny gold coin from his pocket. He pointed to the green box and then extended the coin.

He wants the box. He is trying to negotiate.

Seeing an opportunity present itself, Ohanzee steadily lowered the knife and slipped it back into his belt. Raising his own hands for a few seconds, he then gestured to the green box, which prompted a nod from the small holy man.

Ohanzee reached forward for the box, but instead of retrieving it, he took hold of the edges of the canoe and pushed it off of the rock. The holy man vigorously shook the coin, which prompted Ohanzee to release the canoe to retrieve his knife.

For another few heartbeats, the two stood at a standstill as the current gently turned the canoe parallel to the shore before holding up on a few submerged rocks, leaving no obstruction between himself and the white man.

Sensing the same, the holy man pointed with both hands to the campfire on the other side of the river.

He is right. I am as much at his mercy as he is at mine. Even if I could overpower the man now, his friends have rifles. It is suicide.

Again, the man with the face of a boy but the hair of an old man pointed at the box.

He could have backed away or simply jumped into the river to save himself.

In his life-and-death negotiation with the small American, Ohanzee suddenly saw a way out. He gestured to the box and then invisibly lifted it out and to the rock beside the canoe. The man smiled and nodded, extending the coin toward Ohanzee in a feigned toss.

That will do. Steadily and cautiously, Ohanzee again grabbed the edge of the canoe, which now supported by water, easily moved back toward him.

With a final threatening knife jab, Ohanzee tucked the blade back into the belt. Raising his hands to the holy man, he bent over to reach inside of the canoe. Right beside the green painted wooden box, there was a long wooden paddle.

Ohanzee could hear his heart beating in his chest as he debated his actions.

I am already a dead man, sentenced to the fires. What else do I have to lose? I would rather die by bullet than be slowly tortured over the Chippewa fires.

Suddenly resolved, Ohanzee reached for the paddle instead of the green box. When he stood back up, he swung the paddle with all his might, catching the holy man squarely across the cheek.

Although not a hard blow, the little American fell backwards against the rocks, a strange grunt-like groan coming from his body as he fell.

"Nicollet?" a voice called out in the darkness.

THE ALCHEMIST'S MAP

Paddle in hand, Ohanzee knew better than to continue his attack. Instead, he jumped into the canoe, and with the leverage of the paddle, pushed off the rocks and into the currents of the Crow Wing.

"Nicollet? Is everything all right?" another American called out. With frantic strokes, Ohanzee passed within the light of the campfire long enough to see the gathered men. In shock, they suddenly locked eyes with him.

A moment later, he was alone in the darkness.

Shouts echoed behind him.

Then a bullet whizzed by, prompting even more frantic paddling.

For ten minutes, he could hear them behind him in the darkness.

For an hour, the noises grew fainter.

For the next three hours, Ohanzee heard nothing but his own breathing and his heart pounding in his chest.

By dawn, his arms ached and his head pounded.

If those men are following me, they will only be moments behind. If I pull off of the river, they will be on me in moments.

In the dim light of dawn, Ohanzee spotted a dry creek bed with rocks at its mouth.

This will have to do.

He pulled the stolen canoe onto the rocks and gravel, but the weight of the stolen merchandise almost proved too much once he had pulled the canoe fully out of the water.

He looked up the dark river valley but saw nothing.

Finally, he pulled the canoe into the tight little ravine, where soft sand made the pulling much easier. Hauling the canoe thirty yards and out of sight of the Crow Wing, Ohanzee scrambled up the ravine to a good hiding spot.

Hours passed and the sun peeked over the ravine.

The expedition had not followed him.

They had simply given up, or they tended to their wounded colleague.

Either way, Ohanzee spent the afternoon looking down upon the stolen canoe and the mysterious green box.

Finally, driven by curiosity, he walked back down to the canoe.

But instead of finding anything of value, he found a box filled with paper. Only one of the pieces of paper even meant anything: it was a drawing of five rivers that converged into a single spot.

Mahkato, Ohanzee smiled, seeing the drawing as a good omen. If he could reach Mahkato, he would almost be home.

Then, at the bottom of the green box, he found a wampum belt he recognized. *No… what have I done?*

CHAPTER TWENTY-EIGHT
CROW WING RIVER
1836

The Seven Fires is a religious prophecy of the Anishinaabe people. According to the legend, a series of prophets delivered messages to their ancestors while they still lived along the shores of the Atlantic Ocean. The warning was clear: either leave their homelands or face doom and destruction.

From the onset, the Anishinaabe knew how their quest would end, for the prophets described their final destination as a land where the food grows on the water with a turtle-shaped island. After departing the Atlantic, there would be seven stopping places, marked with a collection of tropical cowrie shells, or Miigis shells, to identify the next stage of migration.

By 1836, the Anishinaabe had visited six stopping places: Montreal Island, Niagara Falls, Lake St. Clair by Detroit, Manitoulin Island, Sault Ste. Marie, and Madeline Island. Along the way, over the thousands of miles of terrain, many of the Anishinaabe stayed behind, becoming separate nations such as the Potawatomi, Odawa, Algonquin, and Mississaugas. Those who faced the Dakota in the territory later known as "Minnesota" were the Ojibwe (Chippewa). Despite the descriptions of the prophecies, the specific location of the Seventh Fire (and seventh stopping place) was disputed.

While the Seven Fires prophecies predicted the cross-continent migration of the Chippewa and the arrival of the French, English, and Americans, it also contained a religious prophecy detailing the arrival of a mysterious figure in the era of the Seventh Fire, who would make a decision to either set things right and usher in an Eighth Fire for all mankind or choose poorly, bringing death and destruction.

For the Chippewa Midē' Chagobay, the opportunity to meet Nicollet allowed him to study the strange man. Prior to the attack on Nicollet and the theft of his canoe, Chagobay had seen the wampum belt in Nicollet's possession that was once carried by the traveling shaman, Sha-Koo-Zoo-Shetek.

What does this mean? Is Nicollet the one? Will he heal our lands?

Joining the expedition had been easy for Chagobay. With war brewing between the Chippewa and Sioux, Chagobay's presence offered the expedition a measure of extra protection. He'd brought his own canoe, and his little son, Nanakonan, a prolific hunter and fisherman, provided meals for the whole expedition.

Chagobay also intimately knew the Mississippi River and its tributaries, so he could provide Captain Lyons accurate information for campsites and give Nicollet names and descriptions of every creek and river that fed the Mississippi.

THE ALCHEMIST'S MAP

The men of the expedition despise me, Chagobay decided, but he could not determine if it was protectiveness over Nicollet or other reasons why they looked at him with scowls and hatred.

When the rogue Sioux spared Nicollet at the Crow Wing River, Chagobay saw it as a sign and further opened himself up to the Star Man.

Nicollet prayed each morning, yet he also seemed to live at one with nature, loving every tree, plant, animal, rock formation, and even the stars in the sky with all of his heart.

Heal the nations, Chagobay often repeated in his mind the words Shetek had said to him before departing. *This could be my opportunity to fix the wrongs of the previous generation. But only if Nicollet is the one.*

With the giant Métis, Brunia, serving as translator, Nicollet would spend hours trying to understand the beliefs of the Chippewa people, pressing Chagobay relentlessly for information, especially information on Turtle Island. In return, Nicollet taught him how to use the scientific equipment, and together, they would measure the stars and air.

Hour after hour, day after day, Chagobay watched and wondered.

Is he the one?

Once, along the bank of the river, Nicollet pointed and forced the entire expedition to halt while he inspected something—*pewabic*.

Nicollet rolled the blue mineral on his fingertips and packed away small samples in tins. For the next hour, he investigated the rocks along the river, as if searching for the source of the tiny spring that bled blue. He remained silent for almost an hour after that before he opened his mouth.

By that time, Chagobay had already decided.

The Great Spirit has sent him to me for a reason. The blue earth confirms it.

CHAPTER TWENTY-NINE

LAKE MANITO
1836

Despite the raging storm, Nicollet remained dry under his canvas wedge tent, thanks to the three inches of pelts that kept him off the ground. Even with the elevated ground and tight construction, he listened to the rolling thunder, wind gusts, downpours, and then the steady drip of water from the pine boughs above him.

What is the sense of comfort if my mind won't let me find some sleep?

With the departing storm darkening the dawn, Nicollet relied on a few matches to orient his walk from the tent to the canoe guarded by Jim Taopi. Although he'd lost the green chest, sketches, and Shetek's priceless wampum belt, his scientific equipment and specimens remained, including the samples of copper vitriol.

THE ALCHEMIST'S MAP

So many "Longue" rivers.
Countless watersheds.
But to find Fort L'Huillier, I must find vitriol.

Nicollet's fingers dabbed at the blue earth, wondering about its chemical origins. In the span of two comets, science had gone from magic to chemistry. In nature, blue occurred least often, but Nicollet doubted he'd find a unicorn under the microscope.

When a shadow moved, he dropped the specimen tin. He stooped to quickly right the container before the blue dirt spilled out.

Nanakonan, the Midē''s son, stood there with a grin and gestured for Nicollet to follow him to the edge of the camp.

Chagobay, dressed to rival Cardinal Croÿ-Solre, looked rested and eager. "A new path," he said, pointing to the northwest.

Nicollet shook his head. Thanks to months of tutelage from Antoine Clément and the Jesuit missionaries in St. Louis, Nicollet had learned enough Anishinaabemowin to converse with the Chippewa as well as he could with their Potawatomi cousins. "North Star. Leech Lake," and then Nicollet pointed to the northeast. "Mississippi River."

"There is a better path. The Crow Wing River flows west. We will portage."

Lyons will not agree until we rescue Reverend Boutwell and his wife. The Mississippi River route will be faster.

"Blue earth," Chagobay pointed to Taopi's canoe and then to Nicollet. "I can show you more."

❧

For as far as Nicollet could see, a field of reeds swallowed the river. The low banks allowed the main channel to spread out wide and shallow, which also allowed the spring and summer growth to choke the entire river.

What is Chagobay looking for?

Had they only needed to continue upriver, it would have been difficult but ultimately possible. But Chagobay had insisted on a new route.

Even though Captain Lyons said the detour was not part of their mission to rescue the Boutwells, he quickly relented just to lighten the depression that had swept over Nicollet after the theft of his canoe.

Lyons huffed at the delay, which was noticed by both Chagobay and Nanakonan, who whispered to his father. A moment later, Chagobay lifted his son onto his shoulders.

From up there, Nanakonan smiled broadly at the grim-faced men and then down at Nicollet, who found strange beauty in the boy's efforts and enthusiasm.

Atop his father's strong shoulders, Nanakonan looked to the edges of the wide shore for a channel from a hidden lake.

Unlike most outlets which carved deep ravines, the shore was evenly flat, rocky, and wooded. *Even if the boy does spot it, there is not enough water for our canoes to pass.*

"There, there, there!" Nanakonan shrieked wildly, pointing so his father could see the flat rocks where the water cut deeper into the shore.

Behind him, the men broke into applause. Even Nicollet smiled and bowed to Nanakonan.

With Chagobay using the poles to push the canoe toward the flat rocks, the wild rice reached up like a million fingers trying to keep the expedition from proceeding.

Twenty yards from the rocky mouth of the stream, the water deepened and a distinct channel formed within the reeds. Nanakonan climbed down from his father's shoulders. Nicollet smiled warmly at him, and the boy reciprocated.

Having spent two hours looking for the tiny outlet, the men continued up the stream just a few minutes before pulling off onto a solid bank

THE ALCHEMIST'S MAP

to prepare some lunch. Nicollet listened to Lyons, Colton, and Faribault argue for a few minutes about the wisdom of leaving the Mississippi River. After feasting on a pike Nanakonan had speared, Nicollet found Chagobay standing in the pines.

"Last night, before the storm, you told me you were a Wâbĕnō. Brunia could not explain this to me. How is a Wâbĕnō different from a Midē′?"

Chagobay carefully measured his words. "We are servants of Manabozho, chosen by our spiritual gifts to help fulfill his will."

"So why did Manabozho choose you?"

"He chose me because I carry the blood of the Wijigan, which is needed for the Seven Fires prophecy to come to an end. If my people are to survive certain doom, I must do my part to bring the prophecies to an end, which is why Nanakonan must have a serious mind instead of always acting like a child."

"But he is a child."

"And that puts him in great danger. Only a disciplined Wâbĕnō can control this manito, or else it will turn and kill anyone who disturbs it."

Is that what Chagobay fears? From what he'd read, a manito was akin to the Horned Serpent that lived in the depths of the water, much like the biblical Leviathan. "You are a good father to want to protect your son."

By the time Nicollet and Chagobay returned, Big Moe Maxwell had collected and cleaned the plates from the nine of them. An hour later, after camp was packed back into the canoes, Nicollet noticed a smoldering fury again return to Chagobay's eyes as they led the tiny armada through the creek.

Nanakonan sat behind his father, huddled meekly in a ball. Behind him, Nicollet watched the reed-lined banks finally begin to widen as they approached the lake. In the rear of the canoe, Maxwell steadily pushed his paddle through the water, unaffected by the beauty of the place.

In the canoe behind them, Brunia began to hum an old folk song soon to be joined by Nanakonan. A few moments later, even Captain Lyons began to hum it also. In that magical moment, all three canoes fell into synch with the singing and paddling.

"Quiet!" Chagobay turned with enough fury in his eyes to silence even the fierce Sergeant Taopi. "There must be no singing at this place."

Something is wrong, Nicollet realized. *Chagobay acts frightened.*

None of the men had seen the Chippewa holy man act in such a way. Lieutenant Colton traded his paddle for his rifle.

Like other lakes in the Big Woods, it was surrounded by a canopy of pines and outcroppings of granite shores littered with boulders. For hundreds of yards in all directions, the southern shore was lined with a massive field of wild rice, with a deeper channel leading them toward the center of the lake. When the water finally deepened, a strange bed of flowering lily pads filled the channel.

Chagobay lifted his paddle, allowing the canoe's momentum to drift them through the beautiful array of flowers. The men mimicked Chagobay, with nary a paddle dipped, and the canoes eventually slowed to a crawl.

Behind them, the Sioux guide Jim Taopi whispered, "Tewapa," without any of the others questioning his meaning. A light eastern wind pushed the canoes through the field of flowers, and once past, Chagobay finally dipped his paddle into the water and angled them toward the oak-lined southwestern shore.

"Why did you not touch the lilies?" Nicollet finally asked.

Chagobay thought over the question for a few moments, and as they neared the shore, he finally gave his answer. "The lilies might look beautiful, but their roots extend to the bottom of the lake, echoing like the

THE ALCHEMIST'S MAP

strings of your fiddle. If Nanakonan did not already awaken the manito with his pike, the lilies would have announced our arrival. The spirit that dwells here is too powerful for me to control, so we must not let it know I've brought you here."

Nicollet looked to the steep cliffs behind the wild rice field, and across the seven-mile lake, he could see a low field of stone.

What does Chagobay want me to see?

With the entire expedition feeling the strange tone, silence continued as they paddled across the large bay to an island with a green, oak-covered hump.

"Mizheekay. Turtle Island," Chagobay nodded as they pulled the three canoes onto the shore and out of the water.

After supper, Captain Lyons and Corporal Faribault began to argue.

"The water level is too low," Faribault insisted, looking at his primitive map. "We need to get back onto the main branch of the Crow Wing River if we are to reach Leech Lake."

"We shouldn't stay here," Taopi nodded. "My grandfather once told me it is the Place of Souls."

Or Spirit Lake? Even the stoic Taopi is shaken? Nicollet watched as Chagobay chose to stare out at the lake rather than debate the men.

Any river potentially led to the headwaters, and from what Chagobay had told him, Lake Manito had a tributary river that led north toward Leech Lake where its headwaters were located.

Nicollet also felt as if Chagobay was holding back vital information, so just before nightfall, he pulled Chagobay aside to ask him questions.

"Does the manito have a name?" he asked.

"Yes, but his name is cursed. My grandfather once spoke the name of the manito, and it brought death to my entire clan, leaving only my brother, his daughters, and Nanakonan to carry on the sacred quest of my people until the Gitchi-Animikii arrives."

"What is the 'Animikii?'"

"It is the Great Thunderbird, the one who will fight the water serpent and throw him into the Land of the Midnight Sun where he belongs."

"The Land of the Midnight Sun?"

"It is the place where the souls of our people go when they die. Long ago, when the world was still new, the manito found here walked upon the earth with human feet. He was a mighty hunter that lived in a land far to the north, before there was summer or winter. He was also a powerful Jeśsakkīd, a sorcerer, who first learned that humans had souls. Afraid of his own death, this evil sorcerer learned how to trap the souls of the dead, keeping them from descending into the Land of the Midnight Sun where they could find peace."

"He wanted to cheat death," Nicollet echoed.

"Yes. He wanted to stop time, which is why he was also called the Wintermaker, refusing to allow the next summer to ever come. One day, a mighty warrior came to challenge the Wintermaker to combat, and to free the souls he had captured for himself. The evil one fled, and the great warrior followed. Now, the Fisher Cat guards the northern sky until the coming of the Great Thunderbird, who will pull the Wintermaker from the sky and send him to the Land of the Midnight Sun where he belongs."

Orion, Nicollet realized, *the warrior.* "Show me the Fisher Cat."

Chagobay pointed to the northern sky. "We call it Ojiig."

When Nicollet saw that Chagobay pointed to Ursa Major and not Orion, he became so overwhelmed that he began to weep. *Champollion would adore this man. Imagine the tales they could tell. Champollion would know what to do.* "Surely you do not think the Great Spirit has sent me to help you. Only a great fool would lose the wampum belt of Shetek," he confessed and wept for another minute. *What would*

THE ALCHEMIST'S MAP

Stewart say now? He is the warrior, not me.

Chagobay put a hand on his shoulder, prompting Nicollet to compose himself. "During the battle between the Fisher Cat and the Wintermaker, the Water Drum was left behind for the Great Thunderbird to finish the fight one day. The Water Drum can command the souls of the living or dead, on earth or in heaven. I would like you to see it."

CHAPTER THIRTY

LAKE MANITO

1836

Just before daybreak, Nicollet woke to find Chagobay and Nanakonan ready and waiting. The cautious Midē´ insisted to Nicollet that only he could come with, and except for Brunia, who eyed him cautiously as he tiptoed from the camp, no one was the wiser to their departure.

When they crossed to the north shore of Lake Manito, Nicollet and Chagobay put away their paddles and took out their long poles. They passed through a valley flanked by tall cliffs on both sides. For a mile, they pushed their way through the river until they finally came to a wall of rocks strewn across the channel almost like a primitive dam.

"My brother and I spent a summer rolling boulders into the river," Chagobay explained, "trying to create a dam that would raise the river

THE ALCHEMIST'S MAP

level high enough."

"Why would you do that?" Nicollet asked and Chagobay just raised his eyebrows.

"We were tasked with keeping the Water Drum hidden until the Great Thunderbird came to retrieve it. Come, I will show you."

None of this matches what Lahontan or Le Sueur described. He is not leading me to Fort L'Huillier.

Chagobay led Nicollet and Nanakonen up into the rocks and then pointed. "Bad medicine. Even in death, the Wintermaker's magic is working against me, forcing me to make a choice."

There, twenty feet ahead of where they stopped, a brilliantly blue mound of sand glistened in the morning sun.

Vitriol! Just like what Baron Lahontan described. Tucked into a deep valley, where natural erosion could expose copper to the elements, the mound of vitriol appeared both natural and supernatural. "Why do you think this is a sign of the Wintermaker's magic?"

Chagobay's fear was palpable. "The magic of the Water Drum is so strong that it will transform any substance near it. In life, the Wintermaker tried to control this magic—and failed. I brought you here to help show me the way forward. The Water Drum's capacity for good or evil could unbalance the world. In the hands of the Great Thunderbird, it could set things right, but if the magic inside is unleashed, it could bring the Wintermaker his ultimate victory over death."

The clues don't fit the narrative. This is not Fort L'Huillier. Nothing about this place matches what Lahontan or Le Sueur saw, save for the vitriol. At the river's edge, Nicollet studied the vitriol and its surroundings.

While odd, the mound could certainly be a nodule of copper exposed by a landslide in the river valley. *Is there a natural explanation rather than latent magic bubbling up from the deep?*

Nicollet walked forward and stood over it for a moment and then laughed at the incredulous sight. *Very different from what I found along the Mississippi.* Hydrated copper sulphate, or even the patina from corroded copper, had a grainy or powdery appearance. Plus, there would be a source of the chemical reaction, but what he saw amongst the rocks seemed almost poured out from a phantom beaker. Kneeling, his fingers delicately touched the blue substance. "It is oily," he said, rubbing his fingers together.

Nicollet's eyes darted up. A trickle of water came down from the face of the cliff, cutting through the soft sandstone to reveal the granite that formed the valley.

The substance looked like sand, and although the formation was strange, the vitriol could have simply mixed with the sand. A trickle of water came from a fissure in the cliff above the vitriol. *The source?*

"Strange," Nicollet said and then bent down. He quickly retrieved a canister and filled it to the brim with the blue substance.

He handed it to the boy. "Nanakonan, could you bring this back to the canoe. I want to inspect this fissure a little bit more."

Nanakonan bounced across the stony river bottom for a few yards before climbing the edge of the cliff. Following the blue-bleeding rocks, Nicollet struggled to find a scientific explanation for the miracle. With Chagobay's help, he carefully climbed over several boulders.

"It could be a copper mound exposed when this rock eroded away," Nicollet shouted out another explanation, mostly to himself. "There could be a copper nodule up here slowly eroding."

Near the top of the cliff, Nicollet spotted a small cave. *Ah ha, the source of the bleeding.* Its dark mouth opened wide enough for a man to enter, slightly hunched.

Chagobay nodded. *Perhaps formed by a fissure or spring, which would explain the residue collecting below it.*

THE ALCHEMIST'S MAP

Before Nicollet could climb any further, a strange splash formed in the pool behind them. The sound hadn't come from the canoe; it had come from upstream.

Ten warriors appeared on the ridge, five on each side. Nicollet and Chagobay froze where they stood, and that was when four canoes came around the bend.

"Pillagers," Chagobay whispered.

"What does that mean?" Nicollet asked, wishing he had Shetek's wampum belt.

"You should pray to your God."

CHAPTER THIRTY-ONE

LAKE MANITO
1836

The Undine wrapped Nicollet in her arms, pressing his wounded head against her bosom while she caressed his wispy curls. She hummed an old French melody that reminded him of one his mother used to sing while in the kitchen.

He knew the face she wore also, one he saw whenever he looked upon the likes of Juliana Leeves, Mary Ann Eastin, or even Elizabeth Tolliver.

"Where am I?" Nicollet asked, realizing that a blanket of fog replaced the Pillager warriors that had just surrounded him.

"You are far, far from home, mon amour. What are you doing in such a foreign place?" The Undine's voice poured from her lips like a

THE ALCHEMIST'S MAP

song, and Nicollet closed his eyes again as it rolled over him.

"I am proving my worth. I will solve the unsolvable mystery."

"Ah, my sweet Nicky. You were always such a smart boy. What mystery do you plan to solve?"

Nicollet felt a chill run through his body, but not because he dreamed of ice. He'd been struck in the head by one of the angry Pillager warriors and lost consciousness. So he fearlessly sat up and looked at the woman who held him in her arms.

"Who are you?" he asked, looking at her strange blue eyes.

"Don't you remember me? I have been waiting for you under the waves."

Nicollet felt his throbbing head, but his fingers touched a wound that did not bleed. "I see your face, but it belongs to another, and I already know her name. Are you supposed to be the evil spirit that haunts this place? An Undine? Or are you just a figment of my imagination?"

The Undine reached out a gentle hand that glistened. "My dear Nicky. You should have listened to your friends. The frontier is no place for the likes of you. Go home, before it is too late."

The throbbing in his head worsened.

Soon the tender blue eyes of the Undine vanished, and a blinding light burned away the fog.

"Wijigan," he heard a voice shout, and when he opened his eyes, he saw Chagobay on his knees, a Pillager warrior holding him up by the hair.

The angry men spoke so fast that he could only focus on the bloody gash near his hairline.

His arms and ribs ached, a sign of a beating following the strike to his head. They tied him up, loaded him into a canoe, and paddled north up the narrow river. Every once in a while, Nicollet discreetly glanced to the ridge to see if Nanakonan followed them. The boy had vanished along with the vitriol when the Pillager warriors had arrived. *I can only hope he went back to find the others.*

After several miles, the land flattened and the river narrowed to a stream. In this low area, the Pillagers had made camp, forcing Nicollet and Chagobay out of the canoes to an even larger and angrier crowd.

"Wijigan!" they again snarled, beating Chagobay twice as often as they beat Nicollet. "Do you mean to bring ruin on our people?"

One of the men waved a war club, wanting to kill Chagobay right there.

Another wanted to create a pyre to burn Chagobay.

Others only wanted to kill Nicollet.

Finally, it was decided Chagobay would die.

Hearing the decision, Nicollet threw his arms around Chagobay and endured another beating. When they saw he was unwilling to let go, the attacker finally relented, looking back at their young Pillager chief for guidance. Neither the cruel chief nor any of the other braves met the man's mystified gaze, however; instead, they were all looking upriver at the canoe flying two large flags—an American one at the bow and a British one at the stern.

As much as Nicollet hoped for Captain Lyons, or even another party of Major Tolliver's, his rescue consisted of only two Chippewa braves. The two braves didn't speak a word as they interrupted the war party. In fact, they did not even draw weapons but fearlessly steered right into the throng.

Jumping out of their canoes, the men looked around for a moment before locking eyes with Nicollet. "In the name of Chief Flat Mouth of Leech Lake, we claim these prisoners."

CHAPTER THIRTY-TWO

LEECH LAKE
1836

Nanakonan managed to navigate the big canoe all the way across Lake Manito until he reached Turtle Island. As he approached, he could see the large Métis, Brunia, staring out at him.

His lungs and arms ached, but even if he'd been able to shout, he decided against it. *The Pillagers will kill my father for bringing Nicollet here. They must not know he brought others, too.*

As the canoe slid onto the shore, he hunched over in exhaustion. Brunia's strong hands clamped onto his arms, lifting him up from his seat.

"What happened to Nicollet? Where did your father take him? Where is he?"

Located one hundred twenty miles due west of Lake Superior, Leech Lake is Minnesota's third largest body of water with a hundred thousand acres of water and one hundred ninety-five miles of shoreline, thanks to jutting peninsulas, bays, and islands. Isolated from major watersheds, it had quickly become the center of the Chippewa nation in northern Minnesota by the 1750s.

When Joseph Nicollet and Chagobay arrived at Leech Lake, Nicollet learned that everything Major Tolliver feared had come true. Forty miles from where he had been abducted, thousands of Chippewa warriors lined the shores of Leech Lake. Nicollet finally understood the magnitude of the situation; each day that passed without justice for the murdered Chippewa women brought more and more chieftains to Leech Lake.

The two young men who had come to claim Nicollet and Chagobay for Chief Flat Mouth fearlessly marched the pair down the inside of a peninsula on Leech Lake's most western arm, trailed by Chief Bad Earth and the other upset Pillagers.

"Flat Mouth's son has returned," Nicollet kept hearing from onlookers as he followed the two men carrying the large flags.

Finally, he saw a half-circle of ornate chieftains awaiting his arrival. One of the chieftains raised his spear and shook it, bringing a roar from the crowd that made Nicollet's bowels tighten.

"Father, I present these two prisoners, who I have rescued from Chief Bad Earth."

A smaller man with thin eyebrows and a protruding jaw nodded. "Give them food and water," he said, but his eyes watched Bad Earth the entire time. "Come, Bad Earth. Sit at my fire and explain your recent actions."

The young chief who'd laughed as his braves beat Nicollet now seemed worried. "Kaghino's mother and wife were murdered."

Several grunts and grumbles threatened to stop the young war chief before he began, but Bad Earth set his jaw and continued, "The Sioux are killing Pillagers on our lands, so I protect it from enemies until you decide to act."

"Your men would not be enough to stop the Sioux," Flat Mouth declared. "Even now, I hear stories of them gathering in the west because your men harassed the Sioux along the border—without my permission. And now you take an American prisoner?"

"This crazy old Midē′ brought the American to Lake Manito," Bad Earth argued. "Isn't it your decree that no man or woman set foot in that place?"

"It is, but I will not have zealots such as yourself allowing the Americans and Sioux to unite against us in common cause."

"I understand mighty Chief Flat Mouth must protect his people, but I believe the old Midē′ I found is one of the Wijigan Clan."

"You believe…" Flat Mouth muttered angrily and shook his head. "I will not allow our people to be threatened because of silly superstitions. Bring the American here. He will explain his actions as well."

CHAPTER THIRTY-THREE

LEECH LAKE
1836

Nicollet took a deep breath to will his bruised arm to action. He brushed off the dirt from his jacket, and with a scarf, removed the trickle of dried blood from his forehead and eyebrow. He swept his curly hair back from his eyes and held his chin high despite the pummeling he had taken.

"Are you from the stone fort?" Flat Mouth asked.

Nicollet smiled and began to explain, but halfway through his explanation, Flat Mouth raised his hand. "Go get the translator Black Jacket. This man's words hurt my ears."

A young man ran off and quickly brought back an old Chippewa quite literally dressed in a black jacket. "Translate his words for me,

THE ALCHEMIST'S MAP

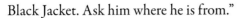

Black Jacket. Ask him where he is from."

Nicollet looked around for Chagobay, but could not find him.

Black Jacket repeated the question, and Nicollet answered, waiting to see how his translator treated him.

Clear communication is good, as long as I can trust this fellow. I will explain that I am from the Savoy region of France, which should endear me to the Chippewa.

"He says he is from the mountains, but I could not understand which mountains he meant," Black Jacket explained to Flat Mouth.

"Ask him if he is from the Stone Fort."

So Black Jacket asked, and received another complicated answer to translate. "He says he is not from the Stone Fort. He says he is... from the stars."

From the stars? No, I am an astronomer.

"From the stars? See, Americans are liars. Where is the justice and peace promised by the gentle words of the American president?"

"I am not American," Nicollet said in Anishinaabemowin. "I do not speak for those at the fort."

With the two flags propped at his left and his right, Flat Mouth rose and violently tossed the American flag to the ground. Then he reached to his chest, removed a golden medal, and tossed it at Nicollet's feet. "Tell this man that I have the power to destroy every American between here and Lake Gitche Gumee. If I had not made a promise to bury the hatchet, I could have torn down his stone fort. Yet they threaten me to strike down the first one who starts a war. He threatened to reduce the first village to start a war to ashes. Where is the justice of the Great Father, this American president?"

"Tell him I'm French," Nicollet said to Black Jacket and then rose. He walked over to the British flag and, with a tug, let it drop to the ground before returning to where he earlier knelt. Then reaching into his red vest, withdrew a large piece of jewelry and extended it to Flat Mouth.

"Tell Chief Flat Mouth that I am not from the Stone Fort. I come from across the sea. I have only come to look at the stars. I speak for neither the British nor the Americans. This medallion, which I give as a gift to Chief Flat Mouth, is proof that I do not speak with a forked tongue."

Nicollet waited for Black Jacket to translate.

Cosette, you save me once again! Flat Mouth took the locket given to Nicollet during the riots of the July Revolution. *It is time to cash in my lucky charm.*

"Naponeon," Flat Mouth muttered with a smile.

"Yes, yes, that is Naponeon," Nicollet repeated, not wanting to correct the powerful leader. "He was a great warrior of the French, who once helped the Chippewa like a father helps a son."

Flat Mouth turned the figure painted upon the white stone. "Well, it is strange, on whatever side I turn it, the figure looks at me and seems to say, 'Thou art my brother warrior.' Send the Frenchman to my tent. My wives will feed him and treat his wounds and we will talk. Tomorrow, when Chief Solid Ground arrives, we will continue to speak about matters of war."

Although Flat Mouth's wives stuffed Nicollet with duck and deer, the dull pains throughout his body left him nauseous. Nicollet rose at the break of dawn and prayed along the edge of the woods. With thousands of Chippewa gathered on the peninsula, many of which watched him pray, Nicollet entertained no plans of escaping.

What of Chagobay?

What do I do now?

As he prayed for wisdom, he heard footsteps approaching, and when he opened his eyes, Chief Flat Mouth stood over him, still clutching the locket, with the translator Black Jacket behind him.

THE ALCHEMIST'S MAP

"Why do you hate Americans?" Nicollet asked.

"We hate them because they establish military posts to protect the natives but instead they keep them like dogs. Yet I withhold my hand, preventing our young ones like Bad Earth from exterminating the Americans, even though they put us in prisons, whip us with rope, and tie cords around our necks and hang us."

Men like Benton, Poinsett, and Abert. "Not all Americans are like this."

"Yes, they are. Even Mr. Boutwell, who came to us in friendship, wears a mask. Now, I no longer know whom to trust. The agent from the Stone Fort or the agent from Lapointe."

Boutwell? Are they already prisoners of Flat Mouth? Nicollet wondered, but also contemplated Flat Mouth's other words. *Lapointe. He means Schoolcraft.* Major Tolliver's worries had been well-founded. "I cannot speak about the agent from Lapointe, but I know the agent in the Stone Fort to be a man of integrity, who only wants what is best for your people."

"Then why does he withhold goods from us?" Flat Mouth asked. "The agent at Lapointe does not deny us, and now the young men from my village have heard about it. I want the agent from the Stone Fort to offer goods as a token of good faith between us. We do not know if the agent is telling falsehoods of his own or if Washington orders him to tell them. We beg you to write to our Great Father telling him of our intentions."

"Me?" Nicollet recoiled. "Why me?"

"Our fathers always said they would love to see the French again, they who first visited this land. We long for the French of the other shore, that they may return and save us from the Americans. However, these are strong words. I do not know who to trust, so will *you* tell them?"

I am not a diplomat, but how can I deny such honest requests? "Yes, if they are fair words."

"Will you write down what we say to you?"

"Yes."

So that afternoon, a great coalition of Chippewa chiefs, including Bad Earth, Strong Head, and Solid Ground gathered with Flat Mouth to discuss what should be done.

For an hour, the chiefs repeated and restated their grievances with the Indian Agents, the United States government, and their enemies, the Sioux. Nicollet patiently wrote down the grievances in his letter, which extended for multiple pages.

Nicollet wrote down the final words. "I promise you, Chief Flat Mouth, that Tolliver will hear these words, but that is all I can promise. I am certain Tolliver will capture these murderers and show you good faith, or your hand will be able to strike down any of these who wrong your people, but before I can return to the Stone Fort, I wish to see where the Mississippi River begins."

"It is only a few days west of here," Flat Mouth said. "I will allow it. Now, let us speak plainly as men."

Flat Mouth put his hand on Nicollet's shoulder. With a gesture, the pipes were lit and the chieftains smoked quietly for an hour. During that time, Flat Mouth had his set of fine china brought out, and Nicollet drank tea with the other chiefs.

At the end of the session, a weary and worn Chagobay was marched to the edge of the camp. Nicollet rose and rushed over to the prisoner, throwing his arms around him in a hug and then gently touching his battered cheek. "What will happen now?" Nicollet asked as he returned to the strange tea party.

"There are some who wish me to punish Chagobay for bringing you into our sacred places without consent, but I see that this Midē´ only performed the will of the Great Spirit, so I will allow him to remain your guide as long as you wish to travel in our lands."

THE ALCHEMIST'S MAP

"I do wish it," Nicollet said.

Chagobay was released from his bonds, and he fell to the ground in relief and exhaustion.

From the edge of the camp, a white minister and his wife appeared. Flat Mouth rose and put a gentle hand on Nicollet's shoulder once more. "Take heart, Reverend Boutwell has come to rescue you from this ordeal. He will bring you to your worried American friends so that you can continue your journey and then bring our letter to the Great Father Tolliver."

The expedition is near?

Nicollet rose and walked over to help Chagobay from the ground.

The wide-eyed young preacher held an incredulous grin. "I hear you've come to rescue me," Boutwell said. "Or is it I who have rescued you?"

"It has been a challenging few days."

"Black Jacket tells me you still wish to see the headwaters," Boutwell said.

Lake Itasca, yes. "Yes, I am a mapmaker who joined Tolliver's rescue party for you. Things were going smoothly until I met the Pillagers."

"Are the Sioux really preparing for war?" Mrs. Boutwell asked.

"Tensions at Fort Snelling are high," Nicollet admitted, "But Flat Mouth has given me a list of conditions that could lead to peace."

"You?" Boutwell scoffed. "George Fanshaw said your reputation as a scientist is tarnished, so what gives you any authority as a diplomat?"

Fanshaw? "Chief Flat Mouth wishes it due to his mistrust of the white men he's met," Nicollet said with enough sarcasm to rankle Boutwell even further. "How do you know Fanshaw?"

"I accompanied Henry Schoolcraft to the headwaters in 1832, but for some reason, the government felt the need to send Fanshaw to verify Lake Itasca hadn't moved. What a Frenchman means to accomplish is a bit suspicious. Perhaps I should look over Flat Mouth's terms?"

"No, you and your wife can hear them when I return to Fort Snelling, but now, the watershed waits for a true scientist. Give Major Tolliver my regards."

CHAPTER THIRTY-FOUR

LAKE ITASCA

1836

Brunia led the way, alone. On his massive shoulders, the lead canoe pushed through the branches and the brush to create a path for the others to follow. Despite the beating, Chagobay held the nose of the second canoe with Big Moe Maxwell holding the tail.

Maxwell might be a thief, but he can at least spare Nicollet the burden of portaging, Brunia decided.

Trailing behind the path forged by Brunia, the canoes of the two soldiers, Colton and Taopi, floated through the air above the stony ground. *Still too many spies.*

Somewhere in the distance, several canoes carrying eighteen of Chief Flat Mouth's warriors dallied, knowing that the fragmented expedition could quickly be found should danger arise.

We could still become hostages, if Flat Mouth willed it.

Behind the three canoes, Brunia could see Nicollet walking with his sextant on his back, in a leather case thrown over his right shoulder as a knapsack. Despite not being given the duty of portaging the canoes, he carried a heavy load of equipment whenever they crossed land. The barometer was slung over his left shoulder, along with his cloak that helped protect his other pieces of important equipment.

Under his arm, he carried his portfolio of astronomical and meteorological notes and a basket that contained his thermometer, chronometer, pocket compass, artificial horizon, tape line, and other small devices.

On his right side, a spyglass, powder flask, and shot bag hung; in his hand, an umbrella despite the fact the rain had held off for much of the morning.

Mile after mile, Nicollet lugged his portable observatory with him, relentlessly working through any break to get his measurements and record them in his notes.

He still plays the part of the single-minded scientist, but I wonder what he saw at Lake Manito...

"Do you see that rise in the distance?" Nicollet called out. "That is our watershed."

"What do you say, Chagobay?" Brunia asked the trailing canoe.

"No, the Mississippi comes in from the north of the lake."

"Schoolcraft's lake?" Colton asked from the third spot.

"Yes, Corporal Colton," Nicollet said from the very rear. "Schoolcraft's lake is just on the other side of the hill. Math does not lie."

Schoolcraft—the villain who sabotages everything. Despite never having met him, Brunia despised him almost as much as Major Tolliver did.

Nicollet yelled up to him, "If the true headwaters are south of the

THE ALCHEMIST'S MAP

lake, I must stay here for a while and collect measurements. Brunia, I'll catch up to you at the top of the hill."

The little fellow is wearing out. I suppose I have kept a steady and demanding pace since leaving Leech Lake.

"Don't get yer hide lost in these woods," Maxwell grumbled.

"How could I get lost? I am a mapmaker," Nicollet said in jest and loudly set down his haul of equipment.

Big Moe remained sore at Nicollet for giving their coffee to Flat Mouth when he was reunited with Captain Lyons' party. Brunia had secretly tracked them all the way to Flat Mouth's camp at Onigum, and then he returned to guide the Americans back to Leech Lake. Once Nicollet was found, Reverend Boutwell and his wife, Hester, returned with Captain Lyons and Faribault to Fort Snelling, along with little Nanakonan, at Chagobay's insistence. Brunia, Maxwell, Taopi, Chagobay, and Colton were allowed to continue to the source of the Mississippi with Nicollet.

After reaching the rise, Brunia set down his canoe and waited for the scientist to catch up. Twenty minutes after setting down the canoe, clanking resumed in the woods to the south. A few minutes later, Nicollet appeared.

Chagobay helped him unpack the equipment and then pointed. "Do you see that lake in the distance? North of it is the source of the Mississippi."

"Schoolcraft's lake?" Nicollet said. "That is an arm of Itasca?"

Chagobay nodded and watched as Nicollet took out his barometer and took measurements, all while shaking his head. "I might have been convinced it was the source if I'd traveled by river like Pike, Cass, Beltrami, Schoolcraft, or even Fanshaw. But our portage reveals a different truth."

Nicollet jotted down his measurements in his notebook and then picked up his canteen, but not to take a drink. Instead, he walked over to Brunia, uncapped it, and began pouring it onto the ground. "This is the watershed that creates the Mississippi River."

Nicollet pointed to a small body of water at the bottom of the hill. "The water from my canteen will trickle down this hill to *my lake*. From there, it will follow that little creek a thousand feet or so until it reaches Schoolcraft's lake, Itasca. The math is not wrong, Chagobay. This is the top of the world."

But will Nicollet find what he truly seeks? Brunia wondered as he watched Nicollet put away his canteen.

"Congratulations, Professor Nicollet," Edgar Colton smiled.

"Merci, but alas, I've come too late, for what the people believe is true, and Schoolcraft has already declared a different truth." Nicollet shrugged and sat down next to his remaining companions. "Do you see that slight rise to the west of my little lake, Edgar?"

The sharpshooter focused his eyes and nodded.

"That is the Hauteurs des Terres. From that little rise, two of North America's most important waterways are formed. To the north and west, the little creeks form the Red River, which flows thousands of miles north until it empties into Hudson Bay. Below us, the Mississippi River begins, flowing thousands of miles until it empties into the Gulf of Mexico. It is all downhill from here, gentlemen."

The top of the world? Brunia reflected. *The mountains of Montana felt so much higher.*

After a meal of roast venison, the men watched the glowing coals with a sense of contentment. Maxwell, whose belly was sour, retired to his tent first. Half an hour after they ate, Nicollet finally changed the subject and spoke openly to the Midē′, Chagobay.

"Tell me, Chagobay, what does the word 'Itasca' mean?"

"'Itasca.' There is no such word for the Anishinaabe. Perhaps it is Sioux?"

THE ALCHEMIST'S MAP

Taopi looked up from the fire, whose light gave his crushed face even more sinister shadows. "It is not a Sioux word."

"Really? Brunia? Do you know it?" Nicollet asked.

Leave me out of this, Brunia thought and shook his head.

Nicollet nodded and said, "Then I really have to make a visit to Madeline Island to discover the meaning from Schoolcraft himself. Life has given me too much cause to meet him."

The next morning, the men finished portaging the three canoes down the hill to Lake Itasca. Their canoes silently glided across the surface until they reached the shores of a turtle-shaped island. There, after Nicollet took careful measurements with his tools, they explored it for a few minutes.

Then, Chagobay cried out from the center of the island, drawing all the men to his cries. "Look," he pointed.

Nicollet knelt and studied the sight, and after a moment, turned to his guides behind him. "What is the meaning of this?"

"See?" Taopi laughed at the Midé'. "Your people will never find it."

As Taopi ambled away, Brunia found himself staring at seven white buffalo skulls.

Nicollet asked, "What does this mean?"

Chagobay scowled. "It means Taopi is probably right."

"Why? Explain this for me."

"The Wijigan Clan left these here generations ago to tell those who followed that this is *not* the location of Turtle Island, or Spirit Lake."

The Chippewa seek Turtle Island, and the Sioux once guarded their Spirit Lake. No wonder war lingers in the air.

"Who are the Wijigan?" Nicollet asked Chagobay while Taopi waited by the canoes.

"They were the Skull Clan, keepers of the ancient truths about the Seven Fires," Chagobay sighed and began to walk away, but then he stopped and turned to explain. "Chief Black Horse of the Sioux, despite losing the war for the Great Forest, returned and killed all the Wijigan, who took the secrets about Turtle Island to their graves."

Unless some of them survived, Brunia decided. *This strange heretic distracts Nicollet with half-truths.*

Chagobay walked away, as did Colton, leaving Nicollet and Brunia to ponder the truths about the buffalo skulls.

Nicollet looked around to make sure all the members of the party were accounted for. "So, Antoine?" Nicollet spoke softly to him. "It appears Sir William was correct about me wasting my time with the Mississippi. What should I do?"

Brunia. Here, I am Brunia the Métis. In St. Louis, I am Antoine Clément.

CHAPTER THIRTY-FIVE
FORT SNELLING
1836

If I am to become a man of power, it seems there is no other choice, Hank Sibley decided, sitting alone in his kitchen as the sun slowly rose in the east. *Shit.*

Across the river, Sibley could see a few lights appear from Fort Snelling as their day began also, but his two-story stone house was silent, except for the soft breathing of Red Blanket Woman in the corner.

As she slept, Sibley settled in the adjacent room to sip his coffee and reread the letters in front of him.

Weeks earlier, Ramsay Crooks had said to him, "Enjoy your young bride while you can. Our world is soon coming to an end."

Ramsay Crooks, the current president of the American Fur

Company, had stopped to visit during early August to ascertain the tensions between the feuding Chippewa and Sioux—and also to collect his daughter, Hester Boutwell.

"Have you heard what is happening in the Columbia District? The Hudson Bay Company is undercutting our agents and destroying the fur trade in the process. There is a reason Astor sold his shares of the company."

Crooks had then tossed a hat at Sibley. The silly-looking thing had been over a foot tall with a five-inch brim around it, wrapped in black silk. Silk—the fur of the future.

"It doesn't matter if you are one of the best managing agents in the company," Crooks had explained while smoking his pipe. "In five, ten years, the industry will collapse, leaving you with nothing but an aging squaw."

"I have taken her as a wife as a sign of good faith. It was the only way to avoid a war."

"What would a war really matter?" Crooks had cynically asked. "There would simply be fewer savages for us to deal with afterwards. Think of your future, Hank. Stop being the loyal agent and start thinking of yourself."

Then Crooks had handed him an unexpected letter.

Reading it again, Sibley almost jumped when Red Blanket Woman walked past him to the door, carrying her chamber pot. When she returned, she immediately went into the kitchen to begin breakfast.

What will happen to you when this is over? Sibley wondered. Ramsay Crooks left Fort Snelling, but Sibley knew all was lost if young Mrs. Boutwell was harmed. The actions of a single murderous Sioux threatened to bring an end to his world much faster than even Ramsay Crooks anticipated.

Red Blanket Woman filled his cup with hot coffee, her face

THE ALCHEMIST'S MAP

emotionless in the process.

She doesn't want you, fool. The only reason she is even here is because there was no other choice. Her father knows this. All of the damn Sioux know this. But you... you had a choice.

Shortly after breakfast, the knock at the door finally came.

"Good morning, Mr. Sibley. I hope I didn't come too early," Captain Lyons said.

"Of course not. Come in, Lyons. Let's hear all about your adventure rescuing the Boutwells."

Despite the warmth of the cabin, Lyons wore long sleeves to cover his pox scars. The only exposed skin was his hands and the flesh around his eyes. Red Blanket Woman brought them some slightly burnt biscuits, which Sibley shrugged off.

It took half an hour before the cautious officer finally relaxed enough to provide information without coaxing. "You should have seen Nicollet at Onigum when we found him. He had all of those Chippewa chiefs under his spell. Even after I arrived with the authority of the United States government and the American Fur Company, those chiefs still deferred to Nicollet. I think all of those measurements and studies were all a masquerade. Think about it... what if he was an agent for the Hudson Bay Company? Or the British Empire? Who would suspect a Frenchman of such things?"

You moron. You will only ever be a puppet and never a puppet master. "Has Reverend Boutwell departed for Madeline Island yet?"

"No. Although Mrs. Boutwell wants to go home to Madeline Island, the Reverend is convinced war will begin any day, so he insists on staying over the winter."

"Tell me why Boutwell was suspicious of Nicollet," Sibley said.

"Apparently, Nicollet was with the chiefs for quite a while after coming to Onigum. The mapmaker quickly turned into a diplomat.

Boutwell worried why such a man would come on his own volition to the region."

"What of Nicollet's studies? What was his routine?"

"The man would stay up late into the night, using his instruments to measure the stars. He was constantly scribbling things down in his notebook. Once we met this Chagobay fellow, Nicollet claimed God had given back everything that was taken away."

"What had been taken away?"

"The canoe of supplies that was stolen contained a lot of personal items for Mr. Nicollet. He had a collection of old maps and books in that little green chest of his. In those first few days, he was constantly comparing his measurements to these maps. If I was to guess, he was looking for something found on these maps."

Son of a bitch. The puppet masters back east—Astor, Delhut, and his father—worried about Nicollet, but Sibley did not yet understand their reasons. He knew if he gave them the right answers, he would gain their trust. "Could they be maps of Chippewa tribes?"

"Possibly. He only had them for a short time, but he did show the Midē' the chest. So do you see my worry?"

Could that be what they worry about? Is Nicollet a warmonger sent to stir things up with the Chippewa? "Tell me how you managed to lose Nicollet."

"It was that Medicine Man. He kept insisting that he had something of value to show Nicollet. Instead of following the Crow Wing River due north, he took us to some lake."

"Do you remember the name of this lake or where it was located?"

"Honestly, Mr. Sibley, we visited so many lakes and rivers that they all seemed to blur together. I could probably find the general area, but even Chagobay struggled to find it and he knew where the lake was. Besides, the Pillagers almost killed Nicollet and Chagobay for visiting

THE ALCHEMIST'S MAP

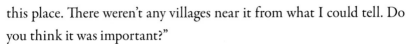

this place. There weren't any villages near it from what I could tell. Do you think it was important?"

What I think does not matter. I now have a chip to play, but who do I give it to? "Who knows? So how many days was he unaccounted for?"

"Just a handful. Chagobay's boy found us and told us what happened, so I decided to go to Leech Lake via the Mississippi River instead of the Crow Wing. By the time we did find him, Chief Flat Mouth arranged an escort to take him to the source of the Mississippi all on his own. I had rescued Reverend Boutwell and his precious wife, so we parted ways."

It is a good thing I was thorough, then, Sibley decided. "This letter came to me but it is meant for you."

Lyons tore it open right in front of Sibley. *Simpleton.*

Moments later, Lyons' shoulders dropped.

"Bad news?" Sibley asked.

"I am to be stationed at Fort Pierre Chouteau on the Missouri River."

"Congratulations," Sibley said, shaking his hand. *The puppet masters move their pieces on the chess board.*

A few days later, Sibley's contingency plan fell apart when Old Bets brought Big Moe Maxell across the Mississippi without Nicollet.

"What is the meaning of this?" Sibley asked. "I hired you to stay in the man's back pocket. What has happened?"

"Mr. Nicollet is safe. He and an entire coalition of Chippewa chiefs are gathered just north of Fort Snelling to talk peace with Tolliver. Taopi and Faribault are up at the fort right now letting Tolliver know. I've come to get what's mine and a little more."

"You'll get exactly the amount agreed upon."

"I'm not a greedy man, but… I just want some good whiskey and a young squaw to warm my bed like you have. I think I know what Mr.

Nicollet is doing, and it isn't about making his map. I pretended to be sleeping, you see. I even groan and mumble in my sleep to fool 'em. But I hear things. I remember things. Things that cost money."

From a distance, Sibley heard a horn and then a bell. He stepped right past Maxwell and stood along with the half-dozen traders at Mendota who all nervously looked to see the cause. It was then that Sibley noticed the Sioux had again slipped away into the woods.

Knowing that his two-story stone house provided Red Blanket Woman adequate protection, he left her behind with an agent and rushed to Old Bets' ferry to cross over the Mississippi. When he reached the summit of the hill, he found the walls manned by Major Tolliver's soldiers but the doors of the fort wide open.

Outside, two platoons of soldiers stood in formation, flanking both sides of the gate.

Major Tolliver and the other officers stood beneath a large American flag as they looked to the woods north of the fort. Then, a long procession of Chippewa slowly and steadily came marching out. After a few minutes, Sibley estimated the number to be at least three hundred.

Leading the procession was Chief Flat Mouth, decorated in his finest attire. Flanking him were the other Chippewa war chiefs. A few yards behind the great chiefs, Sibley saw the distinctive red vest of Joseph Nicollet.

Obviously not a warmonger.

Inside the fort's open doors, Sibley saw Sergeant Taopi and Edgar Colton.

As the chiefs presented themselves to the officers, Nicollet, Brunia, and the translator Black Jacket stepped forward.

"Chief Flat Mouth of the Leech Lake Chippewa has come to speak to Tolliver about peace," Black Jacket began. "Flat Mouth says it is Providence that has guided Joseph Nicollet to his shores. Because

THE ALCHEMIST'S MAP

of him, we will sit down and light a great fire so that we might discuss our grievances."

"You are welcome to stay at Fort Snelling," Major Tolliver graciously offered. "Your men may stay on the north banks of the St. Peter and the Sioux will stay on the south banks of the St. Peter. I thank you for bringing Professor Nicollet back to us and watching over him on the journey. Come!"

As soon as the translation was made, the formal processional ended and the Chippewa chiefs approached the entrance. Knowing there would be grievances from the chiefs about their treatment by agents such as Maxwell, Sibley followed the throng into the fort.

Elizabeth Tolliver threw her arms around Joseph Nicollet and even had the audacity to kiss him, which caused all the men to laugh.

A ten-year-old Chippewa boy stopped Nicollet in his tracks. Taopi and Colton stood at a distance, watching the encounter. Nicollet knelt and embraced him as if his own son. Sibley could not quite hear what they were saying, but he could clearly see the boy extend a small metal canister.

Nicollet studied it for a moment and then hugged the boy again before whispering something to the giant Métis, Brunia, who walked off with the boy.

As the assembly broke apart, Sibley discreetly walked up to Edgar Colton. From his pocket, he retrieved another letter entrusted to him, this one also sealed with wax from a masonic ring.

Unlike Lyons, Edgar Colton just took it and slipped it in a pocket, never even acknowledging Sibley or the letter.

This man knows how to keep a secret.

CHAPTER THIRTY-SIX

MADELINE ISLAND
1837

Could it be true? Henry Schoolcraft wondered. *Is Nicollet truly coming here?*

The elders whom Schoolcraft had met along the banks of Chequamegon Bay spoke of an evil spirit that had gained a foothold among the people who lived on Madeline Island. If the tales were true, the Chippewa had once turned to cannibalism and black magic in order to gain power and wisdom to defeat the Sioux.

Will I need to turn to sorcery to deal with the likes of Nicollet? That infernal man!

For almost a year, tales of Joseph Nicollet filled his correspondence. Despite the threat of war, Nicollet had still managed to reach the

THE ALCHEMIST'S MAP

headwaters. While in the north woods, Nicollet averted the brewing war between the Chippewa and Sioux, resulting in proud Chief Flat Mouth returning to the negotiation table with Tolliver and strengthening his position.

Even after his return from the headwaters, Nicollet lingered at Fort Snelling, spending the winter ingratiating himself with Tolliver and Sibley whilst also studying the Indian tribes.

Have I wronged him somehow? Is he so hell-bent on destroying my reputation?

Then, Schoolcraft learned that in order to create a "proper map," Nicollet wanted to examine the St. Croix River Valley, which would lead him to Madeline Island.

But does he come for me? Or to visit the Sixth Stopping Place?

Sibley claimed in a letter that the expedition appeared to be scientific and practical—Nicollet was part of a group escorting William Aitken, Reverend Boutwell, and his wife Hester back to Madeline Island.

When the guests arrived, the island came to life with excitement, but Schoolcraft sat alone in his office. *I will not suck up to this French fop. Nicollet must come to me.*

Which he did, on the third day of his stay.

"Ah! The Great Diplomat! Welcome to Madeline Island, sir," Henry Schoolcraft said gregariously, even though he was sick to his stomach. His handshake tried to crush Nicollet's hand into pieces, and the welcoming slap on the back was strong enough to dislodge a bone from a choking man's throat.

"Bonjour! What a fine home. It seems more at place in Baltimore than here on the edge of Lake Superior," Nicollet replied. After small talk about the weather and Nicollet's weeklong journey from Fort Snelling, the two men sat drinking wine.

"I somehow imagined you to be a man in his twenties," Schoolcraft said. "Unless I'm mistaken, you might even be a few years older than me. How old are you, Nicollet?"

"This past year, I turned fifty-one."

"Fifty-one, yet you travel all over the frontier like a young man. I should be thankful you're *not* a man in his twenties. Imagine how easily you would undo my legacy then."

"Jamais, Mr. Schoolcraft, I can assure you that—"

"I only tease, Nicollet. You are no threat to my ego. If anything, I should be thanking you for the little miracle you worked last year at Leech Lake—war was averted and not an ounce of blood was shed."

"There were two women murdered," Nicollet said. "I can assure you there was more than an ounce of blood shed."

Does he truly love the Indians? Perhaps Delhut is wrong about the man. "Even so, the United States owes you a great deal, *Ambassador* Nicollet. The fur trade continues. Peace flourishes. A great boundary owned by the United States now exists between the Chippewa and Sioux. All in exchange for... hunting rights? Diplomacy at its finest."

Schoolcraft raised his glass, but Nicollet did not reciprocate. *Has he come to confront me? What does this little fellow want?* "Now that war is averted, I hear you will be returning to Washington along with Major Tolliver to present this treaty. Does this mean the esteemed Nicollet will officially turn from mapmaking to diplomacy?"

"I've actually been giving thought to writing about the customs of the Chippewa."

Bastard! What have I ever done to wrong this man? He first challenges my work in mapping the headwaters, and now he challenges my efforts to study the Indian. He does not seek the Philosopher's Stone—he means to ruin my good name. "My wife is part Chippewa and a writer. I've also given thought to writing about the Chippewa."

THE ALCHEMIST'S MAP

"You have? I met Jane yesterday, and she is clearly the best of both the Irish and Chippewa people. You are blessed to have such a literate and lovely wife."

"My thanks, but see here—life is so short, Professor Nicollet. Perhaps you should stick to matters that suit your existing abilities. What is the line from Macbeth? 'I have no spur to prick the sides of my intent, but only vaulting ambition.'"

Nicollet merely shrugged. "Big results require big ambitions. Doesn't the Psalmist write: 'Delight yourself in the Lord, and he will give you the desires of your heart.' I trust that God will not torment me with dreams that cannot be attained."

Schoolcraft seethed, but masked it with a swig of his wine. "I was told you were robbed during your expedition."

"Dieu merci, none of my equipment was in the canoe, nor were any of my scientific journals. Mostly, I lost personal items and luxuries, which of course greatly saddened me, but had little impact on my true purpose."

"Your true purpose," Schoolcraft repeated. *He's come to understand something. If it deals with the Drummond Map, I must discover this purpose.* "So did you produce a superior map using your sextant and barometer?"

"I believe it will be quite satisfactory, but it will take some time to calculate the nearly two thousand astronomical and barometric observations I've made. I would hate to repeat the glaring errors done in the past. Modern cartography will be more than just ink sketches on paper. While I was in St. Louis, I read your book, *Narrative of an Expedition Through the Upper Mississippi to Itasca Lake*."

"What of it?" Schoolcraft snapped.

"I'd regret traveling this far without taking time to ask you about it. I've spent considerable time with guides who were both Chippewa and

Sioux, and none of them claimed the word 'Itasca.'"

My little riddle. "Nor should they. The word is a play on words, an invention of mine."

"An invention?"

"Yes. Did you find the lake at the headwaters of the Mississippi, which I dubbed 'Itasca?'"

"I did. I explored the entire area to understand the elevation of the watershed. I actually found a smaller creek feeding the lake—the truest source of the Mississippi River, higher than the lake itself."

"Did you?" Schoolcraft asked, pushing his ego aside. *Find out his intentions. Learn what he has discovered.* "Did you visit the island?"

"Yes, we visited the island."

"Then you must have seen the skulls. Do you know the history of *this* island?"

"Madeline Island? A bit. Part of the reason I came is because of the fascinating tale of the Seven Fires."

"So what do you think? Is my island on Lake Itasca the legendary Turtle Island and the Seventh Stopping Place?"

"If I were to guess, I'd say that honor belongs to the stone island of Mille Lacs. One of my Sioux guides said it was sacred to them, and was also the location of a key battle more than eighty years ago. Although... I've also heard of an island near the westernmost tributary of Lake Superior. When I return, I hope time allows me the opportunity to map it also."

He didn't find anything either. If Delhut is correct, Nicollet saw the Drummond Map and went to the same places we've been. Even now, he is making plans to visit other divides. Curious. "So, you'd like to understand the mystery of 'Itasca?' To the layman, 'Itasca' is as foreign as 'Mini Waken Chante' or 'Wokiyan Oye,' but to others, it is a multi-layered pun."

THE ALCHEMIST'S MAP

"A pun?"

I'm surprised he didn't crack my code. "My original map was labeled with the Latin words 'Veritas Caput.'"

"The truth about the head," Nicollet translated. "You made a reference to the headwaters of the Mississippi."

A pun has two meanings, Professor Nicollet. Clearly, he is not an agent of the Periphery. Did he come out of mere curiosity as Humboldt's apprentice? "The truth about the head," Schoolcraft repeated. "Shortened to 'itas' and 'ca.'" Henry Schoolcraft raised his glass and saluted Nicollet, "So now you know the truth about the head."

Once he finished his drink, he pressed for more information. "So what are your plans for the future?"

"As you've heard, I will accompany Major Tolliver back to Washington to present the treaty to President Van Buren."

"You will find Washington much different than when you left it."

"Yes, political change is so very democratic in this land. With my success in mapping the Mississippi and St. Croix, I hope I can show Colonel Abert that my techniques are far superior to those of George Fanshaw."

"Do you know Fanshaw?" Schoolcraft asked.

"Only in passing," Nicollet said with a wry smile. "I've heard he has gone to oversee the theft of Cherokee Lands, which means Colonel Abert needs a new scientist."

Nicollet means to return? Clearly he did not find anything at the headwaters. "Be careful of those politicians. Their zeal for Manifest Destiny robs them of their senses."

Either he is innocent, or he is being coy. If that is the case, he means to explore other rivers to find Fort L'Huillier, the Rivière Morte, the Undine... "I wish you the best of luck in acquiring these funds, as well as luck in your future expeditions. Where will you go?"

Nicollet sighed dramatically. "If I do manage to find funding, I think it is only proper to map the St. Peter River."

"Into Sioux territory?" Schoolcraft clarified, then reached for the wine bottle. "Then I drink to your health." *A man his age will never survive... and then I will be rid of this thorn in my side.*

CHAPTER THIRTY-SEVEN
NAMEKAGON RIVER
1837

Nicollet left Madeline Island the next day, with Lieutenant Colton escorting him back to Fort Snelling. The two of them had to portage a small birch bark canoe twenty-five miles through field and forest until they reached Lake Namekagon, from which issued the Namekagon River that would bring them back to the Mississippi River and Fort Snelling.

While the two portaged the canoe above their heads, Nicollet thought of Lake Manito. The previous summer, Chagobay had insisted they travel far off for him to see the vitriol, only to be interrupted.

I must find an excuse to return to Lake Manito, but at a time when men like Schoolcraft and Sibley are not watching me so closely.

Yet all he had from his expedition were two tins of copper vitriol. While copper was an important clue, none of the other clues from Le Sueur, Lahontan, or the Alchemist's Map seemed to fit.

Lake Itasca had even fewer similarities.

If the Mississippi River is not the place where water flows in all directions, then it is also not the place where Lahontan found the Undine or where Le Sueur mined copper. Could it be Stewart's Missouri?

Colton struggled with his breath and stopped walking for a moment. Although a young man just past his twentieth birthday and built with stocky strength, Colton had weak lungs. The two traveled almost three miles since their last stop, so Nicollet was glad to take a break.

When Colton regained his breath, the rosy-cheeked soldier wiped off his sweaty brow but kept a keen eye on the woods.

"Something wrong?" Nicollet asked his guide.

"I thought I heard something a while ago."

"An animal?"

"More like a dog, from the sound of it."

"A dog in the wilderness?"

Colton smirked. "An Indian, most likely."

The comment chilled Nicollet. "You see the Indian as a dog?"

Colton nodded. "They're all savages in my book. I know you think highly of them, especially Chagobay, but you didn't see what Chief Black Hawk did when he crossed back over the Mississippi to reclaim his land. My brothers and I collected Indian scalps until we were old enough to join the militia. I was at the Battle of Bad Ax when we crushed Black Hawk's army."

"You should be proud."

"I am," Colton snapped and then huffed loudly. "We've rested long enough. Lake Namekagon is just a few more miles. I want to get there before dusk."

THE ALCHEMIST'S MAP

Colton returned to the bow of the canoe and lifted it above his head, allowing Nicollet to slip under and raise the stern. Unlike portaging with other men in the earlier expedition, portaging with Colton meant a balanced load since the stocky Wisconsinite had only an inch on him.

There were several western tributaries along the Mississippi River. The St. Peter is the most obvious based on Lahontan's description of a "Long River," but the Des Moines also has a headwater in Dakota territory. And the smaller tributaries? Could it be one of them?

The slope of the forest floor grew steep, and after the trail wound to the right, the wall of woods suddenly opened to reveal a large lake.

"Is that it?" Nicollet asked.

"Yes, but we need to keep going."

So Nicollet took a deep breath and forced his legs to go a little further.

Without notice, Lieutenant Colton tossed the nose of the canoe off his shoulders, toppling Nicollet to the ground and trapping him under the full weight of the canoe. When Nicollet regained his senses, he rolled the canoe off of him, only to see Colton pointing a pistol at his face.

"What is the meaning of this?" Nicollet asked, but in his heart, he suddenly understood why Schoolcraft had been so cordial.

"I'm sorry for making you do all of this work only to kill you, but I didn't want to portage on my own."

"Kill me?" *Is he serious?*

"Could you step away from the canoe? I don't want to have to explain any traces of blood when I get back to Fort Snelling."

Mon Dieu, so this is how I die. "Major Tolliver is expecting me to return by the end of the week. He's waiting for me to join the delegation leaving for Washington."

"And I have a letter telling him you've already left for Washington on a boat going through the Great Lakes," Colton said as he patted his chest pocket. "Now, step away from the canoe."

Before Nicollet could force his quivering legs into action, a thunderous rifle blast filled the air and an explosion of blood and gore burst from Colton's chest. Spurts of blood sprayed several feet from where he stood.

Before Colton even fell to the ground, a streak appeared from the edge of the trees. Nicollet's wide eyes could only focus on the raised hatchet that came crashing down on Colton's rosy face, turning it into pulp with several strong strokes.

When the attacker's face turned, Nicollet looked into the dead grey eye and scarred face of Taopi.

Nicollet passed out from the terror.

Moments later, Taopi stood in front of him, offering him a hand up. "I've followed you since the day you left Fort Snelling. I was told to keep you safe, but I didn't think Colton would be the one to try to take your life."

"Neither did I," Nicollet said, and took Taopi's outstretched hand. When Nicollet rose to his feet, Taopi marched over to Colton's corpse, using his foot to roll it over. He pulled back the jacket and found a letter, already half-stained with blood. "Do not let him return to Washington... Make sure he has an accident..."

Colton was ordered to kill me? "Who sent *you*?" Nicollet asked, turning back to Taopi. "Who sent you to watch over me?"

"Professor, we need to hide his body and never speak to anyone of what happened here. Edgar Colton abandoned you in the wilderness, and I happened to find you on my way up to Madeline Island."

Taopi took hold of Colton by the boots and began to pull him off the trail. Nicollet followed after. "Were you sent by Major Tolliver? Is that why you followed me?"

Taopi kept dragging the limp body until he neared the shore where the waters of Lake Namekagon revealed a shore of rock and boulders. The Indian scout began to roll away stones to create a cavity.

THE ALCHEMIST'S MAP

"You're a spy, aren't you?" Nicollet asked, astonished at how his traveling companion had kept such a low profile. "Was it the priest, De Smet, who told you to watch over me?" Nicollet asked.

"No, Faribault is his man." Taopi continued to toil, and Nicollet joined him in moving the stones out of the way. After they pulled Colton's body into the shallow cavity and covered it with rocks and stones, Taopi finally answered. "I find it hard to believe that you are Wishwee, the one who comes from the stars to battle No Soul, but Chief Wahanantan believes it to be so, and I will lay down my life so that you may fulfill your destiny."

"Chief Wahanantan?" Nicollet repeated, remembering De Smet's challenge to find the elusive Sioux chief. "Then I have a few questions for you."

CHAPTER THIRTY-EIGHT

ALBANY, NEW YORK
1838

From the Apostle Islands, the waters of Lake Superior flow through the narrow rapids at Sault Ste. Marie to Lake Huron, where they join the waters of Lake Michigan. On the extreme southern reach of Lake Huron, the waters pass through the Detroit River, past Lake St. Clair, and into Lake Eerie. Upon going over the Niagara Falls, the waters enter Lake Ontario, which narrow into the St. Lawrence River.

Because of its strategic location to both Lake Ontario and the St. Lawrence River, Albany shifted from a key military outpost to the seat of government for New York by the winter of 1837.

It somehow reminds me of Kuban along the Black Sea, Krasdan Krai reflected. Despite the deeply wooded valleys of rural New York, his

THE ALCHEMIST'S MAP

childhood village and the grand home of George Fanshaw could have been on different planets.

Once the carriage stopped, Krai secured his satchel and walking stick. Krai ignored the driver's son and his effort to help him from the carriage. The boy handed him his top hat, which he slipped onto his head for the short trek across the yard.

"I'll be staying in town," Krai said when he saw the boy climbing onto the carriage to get the other bags. "This should only take a few minutes."

"Yessir."

George Fanshaw stood at the front door already, watching Krai approach. The tall Englishman had drinks ready and waiting but his solemn expression contrasted greatly with the gesture.

Does Fanshaw think he's a loose end? Krai did carry his dagger, pistol, and poison, but these were not the instruments he'd use to dispatch the official United States Geologist.

"Mr. Krai, welcome to Albany. The letters said you would not be staying, but my wife made some refreshments for you nevertheless."

The obligation of hospitality is one of my old tricks, a lesson he'll understand when I leave every drop and morsel exactly as I received them.

The walking stick and satchel prevented Fanshaw from shaking hands, leaving him to only gesture to the plush chair on the porch. Krai set the heavy bag down at his toes and leaned the ivory head of the walking stick at his side. Inside the fashionable item was a narrow blade that could pierce a man's throat from across a table. "You've done quality work in recent years."

"Thank you, Mr. Krai. It has been a grueling few years, and only in recent weeks have I felt like my old self."

"Your work in identifying malcontents and subversives within the Cherokee Nation has reaped great rewards. We believe that by next

May, the remnants of the Cherokee Nation will be moved from Georgia to Oklahoma without any resistance."

"Cut the head off the snake," Fanshaw said, "and the body will die. To Lady Columbia."

Krai raised the cup but did not sip, which Fanshaw silently took note of. Krai then reached down for the heavy satchel and set it between the cup and plate of food. "Your back pay and severance pay."

Fanshaw blinked as he sorted through the message, but did not reach for the tens of thousands of dollars in front of him. "Is he not pleased with my work?"

"Quite the opposite, he was thrilled to read about your tour of the region, especially your trip on the... how is it said? Minnay..."

"Sotor," Fanshaw finished. "Minnay-Sotor. It means 'clear blue water,' which was certainly not the case. If he is pleased with my work, then why is this considered severance pay? I am a devoted disciple of—"

"Your zeal is noted, which is why your time here in America is coming to an end. Think of it as a game of chess, in which an important piece is simply being moved to another region of the board. As always, he is thinking decades ahead of the present. In that satchel, you'll not only find a reward for your tour of the Minnay-Sotor territory, but also money to return to England with enough funds to buy a vacation home in France."

Fanshaw reached for the bag and slid it across the table, eyeing it cautiously. "In what capacity will I be returning to England?"

"Your time as United States Geologist and explorer has made you the perfect diplomat to negotiate northern border disputes between the United States and England."

"Really? An American diplomat in London?"

"Yes, our next phase appears to be the Upper Missouri River in the Rockies."

THE ALCHEMIST'S MAP

"The Oregon Territory?"

"Yes, I just returned from a terribly boring trip up that forsaken river last spring."

"You went up the Missouri?"

"Yes, I took a steamship from St. Louis all the way to a remote outpost called Fort Union to remove a pawn from the chessboard. We do our duty to humanity, don't we?"

"That we do," Fanshaw agreed morosely.

"A few years ago, prior to your expedition, you were given copies of a map to aid in your geological assessment. Have you destroyed those copies as instructed?"

"Destroyed and forgotten."

"Good," Krai nodded, only to feel the lingering agitation of the small rock in his shoe named Nicollet. "Unfortunately, there has been a bit of excitement in Washington in recent days. Joseph Nicollet returned from Fort Snelling as part of a diplomatic entourage negotiating a treaty between the Chippewa and the Sioux."

"Yes, I've heard."

"It received so much attention that Colonel Abert had no other choice than to hire Nicollet to save face after Nicollet bragged about the veracity of his map compared to those of his predecessors."

"He is an arrogant man. I wrote to Abert that he had made a monstrous blunder in hiring Nicollet. I met the man once in St. Louis."

If only I'd found him in St. Louis. When Krai arrived in St. Louis to locate Nicollet himself, he learned the mapmaker had already gone on to Fort Snelling without any funds. Krai waited for a year, only to receive another covert mission—the trip to Fort Union. When he returned from the mission, Nicollet had already gone through St. Louis and up the Ohio to return to Washington D.C. "Yes, arrogant, but also a very capable man. Now that he has government funding, there will be little preventing him from following his imagination. With that being said, I have a very serious question to ask."

Fanshaw swallowed hard and nodded.

"Will Nicollet find Fort L'Huillier?"

Fanshaw had to temper his reaction, which began with incredulity, shifted to fear, and finally settled into stern confidence. "The legend is a lie. There certainly is no copper, the seven-mile volcanic mountain cloaked in mist is a dream, and this place where the waters flow in all directions is an impossibility. Nicollet will only find mosquitoes, sunburn, and hostile savages."

If any savages remain by spring, Krai added, grabbing his walking stick by the ivory head carved into the likeness of a skull.

CHAPTER THIRTY-NINE

MITU'TAHAKTO'S
1838

Kit Carson's eyes were open but the nightmare did not end. A year earlier, the Mandan village of Mitu'tahakto's had been a thriving community along the banks of the Missouri River, but now it was a ghost town. The Angel of Death had claimed much more than just his beautiful wife, Singing Grass.

With her arms wrapped around his waist, his daughter, Adeline, proved to be far luckier than the residents of the village, which had now been swallowed up by untamed vegetation from the Mandan farmers. Unlike other tribes on the prairie, the Mandans left behind homes of earthen domes, decorated with white buffalo skulls and ornamental poles that reminded Carson of flagpoles.

He heard a voice, and his rifle stock leapt to his cheek.

An Arikara boy stepped around the corner of a home with an arm full of vegetables, only to freeze in his tracks when he saw Carson staring at him from behind the sights of his rifle.

Two other Arikara youths came around the corner and also paused when they saw the horse and rickshaw behind it. Carson's pile of furs was all that he had left, and he meant to protect it. But the three youths were the only living souls he'd seen in months. "Who are you? Where do you come from?"

Like poor Adeline, the boys had survived smallpox over the winter and were left with the facial scarring. The Arikara boys told him what had happened here and elsewhere on the plains.

Of the two thousand Mandans who lived in Mitu'tahakto's, only twenty-seven survived and had been taken in by their neighbors to the north. During the terrible winter that followed, the Arikara had learned of the fates of other neighboring tribes. To the west, two-thirds of the Blackfoot had died and a third of the Crow. Along the upper Missouri River, half the Assiniboine and Pawnee had died. Half of the Arikara's own tribe had died, as well.

"What of the Sioux?" Carson asked.

The Arikara boy shook his head. "It's difficult to say, but the Lakota in the west and the Dakota in the east were not spared."

Carson nodded. "We've just come from Fort Union, and it is worse up river. Have you been to Fort Clark?"

"They kept us away with their guns."

The furs in the rickshaw were enough to purchase passage on the next steamer. He could then bring Adeline back to his family in Missouri.

A year earlier, Carson had shared drinks with a man by the name of Captain Daniel Lyons, who bragged about being part of the Nicollet

THE ALCHEMIST'S MAP

expedition. The same man later sold him infected blankets, killing his precious Sweet Grass and scarring their daughter forever.

Once Adeline is safe, I will find Lyons and kill him. If only I could kill him a thousand times. If Lyons remained at Fort Clark, no man alive could stop his wrath, but Carson doubted fate would be so kind.

CHAPTER FORTY
ST. LOUIS
1838

Father Pierre-Jean De Smet felt his fists clench as he walked down the streets of St. Louis, but so much had changed in the four years he'd been gone that he had to ask directions.

In a town I helped build, no less.

It was no longer the charming metropolitan filled with hope. No, now it was just like every other city—filled with corruption and vice. A journey of almost twenty thousand miles ended with a loud knock on Joseph Nicollet's hotel door.

A young military officer with hair parted down the middle answered the door. Before he could even ask, "Can I help you?" De Smet had noted the differences in the uniform from others he'd seen. It

THE ALCHEMIST'S MAP

belonged to the United States Corps of Topographical Engineers.

"Who are you?" De Smet asked.

"Lieutenant John C. Frémont," the young man said. "And who are you?"

Joseph Nicollet answered. "That is Father De Smet, Johnny. A friend and an ally. Invite him in."

Nicollet had also changed during the time De Smet was abroad. His curly black hair now represented the minority in a head of dark gray. He wasn't as plump as he'd been; his skin was tan and his frame seemed taut after two years in the North. The man seemed even more energetic and the twinkle in his eyes conveyed unbridled optimism.

"Please come in, Father De Smet," Frémont said, stepping aside.

Along with Frémont, two others sat in the room. Nicollet wore a new outfit, including a bright blue vest beneath his jacket. In the corner chair, a tall, smooth-faced Métis sat in modern clothing. *A Cree, by the looks of him.*

"I looked for you at White Marsh, where you were all but a memory," De Smet said coldly in reference to the Jesuit complex back in Maryland. "We have private matters to discuss, and I do not know these two men."

"Then let me introduce them," Nicollet said, rising from the couch.

"I do not want introductions; I want them to leave."

Nicollet's smile vanished and his back straightened a bit. "As it so happens, Antoine was leaving anyway." Nicollet first shook hands with the tall Métis but then pulled in for an embrace. "I will find a way without you. Stewart needs you more than I do at this point. It warms my heart to think of you in a Scottish castle. Farewell."

Lieutenant Frémont stood his ground, watching as the tall Métis walked out the door.

"See to our provisions," Nicollet said to Frémont. "Our steamer returns to Fort Snelling in two days, and I do not want anything misplaced or left behind."

"Yes, Professor Nicollet," Frémont said, and closed the door solidly behind him. De Smet could hear the military boots echo down the hall.

"You are in league with the Devil," De Smet announced.

"Devils, in fact. I am surrounded by devils," Nicollet boasted, returning to the couch, gesturing to the chair that had been filled by Frémont moments earlier. Upon the table were layers of maps, old and new. "One of the devils attempted to kill me a few months ago. When the man's blood splattered on my face, it may as well have been Lady Drummond's blood, for I am still trying to escape from her shadow. I assume you've spoken to your superiors in Rome."

"Yes, and Conrad Simmons agrees that you are a madman."

"I am only trying to keep myself alive."

"And?"

Nicollet smiled wryly. "I hope you understand why I still cannot accept your help. Exploring the headwaters of the Mississippi is only the beginning."

"Yet you will accept the help of politicians who are only using you for their own foul purposes."

"Awareness of a trap makes it easier to avoid," Nicollet mused. "I've seen the face of my enemy, Father, and I know I am being used. Dangling promotions in front of ambitious men will get them to do the most foul things."

"Yes, I know. One of the men on your foolhardy trip up the Mississippi was one of my men."

"Your man? You mean Davey?"

Perhaps he is not a total fool. "Frémont is not to be trusted."

"Frémont is predictable. The others want me to find it. They've been looking for quite a while with no success, and I offer them a little bit of hope, which is why they now help me. Knowing they are watching, I will muddy the waters and leave them bewildered. Do you remember speaking to me of Chief Wahanantan?"

THE ALCHEMIST'S MAP

"Of course," De Smet said, having heard all the strange legends prior to departing. "I believe he is key to understanding all of the legends."

"Correct ou d'accord, for Chief Wahanantan had enough wherewithal to send a spy into my camp, one who saved my life. The spy waits for me back at Fort Snelling, and when the opportunity presents itself, he will take me to Wahanantan, who wishes to speak to me."

De Smet walked up to the stack of maps on the table, some familiar and some obscure. "I wish I could join you on this expedition instead of tending my flock. Simmons was right when he picked you, even though I could not see the wisdom at the time, but there are factors you do not yet understand."

"Really? What sorts?"

"I need to speak plainly to you about a common enemy we share."

CHAPTER FORTY-ONE

FORT SNELLING
1838

Sergeant Jim Taopi sat under a cottonwood tree sharpening his knife when a cannon announced the coming of a steamer up the Mississippi. On the opposite bank, Old Bets emerged from her shack in anticipation of ferrying parasites from the landing below Fort Snelling.

Nicollet took too long to return.

With Major Tolliver still in Washington, D.C., chaos greeted the big paddle ship as it came around the corner. Soldiers from Snelling, refugees from the Red River colony, traders who'd wintered in simple shacks, Sioux from nearby Kaposia, Indian Agents, and even Hank Sibley soon appeared by the docks.

Taopi spit on his whetstone and continued sharpening the knife.

THE ALCHEMIST'S MAP

Two months earlier, Sibley had received a letter that Nicollet would return with a fully funded expedition, which brightened everyone's mood, for it meant an influx of government money would be arriving with the paddle ship. Since that day, Sibley had been arranging for wagons, horses and mules, and rations, as well as men for the expedition.

Dozens of voyageurs had lined up at Sibley's house, hoping to be selected as hired hands for the expedition west. A few days later, Hank Sibley came to Taopi.

"I'm looking to hire a Sioux guide for the Nicollet expedition," Sibley had said. "You're already familiar with the man, and we need someone who knows the Sioux tribes west of here. Red Blanket Woman said you spent time with many of these tribes as a young man."

Taopi nodded. "Major Tolliver has already hired me for his purposes. If you're looking for a proper guide, Joe Laframboise is heading back out to the Great Oasis. He knows the territory. Or Renville. He lives out on the upper St. Peter." He paused, caught on something Sibley had said, "Red Blanket Woman told you I spent time on the prairie?"

"She's more than just a pretty face. Both Renville and Laframboise are intent on heading back as soon as the spring floods recede. I know you're Tolliver's man, but I could arrange for a small bonus on my end."

Sibley wanted to hire men cheaply so he could pocket the profits, and after stubbornly refusing the entitled manager, Taopi managed to negotiate the selection of the other men, except for Big Moe Maxwell, whom Sibley had already hired as the expedition's cook.

With his eight voyageurs ready, Taopi now watched as Nicollet's men disembarked from the ship. Crates of supplies, including a massive yellow telescope, were brought to the wagons Sibley had procured. Knowing Nicollet would not be so foolish as to introduce Taopi to the others, he simply watched and noted them.

There was a young officer, dressed in a uniform Taopi had never seen.

The enthusiastic young man barked out orders like a seasoned general.

A well-dressed teenage boy came next, nervously following the crowd as it flowed out of the ship. Next came a pair of wide-eyed tourists, who let others carry their bags while they took in the scenic view below Fort Snelling. In their zeal, he heard French phrases uttered.

Walking the plank with Nicollet was another gentle-looking man, with a bright blue bowtie and dark, swept hair. Although a few years younger than Nicollet, he lacked the elder scientist's confidence. Finally, the ship began to take on cargo and passengers heading back to St. Louis.

No Brunia on this trip, Taopi observed. *I will have to deliver the terrible news to Nicollet myself.*

Taopi followed the crowd back up the long slope to Fort Snelling, knowing he needed to be an afterthought to Nicollet. Hank Sibley soon stole Nicollet, the young lieutenant, and the other three gentlemen back to the company outpost so that Red Blanket Woman could provide them a hearty supper.

By the next day, Taopi learned the names of the men who would be joining the expedition: John C. Frémont, an officer in the United States Corps of Topographical Engineers; Viscount de Montmort, a French attaché; Captain Gaspard de Belligny, a French tourist; Eugene Flandin, the son of a wealthy French merchant; and Karl Geyer, the man in the bowtie, a German botanist Nicollet had recently befriended during his stay in St. Louis.

Edgar Colton had been at Snelling for more than a year before he turned into a snake. I wonder if I will have to bury any of these men in time?

With his oversized hat protecting his scars from the sun, Taopi sat in the shadows of the western gate, watching people come and go. Finally, Nicollet and his pack of gentlemen passed by on their way out.

"Sergeant Taopi," Nicollet said, stopping. "I've been told you are

THE ALCHEMIST'S MAP

going to accompany us on the expedition. Johnny, this is Sergeant Jim Taopi."

The young lieutenant grew wide-eyed when he gazed upon Taopi's deformed cheek, so for good measure, Taopi removed his hat to reveal the patch of pink atop his head left from a Chippewa blade. "Lieutenant."

"Johnny, could you bring the others over to Mr. Sibley? I'd like to review the supplies with Sergeant Taopi for a moment."

As Frémont led the gentlemen away, Taopi put his hat back on and stood up with a grunt, walking back through the gate ahead of Nicollet.

Nine wagons waited in line from the storehouse all the way to the blacksmith shop. When Taopi reached the lead wagon, he leaned against it to face Nicollet.

"Nine wagons? I was led to believe we only had funding for seven."

"That's true, but a week before you arrived, traders came with news that there were war parties attacking posts in the west."

"War parties? Again?"

"Death has come to the prairie, and now the enemies of the Seven Council Fires test the resolve of my people. We're not sure of the details, but neither Renville nor Laframboise wanted to risk losing their own supplies, so they've added their wagons to our expedition to make nine."

"What about the men you hired? Can we trust them?"

"We know Moe is a thief and agent of Sibley, but the others are just simple men looking for an easy way to make money. There is some bad news I must tell you, though."

"Yes, I've heard all about the rumors of illness on the prairie. I've brought vaccines for any Indian willing to receive it."

Too late for that, I am afraid. "It is another matter."

"Have there been questions about Corporal Colton?"

"Yes, especially from Sibley, who is paying a small ransom for anyone who can find the whereabouts of Corporal Colton."

"Sibley is an intermediary for someone looking for Colton. Have you learned anything else about the letter in his pocket? Was Colton paid by Schoolcraft?"

"Schoolcraft and Sibley have been in constant correspondence, but Schoolcraft never once inquired about Colton. I do not think he was involved in the assassination attempt."

"That would certainly surprise me. If you knew Schoolcraft as well as—"

"You have other enemies besides white men. You will not be able to return north. Evil has spread through all the lands. Chagobay is dead," Taopi finally said. "His own people killed him."

CHAPTER FORTY-TWO

SWAN LAKE
1838

On the other side of the prairie, hundreds of miles to the east, Chief Sleepy Eyes grit his teeth as a wave of pain passed through his body. His hand gently supported the wound at the bottom of his ribcage as he sat up, and except for the blinding flash of pain, the scar seemed to hold his torn muscles.

Will this wound ever heal?

At the door of his teepee, his eldest surviving son stood wide-eyed as he watched his father rise from his bed. Once Sleepy Eyes caught his breath, his son answered him.

"They have crossed the Minisotah River," Manza Ostag Mani told him. Looking at his son, Sleepy Eyes knew the boy would soon be of fighting age. He had named him "One Who Walks with Iron," but his son was not yet a killer. *I hope he never has to kill a man face to face as I have.* "Are you certain it is him?"

"He wears a green vest instead of a red vest, but he has curly hair and no beard, and whenever they stop, he measures the sky and stars. It must be Nicollet, the Great Sorcerer."

"Bring me my war bonnet," Sleepy Eyes demanded, fighting the nausea that passed after he rose from his sickbed.

Pretty Water, his wife, stood up as if to block his passage. "You are not leaving here. Your wound has only begun to heal."

"Bring me my war bonnet!" Sleepy Eyes shouted, only to wince in pain. Iron Walker ignored the glare from Pretty Water and obediently left to bring his father's headdress and other ornamental clothing. "Help me out of these rags."

Pretty Water stood with her arms crossed, tears in her eyes. She'd been strong enough to help run the village for the past months, yet resigned herself to the command of her chief. She dutifully helped Sleepy Eyes from his sickbed and pulled the cotton shirt over his head and shoulders.

Sleepy Eyes looked down at his wound. Just inches below his heart, the pink wound still showed signs of infection. *Perhaps I am cursed for going where I should not have gone.*

Although the wound had quickly closed the previous fall, it had become infected twice during the winter and had to be lanced. A month earlier, inspired by the warming weather, Sleepy Eyes had gone hunting with his son, only to see the wound fester and swell again, bringing with it a terrible fever.

"He should be coming to you," Pretty Water insisted as she washed the wound a final time. "You are the chief here at Swan Lake. You rule in the land of the Sisseton."

THE ALCHEMIST'S MAP

"This Nicollet is special. He is a servant of the Great Spirit, and I will humble myself by going to him," Sleepy Eyes insisted.

"How can you be sure?" Pretty Water asked as she slipped new deerskin clothes onto her husband's massive frame.

"Taopi told me everything I need to know about the man." *And a dead Tizaptanon told me the rest.*

"Is that why you waged war and risked your life last summer? Because of the testimony of a half-breed?"

I did what needed to be done. "Taopi is an honorable man, a man who can be trusted. Everything he spoke to me was true. I knew what I was doing when I rode south."

"I hope you know what you are doing now. Your people need you; your family needs you."

If I do not fix this, there will be no people. I must lift the curse brought by the Serpent Star. Sleepy Eyes kissed the top of her head. "There is no danger today. I will ride out with a dozen of my best warriors under an American flag."

This time, Pretty Water did not argue, and by the time Iron Walker returned with the headdress, Sleepy Eyes was fully clothed. The war bonnet added another foot to his already unmatched height of seven feet. When he had received it from his father, it had dozens of bald eagle feathers, but after three decades as chief, his bonnet now flowed down his back. Each carefully wrapped quill marked a significant victory during his life.

After the headdress was placed, his wife and son continued to adorn their patriarch with frilled aprons painted with red and blue. "Fetch the letter, and your sister," Sleepy Eyes said.

Iron Walker left immediately, but Pretty Water stood with her hands on her hips. "Why are you bringing Yellow Medicine with you?"

"Laframboise will be with them, and after I ignored his counsel last summer, this will set matters straight."

"She is your youngest daughter."

"I know."

A few moments later, after his son found and pinned the blue eagle upon his chest, Sleepy Eyes stepped out of his lodge to where Yellow Medicine stood, her head low. Nearly a hundred men, women, and children waited with wide eyes outside of his lodge. His head held high, Sleepy Eyes bathed in the moment as they whooped and hollered their chief's return from death's bed.

My people need a victory, Sleepy Eyes realized. *I hope they understand what I am about to do.*

Despite the pain and consequence, Sleepy Eyes vaulted onto his horse, again inspiring those who watched. "Fetch a horse," he said to his son. "You are coming with us."

The war party rode furiously out of the village to impress the children, but by the time they reached the Cottonwood River, they were slowed to a trot. Two of his scouts had rode ahead, and at the confluence of the Cottonwood and Minisotah rivers, they returned.

"There are nine wagons camped just east of Swan Lake," the eldest of the scouts informed him.

"Go inform them that Chief Sleepy Eyes is coming."

An hour before dusk, they found the party. Even though there were enough men in the expedition to neutralize his dozen warriors in just a few minutes, none of them even held a gun.

From a distance, Sleepy Eyes recognized the thick mustache of Joe Laframboise, who often traded with his people along the Cottonwood River. He also knew the dark-skinned, short-haired son of Joseph Renville, another man of good reputation.

"Greetings, Chief Sleepy Eyes of the Sisseton," Laframboise began. "We come as friends and welcome you to join us at our fires. We have good will and presents to exchange."

THE ALCHEMIST'S MAP

Sleepy Eyes heard the words but looked right past the fur trader to the clean-shaven little man. With wide eyes and curly hair, the man in the green vest looked more like a boy than a man, but after his conversations with Taopi, Sleepy Eyes knew he had indeed found Nicollet.

The stench of the Americans was palpable, masked only by the roaring fire and the smell of game killed from the hunting grounds of his people. The toothless man who brought him a plate of food smelled the worst, but Nicollet, sitting four seats away from him at the fire, smelled as if he had stuffed his vest with lilac blossoms.

For an hour, Laframboise dominated the conversation, speaking to him in Sioux, repeating again and again that they meant no harm or disrespect with their expedition. On the edges of the camp, he spotted the grim Taopi standing with the other men. The longer Sleepy Eyes waited, the more gifts piled in front of him. Laframboise understood who ruled the territory, even after the terrible winter.

"It fills my heart with joy that Laframboise has returned from the Stone House to his home in the land of the muskrats," Sleepy Eyes nodded. "I have brought my youngest daughter, Yellow Medicine, who will bear him strong children that will make him proud."

Sleepy Eyes watched as the hardened fur-trader softened into a puddle of tears at the notion. "You honor me with a gift that cannot be matched."

"You are a friend of the Sioux, and if we are to survive the coming days, we will need friends such as yourself, as well as Nicollet."

Sleepy Eyes reached into his pocket and handed Nicollet the letter.

"It is a letter from President Monroe," Nicollet explained to the others. "It says that Chief Sleepy Eyes of Swan Lake is a 'Friend of the White Man.' Tell him that I have also been a visitor to Washington."

Sleepy Eyes did not need to wait for Laframboise to translate. Having received a vision from the Great Mystery, Sleepy Eyes had changed from the ways of his father, knowing that a flood of White Men was coming. Thirteen years earlier, he had traveled all the way to Washington to witness the majesty of the White Man, and since returning, learned as much English as he could to help guide his people through the coming days. Although he struggled to find the right English words, he understood most of what the men said.

Nicollet handed back the letter, which Sleepy Eyes tucked back into his pocket. "You will have safe passage through the land of the Sioux," Sleepy Eyes promised, "but I cannot guarantee your safety farther west, because where you go, our enemies throng. For that reason, I will give you my son, Iron Walker, who is the dearest thing to me on earth. My heart will rejoice if he dies fighting for the whites."

Laframboise quickly translated to Nicollet, who immediately shook his head. But the present was not negotiable, which Laframboise explained, to which Nicollet finally replied, "I will answer for his life with mine or remain on the prairie with him."

Taopi was right about this man, Sleepy Eyes thought after hearing the sincerity of Nicollet's words, *even if he smells like flowers*. So when Nicollet produced a barrel of gunpowder, the limits placed on the gift did not surprise him.

"This is only for hunting," Nicollet explained through Laframboise. "Your scalp will hang in your enemy's lodge if you carry it with you to war."

Despite being a little man, Nicollet spoke fiercely.

Sleepy Eyes waited deep into the night before unveiling his true purpose in the visit. Laframboise retired to sleep, and that was when Taopi approached Nicollet, taking over the duty of translation, and both soldier and brave slept in the shadows of the fire, their bellies full.

"Two years ago," Sleepy Eyes explained through Taopi, "I heard rumors of war brewing between the northern Sioux and the Chippewa.

THE ALCHEMIST'S MAP

I also heard about a Frenchman who brought peace between the two nations at the Stone House. But last fall, I heard about a Tizaptanon man bragging that he had killed Chippewa women on the Crow Wing River. Knowing that the Tizaptanons protected this man, I sent a messenger to demand this man be brought forth to answer for his crime. The Tizaptanons sent back my messenger pierced with many arrows."

Sleepy Eyes waited for the story to be relayed to Nicollet, who began to cry softly before wiping away the tears.

Taopi explained the reason to Sleepy Eyes. Although war between the Sioux and Chippewa was averted, the Pillagers still had unfinished business with the man they viewed as a heretic. When Chagobay traveled back to his home along the Crow Wing River, a band of Pillagers fell upon Chagobay and young Nanakonan, and convinced of Midé' priest's disloyalty—both for working with the Americans and for belonging to the heretical Wijigan Clan—they placed Chagobay in a pyre.

Once the fires raged, they released Nanakonan, offering him a chance to free his tortured father. Twice the boy entered the flames to try to free his father's bonds as the cruel men laughed, and on the third attempt, now badly burned, the boy ran through the flames and out into the woods.

Nicollet raised the curly hair above his brow to show Sleepy Eyes a scar above his hairline.

"Yes," Sleepy Eyes nodded. "You are lucky to have lived. I rallied my men and waged war upon this band of Tizaptanons who protected Ohanzee, this murderer and sower of war. We found him hiding in an unholy land surrounded by many waters and rivers. We set up a net, spreading our forces thin. Knowing the Tizaptanons are cowards, we waited until this net was cast before riding into their camp. At the Burned Fort, I found your attacker. Leaping from my horse, I fought him to the death, despite being greatly outnumbered. One of his friends stabbed me in the side after I laid this killer low, but unable to subdue me, they fled. Most of them were routed, fleeing like ants exposed to the sunlight."

Again, Sleepy Eyes waited for Taopi to translate. When he finished relating the tale, Nicollet became speechless.

That was when Sleepy Eyes turned to retrieve the first gift. "Knowing how you brought peace to the land, and what had happened to you back at the Crow Wing River, I give this gift to you to carry with you into the lands to the west."

The leather pouch was given to Nicollet, who opened it and removed the long hair and scalp of Ohanzee.

"Now the cowardly Tizaptanons will know to fear both the President of the United States and Sleepy Eyes, chief of the Sisseton at Swan Lake." Sleepy Eyes then whispered to his son, who stood and walked away from the fire. A moment later, he returned with a green wooden box that he set next to Nicollet.

"After slaying Ohanzee, I found this wooden box filled with books and maps," Sleepy Eyes explained as Nicollet's eyes grew wide. "I knew that it must belong to Woktchan Witchashton."

"Woktchan Witchashton?" Nicollet repeated, clutching the green box on his lap.

"I don't quite know how to put it," Taopi explained. "They call you 'the Magician Spirit,' 'the Great Man,' 'the Philosopher.' 'Woktchan Witchashton'... a Magi."

"Yet it is Sleepy Eyes who has produced the only true miracle," Nicollet added. "I thought this chest was lost to me."

Sleepy Eyes watched as Nicollet carefully opened the chest, which included the wampum belt that belonged to one of the Glusta. Nicollet looked over his shoulder to see who else had stayed up late into the night. After a night of feasting, most of the party had fallen asleep or drifted

THE ALCHEMIST'S MAP

away from the fire, leaving them alone.

Nicollet's fingers gently sifted through the manuscripts and papers, until he finally closed his eyes and prayed to his God in the sky. For the past several months, the chest had been a source of intrigue for Sleepy Eyes, who poured over its contents while healing from his wound.

"Ohanzee hunted for the same thing you seek," Sleepy Eyes explained, causing Nicollet to close the chest. Nicollet picked up the dried scalp of the murdered man, studied the mass of hair for a moment, then slipped it back in the leather pouch.

"You seek Mahkato," Sleepy Eyes said.

"Mahkato?"

"The place where the earth bleeds blue," Sleepy Eyes answered. "For many nights, I stayed awake, unable to sleep because of the wound to my ribs. While I could not read the words in your books, I could see the drawings made by the men who had visited Mahkato."

"The drawings found in these books are fictitious," Nicollet said. "They describe a land where the rivers flow in four directions."

"Yes, and that place is Mahkato."

Nicollet shook his head. "No, I followed the Mississippi River all the way to the source, and all I found were swamps and creeks. There was no Spirit Lake or Turtle Island at the end of the quest."

"Yet you head into certain danger, past the land of the red pipestone, to seek out the Plateau Du Coteau, where the waters flow to the north as the Red River and to the South as the Minisotah River. I tell you again, you seek the same thing as Ohanzee."

The small man took a moment to gather his thoughts. He looked to the stars for a moment before peering across the fire to Sleepy Eye. "Tell me more about Mahkato."

"For a long time, the Dakota fiercely protected this location from enemies of all sorts. But now it is a cursed place... a place where an evil spirit slumbers. Fools like Ohanzee have only angered the spirit, pouring out disease and pestilence upon our land. I prayed to the Great Mystery that he would send one to cleanse and purify our land."

Nicollet then pulled out the wampum belt of the Glusta tribe. "Do you know this?"

"Yes," Sleepy Eyes admitted. "The Glusta came to me to seek permission to enter the Haunted Valley. He wished to look for clues about the Key of Death."

When Taopi finished translating, he spoke directly to Nicollet. "At Mni Wakan, one of the Glusta came to Chief Wahanantan, saying that the sign in the stars meant Wishwee would come looking for the White Egg."

"I am not this Wishwee fellow," Nicollet declared. "Does Chief Wahanantan expect me to find this White Egg?"

When Taopi did not answer, Sleepy Eyes answered, "The Great Mystery has given you special magic to help you find what is lost. It is good you have come. Continue on your journey to the Place Where Water Flows to Opposite Sides. There, past the Red Pipestone, you will find our great chief, Wahanantan. He still knows the old ways, even though the time of the Seven Council Fires is over. Ask him your questions."

At this, Nicollet became silent, his eyes drawn to the heavens and fixed on the North Star.

CHAPTER FORTY-THREE

PIPESTONE

1838

I have failed him, and now he will never trust me, Frémont thought as he reached down with a gloved hand to rip a plate-sized piece of buffalo shit from the prairie floor. As he pulled the buffalo chip from the grass beneath it, the chip split in half, releasing odor from its moist center. Frémont tossed it away, knowing that only the older chips could be successfully dried for fuel.

Frémont tried to first clean his gloves off on his pants, then on the prairie grass, before picking up his sack of dried fecal matter he had collected. In the distance, he could hear chuckling.

Perhaps they are all right. I will never become more than a servant. Frémont searched the horizon for the small clump of trees where the men had made camp, but he became temporarily lost in the sea of grass that stretched out like the surface of a lake.

Someone whistled sharply.

Frémont spun in a circle so quickly that the sack swung around and clunked him in the side; he waved when he saw the little line of smoke and the distant clump of trees.

Walking through waist high grass, Frémont understood why there were few trees in such a place. Summer grass smothered the earth like a wet blanket, making even a casual stroll laborious. Once the grasses dried, a spark could light a fire that would have burned any tree that managed to emerge from the grass.

The three families of Sisseton Sioux they found at Pipestone Quarry had already claimed what little dry brush existed. Wanting to create harmony with their fellow pilgrims, Nicollet refused to accept their gift of firewood, choosing to send Frémont on his daily errands instead.

If Nicollet is ever to trust me, I'll just tell him the whole truth.

With his bag of buffalo chips, Frémont returned to the camp, hoping to restore his place amongst the men.

A week earlier, at a lake Nicollet dubbed "Shetek," tragedy brought him under the protective wing of the professor.

After riding for days across open prairie before finding the headwaters of the Des Moines River, the beauty of Shetek quickly soured. Laframboise and Renville both raised alarm when a village of Sioux nearby turned out to be totally abandoned. Then, Nicollet visited a large island in the middle of the lake, only to return moody and agitated. Wanting to lighten the mood, Frémont went out hunting with the others.

While hunting the uppermost tributary of the large lake, Frémont's feet had become stuck in the mud. Although he was only in three feet of water, he lost his balance and fell backwards, almost drowning.

THE ALCHEMIST'S MAP

When he woke, he found himself at Nicollet's fire.

"Do you want to be a hunter or a scientist?" Nicollet asked him.

"Can I be both?" Frémont mused, but Nicollet did not laugh. "I took this commission so I could learn from you."

"Then focus on the science, and I will teach you how to properly make a map."

With Nicollet's ephemeris filled with astronomical data detailing longitudes, latitudes, and charts of astronomical objects, Frémont quickly learned the book was almost more valuable than the yellow telescope that rode in its own wagon. Once he finished studying the book, Nicollet would teach him how to use the sextant and the barometer.

Two days ago, however, Frémont lost the book and found himself alienated from both the voyageurs and the scientist, which was how he ended up collecting buffalo chips for fuel.

Swinging the bag to his other shoulder, Frémont returned to the camp with at least two days of fuel. The lighter the bag, the better it would burn. And the bag was both massive and light.

Glancing to the south, Frémont saw the first of a dozen horses just fifty yards from where he stood.

Indians!

Even at fifty yards, Frémont knew they were not Sioux. The approaching caravan was led by men with shaved heads with plumes of black hair rising like spines down their necks. With the horses attached to pole carts, no one in the party rushed out to kill him, but Frémont nevertheless dropped his bag of dried dung, drew his pistol, and stood his ground.

I will be a shield for Nicollet.

In the distance, the camp of Sioux stood at attention, but only Frémont had armed himself. He raised the gun above his head and then steadily put it back into its holster.

With a gesture, Frémont welcomed the strangers closer, picking up the bag of dung.

"Who are they? What do they want?" the excited tourists asked from beside the guide, Joe Laframboise.

"They are Missouri," Laframboise explained without even turning. Although not a large man, the frontier had turned him into a dried piece of leather. "They have come a long way north to find this sacred place."

"Are they going to attack?" Frémont checked.

"Of course not. The Pipestone Quarry is the closest thing the Indians have to a church. Tribes from hundreds of miles in all directions visit this place, knowing that the Great Spirit gave it to them. None of them would dare profane such a place with bloodshed. They come here for peace, not war."

"We should go talk to them," Nicollet said to Laframboise. He walked over to the food supplies and took a crate of food from the bewildered Big Moe and handed it to Iron Walker. With Laframboise and Renville flanking Nicollet, the three men led the young Sioux prince out to the approaching Missouri Indians.

"Keep a close eye on the horses tonight, boys," Big Moe muttered through his rotting teeth. "These Indians will rob us blind and leave us to die on the prairie, if they can. Don't believe any of this hospitality they are about to show. They will sneak up tonight."

After a few tense moments of waiting helplessly for Renville and Laframboise to translate their intentions to the Missouri Indians, Frémont joined Nicollet and the others to speak with them.

Even though no one could bridge the language gap between the English, French, Sioux, and Missouri languages, a deal was struck after Nicollet finished hugging each of the weary Missouri travelers.

The Missouri continued on to a spot at the far north side of the quarry, where they gathered into a circle. The three families of Sisseton

THE ALCHEMIST'S MAP

Sioux watched them closely for an hour before continuing with their own routines.

Frémont strolled from wagon to wagon and tent to tent, searching for his purpose. Most of the men ignored him as he stood and stared, but Nicollet called out gently, "Johnny."

"Yes, Professor Nicollet."

"I would like to apologize for my harsh words the other day."

"I understand," Frémont nodded, still showing the guilt he felt for having lost the book. Nicollet continued to pass his metallic utensils through his little flame. "What are you doing, Professor?"

"During my negotiations with Secretary of War Poinsett about the parameters of this expedition, I was afforded two crates of smallpox vaccines, to administer as I saw fit. The Missouri Indians have traveled hundreds of miles in order to quarry stone for a new peace pipe to use at their religious services. Tomorrow, I will give them 'good medicine,' if they want it, to help them survive the epidemic killing so many of their people."

"I thought Renville said all of the good stone for pipes has been harvested by the Sioux already."

"It has been," Nicollet shrugged as he continued cleaning the needles and syringes. "But it seems that the Great Spirit has been hard at work bringing all of us together here at this place."

"You mean God?"

"Yes. Call Him what you will. The Missouri said this place is holy, created when the Great Spirit cast his lightning to the ground, revealing the sacred red stone below the surface. Do you remember the terrible storm we encountered when we arrived? How it almost overturned Renville's wagon?"

"Yes, but the Sisseton women claimed that the buffalo herds wore a path through the prairie, revealing the red stone long ago."

Nicollet nodded. "So it is your view that one story must be right and the other story must be wrong? Many of my friends think like you do, Johnny. Life must fit one paradigm or another. But sometimes multiple theories can fit the same evidence. The day you begin to *assume* is the day your mind closes to possibility, and before you know it, you cannot see the path set before you by the Great Spirit."

Frémont stood, baffled by Nicollet's point.

"The Missouri, for instance, traveling up through the lands of the Iowa, lost their way, missing the Rock Rapids that would have led them back to these sacred lands. Instead, they followed Kanaranzi Creek far to the east, leading them blindly over the lands we had crossed, where they found this."

Nicollet reached down and tossed a thick leather-bound book at Frémont's feet. Recognizing it immediately, Frémont picked up Nicollet's ephemeris.

"Take a moment to consider the odds of this book being found out on the open prairie, on the eve of the most important celestial event of the past six years, and then tell me you do not believe in the Great Spirit."

Dumbfounded, Frémont stood holding the book—destiny transformed. "Professor Nicollet, there is something you must know about my place on this expedition."

"Involving Secretary Poinsett?"

Does he already know my true purpose? "First, he sent me away from you, and now, he wants me to spy on you. He placed me under the command of Colonel Abert, knowing I would be placed on your expedition. He wants me to steal the secrets of your new science."

"I accepted the funding, knowing your loyalties were most likely divided."

"They are not divided, Professor. I am only your servant from this day forward."

THE ALCHEMIST'S MAP

"I do not want a servant. I only want you to be the man you were meant to be." When Nicollet looked back down, he had already moved from the box of vaccines to another more sinister crate.

"What are you going to do with that?"

Nicollet smiled before opening the crate of dynamite. "It is the custom of the Missouri for the one chosen to work in the quarry to fast and purify themselves for three days beforehand. They must abstain from all contact with the opposite sex. They must then proceed with a ceremony of prayers and offerings to the spirit of the quarry.

"The Missouri give the spirit food and smoking materials so that he will let them have good stone; stone that will not flake, that is clear red, compact, and uniform.

"If, by ill fortune, the chosen worker only finds thin, brittle sheets of stone, this man is found to be impure—a liar who has misled the others by vaunting a chastity of which he is not capable. He is obliged to retire, and another takes his place who mines deeper or chooses a better site. Johnny, do you understand what I'm saying?"

"Not really, Professor Nicollet."

"I have decided that you will be our virgin representative, who will search for this elusive Catlin stone which they use to make pipes."

"A virgin... You haven't heard the gossip, have you? Wait, is this my penance?"

"Non!" Nicollet laughed. "I am giving you the honor of joining the Missouri on this sacred endeavor. I will not see our Missouri friends, who have returned this precious book on the eve of the Occultation of Spica, fail and return home empty-handed."

"But what are you going to do with the dynamite, Professor Nicollet?"

"Prepare yourself, Johnny, for in three days, you will be transformed into Thor, the God of Thunder and Lightning."

CHAPTER FORTY-FOUR

PIPESTONE
1838

That night, while the voyageurs danced, sang, wrestled, and laughed around their buffalo chip campfire, Nicollet and the gentlemen gathered at the center wagon around the large telescope.

When the clouds scattered, Nicollet quickly went about his business, explaining the details to the botanist, Karl Geyer, as well as to his topographic apprentice, young Frémont.

"For the first time in six years, I am prepared to observe and compare the longitude of a place deduced by three methods: chronometer, lunar distances, and the eclipse of a star."

Captain Gaspard de Belligny, who studied the scientific methods of

THE ALCHEMIST'S MAP

Nicollet's map-making for the French government, patted Frémont on the shoulder while Nicollet searched the heavens for his star.

The Great Spirit had indeed smiled on Frémont's blunder.

Should I forgive him, though? If I trust him with the truth, will Frémont end up like dear Chagobay?

It was the Fourth of July, and it was time for bastard Johnny Frémont to fully be reborn as "Lieutenant John C. Frémont."

With Big Moe part of Nicollet's seemingly cruel joke, Frémont had been given no food or nourishment in order to prepare himself for his big moment with the dynamite. Even though the dirty voyageurs had been allowed to enter the quarry to bore holes, they were still allowed to eat, drink, and be merry, but Frémont spent most of his time under the wagon, his belly groaning and gurgling for lack of food.

Joe Laframboise and one of the voyageurs even returned with an obscene bounty of food—two great Canada geese and eight ducks—which allowed them to share with both their Missouri and Sioux neighbors.

But not with Frémont.

After supper, Nicollet called his apprentice over to his laboratory wagon. "Do you know what today is?"

"The day I get to eat."

"No," Nicollet smiled.

"The day I light the dynamite?"

"No."

Frémont just shook his head.

"Today is the birthdate of our country. I came to this country as a penniless traveler, but you were afforded the honor of being born in this country. You've made all of us proud with your sacrifice, so let me make you a little treat."

Nicollet procured a tin cup. "I was saving this for a special event, but it can be our little secret. Something to get you through until tomorrow."

Frémont nodded, unsure of the plan.

Then Nicollet wore his wizard's hat. After filling the cup with water, he added sugar, and then began to carefully measure out small doses of other powders and chemicals, until finally, with the addition of a little soda, the caramel-colored water began to fizz and pop, bringing the cup to life.

"Drink," Nicollet smiled with assurance.

"Will it hurt?"

Nicollet laughed. "No, it will not hurt. I have found this little chemical concoction to be quite refreshing and filling, especially for an empty stomach."

Frémont's caution turned to surprise once he tested his first sip. He quickly swallowed down a gulp, then another, and another, before an unexpected belch caught him by surprise. "It is delicious."

"Sip it gently," Nicollet said, sending him back to his spot under the wagon. "Later this afternoon, you will bring thunder and lightning to the prairie."

Independence Day proved to be hot and dull—until it was time for the dynamite.

With the eyes of the scientists, voyageurs, Missouri, and Sioux upon him, Nicollet gave Frémont some last-minute instructions.

When it came time to light the fuse, Frémont bolted faster than a jackrabbit back to where the men cowered in safety.

"You did light it, Frémont?" Laframboise questioned, and for a second, Frémont's eyes grew wide in self-doubt.

But then the thunderous explosion shook the quarry, sending stone shrapnel high into the air only to come down like a red hailstorm.

The reverberations were soon swallowed up by cheering from the men.

THE ALCHEMIST'S MAP

Nicollet bolted across the field, waving to the Indian tribes to come quickly.

The blasting had produced a fresh vein of red mineral for their pipe, which was easily harvested by the chosen members of each tribe. Afterwards, Nicollet's fiddle filled the air, and three nations celebrated Independence Day with music.

Just before Big Moe's supper, Frémont hiked to the top of the distant bluff overlooking the quarry. He waved a large American flag, which was greeted by a chorus of "Hurrah!" from the voyageurs.

But then he did something unexpected.

A twenty-three foot pillar of red stone, looking like a chimney, stood alone in front of the bank of stone. Carefully judging its distance, young Frémont took a running leap, flag in hand, only to land on the two-foot sloping platform on top of the chimney. After teetering for a moment, Frémont rose squarely atop the chimney rock, proudly waving the flag to even louder celebration.

"Come," Nicollet said to the others. "The fool won't be able to get a running start to leap off the chimney. He'll need our help."

True enough, Frémont's descent was far less glorious. After creating a human ladder along the base of the pillar to retrieve him, Nicollet, Renville, Geyer, Laframboise, and Flandin sat with Frémont in the red rubble at the base of the chimney.

"We should mark this day," Laframboise said, holding a big knife. "Come."

They followed Laframboise to the wall of stone and watched him carve his initials in it. Then he handed the big knife to Nicollet.

Nicollet paused, remembering how François Champollion had once bragged about adding his name to a list of Pharaohs.

A chance at immortality.

Or blasphemy?

When the five men finished, the big blade was handed to Frémont.

"Go ahead," Laframboise told him. "You've earned it."

Frémont carved his first name and smiled.

The moment quickly ended when they all turned to the sound of a galloping horse. Taopi rode up from his scouting patrol and said, "There is trouble to the west."

CHAPTER FORTY-FIVE
GRAND OASIS
1838

The Coteau des Prairies is a glacial ridge two hundred miles long, and at places, a hundred miles wide. It abruptly rises nine hundred feet from the prairie, which is why Lewis and Clark described it as the "mountain of the prairie." With its highest elevation in the north near the border of North Dakota, the ridge gradually slopes away to the south toward the Missouri River in northwest Iowa. The Sioux River sits atop the ridge, running the entire length from north to south. Because of its steep slope in places, it is the headwaters of several rivers that flow in all directions.

The Nicollet Expedition of 1838 intended to study the elevation of the Coteau des Prairie near Sioux Falls, which was the unofficial border between the eastern Dakota and the western tribes of the Yankton, Yanktonnan, and the Lakota of the open plains.

With the startling news delivered by Taopi, everything halted, including the wagon train, and for three days, riders scouted ahead while the voyageurs nervously cleaned their guns and stared down every blade of grass that moved in the breeze.

Baron Lahontan's map showed the "Rivière Longue" flowing from the west of the Mississippi River, making the Minisotah, Des Moines, or the Cannon rivers likely matches. It first noted a "Separation des Cartes," indicating a continental divide of sorts.

Like what I found at Lake Shetek. It was at a divide that Lahontan labeled a waterway "Rivière Morte," or "River of Death." The distinctive headwater for the River of Death began in a pronounced ridge that ran from north to south.

On the map, Lahontan left a mark indicating the place where he saw the copper vitriol bleeding openly upon the earth. Nicollet mulled it over while the group sat in a state of apprehension.

Visit the interior of the earth; by rectification thou shalt find the hidden stone.

The Undine.

When Laframboise came galloping back to the camp, everyone, especially Nicollet, waited to find out what had happened to the Grande Oasis outpost. Big Moe Maxwell immediately gave the hungry guide a cup of water and a bowl of stew.

"It was not the smallpox," Laframboise said before taking in the first bit of nourishment he'd had in two days.

Dieu merci, Nicollet prayed.

Junior Renville sighed in relief, hearing it wasn't the disease. His home was north, near the headwaters of the Minisotah, yet on the vast prairie, was considered a neighbor to the Laframboise outpost of Grand Oasis.

THE ALCHEMIST'S MAP

"So your wife and son are well?" Nicollet clarified.

Laframboise explained, "Red Fox and Lowell are fine, yes. Taopi was right—the entire post was burned to the ground, but not because of smallpox. Many of the provisions were buried, and the clues left behind indicate that they traveled north."

"To Lac Qui Parle," Junior Renville said with a smile.

"Yes, it appears both of our families wintered safely. But there is other news," Laframboise said as he shoveled down mouthfuls of stew. "I met a Sioux warrior that had traveled south from Lac Qui Parle."

Now Iron Walker perked up, hearing news of one of his father's men.

"Hearing about the smallpox epidemic on the prairie, a roving band of Fox Indians came up out of Iowa looking to take advantage of things. I would bet that is why they burned down all of the buildings at Grand Oasis."

Taopi muttered the reason, "To leave the Fox nothing but ash."

"Sioux war parties have gone to The Falls, where they plan to ambush this raiding party. So we will not be able to map the base of the Coteau, Mr. Nicollet."

"What are the other options?" Nicollet asked, knowing all hopes of finding the Undine meant exploring every watershed and "Spirit Lake" he could find. He also needed to produce results or risk losing his governmental funding.

"The Sioux hunter said that Waneta of the Yankton has come down from Devil's Lake to visit with Renville Senior at Lac Qui Parle."

"Waneta?" Nicollet repeated, pronouncing the syllables slowly. "Is this the same man as the legendary Chief Wahanantan?"

"It is his son," Taopi said, and then turned to Laframboise, "Why would he be so far from his father?"

Laframboise set his spoon down and ran his hand through his thinning back hair. "The reason Waneta has come south from Devil's Lake is that a band of five Tizaptanon families have gathered on the northern edge of the Coteau, near a place called Two Woods Lakes. They are unpredictable and dangerous."

Nicollet asked, "How close would we come to Two Woods?"

"If you are to properly map the Coteau?" Laframboise sighed and answered. "Within ten miles of their camp. The odds of them finding our wagon tracks would be quite high."

"How many would there be?" Nicollet asked, knowing his decision held his own life and the lives of others in his hands.

"Five families? There could be fifty of them."

"Will they be heavily armed?"

"They would undoubtedly have ill-gotten weapons. These men are outcasts from society, and thus see everyone, including a scientific expedition, as their enemy."

So much risk. "How far away is Lac Qui Parle from here?"

"It is more than sixty miles due north, but that would take us far away from the Coteau Des Prairie, our destination. If we head straight west for forty miles, we will find this great ridge, where it only becomes more defined the farther north we head."

Nicollet took a moment to decide. He looked at young Frémont, and then over at the German botanist, Geyer. "This is a scientific expedition. We need to measure the Coteau."

"Don't worry about the savages, Professor Nicollet," one of the voyageurs boasted. "They wouldn't come within a hundred yards of our wagon train."

"We'll protect you, Professor Nicollet," another added, and soon all the voyageurs threw in their support.

Nicollet felt their confidence. *And I can use this as a plausible excuse to remove spies from the expedition.* "Since we are heading into possible danger, we will send a wagon with Yellow Medicine, Iron Walker, and

THE ALCHEMIST'S MAP

Flandin under the protection of Captain Belligny and the Viscount to Lac Qui Parle, where they can tell Mr. Renville our plans, and perhaps get Waneta to wait for us."

"Then it is settled. Tomorrow, we will divide our expedition and adjust our heading," Laframboise declared, nodding approval at Nicollet.

And I will find out why Lahontan called it the "River of Death."

CHAPTER FORTY-SIX
THE COTEAU DES PRAIRIES
1838

Day after day, Nicollet filled the blank white pages with ink, but his map did not match the designs of Baron Lahontan.

At the base of the Coteau's sharply ascending wall, the expedition found a beautiful lake tucked into the crease of land where they camped.

"It's so beautiful," Frémont said aloud.

The voyageurs then promptly harassed the young officer about his declaration until Frémont retreated to Nicollet, who was gathering his data in his book.

"So, Johnny, when we return from our mapping expedition, is there someone other than this lake that holds your heart?"

THE ALCHEMIST'S MAP

Frémont shook his head. "Yes, but I'd stand more of a chance with this lake."

"Ah, a brave knight falls in love with an aquatic enchantress. What is the name of your Undine?"

"I met her in Washington just before we departed, but she is far too young for me."

"By the time we return, she may be a woman, ready to marry," Nicollet offered.

"Well, there is another problem. Her father."

"Star-crossed lovers? Whose daughter is she?"

"She's the daughter of Senator Benton of Missouri."

"Ooh la la."

"You know him?"

"I do. Before Colonel Abert offered funding, I tried many times to acquire funding from Benton. He is a formidable man whom I inadvertently called a 'vampire' while in his presence"

"As I said, I'd have more of a chance with this lake."

"We shall name her 'Benton,' then—in honor of the daughter, not the father."

"You'd do that?" Frémont smiled at his mentor. "Thank you, Professor Nicollet."

It wasn't the only lake to receive a symbolic name from Nicollet.

After Nicollet made measurements of longitude, latitude, and barometric pressures to determine elevation, the smaller caravan again rolled up the spine of the great ridge, where Laframboise showed them the Big Sioux River as well as the massive lakes that formed along the top of the continental divide.

Hoping for information from the local Yankton Sioux about the Tizaptanons to the north, Laframboise set up their camp on a narrow isthmus between four lakes, where the Yankton commonly camped.

"This lake is as large and beautiful as the lakes in the land of the Chippewa," Nicollet said.

"What is this lake called?" Geyer asked Laframboise.

"The lake is called 'Unkce,'" Laframboise answered.

"Really, what does it mean?"

"Oh, it means 'much cactus' in the Sioux Tongue."

"Cactus?" Geyer grew excited. "I shall have to find this 'unkce' and study it. How do you spell that?" the German botanist asked, pen and ink at the ready.

"U-n-k-c-e," Laframboise spelled it out slowly. Nicollet and Geyer noticed how Junior Renville started to laugh.

"What?" Geyer asked.

"We are staying at Lake Unkce," Laframboise said confidently. "Put that in your notebook."

"Don't, Mr. Geyer," Renville finally stopped him, throwing a small rock at Laframboise, who burst out laughing.

"I'm sorry, Mr. Geyer. I was just having fun with you," the crusty guide finally said. "The Sioux call this place 'Unkce'ota,' which means 'prickly pear.' It is a type of thistle that can poke through a moccasin. 'Unkce' by itself, however, means 'shit.'"

"Lake Shit?" Geyer repeated, and all of the men devolved into laughter.

"That's right. Lake Full of Shit," Laframboise said.

Nicollet reached for his own notebook and began to jot. A few days earlier, while Nicollet studied a boulder deposited upon the top of a hill, Frémont and Laframboise had openly debated the Great Flood of Genesis, with Frémont turning to the science taught by his former mentor, Joel Poinsett. "Science doesn't lie," Frémont had argued, "even if the man does." Neither man acquiesced during the debate.

Nicollet had remained silent, knowing that as Secretary of War,

THE ALCHEMIST'S MAP

Poinsett held the purse strings for the expedition. Yet he also knew what De Smet had told him: Poinsett planned to remove all Indians and erect a series of forts across the prairie.

Now, Nicollet took the opportunity to bridge the tension between Frémont and Laframboise. "I have decided what this lake shall be called on my map. Far in the north, I named the Chippewa lakes after many of my friends, such as Tolliver, Sibley, Gratiot, and even my old nemesis, Arago. So a lake whose name varies from being 'prickly' to being 'full of shit' shall be forever known as 'Lake Poinsett.'"

Laframboise laughed and Frémont nodded with approval at the joke crafted for them.

Big Moe stood from his fire and looked to the setting sun, scratching his hair under his cap. "That doesn't look good."

Nicollet looked to the west and saw that one of the voyageurs was dragging Jim Taopi back to camp.

CHAPTER FORTY-SEVEN
LAKE POINSETT
1838

O*ur expedition travels upon the edge of a knife.*
Nicollet opened his green chest when the others weren't looking and discreetly removed the light object from the leather pouch and tossed it onto the fire.

For a moment, it just sat there in the embers and ash, and Nicollet quickly looked over to Big Moe, hoping he would not have to explain it.

Then the human hair blazed, and the dry scalp ignited. By the time Moe returned, the dried scalp of Ohanzee appeared as nothing more than a darkened piece of coal.

Laframboise tucked two rifles into his saddlebag and also armed himself with two pistols, giving him more than a dozen shots at his

THE ALCHEMIST'S MAP

future disposal. Junior Renville was similarly armed, although he carried something Laframboise did not—an American flag.

"If we don't return by lunch, pray for us," Laframboise said and then galloped off to the east with Junior Renville in tow, the flag streaming above them.

Once the scalp of Ohanzee had vanished from the earth, Nicollet walked back over to the wagon where fierce Jim Taopi shivered like a child under a shell of blankets.

The other men remaining in the camp were silent. *I have put us all in danger, but Taopi once saved my life—now I must save his.*

Two days earlier, the limp body of Taopi was dragged back to camp by a voyageur after finding him in a shallow inlet of Lake Poinsett where he'd been duck hunting. The intense fever that gripped Taopi was evident when he was set beside the campfire, but neither the voyageur who found him nor anyone else knew if Taopi had lost consciousness prior to falling in the water or if the fall in the water had caused his fever.

When his water-logged lungs had coughed up blood, Laframboise offered a solution—to quickly turn back to the east for the home of Joseph Renville at Lac Qui Parle, where Taopi could receive medical treatment.

Would I have done the same for any of the other men? Nicollet wondered as the morning slowly dragged on.

The path to Lac Qui Parle came at a steep cost—the expedition had to pass by Two Lakes, where the five families of renegade Tizaptanons camped. Laframboise, who had Odawa blood, and Junior Renville, who was part Sioux, had immediately volunteered to ride ahead to declare their peaceful intentions.

Frémont sat cleaning his gun when the sound of horses returned from over the hill.

Laframboise and Renville had survived.

"I counted almost fifty teepees camped along the lake," Junior explained with a voice cracking in fear.

"Are these the same men who killed Louis Le Blanc last spring?" a voyageur asked.

In Spring of last year, French trader La Blanc and a group of his men were killed in a run-in with a band of Tizaptanon warriors. Tensions between the renegade zealots and everybody else remained as high as ever.

"They are, but luckily they also knew and respected Junior's father, so we are strangely fortunate."

"We explained that we were scientists, not the military, and were not searching for any fugitives from justice. The chiefs appreciated our efforts not to disturb the women and children on our way to Lac Qui Parle, and the meeting was almost concluded until they learned Joseph Nicollet was with the expedition."

"Me?" Nicollet said, almost flinching. "How do these men know me?"

"I am sorry, Professor Nicollet. Chief Thunder Face wants to meet the one who they call 'the Great Sorcerer.' He insisted we bring you to their village, so that they might dance and smoke with you. It was the only way he'd let us pass."

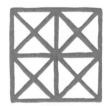

CHAPTER FORTY-EIGHT
TWO LAKES
1838

Two Lakes, despite what the name implied, turned out to be a cluster of four small lakes. From the hill where the wagons stopped, Nicollet could see the descending slope of the Coteau, which led toward the Minisotah River and Lac Qui Parle. Part of him wanted to just keep riding, but it appeared he had no other choice but to meet with the renegade chief.

At the bottom of the hill, nearly a hundred men on horseback waited for the arrival of the Great Sorcerer.

"These men are religious zealots," Junior Renville reminded Nicollet as they rolled down the hill in a single wagon. "They are stubborn and superstitious, and if you offend their ways, they will not hesitate to kill every last one of us."

"I understand," Nicollet affirmed once again, setting the wampum belt over his shoulder. "I have already met one far away at the Crow Wing River."

The tension hung heavy in the air as Nicollet arrived at the camp. But then Nicollet rushed forward and embraced their fierce chief, much to the chuckles of the chief's tense family members.

The bewildered chief looked around, took a deep sniff, and declared to his friends and family, "He smells like flowers!"

At the command of Chief Thunder Face, the women and children began to sing, the riders began to circle and scream, and the elders of the village stood to welcome Nicollet to their fires. Laframboise stayed on his left and Junior Renville stayed on his right, and the three of them left their wagon in order to sit at the fires.

After Nicollet offered up the last of their sugar and coffee as gifts, Thunder Face shouted out, "Dance, dance, I say his name. Dance for the Great Sorcerer."

While they danced feverishly for Nicollet, all three men were stuffed with food, which Nicollet finished to the last morsel. Once the meal was done, Nicollet stood up and went over to Big Moe's food supplies, picking the last of the wrapped cornbread loaves, which he broke off in pieces and began to distribute to all the women and children, whom he patted on the head like a small doting grandfather.

Once done, Nicollet sat back down next to Laframboise, whose mouth was agape.

"See!" Thunder Face shouted loudly after the dance concluded. "He, by himself, looks after everyone. Never have we seen a white man as good."

On and on into the night, the poor renegade tribe stuffed their guests with dog meat and breadroot, while they pressed Nicollet for

THE ALCHEMIST'S MAP

information about himself and his purpose for coming to the prairie. What Junior Renville couldn't translate, Nicollet explained through sketches and illustrations.

"You have spirit," one of Thunder Face's brothers declared to Nicollet. "You are not proud; you treat us as equals while the others have us eat beside the poor, who they scorn."

Nicollet knew they were prodding him for more gifts, which seemed to upset Laframboise, who wanted to leave as soon as possible. But Nicollet had no problem raiding Big Moe's food stock for pork, cereal, and grain if it meant saving the life of Taopi.

"See if I speak the truth," Thunder Face finally declared between dances. "Will you all believe me now? Don't I know better than any of you? I guaranteed that he would come, that you would not wait for nothing! See now all that he does for you. Dance then to please the great man that has come from far away to be charitable to you, to your women, and to your children. This man will return to the American President and let all of them know the truth about us. And when he does, this period of great despair will wash away and a new day will come to our people."

They think I am some sort of savior, Nicollet realized. *What will happen when they learn I am only a man?*

Thunder Face reached into a leather bag and procured a turtle rattle. Holding it in his hands, he said, "Ke-ya is a guardian of life, longevity, and fortitude. When I was born, my mother took a piece of my birth cord and placed it inside of this rattle. She taught me the meaning of time with the shell of this turtle. The thirteen scales on the back represent the thirteen moons in a year. The twenty-eight smaller scales along the edge represent the twenty-eight days from one moon to the next."

Time. It was something Nicollet felt he was running out of, and he wondered what the Watchmaker's Son would think of the Great

Sorcerer out on the frontier. He had not found Lady Drummond's murderer, the Alchemist's Map, the Philosopher's Stone, the Key of Death, the Undine, or even Fort L'Huillier.

Yet when Chief Thunder Face reached over and handed him the turtle rattle, Nicollet felt blessed and content. Gorged and exhausted, he slept better than he did at any other time on the expedition.

Then he again dreamt of the Undine.

The water spirit found him in an old memory of the Chamonix glacier near his home in Savoy.

In this memory, the Undine appeared again in the wall of ice. She moved gracefully within the blue water, approaching the surface of the ice as if looking through the porthole of a sinking ship.

"Do you remember how you were trapped in the glacier for days?" she asked. "It was a warning—a premonition. Now you surround yourself with savages and believe them to be your friends. These thieves will kill you and your friends for the sheer pleasure of it."

"No," Nicollet said to the shimmering image on the other side of the ice. "These Tizaptanons are humanity in their purest form."

"They are murderers and rapists."

"You're wrong. They hold the secret to the past. They are the last link to uncovering the truth about you."

"Me?"

"I might not be the Great Sorcerer, or Wishwee, or the Great Thunderbird, but I know you are not the Undine, or a shapeshifting monster known as No Soul, or the sleeping water serpent. I will learn your secrets before I am through."

"Is that a threat, child?" the Undine asked, pressing her face to the pane of ice.

At that, the ice collapsed, swallowing Nicollet in a wave of blue vitriol.

THE ALCHEMIST'S MAP

"Professor Nicollet, wake up."

Nicollet's eyes opened wide and he immediately sat up on his elbows, but Laframboise cupped his mouth to silence him. "Thunder Face will keep us here for a week, and we are already perilously low on supplies. We are going to quietly slip away and depart before any of them know better. Understand?"

Clutching the turtle rattle, Nicollet nodded, feeling as if the Undine herself had caused Laframboise to pull him away from the Tizaptanon village.

At noon, three of Thunder Face's warriors appeared on horseback on the high bluff of the Coteau, but by the time they returned to Two Lakes, the wagons had added another dozen miles after regaining the flat prairie. Nicollet sat in the wagon bed for the next two days, sulking and pondering his dream of the Undine.

Finally, Nicollet returned to the wagon seat beside Laframboise, who glanced at him curiously as if seeing him for the first time. "What are you doing out here?"

"I'm making a map of the Mississippi watershed," Nicollet said, a little perplexed.

"Why? Why is a fancy man like you pursuing such a foolish endeavor?"

"I would disagree that it is foolish. Back in France, the world is shackled like some caged beast, to be prodded and poked by my colleagues. Out here, it is still wild and free. I see it as a privilege to be out here with you."

"Perhaps Poinsett isn't the only one full of shit," Laframboise muttered. "Your map will lead greedy men right to Thunder Face's village and right to the sacred Pipestone Quarry. It will allow them to shackle this great beast like the horses that pull our wagons. They will ride the beast into the ground and never think twice about the savages. Do not trust your friends in Washington, Professor Nicollet, or they will trod right over you with their dreams of wealth and power."

With his mind spoken, Laframboise seemed to breathe easier, but Nicollet knew he was right. *My map will doom these people, but how else was I to investigate? I can only hope my work can find a greater purpose.*

As they finally neared Lac Qui Parle and the Minisotah River that would lead all the way back to Fort Snelling, a single rider appeared on a hill.

CHAPTER FORTY-NINE
LAC QUI PARLE
1838

Lac Qui Parle is a naturally-occurring ten-mile reservoir along the upper Minnesota River system. The exact meaning of the French phrase is still debated. The literal translation reads "The Lake that Speaks," but why it became known by that name is uncertain. One suggestion is the alluvial bluffs that created the dam are also responsible for echoes, which both Indians and French voyageurs took note of. Another tradition says it received its name because of the strange groaning and whistling of the ice, which because of river fluctuations, constantly shifts during the winter. A Sioux tradition claims that the first visitors to the lake heard voices call out to them but not a single footprint or source for the sound could be located.

Lac Qui Parle's first permanent resident came when Canadian soldier, interpreter, translator, guide, trader, and evangelist, Joseph Renville, built a stockade for a village, replete with a trade house and church. Renville, who was a quarter Indian, married a Sioux woman and fathered eight children, including his eldest, Joseph Renville Jr. The Renville house was known throughout the region for its massive stone fireplace, where the eclectic pioneer entertained guests of all nationalities.

When the Nicollet Expedition arrived on Sunday, July 15th, 1838, they were greeted by the other half of their expedition, a host of worshippers—both white and Indian, and the residents of Grand Oasis, including the family of Joe Laframboise.

For once, Nicollet was not intimidated by the physical presence of a stranger, for Joseph Renville Sr. was a small man with an almost delicate constitution. He had a thick head of gray, bristly hair and wore clothes that were crisp and clean. After only a few hours in the presence of this man, Nicollet determined his intelligence could rival any of the scientists he knew in Paris.

Joining the savant of the prairie were several guests, and for four days, Nicollet exchanged stories with Renville Sr. while Jim Taopi recovered under the care of Mrs. Renville. On the fourth day of storytelling, Nicollet let slip that he desired to meet the legendary chief of the Yankton.

"Wahanantan?" Renville repeated, his mouth agape as he looked at the equally stunned guests. "You came seeking Wahanantan?"

I have failed to find either the Philosopher's Stone or the location of the mine. Wahanantan might be my last chance to unlock the truth. "Oui, on several stops of my journey, I have heard the name 'Wahanantan.' From what I have been told, his people still live wild and free out upon the prairie."

THE ALCHEMIST'S MAP

"Yes, the Yankton still cling to the old ways, despite our efforts to evangelize them and prepare them for the ways of the modern world," Renville said. "But our baffled looks stem from the fact that Chief Wahanantan's son, Waneta—He Who Charges—came here a little more than a month ago."

Of course. "And why is this baffling?"

"If you ever met Waneta, you would understand better. He is a mysterious fellow whose glare could soften the spine of any man. He just rode up to our village and camped under a maple for three weeks. We pressed him about his business, and he said he'd received a vision and was waiting for a man from his dreams."

It can't be me. I can't truly be the Wishwee.

Renville continued with a shrug. "He waited under that maple tree for three weeks before leaving just a few days before your arrival. Now do you understand our reaction?"

"That is quite a coincidence. Where did Waneta go when he departed?"

"Looking for you, or looking for his father. Chief Wahanantan could be anywhere out on the open prairie, but he always comes back to camp at Mni Wakan."

Spirit Lake? Perhaps Mille Lacs was not the only sacred place. "How far is Mni Wakan from here?"

"Too far for you to safely reach and return prior to winter. It is also too dangerous without a stronger escort. You were right when you characterized the Yankton as untamed. The young boys would strip the wheels from your wagons to show their stealthy hunting skills during the two-hundred-mile trip."

If I cannot find the Philosopher's Stone, then perhaps I can find Waneta still lingering nearby. If only I had more time.

With Taopi recovering, Nicollet used his scientific purpose as an excuse to seek out clues from Baron Lahontan's map. With two others, Nicollet traveled by canoe up the final stretch of the St. Peter River, traveling through Marsh Lake and Big Stone Lake before reaching the headwaters of both the St. Peter River and the Red River, which flowed to the north.

Yet there is no blue earth.

At the northernmost tip of the Coteau, the trio explored every creek and stream that fed the waterway that led all the way back to Fort Snelling. Nicollet collected the elevation of the Coteau as well as the elevation of the headwaters.

Yet there is no Turtle Island or Spirit Lake.

At a Yankton village along the banks of Lake Traverse, Nicollet learned Waneta had been in the area a few days earlier.

Yet no tale of Wishwee or water spirits.

Nicollet did find a strange hollow reported to be haunted, but after a few hours, he departed once more with an empty feeling in his gut. After eight days, he knew that the St. Peter River was not Lahontan's Longue River any more than the Upper Mississippi had proved to be. He also knew he needed to return.

So on July 28th, Nicollet watched as Lac Qui Parle village came into sight once again. Three figures waited to greet them.

Nicollet recognized the first figure as Joseph Renville Sr. because of his short stature. The man to his right also became obvious when he saw the distinctive flop hat that covered the scarred scalp of Jim Taopi.

When the canoe landed on the shore, Nicollet was able to clearly see the details of the third man.

Waneta?

The large Yankton stood six foot and three inches, with rich leggings that exaggerated his height. Upon his broad chest, he wore an embroidered tunic befitting his rank as the son of a chief. He wore a buffalo

THE ALCHEMIST'S MAP

skin coat around his broad shoulders and his hair was decorated with feathers. Instead of seeing eyes, Nicollet saw a pair of green glasses on the man's chiseled face.

Could God have crafted a finer human being?

In long strides, the warrior approached the canoe and outstretched his hand to help Nicollet from the canoe.

"Leela ampaytu keen washtay," Waneta said, and Nicollet quickly turned to Taopi.

"Waneta says 'Today is a good day.'"

"Leela ampaytu keen washtay," Nicollet repeated, a bit more uncertain about how it would end.

CHAPTER FIFTY

MURTHLY CASTLE, SCOTLAND
1838

Murthly Castle came into existence as a hunting lodge for King David of Scotland, and in the 14th century, a castle became the centerpiece of the estate. Built along the edge of the legendary Birnam Woods, its reputation as a royal playground extended into the 19th century, when Sir John Archibald Drummond Stewart attempted to reinvest in the property with a new castle designed by James Gillespie Graham.

Following the death of Sir John Archibald Drummond Stewart, the 6th Baronet, his younger brother, Billy, returned to Scotland in 1838 to assume responsibility of the estate and lordship.

Why does the lord of the castle need to lie? Antoine Clément

THE ALCHEMIST'S MAP

wondered as he sweated through the layers of his valet uniform. He threw his silk top hat onto the lawn and stripped off his jacket and vest. *How did Nicollet survive such clothes?*

Clément found a large oak and sat under the shade of its limbs. *A Cree under a tree.*

Back at the castle, Lord Stewart met with other Scottish lords to sell part of the family estate, another castle called "Logiealmond." Stewart tried to explain its connection to Nicollet's quest, but Clément could not grasp it.

What happened to Captain Billy? Did Lord Stewart slowly smother him to death?

When the gentlemen finally left in their carriages, the household servants transitioned to the next event. Lord Stewart glanced once at the solitary oak, but even after the guests left, he did not rush over.

Instead, he walked over to another area of the grand estate where a hundred flags marked another connection to Nicollet.

"It won't be as grand as the Cathedral Basilica of St. Louis," Stewart had promised when explaining it a month earlier. "But it will be a tribute to my newfound faith, as well as to my friend."

The Chapel of St. Anthony the Eremite would be a tribute to an Egyptian hermit, with more references to Nicollet and the quest. *I've given him a decade of my life. Where will be my tributes?*

Finally, Stewart left the stakes and walked over to the large oak tree where Clément fumed.

"It's all settled. My uncle's estate of Logiealmond is sold, and I am once again a very wealthy man."

"Does that mean we will go back to the frontier?" Clément asked.

"Eventually," Stewart said, leaning his arm against the tree. "Nicollet's methodical scientific strategies will cause him to study every headwater west of the Mississippi before he reaches any conclusions, allowing us time to explore another headwater."

"Another headwater? Where are we going?"

"This tale does not end with the discovery of Fort L'Huillier or the Philosopher's Stone," Stewart said. "We are going to Benias Falls along with a few other key stops."

"Benias Falls? What is that?"

"Once, it was believed to be the Gateway of the Underworld. It is the headwaters of the Jordan River. You and I are going to take a trip to the Holy Land before we resume our part in Nicollet's adventure."

CHAPTER FIFTY-ONE
THE HAUNTED VALLEY
1838

Am I James St. Clair or Wounded Man? Sergeant Jim Taopi reached under his hat to itch the place where scar met hair. A carefully-crafted lie had given them five days to discover what the stars wanted. At the end of the five days, Nicollet would be dead or a great secret would be revealed.

The four of them stood on the edge of the Haunted Valley.

Two weeks earlier, Taopi listened as Waneta gave him clear orders from his father, Chief Wahanantan: *Bring Nicollet to the Haunted Valley, and the will of the Great Spirit will be revealed.* Waneta also spoke to Nicollet about Mahkato, but said nothing about the terrible legends regarding the place.

Taopi—Wounded Man—owed his life to the mercy of Chief Wahanantan of the Yankton, and as a result, he obeyed the order, even if it meant the death of his dear friend. The entire expedition departed Lac Qui Parle and traveled down the Minisotah River for the next eight days until they reached the camp of Sleepy Eyes at the mouth of the Cottonwood River. It was there that Nicollet crafted his lie, claiming to Frémont and the others that he intended to vacation with Chief Sleepy Eyes for another five days but would then reunite with the others at the Traverse des Sioux before ending the expedition at Fort Snelling.

Believing the lie, everyone but Joe Laframboise and Karl Geyer went ahead, with Frémont mapping the last segment on his own. The following day, Nicollet, Laframboise, Geyer, and Taopi immediately left Sleepy Eyes' home and headed for the Haunted Valley two days' ride to the south.

Does Nicollet understand the dangers we face tomorrow? Taopi now wondered. *How much should I tell him?*

The Haunted Valley was located more than a hundred miles downstream from the comforts of Renville's home at Lac Qui Parle, and a day's ride south of the great bend in the Minisotah River. As a boy, Taopi knew a punishment worse than beatings or floggings waited in the deep valley, yet now he stood on the edge of a fate worse than death.

I must be brave for my people.

I must be loyal to the wishes of my chief.

If it is the will of the Great Spirit that I die with Nicollet, so be it...

Superstition and fear gnawed at him, and Taopi cradled his rifle in his hands as he looked down at the confluence of the Watonwan and Mahkato Rivers. *An Unktehi lives in these waters, waiting to kill the unsuspecting traveler. How can I protect Nicollet from a faceless evil?*

But loyalty—and two life debts—gave him little choice in the matter.

THE ALCHEMIST'S MAP

"Taopi, are you hungry?" Laframboise asked from the little campfire. "This buffalo meat will go bad if we don't eat the rest today."

"I'm not hungry. How can I eat near this place?" Taopi asked bitterly. Geyer grinned at Nicollet.

"Are you frightened, Taopi?" Laframboise teased.

"You only mock me because the Unktehi that lives here provokes you, so I will forget anything you say."

"What is this 'Unktehi?'" Nicollet asked.

"An Unktehi is an evil water spirit."

"Like a manito?"

"Yes, many believe it is a water serpent, but it is much more than that. Evil dwells near us, which is why Laframboise taunted me. The closer we get, the darker our thoughts will become. We near the domain of No Soul."

"From the story of 'Wishwee and the White Egg?'"

Taopi nodded. "You wish to visit the old soldier fort at Mahkato, but across the river lies the Haunted Valley. If evil does not wait in the shadows, it is because it has already reached our hearts."

Nicollet showed no fear. "I trust Karl as a brother, and Laframboise is as noble as a Knight of the Round Table. I would have them with me, if they are willing. But your counsel I hold over all others. Tell me more, Sergeant. Why does this place concern you so?"

"I have heard stories about this place since I was a child. Evil dwells in this valley, waiting to claim another victim. Laframboise, certainly you have heard the tale of the murderous rampage of John Moredock. This valley causes all, white or Indian, to turn evil."

"What about the story of No Soul?" Nicollet pressed, as if he didn't already know the tale.

Back in Fort Atkinson, Taopi repeatedly heard tales about the Mahkato from more than just the tribes of the Sioux. The Chippewa,

Winnebago, Sauk and Fox, and even Potawatomi told tales about the place where none of them dared hunt because of the ghosts that lived there. His whole life he had avoided this place, but now his nightmares had found him.

Perhaps my heart will calm if I say the story aloud. "There once was a Sioux warrior whose name was Wishwee."

"Wishwee?" Nicollet immediately interrupted. "I thought that—"

"This story is a fable, and I do not know if it is a tale of the past or a prophecy of what is to come. Do you still want to hear it?"

Nicollet nodded.

So Taopi continued, "Wishwee grew up at the most beautiful place on earth, with a calm pool that fed many waters and whose trees were the oldest and most beautiful on earth. But Wishwee's heart grew restless after he visited the Haunted Valley, and he cursed his father's ways and left his village to explore the lands of the earth in order to understand the great mystery."

"Sounds like your friend Poinsett," Laframboise muttered, but a harsh look from Nicollet shut him up, allowing Taopi to continue.

"This young warrior traveled the world, becoming very wise but also very dark. Finally, he traveled to a land far to the north, where the world was old and covered totally in rock and stone. There, Old Man waited, anticipating Wishwee's arrival in his dreams. You see, in the land of stone, where no other life exists, dreams of the past and future echo loudly in the void. So Old Man, who knew the terrible mistake young Wishwee was about to make, tried to stop the future from happening.

"'Stop, young man. The way you seek is filled with darkness. It has already claimed my soul, and the souls of my daughters, and so too will it claim yours if you continue on this path.'

"Undeterred, Wishwee followed the North Star until he came to the cave where the monster slept. When Wishwee finally found No

THE ALCHEMIST'S MAP

Soul, it took the form of a great bear."

"A bear?" Nicollet again interrupted the story. "Are you sure the legend spoke of a great bear far to the north?"

Laframboise smirked and shook his head in resignation. Even Geyer seemed dismayed by this little detail, sighing deeply before looking up at the leaves above them and saying, "Ursa Major."

"Yes, Professor, but No Soul could take many forms. He just took the form of a bear to frighten young Wishwee. But Wishwee was not afraid, because in his travels, his soul had become quite black and no longer had room for fear. He wrestled the great bear, trying to kill it.

"'Fool,' the great bear said. 'You cannot kill me. I am death itself.'

"But the Great Thunderbird then appeared, swooping down to scare No Soul back into the cave, and leaving behind a white egg for Wishwee. Taking the egg, Wishwee returned to the cave where No Soul slept, and once inside, Wishwee smote No Soul, killing him and freeing the souls kept by the monster."

Nicollet turned, attempting to get to his feet, but instead only managed to scramble away from their circle on all fours, where he threw up his supper of buffalo meat. With a grin and an eye roll, Nicollet wiped his chin. "Strange timing for that."

Karl Geyer stood up and walked over to his mentor, rubbing the man's back gently. "It will be okay, Professor Nicollet. It will be okay."

Laframboise seemed ready to curse, his jaw locked and twisted.

Speaking the tale did not help my fears afterall, Taopi realized, feeling the hairs on the back of his neck stand on edge despite the heat of the summer evening and their fire.

"What's wrong, Professor?" Taopi called out to his dearest friend.

"I apologize, Jim. It has been a very long journey for me and my delicate stomach."

"Do you think my concerns are foolish?"

"No, I agree we should approach this place with respect. But your story of Wishwee confused me. The wandering shaman I met was looking for Wishwee because he believed he was a hero who would fight No Soul."

"Stories change in the telling."

Nicollet stood to walk back to the small campfire when he turned. Laframboise grabbed his rifle.

Taopi also heard it—galloping horses.

Luckily, only two figures appeared from the west, yet seemed to know exactly where they would be camped.

One of the two figures Taopi immediately recognized as a companion from the last two months. The other was a man restored.

Iron Walker and Sleepy Eyes.

Fully healed, Chief Sleepy Eyes rode right up on their camp and slid off his horse to land between the four men.

Even though Taopi and Laframboise were armed, the sheer size of Sleepy Eyes, now healed from his knife wound, made Taopi's confidence quiver.

"My friend, I am glad to see you again," Sleepy Eyes began as he loomed over Nicollet, but then he knelt down on the ground, almost cowering until he was lower than the little scientist. "You have left me sad. I asked myself if I was a squaw. I, whom the fear of death, wars, and pain has never stopped."

Sleepy Eyes looked up and out over the lush green valley.

Will he kill us for entering the Haunted Valley?

"You are going to risk dangers," Sleepy Eyes declared. "I will not leave you."

CHAPTER FIFTY-TWO

BLUE EARTH RIVER
1838

Karl Geyer sat alone, angry that Nicollet would not confide in him his secrets. The great scientific expedition of the prairie had abruptly turned into a secret mission akin to robbing the tomb of an ancient pharaoh. Sleepy Eyes, Taopi, and Nicollet whispered, pointed, and drew in the dirt while Joe Laframboise watched the shadows for enemies. Karl Geyer's only companion was his notebook.

Tuesday, August 14th, 1838

We left our encampment at seven-thirty in the morning and crossed the Watonwan branch of the Mahkato River with some difficulty.

> *At the spot where we crossed, the Watonwan is nearly sixty feet, with an average depth of three feet. Its waters are clear and navigation by canoe sure. The meaning of the river is strange, signifying something akin to "he who watches everything." The main river means "Blue Earth River."*
>
> *Here, the river is very interesting. We found stratified banks, twenty to eighty feet high, of sandstone and limestone, filled up with shrubbery. The scenery is beautiful; the river is interrupted often by rocks and rapids. I was unable to ascertain the variety of timber on either side of the river on account of the high water. It is said that the black walnut and butternut are abundant. Red cedar and oaks dress these rocks, as well.*
>
> *We camp at noon, stopping at a large Sandbar Island, which is below a field of rapids almost a half mile in length.*

Nicollet stood on the sandy shore of the Blue Earth River, looking out at the field of boulders.

After carefully preparing some sort of talisman, Sleepy Eyes finally rose from his seat at Laframboise's lunch camp and walked over to where Nicollet stood looking across the thousand fingers of the river.

Nicollet did not want Frémont and the others to come to this place, but why?

Although Geyer couldn't hear what was said over the light roar of the water, Nicollet tenderly patted the massive Indian on the shoulder. Geyer jumped to his feet when Sleepy Eyes gingerly stepped into the current.

"What's he doing?" Geyer shouted over to Nicollet.

"He's making an offering to the evil spirits," Nicollet said as the chief's long legs sank deep into the current. Unlike further upstream, where the Blue Earth had cut through fifty to a hundred feet of bedrock,

THE ALCHEMIST'S MAP

the banks here were only thirty feet high but filled with rocks of various sizes, making Sleepy Eyes' trek across the channel even more precarious.

Taopi, Iron Walker, and Laframboise joined Geyer at the water's edge in case Sleepy Eyes was swept away and into the swirling pool at the base of the rapids, but the tall Sioux kept his footing and soon began to climb out of the swiftly flowing water.

On the other side of the river's deepest current, the Blue Earth River flowed around two massive boulders in its middle. A mile away, the boulders had been visible despite the drop in elevation, but now, the seven-foot giant seemed dwarfed by both boulders. Standing in knee-deep water at the base of the twenty-foot boulders, Sleepy Eyes could find no handhold on the smooth stone, so he skirted around the base of the boulder until he reached the back side, where smaller stones allowed him to climb it like a ladder. Hauling his long, lean torso onto the smaller companion stone, Sleepy Eyes spread his arms and with a thrust from his leg, launched himself up and onto the rounded boulder.

As Sleepy Eyes stood, Laframboise began to clap and soon all five men applauded the efforts of their champion. But then he placed the talisman on top of the stone and began to sing a Sioux prayer.

"What is he saying?" Geyer asked Laframboise, who watched with squinted eyes.

"He prays... to the Great Spirit to protect us from the evil spirits... as we enter the Valley of Death. He... is mentioning each of us by name with a special prayer that we may pass through this place unharmed... and join our companions again... at the Traverse des Sioux."

When the prayers ended, Sleepy Eyes walked back through the water again, where Laframboise and Nicollet waited with extended hands to snatch him from the current.

A mile from the big glacial boulders, the men stopped at a place to cross the Blue Earth River, allowing Geyer a moment to once again make an entry in his journal. While Nicollet's interests always took precedent, Geyer had maintained a careful journal, marking the place and time he collected his botanical specimens. With the wagon full of flora and geological samples, his journal would allow him to publish and lecture for a decade, first in the east and then back home in Germany.

At three o'clock, we reached the confluence of the Blue Earth River and an eastern tributary. The two banks remain forty to fifty feet high, but across the confluence, the bank is an additional sixty feet, making the cliff one hundred to one hundred twenty feet high. Our two guides indicate that the large bluff is the place where blue earth is found.

CHAPTER FIFTY-THREE
FORT L'HUILLIER
1838

Nicollet looked up at the tall bluff from the base of the river and understood how men from the Le Sueur expedition could see a mountain. His heart steadied from the crossing of the river and he prepared himself for the arduous hike up the bluff. Eight years after looking at the Alchemist's Map, he stood a hundred feet from an answer.

He looked back down at his group. *Is the chief crying?*

Sleepy Eyes crouched down on the shore, Iron Walker standing at his father's side. Both Taopi and Laframboise looked away, giving the mighty chief a moment of privacy.

Perhaps this place is indeed haunted. Our greatest warrior is crumbling before my eyes. Having earlier heard the Sisseton chief's confession, Nicollet knew one thing he would find at the top of the hill, however gruesome.

Karl remains neutral. I will bring him with me. "Are you ready, Karl?"

"As always, Professor Nicollet," Geyer said with enthusiasm.

Back in St. Louis, Nicollet had crossed paths with Karl Geyer by chance. With no allegiance to the government, freemasonry, the Order of Eos, the Periphery, the Jesuits, or the Catholic Church, the young botanist lingered in St. Louis hoping to join an expedition going anywhere. *An impartial witness.*

Le Sueur's fabled mountain did not stretch for seven miles, and in just five minutes, Nicollet and Geyer found the slope on the southern side far easier to scale than the steep western face where they had crossed. Even here, though, Nicollet had to grab roots, rocks, and branches for handholds as he ascended the bluff.

"What am I looking for?" Geyer said a few feet behind.

"Oxidized copper residue," Nicollet said. "'Mahkato,' as Waneta called it. Blue earth."

"In a sandstone bluff?"

"There must be some reason for its namesake," Nicollet said, hoping not to be disappointed once again. *Let there be some magic left in the world.*

Once Nicollet reached the pinnacle of his climb, he did find something unexpected. As soon as he stepped out of the way, Geyer echoed his thoughts.

"What in the world is this?" Geyer exclaimed.

"Curious, isn't it?" Nicollet admitted, taking a few steps forward.

Despite having dense vegetation along the slope of the bluff, the top of it was bald, covered only by a layer of waist-high grass. The teardrop-shaped area stretched three hundred feet from nose to tail and

THE ALCHEMIST'S MAP

was a hundred feet across at its widest point. The little sliver of elevated prairie had a harmonious feeling, with small butterflies flitting from wildflower to wildflower.

Atop the bluff, Nicollet also had a better view of the valley. To the west, from where they'd come, he could see the distant valley wall where the Watonwan River met the Mahkato. To the south and east, he could see the course of the converging river, where it met at the steep footing at the base of the bluff. To the north, he could see another valley wall where the flow of all three rivers led to the Minisotah. The area resembled a green bowl nearly four miles in diameter.

Karl Geyer began to explore the grass, more interested in the flowers than in finding any copper vitriol. Nicollet stood with his hands on his hips, finally understanding why previous explorers had declared Fort L'Huillier a fraudulent legend.

"Joseph," Karl Geyer called out suddenly, waving his hands. Nicollet jogged over and stopped in his tracks when he looked down at a collection of skeletons with pieces of flesh and clothing still clinging to their bones. "Where are their heads?"

"Veritas caput," Nicollet muttered. *Itasca, the truth about the head.*

From the edge of the bluff, Sleepy Eyes plowed through the grass towards them, followed by Iron Walker, Taopi, and Laframboise. Soon, they all stood around the corpses.

"These men were Tizaptanon," Sleepy Eyes explained. "We killed them for desecrating a sacred place."

Of course. This is how Sleepy Eyes received his wound. This is how he collected the scalp of Ohanzee, the man who almost killed me. "Why were they here?"

"To hide. Only foreigners would willingly enter the Haunted Valley, or fugitives from the law. The only reason we knew they were here was the smoke from their fire."

"What do you mean, you saw smoke from their fire? Were they camped here?"

"The vile Tizaptanons have strange beliefs and rituals, and from time to time, they return here and burn everything in sight, keeping the hilltop free of trees. My hunters from Swan Lake saw the smoke and alerted me, which is why I came here two summers ago."

According to the legend, Fort L'Huillier was burned by Fox Indians. But what if it was the Tizaptanons? A wooden stockade with wooden buildings—nothing would remain after a hundred and forty years, especially if these wild zealots kept burning it. "Waneta said this place was Mahkato, the place of the blue earth, yet I don't see any sign of blue earth."

"The earth stopped bleeding long ago," Sleepy Eyes said with his head hung low. "For a long time, our warriors continued coming here to harvest this blue paint for our ceremonies, but now the supply is gone."

"Is the blue earth found elsewhere?"

"No, this is a sacred spot. This is the heart of the Haunted Valley," Sleepy Eyes explained. "The most recent explorers visited a spot near the mouth of the Mahkato River."

As they all studied the bald bluff, Sleepy Eyes knelt in the grass. The powerful war chief soon began to weep again, drawing everyone to his side. "We took their heads for profaning this place, leaving them on the edges of the valley as a warning to travelers. I can only pray that the Great Spirit will forgive the barbarity of my actions."

"Perhaps we could give them a proper Christian burial," Nicollet offered, his hand upon Sleepy Eyes' strong back.

Sleepy Eyes consented. "But not here, lest they be tormented by the spirit of No Soul."

Taopi was not pleased. "Professor Nicollet, we only have a few hours of daylight left. We cannot stay in such a place tonight."

THE ALCHEMIST'S MAP

"There is time," Nicollet said, but he also knew his five-day lie was soon expiring, and Frémont's expedition would expect him at Traverse des Sioux in two days.

Laframboise procured a large burlap sack and the five men set about collecting the bones of the slain Tizaptanons.

Nicollet bent down, and after removing some of the grass, he found chunks of coal in the topsoil. *Hardly evidence of a fort.*

While they gathered the bodies and their separated skulls, Nicollet pondered the view from the bluff in all directions. Cleared of trees, it would provide a full view of the valley. An ambitious commander would clear the bluff and also the trees around it.

According to legend, Pierre-Charles Le Sueur first discovered a great mound of copper vitriol hundreds of miles into Dakota Territory upon a river described by Baron Lahontan as "The Long River." With a hired crew of nearly twenty men, they built a fort and then mined this strange copper, sending barges all the way down the river to the Gulf of Mexico.

"So this is what you were searching for?" Joe Laframboise asked softly as they returned from burying the dead.

Nicollet did not answer. Instead, he walked to the edge of the bluff, looking out to the east. With his hands on his hips, he looked down at a series of ponds on the valley floor. "Does this valley flood often?"

"It floods every few years, covering the valley floor," Sleepy Eyes explained. "There are many small rivers that empty near here."

"What is the name of the southern tributary?"

"There are many rivers that flow from the south and east," Sleepy Eyes said. "The Tewapadan, the Tewapa-tankiyan, Psah, Chankasna..."

Nicollet nodded, a smile forming on the corners of his mouth. He ran across the expanse of the grass-covered bluff, standing on the southwestern edge where he could see a river coming from the southeast to meet the Blue Earth flowing from the southwest. He laughed to himself, only to see looks of incredulity from his friends. *A place where the water flows in all directions!*

Nicollet walked to the edge of the bluff to find a stick. In the dirt, he began to draw with the end of the stick. "For a hundred years, everyone has assumed that Baron Lahontan's 'Long River' was the Mississippi, but the source of the Mississippi is just a series of swamps where the water slowly trickles over stone, with no mountains anywhere in sight. So next I went to the Coteau, where the majestic ridge sent the Sioux River flowing south, the Red River flowing north, and the Minisotah River flowing to the east. But not only was there no Turtle Island, there was also no sign Lahontan or Le Sueur had ever been there."

The distinct "V" of the Minisotah River soon took shape, and Nicollet began to fill in the other rivers. "From this bluff, we can look out and see water flowing in all directions. The Minisotah flows to the south, only to turn direction and flow north. The Watonwan flows from the west, only to join with the Mahkato, which flows from the south. From the south and east, the Tewapa-Tankiyan and the Tewapadan join the Chankasna to meet at the base of this bluff. This is the place where water flows in all directions."

Have I finally found the land of the Undine?

At that, Nicollet walked back over to the eastern edge to look down at the ponds again.

"We must go before we all lose our minds," Taopi insisted.

"I'm not losing my mind, Taopi," Nicollet insisted and stared out at the valley for a moment longer. *But where is the Philosopher's Stone? Did Le Sueur take it to France? Was it Chagobay's mysterious Water Drum? Or is it the White Egg of the Sioux?*

When he'd first looked at the Alchemist's Map, it transported him to a place of magic and wonder, but looking down at the valley from the bluff, the lack of tangible magic left him disappointed, however

THE ALCHEMIST'S MAP

beautiful the natural scenery proved to be.

Nicollet went back to his drawing in the dirt and saw something new. The Minisotah formed the first pyramid, the alchemical sign for Undine, the water element. The other rivers flowed from the west and east, forming another pyramid, this one the alchemical sign for Salamander, the fire element.

At the place where Nicollet's group stood, these two pyramids came together, forming a new symbol... the symbol for copper.

Copper.

Just as the drawing of the waterway now had two meanings, Nicollet also searched the valley for two meanings.

"Thirty thousand pounds of ore," the Le Sueur narrative described. *Le Sueur and his men dug for months. Even with annual flooding, there would still be—*

At the bottom of the eastern side of the bluff, opposite the river, Nicollet spotted a small pond. Without any explanation, he suddenly began to run.

CHAPTER FIFTY-FOUR
FORT L'HUILLIER
1838

By the time the others reached Nicollet, he was crying. *I must look like a fool to these men.*

"Professor Nicollet. What is wrong?" Geyer asked, crouching beside him.

"We should just pick him up and drag him away," Taopi said. "Or soon we will all be crying like old women."

They knew what I would find. They all knew I would fail.

Without the restraint of time, Nicollet knew he could have engineered a way to remove the water from the pond, but even if he did and happened to find Le Sueur's mineshaft at the bottom of the pond, he knew it would be a colossal waste of time and energy.

THE ALCHEMIST'S MAP

Le Sueur did not leave Fort L'Huillier empty-handed. "Do you know, gentlemen, we are more likely than not the first white men to stand in this place for more than a century?"

Finding this place was no great mystery. They knew I would not find the Philosopher's Stone because it had already been found—by Le Sueur. "The Mahkato. That is the name of the river?"

"Mahkato Osa Watapa," Sleepy Eyes repeated. "The river where the blue earth is gathered."

Nothing about the area indicated the presence of copper. "But there is no blue earth. You said it yourself—the earth stopped bleeding long ago." *To think, you allowed yourself to believe you were Wishwee, wielder of the White Egg.*

"Professor Nicollet," Taopi grabbed hold of his shoulder. "We must leave this place."

Nicollet allowed himself to be stood up, and soon, all five of them walked along the edge of the pond, heading north toward the Traverse des Sioux. Nicollet mustered no energy to stay, even though he'd most likely reached the destination described on all three maps. His victory had been hollow. There was no proof for any of it, let alone the actual Philosopher's Stone.

Well, that's strange.

Despite the tug at his arms, Nicollet planted his feet firmly so he could get another glance at the oddity. Brushing Taopi and Laframboise away, he turned.

Is that what I think it is?

"We need to go, Professor."

It didn't matter that the sun was setting on the Haunted Valley. *I did not travel to the far side of the world to leave empty-handed.*

He walked back toward the pond, studying the irregularity from both sides.

"What is it?" Karl Geyer asked, joining him as the others stood where Nicollet had begun his retreat.

The entire valley was filled with soft sediments from a thousand seasons of flooding. Although the river was a few hundred yards away to the west, Nicollet could easily imagine spring flooding that would cover the valley floor to the spot he stood, leaving deposits of silt while eroding anything that stood against the flow.

According to Lahontan's tale, he found a massive mound of copper vitriol, where he planted a French land claim.

The mound Nicollet studied was not copper vitriol, yet there it sat along the shore of an unnatural pond. The grassy mound rose almost eight feet from the edge of the pond, with its base claiming an area almost twenty feet in diameter. A thousand years of rain or floods would have obliterated the soft mound.

A hundred years…

"Laframboise, your shovel please," Nicollet said.

"Professor, I must agree with Taopi. We should not stay here overnight. The others will be waiting for us at the Traverse tomorrow, and if we are to avoid suspicion—"

Nicollet could wait no longer. Rushing to the edge of the mound, his fingers began to claw away at the grass until he revealed the soft sediment underneath.

Pierre-Charles Le Sueur had found the same copper mound five years prior to Lahontan, but when he returned, he returned with a professional mining crew. Thirty thousand pounds of copper ore were extracted.

"This would be much easier if you would lend the aid of your shovel," Nicollet prompted Laframboise again.

For the next twenty minutes, they all dug in the sandy mound like maniacal children playing on a beach. As they reached the original

THE ALCHEMIST'S MAP

surface of the valley floor, a strange blue-green substance, only an inch or so in depth, could be found, marking where the excavation had begun a hundred and forty years earlier.

"Visita interiora terrae rectificando invenies occultum lapidem," Nicollet said as he rubbed the oily blue sand between his fingers.

"What do you mean, Professor?" Taopi asked.

"Vitriol. Copper residue. Mahkato Osa Watapa. The place where the blue earth is gathered. Hand me one of the tin containers in my bag, Jim."

I have evidence, even if it is circumstantial.

Taopi quickly knelt and handed Nicollet one of the same specimen containers he'd used up north at Lake Manito. He carefully scooped the vitriol into the tin and sealed it. "It is no wonder the earth stopped bleeding, Sleepy Eyes. Someone dug it all up and sent it down the Mississippi."

Yet a hundred and forty years later, madmen are still chasing after the Philosopher's Stone. If Le Sueur unearthed the stone, something went terribly wrong afterwards. What didn't the Church tell me?

With the tin container in his hand, Nicollet marked it with the alchemical symbol for copper, and then with English letters, he wrote a single word.

Undine.

CHAPTER FIFTY-FIVE

ALBANY, NEW YORK

1838

Jacques Palissy took a deep breath, knowing that the letter contained everything his benefactor sought. He stood from his desk at the post office in Albany and closed his door, turning the lock.

In the decade since coming to America, Palissy had set up a network of spies throughout the postal system. Unlike France, where war had driven the radicals and subversives into secret societies, the plotting in America happened in the open.

Imagine if we'd killed Nicollet, Palissy evaluated. *The enemies of Manifest Destiny would still be hidden in the shadows.*

Now, they came to the light of Palissy's desk lamp.

THE ALCHEMIST'S MAP

TUESDAY, AUGUST 28th, 1838
MENDOTA

To the honorable Mr. Delhut,

The Nicollet Expedition returned three days ago to the comforts of Fort Snelling, and in that time, I was able to gather the requested information about their comings and goings.

True to his word and purpose, Nicollet primarily toured the watershed of the St. Peter River, which he now calls the Minisotah River. Thanks to the observations of my servant, the expedition cook, I also learned that Nicollet managed to visit another watershed along the way—the headwaters of the Des Moines River. Let it be known that at the headwaters of the Des Moines, Nicollet visited a lake with a distinct island, which he calls "Shetek."

Following his detour away from the St. Peter, he next went to the place where the Indians make their pipes, where Nicollet used dynamite to quarry some of the stone. My man closely observed the mining and claims nothing beyond the red pipestone was unearthed. He also saw nothing resembling copper in the process.

After these two curiosities, Nicollet regained focus and mapped the great ridge before returning to the river at Renville's outpost at Lac Qui Parle. While staying here, Nicollet behaved suspiciously when he departed with a single canoe to explore the region around the headwaters of the St. Peter. Although my man did not go with him, he was able to converse with one of Renville's guests, who gave an uneventful account of what they saw. It should also be noted that Nicollet did not return with anything from this outing.

In early August, the entire expedition returned, with Nicollet traveling by canoe down the length of the St. Peter. Nicollet and the wagons reunited at the Cottonwood River, where he remained the guest of a Sioux Chief for five days. After that, the entire expedition returned along the trail from the Traverse des Sioux.

Although Nicollet's purpose has been fulfilled, he has not made plans to return to St. Louis. Although his expedition was a scientific success, it does seem Nicollet has not found what he, or we, were looking for, and he appears to be preparing to explore other watersheds before winter arrives.

Your loyal servant,
Hank

Palissy folded the letter, and began his own letter telling his benefactor about his suspicions of Solomon Delhut of Detroit.

CHAPTER FIFTY-SIX
FARIBAULT VILLAGE
1838

Faribault Village, built at the confluence of the Cannon River and Straight River, was a collection of log cabins and buildings purchased by Jean-Baptiste Faribault from a fur-trader that had gone out of business during the summer of 1837. Although Faribault had officially retired at his new home a short distance from the one built by Hank Sibley, he helped his sons build a new settlement away from the shadow of Fort Snelling.

With the collapse of the fur trade industry the previous summer, and a smallpox epidemic to the west, the region south of Fort Snelling had become largely abandoned, with even the Warpekutey band of Dakota vanishing. Miles from civilization on the edge of the Big Woods,

Jean-Baptiste Faribault had decided to build his city.

Thirty-three years prior in 1805, after years of trading in Canada and Michigan, Jean-Baptiste Faribault had married Elizabeth Pelagie Ainse, the daughter of a British superintendent and a Sioux woman. With the help of his and Elizabeth's now-grown sons, Oliver, David, and Alexander, the village at the edge of the Big Woods quickly grew to twenty buildings that housed several pioneer families and missionaries.

Following this, Alexander Faribault was chosen to lead the ambitious effort of the Frémont Expedition to map the wild Zumbro River while Davey Faribault, who had completed his military service, would lead the Nicollet Expedition up the placid Cannon River.

With winter quickly approaching, Nicollet knew he could not afford to stay long. Two days after arriving in Faribault, his smaller expedition departed to map the Cannon River with a Faribault now beside him on the wagon.

No longer did he have Laframboise, Sleepy Eyes, Renville, Iron Walker, or even Eugene Flandin. Fortunately, Taopi was able to come, and Karl Geyer heartily agreed to join him to collect even more botanical samples, but beyond them, Nicollet was left with the empty friendships of Viscount de Montmort, Captain Belligny, Big Moe Maxwell, and a surly teen Indian guide, Stands on Clouds.

After half a day of silence, Davey Faribault finally said, "I was told you intend to go farther than Lake Tetonka."

Taopi and De Smet trust this family with my secrets. Should I? "Yes. From what I understand, Lake Tetonka is the source of the Cannon River."

"It's the westernmost source."

"Our friend Taopi also told me that the LaPrelle River has its source near Lake Tetonka before it flows west all the way to the Mahkato River."

THE ALCHEMIST'S MAP

"Yes, the LaPrelle starts at Lake Okamon."

"Then I want to travel to the place between these two watersheds," Nicollet said, picturing the Lahontan map in his mind. He had found Fort L'Huillier. Now he meant to retrace Lahontan's journey up the Longue River on his way to the Undine.

The wagons continued to roll through the grass hills that overlooked the flat prairie surrounding the Cannon River. After a prolonged silence, Davey Faribault added, "There is a name for that place."

The Undine? Nicollet secretly wondered. "There is?"

"Yes, it is called 'Waseca,' which means fertile land. Many of the Warpekutey gather there because it is so lovely. We'll make camp there. Where do you plan to go after that?"

"I'm searching for the pot of gold at the end of the rainbow."

Faribault squinted his eyes. "I'm not sure I know what you're talking about, Professor Nicollet."

"Nor do I," Nicollet laughed. *Do I speak plainly with him about the other clues I seek? The Seven Fires quest ends with a turtle-shaped island.* "I met a Sioux man who spoke of a place called 'Mni Wakan.'"

"In the Iowa territory?" Faribault clarified.

"No," Nicollet scoffed, knowing Chief Wahanantan resided there far to the north, yet Faribault seemed to know immediately what he spoke of. *Surely it is not the same Spirit Lake.* "Mni Wakan is nearby?"

"It would take a few weeks to reach it, but half of the distance will be covered simply by following the Cannon River to Waseca."

"How do you know of this place? Have you been there?"

"No, but many of the local Warpekutey stay there during the winter. It is why our territory is now so empty. It is a sacred place to them."

How many Spirit Lakes exist? Nicollet wondered, but understood that these secrets were protected by the Guardians of the Frontier.

Faribault continued, "If we have luck on our side, we can go there and back before the snow flies. What's so special about Spirit Lake?"

"It is difficult to explain," Nicollet said and turned around to look at the wagons following. "What did Father De Smet say of my expedition?"

"I was told you were a sheep surrounded by wolves," Faribault said, frowning. "If you want, Taopi and I can bring you the whole way."

"No. I must not raise too many concerns. I must play the role of mapmaker first and foremost, and you must play the role of guide. Understood?"

Davey Faribault nodded.

The Cannon River flowed in a generally western direction from Faribault Village. Never much wider than twenty yards as it flowed through grassy meadows, it did occasionally open up to a series of narrow lakes. By wagon, it took the expedition four days to reach the source of the Cannon River.

There, in a seasonal village once occupied by Sioux, Nicollet found his nerve to explain more to Faribault.

"I am told by Father De Smet that you are a young man who can be trusted," Nicollet said that evening as the voyageurs prepared supper and the other men assisted Geyer with his botanical collection. "That you are an ally."

Faribault nodded again, staying quiet.

"Don't be ashamed. When I was a young man, and the armies of Napoleon marched on the town of Cluses, my mother stood me before a group of criminals," Nicollet scoffed. "They were actually Jesuit priests, but criminals to Napoleon.

"My mother knew these men would be killed if they were captured. But she also already knew that we were being watched. So she stood me in front of those men and told them that I could be trusted. I took them through winding paths in the French Alps and helped smuggle them out of the country. When I returned some weeks later, my house was

THE ALCHEMIST'S MAP

gone and my mother had been killed, along with... others."

Nicollet paused for a few moments, seeing a pale face looking up at him through water. "So I ask you, young Davey Faribault, are you indeed a man who can be trusted?"

Faribault looked over at him and nodded again.

"Good," Nicollet patted his knee, stood up suddenly, and then shouting out to the others, said, "David is going to show me a spot where the Sioux buried their dead. We will be back in time for supper."

Nicollet smiled and then began walking toward the shores of Lake Okamon.

"Professor Nicollet, I don't know of any burial grounds."

"I know, but it will give us a chance to be alone for a while. Tomorrow, as you know, I am going to unexpectedly continue on my journey to Spirit Lake."

"Yes."

"And you've been very tight-lipped the whole trip. My father would have respected your locked jaw. He always found me to be a bit too social. My younger half-brothers were much more to his liking. Even though I made him proud by smuggling those Jesuit priests, I do not think the rest of my life's choices have made him especially proud of me."

"But you are a renowned scientist."

"My father didn't put much stock in that. Before Napoleon came, he was a watchmaker by trade, and he always reminded me about the value of time. Now that I am older, I understand how precious time truly is. I wasted half of my life watching the world go by before I actually went out and did something. Now, I fear, I don't have enough time left to truly do something of value."

"You worry that winter will come too soon?"

Nicollet laughed loudly, and then noticed Faribault's sincerity. "No, I really wasn't worried about an early winter. I am fifty-two years old, and I am feeling every day of it. I worry that I do not have enough time to unravel this mystery that has been set before me."

Faribault asked no questions but simply walked along with Nicollet. Massive cottonwood trees that towered a hundred feet into the air fringed Lake Okamon. The trunks of these majestic trees were as thick as a man was tall, and as they passed, Nicollet put his hands on them as if greeting old familiar friends.

"I want you to look at this drawing for me," Nicollet said as he pulled the piece of paper out of his vest pocket. "Tell me what you see."

After looking at it for a few minutes, Faribault finally answered, "This is the Cannon River."

Nicollet clapped his hands together. "Ah, but according to Lewis Cass, Zebulon Pike, Giacomo Beltrami, and Henry Schoolcraft, you are wrong."

"So it's not the Cannon River?"

"No, it is the *Longue* River. This is a map made by Louis-Armand de Lom d'Arce, Baron of Lahontan. For a hundred and thirty years, it has puzzled those who have looked at it. Do you see these headwaters? How they form two rivers that flow in opposite directions? Many people believed this was the source of the Mississippi River. Others looked at this ridge where the two rivers form, and believed it was the Rocky Mountains, meaning this is the Missouri River, far west of here. Some have even speculated it to be the Minisotah River."

"But you think they are all wrong," Faribault surmised.

"Baron Lahontan journeyed to a place called 'The Undine.' Are you familiar with this word?"

Faribault shook his head.

"Good. Forget I ever said it. In his journals, he described meeting the Tanuglauk Indians at a place where the earth bled blue from a great mound of vitriol. Have you ever heard of the Tanuglauk tribe?

THE ALCHEMIST'S MAP

Faribault shook his head.

"Or the Gnacsitares and Mozeemleks?"

Again, he shook his head.

"Exactly what those who followed him thought. Only, Pierre-Charles Le Sueur managed to return a decade later, finding a similar place where the earth bled blue. After he abandoned his mine, history lost all records of what ever happened to Fort L'Huillier. Experts began to dismiss both accounts. First they claimed that Lahontan's voyage was a complete fabrication, and later they even discredited Le Sueur, claiming both men made exaggerated accounts."

"What do you think?"

"I think we are standing upon Lahontan's map. I think these little hills are the cause of two rivers flowing in opposite directions. The Longue River is none other than the Cannon, which flows east to the Mississippi. Tomorrow, you will guide me to the other river, which forms near this place where Lahontan met his fictitious tribe."

"The Rivière LaPrelle?"

"Yes. I've labeled it as 'Le Sueur River' on my map, just as I have renamed the Cannon River, 'Lahontan River.' Do you know what Lahontan called the river upon which Le Sueur built his fort and mined the earth?"

Faribault shook his head.

"He called it 'La Rivière Morte.'"

"The River of Death," Faribault answered, translating the French. "'Yunke-lo' is the Sioux name. I assumed it was because of all the trees that plug the river."

"I must seem like a crazy old wizard to you." *The Undine, an ancient water spirit, a white egg, blue earth, Spirit Lake, Turtle Island, Wishwee, a Great Bear, a Great Thunderbird, a Seven-Headed Dragon, Seven Fires, Seven Council Fires; have I gone mad?*

"This is far more interesting than being home," Faribault admitted, which caused Nicollet to laugh so heartily that tears formed in his eyes, ending only when a fit of coughing took hold of his lungs.

"Thank you, Davey. You have quite succinctly put it all back into perspective for me."

Nicollet began walking back to the camp. "I am glad that Father De Smet recommended you to me."

Faribault meekly nodded.

"Perhaps I should have said I am glad that the Lord has found it prudent to send you into my service. You and Taopi are the only ones I can trust with these thoughts of mine."

"What about Mr. Geyer? He seems like an honest man."

"My enemies have taken a great interest in my work out here in the wilderness. Geyer is an honest man, but his loyalties are to science. Because of this, I can trust him with my life, but not with my thoughts."

Supper waited for them back at camp, but Nicollet stopped on the edge of the abandoned Warpekutey village. "Even before De Smet's warnings, I knew my enemies were watching me. Men have long been searching for the Undine, and if I am not careful, I will lead them right to it. Do you understand the need for caution?"

"Not really, Professor Nicollet," Faribault admitted. "Who would want to harm you? What treasure could be found out here on the frontier?"

"That remains to be seen," Nicollet answered.

CHAPTER FIFTY-SEVEN
THE HAUNTED VALLEY
1838

Grey Heron stood motionless, true to his name, waiting for his prey to come to him. Since becoming an adult, he and his band of Tizaptanon outlaws had carried the metal rifles, pistols, and knives of the White Man, yet he knew when to use them and when to use the old ways.

He watched a young buck run through the gravel for a few minutes before climbing back up the sloping bank.

Something is following it.

If the buck had possessed any sense, it would have plunged into the Yunke-lo river and fled to the south. But somehow, it sensed a greater danger on the southern side of the river.

It was right.

Grey Heron, along with his three brothers, four nephews, one uncle, and five cousins lurked in the brush during the day, wanting to avoid detection.

A few moments after the buck disappeared back up the bank, a solitary young hunter—a Sisseton from his clothing—followed the tracks and scampered back up the bank with a rifle in his hand.

This boy will serve as an example to all who follow, Grey Heron decided, stepped out of his hiding place, and crossed the River of Death, hunching as if that would hide him from the Great Spirit.

Three men headed back across the river to flank the boy to the west. Three more climbed the opposite bank and ran out into the field to create a pincer. The remaining eight, including himself, fanned out, knowing they would trap the deer and the Sisseton boy in the spot where the rivers came together.

The hunt thrilled him, and as he ran, he heard his lungs and heart working to keep up with the unsuspecting boy who dared enter the valley. Yet he knew already that the boy's blood would not quench the fires in his heart.

As they approached the big westerly loop of the river, a single shot rang out, echoing through the valley.

When Grey Heron reached the edge of the woods, he found the Sisseton boy gutting his deer out in an open field. In the distance, the tall bluff that had been burned black loomed to the north. If the other Tizaptanons had heard the shot, they would cut from the open field across the southern base of the bluff, trapping the young hunter.

The pincer tightened.

Still focused on his kill, the boy didn't notice four men crossing the river from the west. At the same time, Grey Heron and his men came out of the woods from the south and east. In the distance,

THE ALCHEMIST'S MAP

just below the burnt fort, his brother and nephews came out of the woods from the north to help surround the boy.

But a hundred yards beyond them, a wagon and several riders appeared.

White men.

CHAPTER FIFTY-EIGHT
THE HAUNTED VALLEY
1838

Despite Davey Faribault's warning, the expedition had left the ease of the open prairie to drive the wagons into the Haunted Valley. Five miles to the south, the passage would have been tall grass and wildflowers, but Nicollet's chosen path brought them to a place where a dozen rivers came together in a deep valley.

Having forced the oxen-drawn wagons through the wooded ravines, the wagons again rolled along through the floodplains of the valley.

Nicollet claims to trust me with the story of Lahontan and Le Sueur, Faribault evaluated. *Yet if the story of a copper mine is a fabrication, but what else could they be looking for?*

The sun neared the edge of the valley when Faribault spotted a

THE ALCHEMIST'S MAP

dozen Indians beside the river.

This is trouble.

The voyageurs sensed it too, and began to arm themselves. Their young Sioux guide, who knew the way to Spirit Lake, stood in the circle of hunters, a prisoner.

It's a trap.

Faribault found his own rifle pointed at the chest of the leader. "We come in peace," he said in the Sioux language. "We come in peace!"

The standoff continued as both the voyageurs and the Tizaptanons all shouted out strategies.

Nicollet whispered calmly, which Faribault relayed.

"We are friends of Chief Sleepy Eyes and Chief Black Eagle," he translated. "And we are friends with the soldiers at Fort Snelling. We have not come to take your food but to bring food and medicine."

As Faribault finished relaying Nicollet's message, he realized he'd given Nicollet away as their leader.

The Tizaptanons seized the advantage. "Tell the other white men that we will kill this man first," the leader said of Nicollet. "Tell him to climb off the wagon and come with us or we will kill every man here."

"Our men are well armed. We will not allow our guest to be taken."

Nicollet reached into his green chest to retrieve a wampum belt and put a hand upon Faribault's shoulder, whispering another message for Grey Heron.

"Nicollet says he would gladly offer his life in exchange for us, but first, he wants to know your name and why you threaten him," Faribault said.

The rest of the men looked as terrified as Geyer and the Frenchmen, but their leader remained resolute. "Tell Nicollet that I am Chief Grey Heron of the Tizaptanons. Tell him that I will ransom his life in exchange for the life of Sleepy Eyes, who killed my son Ohanzee on the Burnt Hill."

Grey Heron pointed to the same hill that Nicollet had studied a few weeks earlier.

Nicollet tried to take another step toward his captors, but Faribault forcibly pushed him back toward the wagon. *Does he have a death wish?*

For a moment, the two argued before Faribault turned back to Grey Heron. "Nicollet wants you to know that Sleepy Eyes didn't kill your son. He says that the spirit of No Soul took your son's life."

Grey Heron grit his teeth and appeared to be on the verge of tears—or a suicide attack. "Ohanzee was killed in a knife fight with Chief Sleepy Eyes, who still bears the wound my son gave him. It was not No Soul."

Nicollet then lifted his fop of gray hair to show a scar on his scalp.

Faribault quickly relayed the message. "Your son Ohanzee gave Nicollet that wound up at the Crow Wing River. In the Big Woods, Ohanzee killed women, and almost killed Professor Nicollet while stealing his canoe. When Professor Nicollet looked into your son's eyes, he did not see a man… he saw the spirit of No Soul upon him."

Grey Heron kept his rifle pointed at Nicollet, so Faribault quickly continued.

"No Soul does not want the secrets of the White Egg to be discovered, which is why he drove your son to madness. The spirit of No Soul also drove Sleepy Eyes to the same madness when he killed your son and your friends on that Burnt Hill."

Grey Heron lowered his rifle but kept his hand on the trigger. "How does he know that is where Sleepy Eyes killed my son? Was he there to bear witness? Is my son's blood upon his hands too? Did he goad Sleepy Eyes into the murderous deed?"

"No. Nicollet came to this place *after* Sleepy Eyes had killed your son, but the Great Chief of the Dakota fell on his knees and wept for what he had done. He understood that the spirit of No Soul caused him to do such vile deeds."

THE ALCHEMIST'S MAP

"Lies!"

"Nicollet will take you to the grave of your son, if you wish. After Sleepy Eyes repented of the deed, Nicollet helped him to take the bodies from this haunted valley and bury them in a peaceful place."

Grey Heron dropped his rifle and rushed forward, gripping Nicollet by the lapels of his red jacket and slamming him against the wagon. "This man lies!"

Faribault found himself standing inches from the threat. "He will take you to your son's body. He also says that he is friends with Thunder Face of Two Lakes, and wonders if you know this man."

The name seemed to hit the mark. Pain and frustration swirled on Grey Heron's face.

Grey Heron released Nicollet's jacket, but then quickly reached for a knife at his side. Stepping back a pace, he plunged the knife into the ground and spit at the hilt. "Thunder Face is married to my sister. He was Ohanzee's uncle. How do you know this man?"

Faribault listened with incredulity as Nicollet relayed the story. "The two of us smoked the peace pipe at his camp fire. He gave me his turtle rattle, which is in my chest in the wagon. Would you like to see it?"

Grey Heron nodded, and his men grew tense as Nicollet walked to the wagon. But when he procured Thunder Face's turtle rattle, his men began to whisper their theories.

"Quiet!" Grey Heron told them. "We do not know if this man is telling the truth or if he is a demon in human form." Then he turned back to Faribault. "Have Nicollet lead the way to my son's grave."

"I must go with you. He cannot speak your words," Faribault explained.

Grey Heron nodded, and Faribault and Nicollet walked together away from the tense showdown. A narrow deer trail led south from the open valley, leading up a ravine that ran to the prairie. Not once did Nicollet try to run, and the farther away they were from the burnt hill, the more the tension dissipated.

De Smet is right. Nicollet is far more than just a scientist or diplomat. God has clearly sent him to heal the wounds that threatened to tear this land apart.

As Faribault pondered Nicollet's words about No Soul and the White Egg, he noticed the edges of the prairie begin to appear as the trees thinned. Climbing out of the ravine of the Haunted Valley, Faribault took a deep breath, which Grey Heron did also. There in a field of prairie grass, Nicollet walked over to a patch without any grass yet. There were several graves in the area.

Possessed by grief, Grey Heron dropped to his knees and began to shovel away the dirt. In just a few minutes, he opened the shallow grave, finding a ribcage. Breathing heavily, he scooped away the soft dirt until he found a skull.

In the privacy of the open field, Grey Heron finally broke in front of Nicollet, allowing his screams and wails to fill the air. Faribault knew there was no way to tell which body had been Ohanzee, but the grieving father no longer found motivation for murder.

Nicollet sat down next to his abductor and put a hand upon his shoulder, and for ten minutes, the two sat in silence.

Faribault sat a few paces behind them.

Grey Heron studied the wampum belt. "When the moving star appeared in the sky, the old men said Wishwee would come, but I did not believe them. I only wish you could have come before my son foolishly died. You are indeed the Woktchan Witchastan."

Faribault softly relayed the message to Nicollet, but paused and looked back at Grey Heron when he heard the strange phrase. "'Woktchan Witchastan?'"

THE ALCHEMIST'S MAP

"It means 'Great Sorcerer,'" Grey Heron explained. "Our people were given a task long ago. We were the Santee, Guardians of the Frontier, whose purpose was to protect the lands of the Seven Council Fires, especially sacred places like the Black Hills, Spirit Lake, and the Haunted Valley. One by one, these places were lost to us. My son believed that a sacred treasure had been stolen from the Dakota generations ago, and that it was his purpose to find it before the Wishwee would come looking for it."

"You think Nicollet is the Wishwee?"

"I do not yet know if Nicollet is the Wishwee or just a Great Sorcerer. My son was a troubled man who believed he was the hand of the Great Spirit. Anyone who tried to stop him was a heretic, worthy of death. I think the only reason he stopped himself from killing Nicollet is, even in his madness, he understood who the man was."

"What was the treasure your son was searching for?" Faribault asked.

"The same thing Nicollet is searching for... but he will not find it here. If he wants, I will escort him all the way to Chief Black Eagle's lands on the shores of Spirit Lake near the Iowa territory, but he will not find anything there either."

"How do you know?"

"Because Ohanzee went looking for something there also. His quest only led to his death. Nicollet was right about No Soul guarding the secrets of the White Egg. I pray to the Great Spirit that Nicollet does not die the same way my son did."

"I've already sworn an oath to protect him from his enemies," Davey Faribault insisted.

"Yes," Chief Grey Heron nodded, "but can you protect him from himself?"

CHAPTER FIFTY-NINE

LURA LAKE
1838

W<i>here there is smoke, there is fire,</i> Nicollet thought to himself as he studied the haze on the distant horizon. He turned to the men at camp.

I've put everyone's life in jeopardy.

Things had soured quickly. After arriving at Spirit Lake under the protection of Chief Black Eagle and his son, Red Cap, Nicollet had immediately exchanged gifts and medicine with the migratory Warpekutey, but their young Sisseton guide, Stands on Clouds, had managed to offend their hosts, and Nicollet had had to reduce his payment and dismiss him.

Along the far western tributaries of the Watonwan River, one of

THE ALCHEMIST'S MAP

their mules vanished overnight. Later, they found the butchered corpse of the animal with its eyes gouged out a short distance from where they had camped.

Taopi had immediately volunteered to chase off the vile boy, which was granted, but the next day, clouds of smoke filled the sky behind them as the winds blew a prairie fire closer and closer to their location. Taopi had not returned either.

Leaving Taopi to find his own way home, Faribault had immediately changed their return route, turning due east and avoiding another trip to the Haunted Valley.

After crossing the Blue Earth River far to the south of the Haunted Valley, where the threat of fire reaching them was all but gone, Nicollet had insisted they make camp on the eastern shore of the lake, just in case sparks crossed the river valley and reignited the prairie.

"We need to make a decision," Faribault said loudly enough to gather up the seven remaining men. "This mule will die if we don't give it rest. Even with rest, I am not sure it will make it all the way back to my home, let alone Fort Snelling. Would it be possible to just leave the wagon here?"

Karl Geyer looked sick to his stomach. "I have over four hundred botanical specimens in this wagon. If they are not properly preserved and transported, this expedition will be a failure for me."

"What about you, Professor Nicollet? Is it possible to leave your wagon behind and retrieve it later?"

"How much later?" Nicollet asked Faribault from the spot where he sat, exhausted.

"If we are lucky, we could return with a fresh team of mules and have the equipment back to you in another month... if the weather holds."

Nicollet understood the grim realities. The supply wagon was almost empty but it was the smallest wagon. Nicollet's wagon had twice broken its axle, and they did not have any supplies remaining for a third repair. The third wagon was stuffed with botanical and geological specimens.

So Captain Belligny and the Viscount were sent north with Nicollet's wagon, along with Faribault and Clewett, one of the hired voyageurs. Nicollet kept the other two guides and Geyer, giving the mule, and himself, a couple of days to recover. With the Traverse des Sioux only two days away, Faribault and Clewett could return with extra horses and meet them at Waseca.

"Will you be able to find your way?" Faribault had asked before departing.

Nicollet had laughed. "My dear boy, I am the Great Sorcerer. I am the Last Magi. I am the discoverer of comets. As long as I have the sun and stars, I could find my way to Bethlehem, if necessary."

"And what if your mule dies?"

That had taken the smile off of Nicollet's face. "Oh, don't say such a thing. Well, between here and Lake Okamon are the two rivers where we could hide Geyer's wagon. If the old guy does give up the ghost, we could easily walk the rest of the way by foot. Today is October 6th. We will depart on October 8th. We should arrive with or without our mule by October 10th. It is only a span of five days. I once spent five days trapped inside of a glacier in the French Alps. I will survive a few autumn days upon the prairie."

So the next morning, the other two wagons rolled north while Nicollet and the botanical wagon camped in a grove of oak trees beside an unnamed prairie lake.

Allowing the ailing mule time to rest, the four men found different ways to stay busy. One voyageur went out hunting in the fields north of the lake, firing off a shot every few minutes before bringing back a half-dozen birds for their meals. The other voyageur stayed in camp to tend to the ailing mule. Nicollet stood on the shore of the lake, looking

THE ALCHEMIST'S MAP

out at the wooded island fifty yards from shore.

Behind him, he heard Geyer approach. "I want to thank you for choosing to stay here, Professor Nicollet."

"I understand how important your work is, Karl. I spent my entire career working for Pierre-Simon, Marquis de Laplace, waiting for the day to replace him at the Paris Observatory. In the end, a much more ambitious, deceitful man stole it away from me, leaving me with nothing. I don't want to see you return to Germany empty-handed." Nicollet patted him on the shoulder.

"What are you thinking about, Professor Nicollet?" Geyer asked him.

"I'm thinking that island has a green hump very much like that of a turtle," Nicollet smirked.

"The water would be very cold."

"Yes, but there is a narrow isthmus just below the water. You can see the gravel bar leading all the way out to it."

Geyer turned back to glance at their voyageur companions busy with camp. "We'll be able to warm our feet by the fire when we're done. I'm willing if you're willing."

Soon, both men were stripping off their shoes and stockings, rolling their pant legs all the way up to the knees. Nicollet gasped when he took a step into the water and began to lead the way.

Surrounding them, big lily pads filled the shallow waters of the bay. Instinctively, Geyer pulled the aging plant up by the roots. "The Sioux call this lily 'tewapa.' The lake is called 'Tewapa Tankiyan,' or 'Lake with the Crooked Lily Roots.' Chief Sleepy Eyes told me his people would come down here and harvest the plants."

"Really?" Nicollet paused, pulling up a lily pad himself. An old flower, its petals now dry and rotten, fell apart with a brush of his thumb. "For what sort of ailments?"

"Not for ailments. To aid them in visions, apparently."

"You don't say. Curious."

Thoughts of Chagobay filled his head, and Nicollet tossed the plant back into the water and continued trudging his way across the isthmus until they found the sandy shore of the island, which had fairly steep slopes despite its small size.

"Have I told you the Anishinaabe legend of the Seven Fires?" Nicollet asked as they began to study the red and golden leaves of trees surrounding them.

"The Oceti Sakowin?"

"No, not the Seven Council Fires of the Sioux. I speak of their enemies, the Chippewa. When I was in the north, I met a wise priest named Chagobay. He told me how his people received visions of the future in a time when they lived along the Atlantic. For countless generations, the Anishinaabe nation steadily migrated westward, looking for signs and omens to guide them from home to home."

"What sort of signs?"

"Islands. They left their island home in the east and were sent looking for an island as their final destination. They called it 'Mizheekay,' or 'Turtle Island.' Along their exodus, they would find islands where sacred Miigis shells would be scattered."

"Miigis shells?"

"Cypraeacea, a class of gastropoda."

"Aren't those tropical snails?"

"Indeed," Nicollet replied with a grin. "The Anishinaabe were said to have searched hundreds if not thousands of lakes and islands, searching for these Miigis shells sprinkled upon an island where there should be none."

"It sounds like the stuff of fables... a trail of breadcrumbs."

"It is more than fable. The Anishinaabe first traveled to Montreal

THE ALCHEMIST'S MAP

Island, then to an island near Niagara Falls, then to an island near Detroit, then to Manitoulin Island, then to an island at Sault Ste. Marie, then to Madeline Island, which is where Schoolcraft's trade post of Lapointe is located. Yet their seventh island has proven to be a bit of a mystery."

"You surely don't think it is this little island, do you?"

Nicollet laughed heartily at the suggestion. "It was worth cold feet to find out. But alas... no shells." Nicollet looked from the trees to the fallen foliage over which they walked.

"You are the most enigmatic man I have ever met. Is that why we traveled to Spirit Lake so late in the season? To find the origin of a legend?"

"Of course not," Nicollet again smirked. "We are mapping the hydrological basis of the upper Mississippi River watershed, Karl. That is, and always has been, our primary purpose."

"I can't tell if you are joking or you are serious."

"Well, perhaps I *am* only chasing after fables and legends like Mr. Schoolcraft."

Geyer's forehead wrinkled. "No, Professor Nicollet. Your map will unlock the mysteries of the lands west of the Wisconsin Territory. Your name will be forever linked to these lands."

"Then why do I feel like such a failure?"

"How could you say that about yourself? Look at how far we have come and how much we have accomplished. You are a pilgrim of science. When we return to St. Louis, we will flood colleges and universities with more scientific data than can be sorted through in a lifetime. Your contributions to science are unmatched in the whole of North America."

Nicollet let out a long sigh and, having reached the far end of the small island, turned around to walk the same path they'd just come. "I appreciate your kind words, but I cannot help thinking I should have had a family. Beautiful Juliana Leeves wanted us to be married so we could return to England together. I would have been a much better father than my father. I would have supported my children in any endeavors they pursued. Promise me you will marry, Karl. Science is a lonely mistress."

"I don't know if I am ready to make that promise yet, Professor Nicollet."

Nicollet put a hand on Geyer's shoulder and left it there as he walked. Suddenly, he felt a strange tingle in his fingers. He looked down at his fingertips, rubbing them against each other.

He took his hand off Geyer.

As they neared the place they'd crossed the shallow isthmus, Nicollet rubbed his fingers with his left hand.

"Cold, Professor?"

"No, that's not it. My right hand seems a little numb. As if..."

Before Nicollet could finish his sentence, the little spots in his eyes grew until darkness swept over him.

Back at Fort Snelling, Old Bets waited at the ferry for her passengers to return. Jean-Baptiste Faribault and Hank Sibley had both taken the ferry across the river when the Zumbro expedition had returned. But little Nicollet had not been with them.

Perhaps he was already dead.

The old widow busied herself with a great basket of walnuts, cracking and discarding the thick shells into the water and dropping the nutty fruit into a smaller basket. All along the river valley, the leaves had turned gold and red, a sign winter would soon be coming.

After a few hours, the elder Faribault and Sibley came down the ramp to the launch, signaling Old Bets to shift from one prow to the

THE ALCHEMIST'S MAP

other. In her youth, she'd been as beautiful and slender as Red Blanket Woman. Now, her massive hips became a tool of her trade, for as she walked toward the rear of the ferry, her weight lifted the nose off the landing. With her long pole, she moved the vessel into the water a bit so the weight of the men would not cause her raft to be mired in the mud.

Jean-Baptiste Faribault, Hank Sibley, the thief Maxwell, the bright-eyed Frémont, and Alexander Faribault joined her but paid her no mind, continuing their conversations as if she did not exist. With little effort, Old Bets freed the ferry and began to lead it like a loyal dog across the river. Her second husband, a fur trader, had built the ferry long ago with dreams of filling it with pelts. After his death, it became her primary lot in life.

The men departed without saying a word to her, but she knew Faribault and Sibley would later provide her with gratuities for her services, especially since she wore a cross around her neck and had taken the name "Betsy."

With evening approaching, she secured her ferry with the lock and chain and returned to her little shack built atop a sandstone outcropping. She needed a walking stick to get up and down, but it meant her home was safe from flooding.

Finally, a bit after supper, the young lieutenant departed from Hank Sibley's house and sat upon the chair outside the Faribault house.

A very good sign. The young man knows Sibley is a snake.

When no one joined him, Old Bets grabbed her walking stick and quickly descended the hill to speak with him.

"How kola," Frémont said in her Sioux tongue.

This time, Old Bets ignored him, climbing the three stairs, adjusting a wooden chair, and flopping down in it. Finally comfortable, she looked over at him and said in plain English, "They will kill Nicollet if he stays the winter here."

Frémont stammered as he searched for the right words. "Dear Lord, I did not know you could speak English. Nicollet is in danger?"

"I can read English, also. So can Red Blanket Woman. The evil men know you protect Nicollet, which is why I have come to speak to you. Sibley serves two masters, and one of them is determined to keep Nicollet from ever returning. You need to make sure he returns to the East immediately. He will not be safe at Fort Snelling."

"Who wants to harm him?"

"The same man who hired Red Cheeks to murder him. The same man who hired Scar Face to bring death to the prairie."

"Scar Face? You mean Taopi?" Frémont asked.

Taopi? Should I be trusting this young fool? "No, not Taopi. The other man with scars on his face." *The other young officer... the lion.*

CHAPTER SIXTY
LURA LAKE
1838

In the darkness, the Undine waited for him at the bottom of a deep shaft in the earth. At first, it appeared as the figure and face of Juliana Leeves. She floated, bare-breasted, upon the surface of the water, staring up at him.

"Come join me, sweet Nicky," the Undine called out.

Nicollet found himself standing in a sea of lilies, with the Undine looking up at him from her deep pit within the water. He managed to quietly shake his head.

"Did you really think the Philosopher's Stone would be waiting for you on a turtle-shaped island?"

"It's waiting for me somewhere. I found Le Sueur's mine. I found

Lahontan's river. I found the place where water flows in all directions."

"Yet all you have to show for it are a few tins of copper vitriol," the young woman said. "Turn back now before they kill you."

"Are you afraid I'll find the real Spirit Lake? Is that what concerns you?"

The Undine's icy blue eyes tightened. "No. You and I both know you are not the Wishwee, the one who will fight the shapeshifter No Soul. You're just a boy named Nicky, aren't you?"

Nicollet chucked a water lily at the Undine, but rather than allowing the rotting disk to strike her, she vanished, releasing him from her spell.

Light returned, and the sound of panicked friends filled his ears.

"Professor Nicollet!"

"Help! Something is wrong with Mr. Nicollet!"

"He's being possessed by a spirit."

"What's wrong with him?"

"He is having some sort of seizure. Help me roll him onto his side so he doesn't drown on his own saliva."

Nicollet felt the muscles in his body relax and the sound of panicked friends filled his ears like a strange echo. He tried to open his eyes, but even his eyelids, like the rest of his body, were too tired to answer the call. He groaned a bit but could not speak.

"We need to bring him back to the campfire. I shouldn't have let him cross this cold water at his age. It was foolish of me."

Nicollet felt hands under his armpits and around his knees. By the time they laid him beside the fire, Nicollet's eyes began to focus.

"I saw her," Nicollet whispered. "Mon fiancée."

"His fiancée? Who is he talking about?" a voyageur asked, already boiling a kettle on the fire.

"A woman he once courted back in Paris," Geyer explained. "Juliana

THE ALCHEMIST'S MAP

Leeves. She ended up marrying Edward Sabine."

"No, it wasn't really Juliana," Nicollet whispered. "It was the Undine who called to me. I could see her hiding in the blue depths."

"You stay the hell away from that watery bitch," the voyageur Forsberg blurted out, gently slapping Nicollet's cheek. "Don't follow her anywhere, understood?"

Nicollet blinked repeatedly as the voyageur put his face nose-to-nose with Nicollet's. Nicollet nodded in meek affirmation.

"We'll let him warm himself and get some hearty bouillon in him," the guide said. "And tomorrow, we'll leave for Lake Okamon even if I have to pull the wagon myself."

Soon, Nicollet felt the warmth of the campfire and he fully returned to the land of the living.

Forsberg handed him a bowl of soup. "Eat. It will help you regain your strength."

"You must have had an allergic reaction to the pollen of the lily," Geyer offered from across the fire. "Either that, or you must have experienced a bit of hypothermia after walking through the water. The temperature read thirty degrees Fahrenheit last night, so the water must have been fairly cold."

"Chagobay warned us not to touch the lilies," Nicollet muttered, huddled beneath his blankets. "How could I have been so foolish?"

But none of the three men knew Chagobay, of course, so Nicollet kept the rest of his thoughts to himself.

"Joseph," Karl Geyer began after the four listened to the popping embers in the fire for a time. "What did you mean earlier when you said 'the Undine called to you?'"

Both voyageurs seemed keenly interested in his answer, making Nicollet suspicious of them.

"You're German," Nicollet said to Geyer. "Haven't you ever heard the folktale of the Undine?"

"Yes, I've heard the tales."

"When I lost consciousness, I had a dream that a beautiful water spirit tried to lure me into the depths of the lake to steal my soul."

"See?" one nodded. "I told you a spirit was trying to possess him."

At that, the voyageur pulled out a big knife and walked over to a tree. He pried and gouged the bark of the oak tree until a word began to appear in large six-inch letters: "LURA."

"Lura..." Geyer repeated. "A Basque word for beauty and absolute perfection. A fitting name for the place where Nicollet had a vision."

"No," the gruff voyageur shook his head. "In my Swedish tongue, 'Lura' is a warning for a danger that lurks. I had to warn others about this place."

The shivering stopped, but a fire in his heart began to burn. "I've always tried to do what is right," Nicollet began, thinking of the face in the watery pit.

"I've never known a nobler man," Geyer said.

"But for all my good intentions, I always seem to make things worse."

"Nonsense. Look at the impact you've made during your time on the frontier. You helped avert a war. You've immunized dozens from smallpox. You've become a champion to people who did not have a voice."

Nicollet smiled weakly, then looked back at the flames of their campfire. "My father was a watchmaker in the little town of Cluses. He honed his craft and became a man of esteem in our village. The Baron recognized how the Ancien Régime was changing and that a middle class of specialized businessmen like my father represented the future. For this reason, he proposed an arranged marriage between myself and his daughter, Siréne."

"Your fiancée," Geyer said.

THE ALCHEMIST'S MAP

"What did I know of love? I was young. We both were. I was going to be a watchmaker like my father, marry the Baron's daughter, and live happily ever after... until the revolution came. My mother set me on a path by bringing a group of Jesuits into our house. I helped smuggle them through the Alps to safety, but when I returned, everything I knew was gone, including my sweet Siréne. The Baron met the same fate as my mother, killed by the mob. Sweet Siréne had been raped and thrown into a well. I returned home just in time to help pull her body from the well and give her a proper burial. I've never been able to look at another woman without seeing her face. It is the reason I had to deny poor Juliana's affection. It is the reason I will die alone, Karl."

The next morning, Nicollet woke and looked out over the waters of Lura Lake. Content to let the weary mule rest and gather a little rest himself, Nicollet sat by the fire most of the day while one voyageur fed him, Geyer fiddled with his specimens at the wagon, and the other voyageur walked the shore looking for an easy meal.

In the middle of the afternoon, Taopi came riding up to the camp on a black horse alone. "I did not find Stands on Clouds..." He stopped and stared down at Nicollet, "You look terrible."

Geyer stepped away from the wagon. "Professor Nicollet fell in the lake when he had a medical incident."

"Why are you just camped here?" Taopi asked. "Winter is coming."

"Our mule fell sick," a voyageur said. "We decided to give her a few days rest. One way or another, we were to meet the others at Lake Okamon with new horses from the Traverse des Sioux."

"I assumed," Taopi said gruffly. "After I crossed back over the Blue Earth River, I found wagon tracks heading north, but counted only two sets, which is why I headed back south to find you here."

"With your horse, we could get the wagon to Lake Okamon," Geyer noted.

Nicollet tossed off the blanket and stood. "I understand now why Chief Wahanantan wanted me to come to the Haunted Valley, and it is time that I meet him."

"It is far too late in the season to attempt such a thing," Taopi said. "We will be lucky to reach Fort Snelling ahead of the first snows."

CHAPTER SIXTY-ONE

DETROIT

1839

Twenty years before becoming president, Thomas Jefferson had studied accounts of a long river that led to a great continental divide in the Rocky Mountains. By the time he became president, there had already been crossings of the continent, but Jefferson nevertheless asked congress for a fully funded expedition to the divide and beyond. Commissioning the Corps of Discovery, Jefferson hired Captain Meriwether Lewis and William Clark to lead the expedition. Prior to their departure in 1804, Lewis and Clark were given access to Jefferson's vast library at Monticello and received training in astronomy and cartography.

The expedition departed St. Louis in May of 1804 and traveled up the Missouri River. After passing by the Omaha territory, the expedition passed through the territory of the Lakota, the western Sioux, which Clark described as "warlike" and "the vilest miscreants of the savage race." The Lewis and Clark expedition found shelter with the Mandan nation for the winter before continuing to the headwaters of the Missouri River two thousand three hundred miles upstream from St. Louis.

Solomon Delhut looked down at the Lewis and Clark map on the table, trying to visualize the square inch where the Missouri River began.

"Perhaps we should have hired Nicollet ourselves," Malcolm Gunn said. Despite wearing his small spectacles, Gunn squinted as he read the daily correspondence, making his face shrink up like a rat wiggling its whiskers. Although Delhut and Gunn were close in age, Gunn's head was polished and smooth, leaving only gray hair along the back of his head and near his ears.

"Hired him?" Delhut repeated. "Clearly we should have discreetly killed him back in Paris."

"You are beginning to sound like Schoolcraft. Stop seeing Nicollet as a threat. If we'd killed Nicollet back in Paris, we would have accomplished nothing. The Drummond Map would have still been lost and we would have still been pulling single pieces of grass from the mighty haystack while looking for our needle. By allowing Nicollet to live, he has systematically divided up the haystack for us."

Two decades ago, he and Gunn both learned the secret family legacy involved ancient maps and buried treasure, but now Delhut was a businessman with family responsibilities. Instead of chasing the legacy like a zealot, the older responsibility only left him bitter. "Then why does all of this feel like such a mistake? I can hear my ancestors crying out from the grave."

"Every mile of these expeditions has been catalogued. Not only is

THE ALCHEMIST'S MAP

this a government expedition, but it is also a scientific expedition. When Nicollet finishes, we will have a day-by-day account of his comings and goings. These accounts will become public documents upon his return, allowing us to study every step against our own documents. Neither Nicollet nor our enemies really understand the truth of what we seek and why we seek it."

Delhut set the letters from Sibley down. "Would Nicollet be so stupid as to announce his discovery of the Philosopher's Stone? I don't think so. He would keep those secrets to himself."

"We don't care if he finds the Philosopher's Stone, Solomon. There are more ways than one to pick a lock. Let him push away the haystack for us and hold the needle for the world to see. We would see the spot upon which he stands."

"I see your point, but others are looking also—the one who killed Lady Drummond, for instance," Delhut said, stepping away from the Lewis and Clark map to walk to the other side of the table where the smaller map of Baron Lahontan sat in contrast. "Interpret those letters for me. What is Nicollet doing this time?"

Malcolm Gunn stood up and walked over to the large table. "Three generations ago, our forefathers knew Baron Lahontan had discovered the Undine, but when Lahontan published this map for the world to see, no one knew if he did it to lead others to the true location or throw them off the trail. Having seen the Drummond Map, the Lahontan Map, and the Le Sueur Map, Nicollet has scientifically eliminated the Mississippi River, the St. Peter River, the Des Moines River, and most recently the Cannon River as candidates for Lahontan's Longue River. Now what has he done? Upon returning to Washington, he immediately turned his attention to mapping the Missouri River. What does that tell you?"

"The place where water flows in all directions is found in the Rocky Mountains."

"Exactly," Gunn said with a crooked grin once used for boyish mischief many decades before. "Nicollet is leading us right to the needle. I've already mobilized men to be ready."

"Who?"

"They are Sons of the Dawn also, extended members of the Sinclair family. There is a fur trading colony in Manitoba that we established a while back, which will allow us to get to the headwaters of the Missouri River on the heels of Nicollet, should anything of note be discovered."

"The Order of Eos has men in Canada?"

"At the time, it was a prudent financial move. Now it seems as if the stars have aligned for us. Let the Pied Piper of Savoy lead his merry band of explorers up the Missouri River. He seems hell-bent on doing all of the work for us."

Several hundred miles west of Detroit, at Nicolas Perrot's old fur trading outpost of Prairie du Chien, Wisconsin, a wagon packed with scientific specimens belonging to Joseph Nicollet and Karl Geyer vanished from the face of the earth as it was heading south.

The wagon driver, Pierre Bottineau, took a large bag of pelts and camouflaged the crates to appear as a worthless load of muskrat. Climbing back onto the wagon, he turned the team of horses east, where Sibley's man waited at Fort Atkinson.

CHAPTER SIXTY-TWO

FORT PIERRE
1839

Is it true? Joseph Nicollet is coming to Fort Pierre?

Kit Carson watched from a distance as the steamship *Antelope* came around the bend of the Missouri River.

Fort Pierre was a wooden stockade with elevated towers on each corner of the square. Inside, a trading post, a few homes, and a tall flagpole flying an American flag which could be seen at the center of the court. It was built for accessibility to the river, not for defense or permanence. Two dozen teepees were set up outside the stockade, and as the ship approached, both traders and Indians began to approach the rickety dock.

Vengeance was a delicate matter, so Carson pushed down all his rage and grief to take advantage of the opportunity delivered to him.

A crooked smile, a drooping shock of hair, smallpox scars beneath his beard.

A few weeks earlier, Carson had been at the Green River in Wyoming at a "Rocky Mountain Rendezvous" with a dozen other trappers when he heard from a friend of Captain Billy Stewart that there would be a government expedition departing from Fort Pierre Chouteau in late spring or early summer.

It is a job for old men or young boys, Carson decided, but when he heard the name "Joseph Nicollet," he immediately changed his mind.

Surrounding Fort Pierre, tall bluffs were decorated with stunted trees and brush, sliced in half by the turbid, muddy waters flowing from the distant Rocky Mountains. Compared to the majesty of the Rockies, it was a terribly barren place.

The fort commander rushed to greet an older man in bright clothing—Nicollet, if Carson was to guess. Following him, he saw another scientist and a young officer standing on the dock, overseeing the cargo as it was unloaded from the ship.

For a moment, he thought fate had delivered Daniel Lyons back into his clutches, but the demeanor and appearance of the man in front of him was different than Lyons.

Carson walked between the cut in the river valley where the deposit of sediment dropped another ten feet to the water's edge. Like himself, the young officer had a full beard, albeit a much nicer uniform.

Willie Dixon—an old friend of Stewart—and a few ragged men introduced themselves to the young officer and showed him to the expedition wagons. Carson still had time to join the expedition, but instead, he chose to wait in the shadows, his scalping blade sharp and ready.

For the better part of two hours, Carson watched for either Lyons or the government agent—the one who'd brought the supplies from St. Louis.

THE ALCHEMIST'S MAP

The man with the missing fingers.

Neither stepped off the boat, and Kit Carson found himself alone with a whiskey bottle. He leaned against the packed wagons of the Nicollet expedition, armed and dangerous, when the young officer spotted him from the commander's quarters and boldly walked over.

Bark orders at me and I'll slice off an ear, Carson thought.

"Are you looking for work?"

"I'm looking for answers," Carson said.

"Second Lieutenant John C. Frémont, U.S. Corps of Topographical Engineers. How can I help you?"

"You're with this Nicollet fellow?"

"I am."

"What can you tell me about him?"

"We are on a mapping expedition. We'll be mapping the James River, Devil's Lake, and the watershed of the Red and St. Peter Rivers."

"St. Peter," Carson repeated, remembering the name of the steamer that had arrived at Fort Union two years earlier. "This is a government expedition?"

"It is. We serve under Major Abert of the U.S. Corps of—"

"I heard you the first time. So you fellows are here to figure out how much land you're going to steal from the Indian? Is that it?"

"I wouldn't characterize it like that."

"Well, I would. You're thieves, aren't you?"

"No, mister..."

"Carson, Kit Carson. If you're not thieves, then you're murderers, spreading death to every end of the prairie, just like you did in '37."

"'37?"

"Government men came to Fort Union with supplies tainted with smallpox. From Fort Union, government agents spread disease to every tribe along the Missouri, killing more in one winter than five years of war could have accomplished. You bastards killed my wife."

"Sir, Joseph Nicollet is a friend of the Indian. Last year, we vaccinated countless villages for smallpox. Nicollet counts Chief Sleepy Eyes, Renville, and Waneta as his friends. I can assure you, Nicollet only has the best interests of the Indian in his heart."

"Do you know a man by the name of Lyons? Daniel Lyons?"

Frémont slowly shook his head. "Lyons? Sorry, I don't know the man."

"He bragged about serving under Nicollet. This man, this government man, sold me blankets infected with smallpox. Lyons killed my wife the same as if he'd held a pistol to her head and fired."

"Mr. Carson, there was no man by the name of Lyons with us last year, nor is there this year. Perhaps he served under Nicollet on the 1836 expedition."

"So you don't know this Daniel Lyons? He had smallpox scars, which is why he was certainly chosen to be a harbinger of death."

"Mr. Carson, I sincerely feel sorrow for the loss of your wife, but none of us had anything to do with the epidemic."

"If you find this Captain Lyons... bring him to me, and I will serve frontier justice," Carson said and walked away with a whiskey bottle in one hand and a knife in the other.

CHAPTER SIXTY-THREE
STANDING ROCK
1839

Today, much blood will be spilled upon the open prairie, Chief Wahanantan thought as he stepped out of his lodge to the fanfare of the two thousand Yankton Indians gathered at the hunting grounds.

Outside of his lodge, his family helped him prepare for the day. His son Waneta stood holding his decorated spear while his younger son held a bow and a quiver full of arrows. His daughter stood with his freshly painted horse.

Only his wife did not smile. "Be careful today."

"I will be surrounded by hundreds of my finest braves. What have I to fear?"

But Wahanantan did fear. A deep, penetrating fear chewed away at his bones day after day, stealing away his courage and sucking his heart like marrow.

Show no weakness, he told himself as he climbed upon his horse and held a confident pose. *Remind them who rules.*

As Wahanantan rode south, he could not shake the dream from his head—his days upon the prairie were coming to an end.

But not today. Today I am supreme.

"They are traveling north between the two rivers," one of his advance scouts reported. "If we send out flankers, we can push them in either direction."

"There will be no need for flankers. They have trapped themselves. Today, we will kill as many as possible. Tomorrow, we will know where to find the rest."

Keeping the horses at a steady trot, the heavily-armed mass of Yankton warriors crossed three miles of open prairie before reaching the top of the ridge. There, on the opposite side of the ridge, their prey waited, unaware.

Wahanantan gave the signal and a hundred horses sprinted into the valley below. Screams—both in terror and aggression—filled the valley, and in minutes, the scent of blood wafted up, palpable in the air.

By the time he reached the valley floor, a dozen buffalo from the massive herd had already fallen. The young men of his tribe had ridden hard to prove themselves, leaving older men such as himself to pick off the weaker members of the herd.

For five decades, Wahanantan had annually hunted buffalo south of Spirit Lake. While their neighbors had to rely on trickery or traps to harvest meat for winter, the Yankton used skill and tactic to hunt the buffalo herds that came up from the south each year to feast upon the lush prairie grass growing between the sloughs and lakes of his land. Funneling the herds were two rivers that stretched hundreds of miles

THE ALCHEMIST'S MAP

south to the Missouri River. Combined with the massive ridge that separated his lands from the lands of the eastern Dakota, the herds came like clockwork. With a few days of hunting, his people could disperse for the winter, their food supply secure.

Burnt Earth, his most trusted lieutenant, came riding in hard from the eastern side of the ridge. "We found wagon tracks."

"This far south?" Wahanantan felt the mood of the day change. For the past decade, the throngs of wagons from the distant Selkirk colony grew bolder and bolder. When he was a boy, his father had pity for the dirty children rejected by both Indian and white culture, but the Métis population grew much faster than expected. In recent years, they would fill each wagon with ten buffalo before hauling their ill-gotten harvest back into Canada.

Wahanantan had left two dozen boys to guard the Red River valley, but the Métis must have found a way past them. "I will come with you," Wahanantan finally decided. "I will remind them who rules these lands."

"They will have rifles."

"Show me the way."

So upon the ridge they rode, the herd still scattering like leaves blown by the wind. Atop the eastern slope of the ridge, Wahanantan could see the herd parting around a large boulder on the prairie. But on the boulder, he spotted two human figures.

Burnt Earth noticed them, too, and soon a dozen warriors were heading toward the strange sight. As they grew closer, Wahanantan could immediately see they were white men—but neither Métis nor trader. The older man stood upon the top of the stone, waving his arms in the air. He wore a bright red jacket, making it possible to see him from a mile away.

"Greetings," the man in the red jacket said in Sioux when they came closer. "We are friends of Joseph Renville of Lac Qui Parle." He pointed to the east.

Renville? Burnt Earth and his other warriors shouted out angry questions, which neither man could answer. In fact, the man in the red jacket kept repeating his introduction, and it became apparent it was the only thing he knew how to say.

As the buffalo herd withdrew like a black wave upon a grassy beach, four wagons that were parked on the opposite side of the valley a half-mile away were surrounded by his warriors.

"I know Joseph Renville," Chief Wahanantan answered in English. "I do not know you. Who are you?"

"I am Joseph Nicollet. This is my assistant, Karl Geyer. Those men across the valley are our guides. We were investigating this boulder when the buffalo herd moved south and separated us from our party. We have come to see Spirit Lake, and to visit with Chief Wahanantan of the Yankton."

Chief Wahanantan did not smile but whispered his orders to Burnt Earth that the men were now their guests.

When he spotted his spy, Taopi—the exiled warrior he had long ago dubbed "Wounded Man"—in the wagons with the other white men, Wahanantan knew with certainty Nicollet had been sent by the Great Spirit, and there was much that needed to be discussed.

CHAPTER SIXTY-FOUR
DEVIL'S LAKE
1839

Devil's Lake is a closed water system that is not fed by tributaries. Only at extremely high water levels does the lake overflow and connect with the Sheyenne River. Like Great Salt Lake, which also does not drain, it has a high salinity level. With a surface area of 3,810 square miles, it is the largest body of water in North Dakota.

Although named "Lac du Diable," or "Devil's Lake," by the earliest European explorers, the Sioux knew it as "Mni Wakan," or "Spirit Lake." According to legend, a great Unktehi—a water serpent—lived in the depths of the lake, and once wiped out a whole army camped near its shore.

From a camp on Heart of Spirit Lake, a prominent mountain on the eastern shore, Joseph Nicollet could see thirty miles in all directions.

To the north and east, the Red River tributaries began, flowing to the distant north. To the south, tributaries of the James River flowed all the way back to the Missouri River. Somewhere along those shores, Frémont gathered the scientific data for the region. Nicollet did not need to accompany his apprentice on his exploration—he had an audience with Chief Wahanantan.

The old Yankton chief seemed as prehistoric as the rocks on the slopes of the mountain. Although he still had broad shoulders, age had hunched his back and taken all color from his hair. His arms were still strong and quick but his hands shook whenever he held something. Having met five generations of the chief's family, Nicollet reckoned the chief's age to be over eighty.

Beside Wahanantan, Taopi and Waneta also sat around the fire. After standing in the towering presence of Waneta, Nicollet could imagine the elder chief once in his prime. "It is time for us to speak plainly," Wahanantan finally said.

"It is," Nicollet smiled. "I have visited the Haunted Valley, and I have found the old fort. I have also found places where the earth bleeds blue, but I have not found the White Egg of the Sioux, the Water Drum of the Chippewa, or the Philosopher's Stone of my people," Nicollet glanced at Taopi, knowing none of his secrets were kept from Wahanantan.

But Taopi has not seen everything, Nicollet thought, knowing Taopi never saw Chagobay's cave.

Nicollet reached into the satchel he was carrying and took out six tin canisters. Nicollet tapped out a little from each canister onto a buried boulder until there were six piles upon the stone. "My people call this substance 'vitriol,'" Nicollet began, "and I have searched far and wide for the legendary place where waters flow in different directions. I have found many types of blue earth. Can you tell me which of these six samples is the one that came from the Haunted Valley?"

THE ALCHEMIST'S MAP

Wahanantan touched each of the piles of blue-green sediment. Some were gritty, others spongy, and others sandy. His index finger prodded each before he said, "You are trying to trick me."

"Can you tell?"

Wahanantan leaned back. "Two of these samples are the same."

"Which two are the same?"

Wahanantan pointed to the piles gathered at Fort L'Huillier and another.

"Why did you single out these two piles?"

"There is an evil spirit upon them."

"An evil spirit..." Nicollet repeated. "Like the one that lives in the lake? The Unktehi?"

Wahanantan shook his head. "I have lived a long life, and I have seen how tales can change in the telling. There is no Unktehi here. This place is free from the influence of an Unktehi, but why explain that to white men."

Of course. This body of water does not have a tributary or outlet. It is cut off. "The Unktehi cannot reach this place by water?"

"That is my belief, but evil grows, and so does the power of the Unktehi."

Nicollet pondered all the names and metaphors for evil, comparing them to his own beliefs. His collection of tins represented three years of work. "Not long after I began my journey, a strange shaman visited me in St. Louis, claiming that I had been sent by the Great Spirit. When I arrived in the land of the Chippewa, one of their prophets also believed I had been sent. Even Chief Thunder Face of the Tizaptanons claimed I was a Great Sorcerer. Am I the Wishwee, the star man?"

"Perhaps, but the stars have sent others also. Twice in my life, I have seen the Serpent Star. When I was a boy, the elders told me how they had also seen this strange omen when they were boys."

Three sightings of Halley's Comet—1835, 1758, and 1682. "What happened the last two times the Serpent Star came?"

"For countless generations, my eastern cousins performed a sacred duty, even if its purpose was not known by all. They were the Santee, the Guardians of the Frontier."

By telling tales of a Haunted Valley? "What did they guard? A place? An object?"

Wahanantan glanced once more at the tins, and then he poked at the small fire with his stick. "They guarded time."

"Time? What about the tale of Wishwee? Isn't the treasure a White Egg?"

"The White Egg is only a small part of the tale. As Guardians of the Frontier, they had a purpose, and as long as they performed their duty, all seven tribes remained strong. That is why I say they guarded time. When my grandfather was a boy, a man such as yourself would never have crossed the Mississippi with your life, but now you ride openly upon the buffalo lands because my people are weak."

"What happened in your grandfather's time?" *What happened in 1682?*

"You should know," Wahanantan said, looking at Taopi. "You have been to the Haunted Valley."

"White men came," Nicollet said. "They made a fort and dug in the Haunted Valley. Did they find something?" *Did Le Sueur really unearth the Philosopher's Stone?*

"Yes, they found something, a terrible omen, in fact, but they did not defeat the creature No Soul. Wishwee did not come."

A terrible omen? Nicollet looked at the canisters of vitriol, knowing that Wahanantan had supported a theory that still needed study and verification. "When you were a boy, the Serpent Star also appeared. What happened then?"

THE ALCHEMIST'S MAP

"The White Egg was lost, passing from one nation to another, bringing with it death and disaster. When I was a young man, I rode to war with Chief Black Horse of the Mdewakanton to reclaim the sacred treasure, but its secrets died with those who had it last. Yet, its power festers, and it brings death and illness with it. When the Serpent Star returned, I prayed for the healing of my people. If we have reached the end, and you are Wishwee, then I rejoice that I have lived long enough to see the death and destruction of No Soul."

"The shaman I met in St. Louis, Shetek, told me if I found the White Egg, I should leave it where it rests. What would you advise me to do?"

"If you are Wishwee, you do not need my advice. Wishwee will know what to do with the White Egg."

"And if I'm not Wishwee?"

"Then I task you to become Santee."

"A Guardian of the Frontier?"

"Yes, be a champion for my people. Fight for us. Fight for time."

CHAPTER SIXTY-FIVE

DEVIL'S LAKE
1839

Second Lieutenant John C. Frémont carefully packed away the barometer, tending to it exactly as Nicollet had instructed him. The survey of Devil's Lake was complete, and the men grew restless after a week of inactivity. The fertile lake had a greenish hue to it, and having seen it from all angles now, he took one last look, knowing they would soon be leaving.

Did Nicollet finally find what he was looking for?

Devil's Lake felt like the far side of the world, where civilization seemed little more than a childish dream. In the distance, he could see Waneta and Taopi flanking Nicollet as they returned from the mountain camp of Chief Wahanantan.

THE ALCHEMIST'S MAP

Frémont finished packing away the survey equipment and then secured it in the wagon before returning.

No mistakes.

Nothing gets stolen this year.

This expedition, he wore the guise of expedition leader, giving Nicollet an update of the supplies and their travel readiness before previewing the path they would take across the head of the Coteau to arrive at Lac Qui Parle by the end of August. Last year's fiasco—losing the wagon—almost cost him his career.

Nicollet nodded but did not seem to hear a word Frémont said, but Frémont continued. "I met a warrior of Wahanantan that claimed nothing happens upon the prairie without their chief knowing, so I asked the chief about Geyer's missing wagon."

Nicollet finally seemed to listen. "And? What did you learn?"

"It was not stolen by Indians, as was reported. They thought you found something, didn't they? I was watched every step of the way when we left Fort Snelling last year, but you... you managed to slip away twice, bringing Geyer with you both times. They had to assume you'd found something, which is why the wagon was stolen. Did you find something?"

"It is best I don't involve you, Johnny. Do you remember the day you found me at the Santee River in South Carolina? How we then went to see the burial mounds?"

How could I forget? It is the day I first pledged my loyalty to Nicollet. "What does that have to do with anything?"

"Chief Wahanantan told me how the Dakota people, the Santee, were the Guardians of the Frontier for the Seven Council Fires. The Santee have been at war for a long time, and I have just become one of them."

"Become one of them? How?"

"When my journey began, it began as a quest—a treasure hunt, of sorts. You asked why they'd steal Geyer's wagon. I was shown a map and was asked to find a treasure before evil men found it first."

"What kind of treasure?"

Nicollet slipped his hands into his front trouser pockets. "It is hard for me to say without sounding like a total fool. I've spent the better part of this decade trying to understand it myself, often questioning my sanity. Just when I think I've lost my mind, I find another piece of the puzzle, confirming the insanity. If I tell you, I worry I will lose you."

Frémont shook off the thought. "You could never lose me. I'll be your servant to the end."

"The map that brought me to this place described a possible resting place of the legendary Philosopher's Stone."

"The magical rock that turns lead into gold?"

"An alkahest, yes. In the legends, another byproduct of the Philosopher's Stone was vitriol… copper vitriol."

Nicollet then produced several tins, and upon opening them, revealed blue vitriol in each one. "Ironically, I believe I've identified the resting place of the Stone, but I've been tangled by my own web. I know what to do, but I cannot risk doing it."

"Tell me what needs to be done."

"First, I will return to Washington and shout from the highest peaks about the welfare of the Indian. I will not let them be portrayed as thieving savages or simple brutes. I will wage war in every university and institution that will have me."

"And me? How can I help?"

"When we return, Colonel Abert will want his map, which I must provide, but you… you will begin planning a grander expedition. My next expedition will take me to the source of the Missouri River, far away in the Rocky Mountains."

THE ALCHEMIST'S MAP

"Is that where the treasure is located?"

Nicollet quickly put the canisters away and tucked his journal back inside of his jacket. He patted Frémont on the shoulder. "Of course not, but we will make them believe it is."

CHAPTER SIXTY-SIX

FORT SNELLING
1839

Jim Taopi found one of Junior Renville's canoes still waiting at the Fort Snelling landings, and instead of ringing the bell for the ferry, he climbed into the canoe, alone.

Knowing they were surrounded by enemies at the fort, Nicollet, Geyer, and Frémont had quickly departed for St. Louis—Nicollet and Geyer by ship and Frémont by land to unnecessarily guard another mysterious wagon of plant specimens.

During a single summer, the number of residents living on the eastern shore of the Mississippi had almost doubled. Although just twenty-six years old, Taopi felt as if he'd lived a hundred lives already. With the absconded canoe, he crossed the river and pulled up next to the ferry.

THE ALCHEMIST'S MAP

Night came early now that fall had arrived, and the homes of Sibley and Faribault were lit, the chimneys puffing smoke into the night sky. Taopi found himself climbing the steep path that led to an old fur-trader's cabin.

Old Bets sat on the small porch with a plaid blanket draped around her shoulders. Beside her, Pierre Bottineau, a Métis man in his early twenties with French, Sioux, and Chippewa blood, smoked a pipe.

Seeing Taopi approach, Old Bets rose from her rocking chair with a groan and took a few steps to the edge of her deck. Although the cabin was not home, Taopi nevertheless knew it well.

"What will you do now?" Old Bets asked.

The question had the same effect as a punch to the gut, and his legs wobbled. Despite the unexplained presence of Bottineau, Taopi fell to his knees, wrapping his arms around the legs of Old Bets, weeping into the fabric of her dress. Old Bets brushed away his hat and her old fingers began to comb through his hair, touching the places where a Chippewa ax had stolen his childhood.

"Ina," Taopi said and began to sob, having spoken the word 'mother' in the language of his birth.

Taopi sensed Pierre Bottineau, and wiping away his tears with the back of his hand, he looked up to see the young man now standing.

"Why are you here?" Taopi asked, his tears making him even more terrifying to behold.

"Pierre came to me of his own accord, asking for forgiveness," his mother said.

Taopi stood, stepping past his mother as he ascended the three steps to the wooden porch. His hand found the deerhorn hilt of his knife. "What is your crime?"

"Theft," Bottineau said quickly, offering his two open hands to Taopi.

"What did you steal?" Taopi said, standing so close that Bottineau was forced to withdraw his hands.

"Last fall, I was hired to help bring a wagon down to St. Louis, but at Prairie du Chien, I brought it east, delivering it to Fort Atkinson instead."

Geyer's wagon from the 1838 expedition, Taopi realized. Although it contained priceless botanical specimens, its value was almost worthless to anyone but a scientist.

"Who did you give it to?"

"I... I did not know the man at Fort Atkinson."

"Then who paid you to steal the wagon?"

Bottineau's eyes turned to the stone house. "Hank Sibley."

It was the final straw. The knife sprang from its sheath almost as fast as Taopi pivoted toward the house. His long legs neared a run as he heard his mother calling out for him.

A moment later, he kicked open Sibley's front door.

An infant cried and two dogs barked.

Sibley sat by the fire in a plush chair. One of the exotic dogs snapped at Taopi, and his knife dispatched it with such suddenness that the other dog ran away.

Sibley's eyes widened.

Taopi rushed forward, tossing tables and chairs aside until he lifted Sibley by the shirt, pinning him against the fireplace and holding a knife under his chin.

You've just become an outcast, Taopi told himself about his bold actions, but he knew the man in front of him was a spy. "I know what you've done."

Sibley just blinked in terror.

"There will be no lawyers, no judges, and no juries for your crimes; only my knife will decide your fate," Taopi whispered through his

THE ALCHEMIST'S MAP

clenched teeth. "Now... you are going to make a confession or face immediate justice."

"A confession? I don't know what you think I've done, but I can assure you—"

"Who do you work for?"

"You know who I work for. I am an employee of the—"

"Who wanted the wagon?" Taopi clarified.

"The wagon?"

Taopi pressed the cold blade to Sibley's throat.

"I don't know them. They are friends of my father, and—" Before Sibley could finish, footsteps echoed loudly on the front porch. Instead of Pierre Bottineau, Big Moe Maxwell, wearing pants with suspenders over his hairy white chest, stepped through the doorway with a rifle. At first, the rifle tip stayed near his feet, but then it abruptly drew up and leveled at Taopi. "Put the knife down, Taopi."

The loyal dog has come to his master's aid.

"Not until he tells me the truth," Taopi said.

Maxwell took a few more steps into the room, stepping around the slain dog near the door. *There is no escape now.*

"Put the knife down and we'll talk," Maxwell insisted.

But Taopi knew Sibley was a snake that would somehow wiggle free of any consequence. He wondered if he could throw the knife at Maxwell, wrestle the rifle away, and turn it on Sibley.

It is a foolish plan, one that does not help Nicollet or my people.

With each step Maxwell took toward him, the end came closer and closer.

Taopi turned back to Sibley, putting his face inches away. "Who stole the wagon?"

Through the chaos of a crying baby and barking dog, Taopi somehow heard the cock of a pistol. It was neither one of Sibley's men nor Old Bets nor Bottineau. Instead, he saw Red Blanket Woman, her long black hair unbraided and flowing wildly over her nightgown with a calico blanket wrapped around her body. In her small hands, a pistol pointed at Big Moe Maxwell.

"Put down your rifle," Red Blanket Woman said clearly in English.

Maxwell, ever the coward, lowered it immediately, and when she leveled it at his face, he set it on the nearby table and raised his empty hands.

Ignoring the cries of her child, Red Blanket Woman turned the pistol toward Taopi and Sibley. "Put the knife down, Sugmanitu Tonka. I would not have you murder the father of my child."

Taopi. I am Taopi. Sugmanitu Tonka died when that Chippewa crushed his face and cut off his scalp. Hearing his given name tossed a bucket of cold water over his rage and he realized the barbarity of his actions.

While the blade remained at Sibley's throat, Taopi stepped away from his prey, the knife at the end of his arm's length. Then he took one step sideways, keeping the knife pointed at Sibley.

The pistol's aim did not follow him.

"Pick up the rifle," Red Blanket Woman said, but not to Sibley—she said it to him.

Taopi brushed up against Maxwell as he grabbed the rifle from the table, but before he could do anything with it, Red Blanket Woman said, "If you promise not to hurt the father of my child, I will tell you all about the men who sent him letters."

She was never a peace offering—she was a carefully-planted spy, Taopi realized. "What about your daughter?"

"He would have cast us both aside when the time suited him. Let him raise her as a reminder of what could have been between our two peoples—if greed had not ruined everything."

THE ALCHEMIST'S MAP

Taopi backed up slowly toward the door, being careful not to slip in the butchered dog's blood. As he leveled the rifle at the two faithful servants of the American Fur Company, he felt a small hand upon his shoulder. Red Blanket Woman led him further backwards and out the door.

Once outside, he let go of the rifle with one hand, and taking her hand in the other, pulled her along as they both ran toward the river where a canoe waited to take them away into the protection of darkness.

CHAPTER SIXTY-SEVEN

GEORGETOWN

1839

I think I love him, Jessie Ann Benton decided as her octet finished their performance and applause rained down on her. Returning to her pew along the side of the hall, Jessie caught her breath as the exhilaration ran its course.

The Georgetown Men's Quartet walked onto the stage of the Old North Auditorium, providing Jessie a musical score as she sorted through her feelings.

Her blush calmed slightly, she looked up from her knees and into the large crowd of Washington D.C.'s elites. Amongst the sea of faces, she first caught the eyes of her mother, sisters, and father, so she gave a slight nod and looked back down to her knees.

THE ALCHEMIST'S MAP

After a few measures, she looked back up at the men singing. Most of them were smooth-faced boys, even if they were a few years older than her and approaching twenty. Not a single one of them had a rugged beard or a sharp military uniform.

The United States Corps of Topographical Engineers, she repeated the military branch that had given her trouble a few days earlier.

Jessie looked back up again, scanning the crowd for a moment, only to lock eyes with the handsome second lieutenant who had delivered on his promise to come see her performance.

"Lieutenant Frémont?" Her father had said two days earlier. "Of course I know him. He is the apprentice of Joseph Nicollet."

It had startled her that her father immediately remembered him, so she quickly dropped the subject, lest her father press why she'd seen him at the Georgetown University campus. Although Frémont interrupted whatever his plans were to speak with her for ten minutes, she never found out why he'd been on campus after his celebrated return to civilization.

Jessie sat with the other girls from the Georgetown Seminary until the Christmas concert came to an end, but to her surprise, only her mother and sisters rushed to her side for congratulations—her father had found Lieutenant Frémont.

Don't appear too desperate, she thought as she accepted the praise from her family, but with each glance, she saw a larger and larger crowd gathering—but not because of her father.

Senators, Catholic priests, and Washington elites soon gathered around the handsome second lieutenant.

"Where's Father?" Jessie finally asked, playing ignorant.

Her mother and sisters followed as they crashed the circle surrounding Frémont. She wisely ignored her invited guest and went right to her father, who put aside his political focus to gush about his daughter.

Two conversations continued to orbit in the same space as Jessie took compliments about her singing and appearance and Lieutenant Frémont answered questions about the frontier. The Benton clan ran out of subject matter quickly, and the voice of Frémont caught all those nearby.

"Actually, sir, we named a lake in your honor. Lake Benton. It was one of the grandest lakes I encountered out on the prairie. It stretched on for miles in all directions, and from our camp, I could almost not see the other shore. Near it, we found Lake Abert, as well."

"Did you hear that, Thomas?" Jessie's mother asked. "They named a lake after you."

Frémont glanced at Jessie. He'd told her a different story—that of all the lakes he'd seen two years ago, Lake Benton was the most beautiful, leaving him no choice but to demand Nicollet name it after her.

"Lake Poinsett?" the slender gentleman beside Frémont repeated. "Lake Abert. Lake Benton. Nicollet certainly understands who butters his bread."

They all chuckled at his joke. Jessie looked closer at the man who'd spoken and now remembered the handsome, albeit older, gentleman who'd dropped off a flowering plant to her father. *A poinsettia*, Jessie remembered. *Named in honor of the Secretary of War, Joel Poinsett. Frémont has been ambushed by his boss.*

"You've made South Carolina proud, Lieutenant Frémont," Secretary Poinsett remained at the center of conversation. "Not since Lewis and Clark has Washington been so captivated by the Great Plains. I am honored to have assisted such a promising career, but tell me, where is Nicollet? You've been back in Washington for nearly three weeks, yet Major Abert told me Nicollet's offices remain empty."

"I parted ways with Professor Nicollet at Fort Snelling. He left ahead of me by ship while I personally tended to the wagon of scientific

THE ALCHEMIST'S MAP

specimens we collected along the Missouri and at Devil's Lake. By the time I'd arrived in St. Louis, I was told he'd gone up the Ohio River."

"He's been missing for four weeks?" Poinsett clarified.

"I wouldn't worry about Professor Nicollet. He is most likely entertaining friends in Tennessee for the holidays. I'm sure he'll return by the first of the year so we can begin working on the map and begin planning the next expedition."

"The next expedition?" Senator Benton asked. "You've only just returned."

Jessie felt a flutter of disappointment. *Another expedition would take him away for months—and send him into more danger.*

"I was led to believe your expedition was a success," Poinsett said morosely.

"It certainly was a success," Frémont insisted. "But Professor Nicollet wants to map the Missouri River north of Fort Pierre to provide a complete map of the vast northern watershed."

"Perhaps *after* he provides his map of the upper Mississippi," Poinsett said. "After all, I have forts to build and thousands of miles of land to conquer and civilize." Then he turned to Jessie. "Miss Benton, everything about this evening was simply lovely."

Joel Poinsett took her hand and kissed it before vanishing into the crowd.

Three Jesuit priests stood in the clearing, waiting for Frémont, who said, "I concur with Secretary Poinsett. After months out on the prairie, your voice reminded me of the splendors of civilization. Thank you, Miss Benton, for the invitation."

Jessie melted, which her father seemed to notice.

So did her mother. "Mr. Frémont. In lieu of Professor Nicollet's return, you should come visit our home and regale us with tales of the frontier."

"It would be an honor," Frémont said, and then deftly deferred to her father. "Senator Benton surely knows the locations of my offices, where he can reach me. I bid you all a merry Christmas."

Lieutenant Frémont turned and was swept up by the priests who ran Georgetown, leaving Jessie with a stunning realization: *John Frémont is coming to my house.*

CHAPTER SIXTY-EIGHT
ROME
1841

The Capitoline Museums of Rome are housed in a single building with four massive wings that form a trapezoidal plaza designed by Michelangelo. Built near the center of the ancient city, the archeological museums house some of the most important bronzes, statues, and artifacts in the world. Although opened to the public in 1734 by Pope Clement XII, the museum contains collections featuring Rome's pagan past, including the statue of Remus and Romulus.

On a balcony bench of the second floor of the Palazzo dei Conservatori, facing the she-wolf nursing her adopted human infants, Conrad Simmons waited patiently.

Most of his time was now spent at the Vatican, two miles away on the other side of the Tiber. His days of investigating secret societies were now over, for his superior had recently ascended to the rank of Cardinal thanks to Pope Gregory's support and patronage. Simmons' duties now were administering investigations on a much more global scale, yet one loose string remained—Nicollet.

Giovanni, the old custodian, appeared first from the service door with a broom in his hand. His lively eyes twinkled as he looked over to the stone bench but then he turned to tend to another of the apartments within the museum. A moment later, Father Lupo emerged from the custodial door to join Simmons at the stone bench of the balcony.

"It has been a while," Lupo said. "Who would've thought the Watchmaker's son would have given us so much to talk about."

"What have you learned?"

"Not much beyond what any other man couldn't learn by reading a newspaper," Lupo teased. "Nicollet is using his sudden fame to wage war against the Van Buren Administration, it would seem. Every lecture he gives only fans the flames of his reputation, bringing larger crowds and more honorary titles. Not only has he failed to produce his map in a timely fashion, but there are rumors of a book on Indian customs, which would very much be contrary to the wishes of those who control the purse strings in Washington."

"Yes," Simmons said. "It is why we must withdraw him immediately... for his own good."

"Withdraw him immediately? Didn't you hear me? Nicollet is more of a celebrity as a mapmaker than he ever was as an astronomer. We can't just snatch him off the street without notice. If we faked his death and dropped him off on a deserted island, no doubt a fellow scientist would discover him while studying sea turtles."

"We must try something. We are the ones who put him on this path."

THE ALCHEMIST'S MAP

"I've tried. We've even enlisted the help of our Belgian friend only to have Nicollet refuse our help."

"He refused De Smet?"

"He did. Repeatedly. So do not trouble your soul with guilt. Nicollet seems intent on captaining his own ship through the angry seas. He is making plans for another expedition."

"How could he? With what money? Who would he take?"

"As I said, he has all but gone to war with the Van Buren Administration. American politics can change with the tide. President Van Buren will not win a second term, and this fall, a new administration will control the purse strings. Nicollet seems to have anticipated this."

Father Lupo handed him a letter addressed to Father De Smet written by Nicollet. In it, Nicollet gave an account of the past two years in Washington D.C., including numerous setbacks such as the Corps of Topographical Engineers redeploying Frémont to Iowa. He wrote of the plight of the American Indians and his efforts to educate the colleges and universities about the truth. At the end, he plainly stated his plans to map the upper Missouri River near the Canadian Rockies, which he finished by writing, *"Sound the Trumpets in Rome! For once this first woe passes, the lost key might be found."*

"The lost key?" Simmons repeated aloud.

"I would like to apologize about my earlier reservations about Nicollet. You were right about him. He is a faithful and determined servant."

"Does this mean—"

"He found it? If he actually found it, I do not think he would be trying to warn us. Nicollet might think he knows something, but until he has it, it will be no different than the others."

Woe. Trumpet. Key. "Father Lupo, now I must insist that we recall him so that we might question what he learned as well as question him further about his understanding."

"I would like to see what the Lord intends for him," Father Lupo said. "Let's see what Nicollet discovers with the next expedition, and then we will bring him back so we can speak with him."

CHAPTER SIXTY-NINE
DISTRICT OF COLUMBIA
1841

I have left him in a pit surrounded by vipers, Frémont decided as he walked from Union Station to the map room he once cursed.

After months of exile in the Iowa Territory, banished from Washington for reasons both personal and political, Frémont almost broke into a run.

"Welcome back to Washington, Captain Frémont," a stranger said as he passed by on the wooden sidewalk. Frémont turned around, hoping to catch another glance, but the stranger was gone. Only another hundred yards passed before another complete stranger looked up and smiled.

Again, Frémont neither recognized the man nor had any affiliation with him.

Upon reaching the United States Topographic Engineers' Office, the greetings were based solely on his rank, now a captain. It wasn't until he reached the offices of Colonel Abert that he knew one of his greeters.

After a lengthy chiding, Frémont left Abert's office with his tail between his legs and went upstairs to the offices of the United States Coast Survey.

"Captain Frémont," the men greeted him with smiles, allowing him to be an excuse to stop their tedious work for a moment. Even though many of the men were new, and some much younger than him, they vigorously shook his hand as if they knew him.

Frémont walked up the narrow staircase just as he had done for most of 1840. At the top of the stairs, he found the large office given to them by Joel Poinsett. There, on the massive dining room table, he saw the infamous map of the Upper Mississippi Hydrological Basin.

"Lieutenant Frémont!" Nicollet rose from a plush chair in the corner and nearly ran across the room. Nicollet threw his arms around him, hugging the man tightly. "Have you grown or have I simply shrunk?"

Frémont could see the truth but didn't answer. Despite the bulk of the lavender-scented wool jacket, Nicollet felt rail-thin underneath and his hair was almost white. "It is Captain John C. Frémont, now. I've moved up in the world... after my little reprimand."

"I was worried they had forever taken you away from me... but you've come back," Nicollet gushed, smiling affectionately at his protégé. "Now my plans can continue."

Then Nicollet let go and rushed over to the windows. He flung open the curtains, allowing the light to stream in. Above the table, two sparkling chandeliers cast reflections like the stars in heaven around the room. The massive white canvas almost glowed in the sunlight, and Frémont immediately noticed all of the ink that now adorned it. "You've made tremendous progress since I left. You should be proud... but what in the world did you do to the room?"

THE ALCHEMIST'S MAP

"I simply made it a little more French," Nicollet smiled. "It helped ease the loss of my prized assistant. So tell me all about the West."

The truth will break his heart. Frémont leaned against the massive table and Nicollet leaned against the windowsill, his hands on his hips as usual. "Affairs are bad."

"Then it is as I feared."

"Mind you, I spent my exile surveying the Des Moines, but where there were only three outposts back in 1838, there are now more than thirty settlements. Expansion is happening at a far more alarming rate than even you predicted."

"Any news from Chief Wahanantan? Or Sleepy Eyes? Or Flat Mouth? Do you remember that vile boy who started the fires? I wonder whatever became of him?"

"I never heard. I hardly left Iowa."

"Have you heard the plans proposed by Senator Benton?" Nicollet pressed, grinning slightly when Frémont twitched at the name.

Why does my old friend try to hurt me so? How did I ever wound him? "I've not seen Benton since my return. I try not to think of him."

"Ah, I know better than that, Johnny. Senator Benton has hurt your pride, but your stubbornness will only serve his purposes."

"What do you mean? What has he proposed?"

"He is planning to once again move the Winnebago Indians to act as a buffer between tribes. He is going to push them into the lands of the Dakota. Can you imagine the ripple effect of this ignorant move? After the Van Buren Administration was swept away, I found hope in the promises of President Harrison, but now, your new masters, Benton and Spencer, will create chaos in the West, then offer the military as a solution. Laframboise knew this was coming years before it happened."

"Senator Benton is not my master. Why would you say such a thing after what he did to me?" Frémont realized his voice had risen in anger and quickly collected himself. "Your work is nearing completion, I see. You have Colonel Abert in a twist over the delays."

"Let them wait." Nicollet shook his head dismissively and reached over to a dull green box with his initials on it. Frémont had seen the box on both expeditions he'd accompanied Nicollet on. Nicollet unlocked it with a key he kept around his neck and opened it, glancing up at Frémont.

Inside the box, there was all sorts of clutter: folded and rolled documents, journals, a piece of red pipestone, trinkets, and even a turtle shell. Nicollet found a notebook and took it out. "While you were in Iowa, I have been making preparations for our next expedition. I have prepared a list of materials as well as people I feel we can trust. In order for it to work—"

"Professor Nicollet, Abert's spoken with me. The Tyler Administration wants me to be the public face of the 1842 expedition. If we play our cards right, I might be able to bring you with."

"Bring me with?" Nicollet repeated with a sigh. "I do not think I have the energy for two expeditions."

"Two expeditions?"

Nicollet looked down at his box. "I am losing the fight, Johnny. Last March, Congress had appropriated funds for a new expedition. I was to be its leader, but at a party, I publically began to describe the Chippewa and Sioux to a group of men professing to be my friends. I told them of my plans to take my notes and turn it into a book, defending the Indians to the world as something far different than savage. In the course of a couple of weeks, President Harrison died and you were sent to the Des Moines. I underestimated the will of my enemies."

"I don't understand how any of those things connect."

"As soon as the Indian is gone, the west will be theirs. I returned to Washington believing I could defend the Indian, but now I realize

THE ALCHEMIST'S MAP

I should have gone on the offensive. I should have finished the book and been lecturing. I have wasted too much time. Now President Tyler has opened the floodgates to the West, leaving me behind as a slave to my own creation."

"President Harrison died of pneumonia," Frémont protested. "I was sent to the Des Moines because I overstepped my position in trying to court Jessie Benton."

"Punishment?" Nicollet scoffed. "I was the one being punished. Without you by my side, I was left overwhelmed by this mapping project, leaving me unable to proceed on any other endeavors until it was done."

"Your book on Indian life?"

"And by sending you to the Des Moines, they determined that my apprentice had now become a master. I will not be going with you on the next expedition. I can guarantee as much. I have been making plans for a private expedition."

"A private expedition? To where?"

Nicollet handed him a key.

"What is this for?" Frémont asked.

"It is a contingency if I should be unable to complete the map."

"Why wouldn't you be able to complete the map?"

Despite his aging body, Nicollet's smile still remained strong. "A man can give a speech in the rain one day and die of pneumonia a few weeks later. Even great men are mere mortals, able to succumb to a variety of illnesses. I am on the verge of publishing my map, and in it, I will leave clues for my allies and enemies to discover. Between your trip to the Upper Missouri and the publication of my map, we will create a campaign of misinformation."

"Yes, we will lead them away from what we want to protect. It's why we keep searching west, right?"

Nicollet flipped the pages of the journal to a rough sketch of the monstrosity on the table. "I will attempt to publish my map with these phrases upon it. I worry that they will change my map before releasing it to the public. And as soon as I submit it, my findings will be declared."

Findings?

It took Frémont a few moments to understand. Then he saw the route Nicollet had taken after sending him to the Zumbro. Instead of the Cannon River, he saw the Lahontan River. Instead of the LaPrelle River, he saw the Le Sueur River. A very small "x" identified the location of Fort L'Huillier. And the entire region south of the Minisotah River was labeled as the Undine Region.

He is publishing the location of the Philosopher's Stone.

CHAPTER SEVENTY

DISTRICT OF COLUMBIA
1841

It took two bottles of wine before Nicollet had finished explaining his plans for the private expedition, and even then, he worried he had frightened Frémont away.

Yet Frémont remained transfixed by the contents of the green box, especially the journal, which he slowly flipped through a second time. "So you believe the Philosopher's Stone is some sort of key?"

"It seems the answer to the riddle," Nicollet said, glancing at the tins of copper vitriol he'd unpacked. "So while I am preparing for my expedition, I still need you to continue the quest."

"And you think the Upper Missouri will provide answers?"

"No, but others will think it is Lahontan's Longue River. Do you know the Legend of the Fisher King?"

"It's a King Arthur legend, isn't it?"

"It is. I read the stories when I was a boy and almost forgot all about them until the day Chagobay told me his story of the Fisher Cat who fought a powerful sorcerer that tried to cheat death. Did I ever share this tale with you?"

"No, Professor Nicollet."

"One tale at a time, I suppose. The Fisher King was a guardian of the Holy Grail, but once he was wounded, the land suffered as he suffered. You see, Johnny, the Fisher King was crippled, which kept him from journeying out into the wild. Stuck at his home, only able to fish, he had to rely on other knights to finish the quest for him. Eventually, with proper tutelage, Sir Percival ended up finding the Holy Grail, bringing it back to the old king, and healing both the king and the land."

"In this analogy, do you liken yourself to the Fisher King and me to the young knight? Don't give up on yourself, Professor. You still have journeys left to take."

"I am fifty-five years old, Johnny. I honestly don't know how that happened so suddenly. It seems like just the other day, I met Laplace as a young man in Paris, and now I am Laplace helping a young man begin his career. I've been chasing after one obsession after the other for the better part of four decades... and what do I have to show for it? A green box. Well, it is time I think of someone besides myself for a change."

Nicollet put the contents back in the box and closed it loudly, locking it with a spare key.

"What is that supposed to mean?" Frémont asked.

"Do not trouble yourself with the paranoia of some crazy old wizard. We have plans for a wedding." Nicollet removed his pocket watch and

THE ALCHEMIST'S MAP

looked at it. "I do not have much time to explain, but rest assured, preparations have been made."

"Who is getting married?"

"You are. You and that sweet Jessie Benton will be married by the end of the day."

Nicollet tried to stand but felt the room swim after so much celebratory wine. Frémont looked as if he'd seen No Soul himself climb out of a hole in the floor. "You can't be serious! I haven't seen her for months."

"Please. How do you think you came by her love letters in Iowa? She would bring them to me on her way to Georgetown University, and I would send them off to my friends at the Jesuit College of St. Louis, who would then give them to you. It will bring me great joy to see the two of you happily married."

"You are doing this to upset Senator Benton."

Nicollet smirked. "Yes, but also for you two children. If it is the only good thing I do in my life, I would be satisfied. A colleague of mine, Bishop Van de Velde of St. Louis, is in town on business. He has agreed to marry the two of you this evening at White Marsh."

"What in the world is this?"

"Do you want to marry the girl or not? She certainly wants to marry you."

"Of course I do, but this would be political suicide. Senator Benton would ruin me."

"Not without ruining his own daughter in the process," Nicollet replied as he slipped his primary key back in his shirt pocket.

"He could pay to have me killed."

"Ah, now you are starting to think like a man instead of a boy!" Nicollet grabbed his overcoat and began to collect his belongings. "But he won't do such a thing."

"And why not?"

"Because then he would need me to lead the expedition. I have caught him in my own trap, mon enfant. He has no other choice than to accept you as his son-in-law. If I am wrong, then you will still be happily married to Jessie."

"If you are wrong, you will have your old job back and I will be left behind. Or worse, Benton could shoot me."

"Trust me, Johnny. I am not wrong about this. You will keep them distracted while I finish my masterpiece."

"Yes, so while De Smet and I seek watersheds in the west, your private expedition will sneak in the back door. And then what?" Frémont asked.

A knock came from the doorway and a stranger's voice called out, "Mr. Nicollet, the carriage is waiting below."

Nicollet saw a brooding man in the doorway. "Johnny," Nicollet said, "this is a very good friend from White Marsh. He is going to take you out to Father Van de Velde, where your precious Jessie is waiting."

"What about you?"

"You are about to have the most exciting year of your life; I will be making preparations for the most exciting year of mine. First, I must finish the map that has become both a blessing and a curse. Next, I will continue my defense of the Indians of the Great Plains, and while you explore the Upper Missouri, I will be preparing my own team for a less public expedition."

Frémont stood blinking. "I don't know what to say, Professor Nicollet. You are like the father I never had. I don't know how to thank you."

"I will fight the darkness by bringing a little light into the world." Nicollet took him by the arm and led him off to his waiting bride. "Be sure you do not lose the key to my chest. If I fail, you must find my private journal before they do. Until this map is finished, it is as precious to me as Jessie is to you."

CHAPTER SEVENTY-ONE

CAMBRIDGE
1842

Even after the applause died, the curtains closed, and the custodians began cleaning the lecture hall, a large crowd waited to ambush Nicollet in the College Commons of University Hall.

Although Asa Gray had only recently changed offices from the University of Michigan to Harvard, he still swelled with pride at the reception given to Nicollet.

But even if I must wait all night, I will set things right while I have the opportunity.

While others pressed forward to introduce themselves to Nicollet, Gray waited patiently, hoping for the smallest audience possible before meeting Nicollet on such a shameful pretext.

For the better part of two years, Gray had waited for an opportunity to speak with Nicollet, but the Frenchman was a whirlwind of activity despite being twice his own age.

From week to week, Nicollet would take up new residences, staying with the Bentons, the Tollivers, Ferdinand Hassler, the Jesuits at White Marsh or Georgetown, and private residences in unknown locations. Despite claims of long hours at the Corps of Topographical Engineers offices, Nicollet would give lectures in Philadelphia, Baltimore, Washington D.C., Niagara Falls, and even on a surprise trip to St. Louis.

For this reason, Asa Gray waited for Nicollet to come to him at Harvard.

The crowd waiting in the College Commons was a strange mix. Crusty old professors, ambitious young men, and even a large contingency of female undergraduates from nearby Radcliffe College waited to meet the man.

Although Gray had only recently turned thirty, he'd spent his twenties drifting from field to field and was therefore able to recognize the scientific menagerie gathered for Nicollet's lecture. Astronomers, geologists, botanists, anthropologists, historians, and a few politicians had come to listen to the celebrity.

If Nicollet had a book to sell, he'd be independently wealthy by the end of the night, Gray realized as an hour ticked by.

Gray positioned himself by the exit door, knowing that if Nicollet tired of fame and made a run for it, he'd still be able to speak the words that would undoubtedly stop him in his tracks.

Many in the crowd departed, and Gray found himself standing beside a familiar face. "Dr. Jackson, how have you been?"

Charles Thomas Jackson gave a perplexed look. Five years older than Gray, he'd had the good fortune of settling into his career already. He now had spectacles, a receding hairline, and a full beard but shaved

THE ALCHEMIST'S MAP

lips. Gray had been a young man when he spent a summer working for the Harvard geologist during his survey of Nova Scotia, which is why Jackson finally relented with, "I'm sorry, you are..."

"Asa Gray, Professor of Botany here at your Alma Mater, but I worked with you and Francis Alger on your geological survey."

"Nova Scotia!" Jackson snapped. "It's been a while. So you are a professor at Harvard now? Congratulations."

"Thank you, Dr. Jackson. Did you enjoy the lecture?"

"Yes, he is a peculiar little fellow, isn't he? When he gets worked up, I can barely understand his English. I'd hoped to hear more about his study of the Missouri River, rather than all the talk about Indians, but Professor Nicollet asked me for a favor, so here I am."

"What sort of favor?" Gray asked.

"Oh, Professor Nicollet and I had a chance encounter while he was staying at Niagara Falls, and when he heard I'd studied Nova Scotia, he began to press me on matters of both Indians and geology. During his expeditions, he took samples of copper, and since that is now my specialty, I told him I'd analyze his specimens. He wrote that he'd be coming to Harvard, so it seemed like the right opportunity."

"Copper specimens? Nicollet certainly leaves no stone unturned."

"What about you? Are you a fan, or are you a colleague?"

I feel like a fraud. Gray was still rail-thin as if an emaciated college student, his cheeks still could not muster a beard, and his short dark hair looked the same as it did when he was a volunteer a decade earlier. "I suppose I'm just an anonymous fan, Dr. Jackson."

Gray waited another half hour for the crowd to thin, Dr. Jackson to receive his copper samples, and for Professor Nicollet to finally make his way to the front doors. When he reached them, Gray called out, "Professor Nicollet, I believe I have something you are looking for."

Nicollet's smile vanished, and he quickly whispered something to the man escorting him, who marched through the doors and into the darkness. Nicollet's exodus halted, and the small man put his hands upon his hips before saying, "I do not believe we have had the pleasure of an introduction."

Gray introduced himself and vigorously shook his hand. A few others interrupted for a pat on the back or a brief comment, but Gray stood toe-to-toe with Nicollet, who stood his ground. The College Commons was nowhere near empty, with small circles of conversation still happening, but Gray felt it was private enough to begin, "I believe this belongs to you."

Gray pulled the vasculum from his coat pocket, and with both hands, held the tin cylinder for Nicollet to see. Nicollet's eyes tightened for a moment as he inspected the ornate carving of a field and forest with a distinctly German castle in the background.

Suddenly, Nicollet's eyes darted around the room before he said, "Please put that back immediately."

Gray obliged. "You recognize it?"

"Of course I recognize it, but it certainly does not belong to me."

"I am not responsible for the theft, and received the ill-gotten gains mostly by chance. It took quite a bit of analysis to determine your connection to it."

"The contents?"

"Yes, the contents of the vasculum certainly limited the possibilities," Gray said.

Nicollet stepped closer, this time to whisper. "How did you come by this?"

"As I said earlier, I've only recently begun my professorship here at Harvard and spent the better part of a year studying and looking for suitable employment. When Harvard accepted my application, I sent for my belongings and private specimens I had collected for my professorship at the University of Michigan. Not only were my belongings sent, but there were also four crates of specimens that did not belong to me."

"The University of Michigan?"

"I was to be its first professor of botany, and the board of regents sent me to Europe to create a grand collection. I purchased and collected every sample for them, yet I knew immediately that these samples were not mine. I was on the verge of writing Mr. Schoolcraft and the other regents when I discovered this vasculum with wildflower specimens. Am I correct in assessing they came from your 1838 expedition?"

"As it so happens, the vasculum you have in your possession personally belonged to Karl Geyer. An entire wagon full of specimens from our expedition vanished on the way to St. Louis. There were rumors that it had been sent by accident to Wisconsin, but no one could determine what had happened to it after that. The University of Michigan, you say?"

"Yes, but I can assure you, when I left, none of these specimens were part of the collection. I just wanted to make sure they were returned."

"I'm sure the thief was sorely disappointed to learn the value of the wagon was only in its flowers and ferns, and I am sure whoever delivered these to the University only did so for the betterment of science and learning. Luckily, Karl Geyer will be visiting me soon, and I will let him know our lost specimens have been found. Until then, please keep them safe here at Harvard, Professor Gray."

Nicollet again vigorously shook his hand and then slipped away out the front door to the waiting coach.

CHAPTER SEVENTY-TWO

DISTRICT OF COLUMBIA
1843

By the 1730s, the world had begun to call the thirteen colonies "Columbia," a female goddess based on the Latinized name of "Columbus." Although one of the newest deities in human history, Columbia had roots that reached back in time past the neoclassical fervor discovered during the founding of a new nation.

The Romans once knew her as "Libertas," while the Greeks saw her as "Eleutheria" and "Athena." From the District of Columbia to the capital of South Carolina, she became the visual symbol of the United States—a beautiful robed woman shown holding various objects, such as a light, a cornucopia, a parrot, or even a severed human head. The popular symbol was applied to universities, rivers, territories, companies, and even

THE ALCHEMIST'S MAP

a country during the Spanish American wars of independence. Although symbolically replaced by the Statue of Liberty in later times, her use and conceptual worship left an indelible mark on American history.

While early refugees came to the colonies seeking like-minded believers, others came seeking freedom from the established religions. As a result, Columbia became a new spiritual icon for Manifest Destiny, which sought to bring light, knowledge, and transformation to the North American continent. Through conquest and annexation, the Old World would be reborn as a new heaven.

Having been born in Baku, where his people still worshipped fire as a deity, Krasdan Krai easily took to worshipping the goddess Columbia, even if she was only a concept and offered nothing to humans that they could not provide for themselves. By contrast, Joseph Nicollet still publically worshipped the Old World trinity and once again stood in the way.

"Despite the delays, Nicollet's map is exceptional," the clerk said to Krai, his hands on his hips. "His Report is also finished. I've also set it out for you to see. Both will need congressional approval before printing, but considering the quality of both, I don't see any issues with his work."

Krai recognized Lake Superior in the upper right corner, as well as St. Louis along the bottom of the map. The twists and turns of the Missouri River also remained vivid in his mind, even if the map did them little justice.

Because of Manifest Destiny, another blank space had been filled, even if Nicollet filled it with references to the Old World. "There are always issues and delays with projects such as these."

"Professor Nicollet has been meticulous in his calculations, and after all his efforts, I believe he is ready to move on to another challenge."

"Has he spoken to you about future expeditions?" Krai asked.

"I have mostly inferred. I believe he means to join with Frémont on an expedition to the upper Missouri River," the clerk answered.

"I've heard his health has deteriorated in recent months."

"Yes, he was quite ill for a stretch, but recently, after changing his living quarters and diet, he seems to be a new man."

He is like a cockroach that needs to be stepped on a dozen times. Krai found himself staring down a hundred names, some obscure Indian titles and others he recognized, such as Benton, Abert, Poinsett, Frémont, and Lea. There were two other names that twisted in his belly: Le Sueur and Lahontan.

Despite Nicollet's recent attempts to stop the tide of Manifest Destiny, he'd done little to sway perceptions of the American Indian, and the French pebble in the shoe of Krai's benefactor might have been ignored. Yet putting the names "Le Sueur" and "Lahontan" on the government publication could not be ignored, nor could the most audacious act—labeling a large section with the bold word "UNDINE."

"Is this an Indian word?" Krai asked, feigning ignorance over the term that would send fanatics like the Order of Eos into hysterics.

"It's hard to understand Professor Nicollet some days. In many cases, he took careful measures to give places accurate Indian names, and other times, he'd name a place after someone who met him the day he held a pencil. Undine? I think he wrote about it in his Report to Congress."

"Could you show me?"

The clerk for the Offices of the United States Corps of Topographical Engineers did not know Krai's name, nor he know the clerk's, but the clerk did understand Krai represented wealthy donors who helped advance careers. He found Nicollet's large tome that justified five years of governmental paychecks.

"Here it is," the clerk said after flipping pages. "It's in his summary of his 1838 expedition. It has something to do with a Germanic tale."

A Germanic tale? Not alchemy? Krai slid the open report toward

THE ALCHEMIST'S MAP

himself and leaned down to read the page. His maimed hand held the page from moving.

Nicollet wrote:

> *The term "Undine" is derived from that of an interesting and romantic German tale, the heroine of which belonged to an extensive race of water-spirits living in the brooks, and rivers, and lakes, whose father was a mighty prince. She is moreover the niece of a great brook (the Mankato) who lived in the midst of forests, and was beloved by all the many great streams of the surrounding country. I do not know why I fancied an analogy between the ideal country described in the tale, and that of the one before me; but I involuntarily, as it were, adopted the name.*

Involuntarily? Is he talking of Benton? A girl with a mighty father?

Krai straightened his back while the clerk leaned in to say, "The Undine region certainly sounds lovely."

"Yes," Krai said, "lovely. This is Nicollet's final alteration of the map?"

"Yes, congress has funded printing and publication as soon as it is approved. Will it be approved?"

Krai quickly checked other areas: the headwaters of the Des Moines, the St. Peter, and the Mississippi. A thousand labels were placed upon the map but only one whimsical name—the "Undine."

Involuntarily? For the past dozen years, he'd known about Professor Nicollet's connection to the Drummond map, and having seen it himself, Krai knew exactly why Nicollet placed the words "Le Sueur," "Lahontan," and "Undine" upon it. The map was even marked with many a little "x" to denote where he'd been… if they knew what they were looking for.

Krai felt the weight of his weapons in his pockets, calling to him like hungry birds needing to be fed, but there was no reason to kill the clerk, who had no idea who Krai was or who he worked for.

Yet he also knew Nicollet could not be allowed to travel back west, nor could the map be printed as it was. Now, he'd have to kill Nicollet, *involuntarily.*

CHAPTER SEVENTY-THREE

PLATTE RIVER

1843

Nicollet *will love the Rocky Mountains*, Frémont decided. A hundred miles in the distance, he saw the peaks from the deck of his steamer. He once again travelled the same route he'd taken in 1842, but this time he was equipped to push past the South Pass of the Wyoming Territory and through the Rockies. His goal: a map of the Oregon Trail.

With Jessie's writing skill, he'd turned his trip into a national adventure story in the newspapers, resulting in a second expedition of forty men, a twelve-pound howitzer cannon, and his own Taopi—Kit Carson.

Carson sat alone, refusing the company of any of the other men. Once unleashed upon the Rockies, he would often ride ahead, return for a quick update, and then vanish again. Jessie had made Carson a celebrity, colorfully describing the Indian Fighter and Mountain Man in her newspaper stories, but the bitter guide wanted no part in fame.

He still mourns his young wife, Frémont observed, watching Carson at the nose of the steamer. Carson was medium-height, broad-shouldered, and deep-chested, hardly an imposing figure like Jim Taopi, but he had the narrow eyes of a killer.

The previous summer, Frémont had been looking for one of Stewart's mountain men, Thomas Fitzpatrick, when he ran into Carson, who morosely asked, "Have you found him yet?"

Frémont had all but forgotten the name "Daniel Lyons," but Carson hadn't. Behind every bush, tree, and boulder along the Platte, Carson searched for the enigmatic man who'd brought smallpox to the upper Missouri.

"When this expedition is over, I hope you can return with me to Washington, if only so I can introduce you to Nicollet. He will want to hear all about our adventures."

"You're assuming we will survive," Carson said. Although only four years his senior, Carson seemed to carry decades worth of cynicism. "We'll be going through Shoshone territory, and then only God knows what else."

"Even so," Frémont remained optimistic. "I want you to meet Nicollet. He taught me everything I know about map-making, and much more."

Carson grumbled, only able to connect the word "Nicollet" with the name "Lyons."

Frémont understood the sacrifice he was making for Nicollet. A map of the Oregon Trail could take the better part of a year, and by that time, Nicollet's return to Minnesota would be complete.

With Father De Smet, Baron Stewart, and himself all exploring the

THE ALCHEMIST'S MAP

Missouri River in some fashion or another, the giant Brunia had been sent back to the Minnesota territory for a private expedition.

If successful, Nicollet would be smuggled out of the country, along with the Philosopher's Stone, never to be seen in public again.

Even though Frémont knew he traveled upon another "Longue" river, just as Stewart and De Smet also intended to distract the zealots, he found the legend hard to believe.

Nor could he speak openly of it to a man like Kit Carson.

So the two quietly stood together and waited for the shadows of the Rocky Mountains to return.

CHAPTER SEVENTY-FOUR
BOSTON
1843

Copper is one of the few metals in nature that can be directly used, which made it popular with early humans. Its use can be traced back thousands of years to cultures across the globe.

Another unique aspect of copper is that its natural color is different from most silver or gray metals and instead appears as a robust orange-red color. Whereas iron will rust when placed in contact with water, copper does not react with water. It does react with air, however, creating a green layer of verdigris that acts as a bonding layer to protect the underlying metal.

Copper (II) sulfate, with the chemical formula $CuSO_4 \cdot 5H_2O$, is commonly referred to as copper vitriol and appears as crystals

THE ALCHEMIST'S MAP

that are bright blue. Unlike oxidized copper, copper sulfate contains water and also typically contains four sizes of crystal.

Dr. Charles T. Jackson, a prominent New England geologist, specialized in surveying areas for copper mines as well as determining the chemical quality of samples. For this reason, Joseph Nicollet met with him after a speech at Harvard University several months earlier.

Jackson gathered Nicollet's sample tins and shoved them into a travel bag. Then he went back to his analysis reports, reading over them one more time.

Nicollet is testing me and I don't even know the question he's asked, Jackson realized. *All I have are the answers to this strange riddle.*

Purportedly, Nicollet had taken the samples while on his expeditions in the West, but the only labels on the tins were simple letters, leaving Jackson with a blind analysis. However, rumors floated that Nicollet had approached another geologist, Jacob Bailey of West Point, with the same task. The clue had been a sample of greensand unique to New Jersey, which contained multilocular shells of the family Foraminifera.

My microscope cannot be so easily fooled, Professor Nicollet.

Besides the weak attempt at trickery with the greensand samples, Jackson also found that two samples contained crystals, indicating that they were engineered in a laboratory rather than discovered out in the open wilderness as Nicollet claimed.

I know copper ore when I see it.

Other rumors said Nicollet planned another grand adventure now that his health had recovered. Jackson had intended on delivering the copper analysis during the previous winter, but Nicollet's health had taken a dramatic turn for the worse. Ferdinand Hassler, Nicollet's friend and mentor, wrote that Nicollet suffered from stomach issues, headaches, and even applied blisters. The appointment would have to wait for another time.

All symptoms of arsenic poisoning, Jackson had thought to himself at the time. With the arrival of spring, Nicollet's good health returned. According to the most recent letter, Nicollet currently resided at Galabrun's Hotel, an embassy for French travelers on the outskirts of Washington.

Nicollet had a trip planned on September 15th, forcing Jackson to make his trip to see him over the coming weekend. He wrote to Nicollet that he'd visit on Sunday, September 10th, so he could return his samples and discuss his findings. As a former physician, Jackson also planned to examine Nicollet's health, writing, "Pray take care of yourself; men of true science are not so abundant that we can spare you."

If I pass the test with the copper samples, perhaps he will invite me on his next expedition, Jackson hoped, and set the samples and analysis near the front door beside his travel bags.

CHAPTER SEVENTY-FIVE

BALTIMORE
1843

Saturday nights at Galabrun's Hotel reminded Nicollet of Paris. Unlike the drunken debauchery of the Germanic parties in St. Louis, the guests of Galabrun's showed refined control, bringing a symphony of chuckles and conversation that at times drowned out the fiddle and piano in the corner. Nicollet had left his own fiddle in a storage shed at Ferdinand Hassler's country home, but he also knew his fingers were not as dexterous as they'd once been.

He also did not feel the need to prove himself and was content to watch the younger men strut their talents and boast of their accomplishments. He chose to sit in a booth in the back of the lobby, observing it all, knowing it would be his last weekend of civilized society before he returned to the cold comforts of the wilderness.

Three years of planning and waiting rendered down to a few days.

Nicollet thought of Shetek, Chagobay, Sleepy Eyes, Wahanantan, Grey Heron, and even vile Ohanzee. *First I must find the White Egg—if I am worthy to be the Wishwee they think I am.*

Before he could join the others in St. Louis, he first had to make the journey back to Minnesota. In a few days, the others would meet him at Galabrun's Hotel and then he would vanish from his place in the spotlight.

The waitress set a wine glass down in front of him and said, "Compliments of Mr. Agassiz."

Nicollet looked down at the glass, and from the smell and color, recognized a finer Bordeaux than Galabrun's Hotel served. Although he'd never met Louis Agassiz, he knew the name well enough. The waitress turned toward a dark-haired man still wearing his jacket, seated at a table near the front window. Along with a travel satchel, Agassiz had a bottle of wine and a glass of Bordeaux in front of him. He raised a glass in a salute.

Nicollet reciprocated and gestured to the seat across from him in his booth. Agassiz clumsily struggled with his heavy satchel before collecting the bottle of wine and glass and crossing the busy lobby.

He set the glass and bottle on the table and then vigorously shook Nicollet's hand with both of his. "I apologize for the interruption, but I've been an admirer of yours for a long, long time. If not for the July Revolution—"

"Yes, you and Humboldt left for Berlin," Nicollet recalled. The Swiss scientist had a head of thick dark hair and deeply mysterious eyes with a discerning twinkle in them. Although cleanly shaven, a shadow of a dark beard already presented itself. With broad shoulders and a lean frame, he looked as if he could lead an expedition through any terrain.

THE ALCHEMIST'S MAP

"Please, sit, Mr. Agassiz. Any friend of Humboldt's is a friend of mine."

"I am sorry to intrude like this, but when I heard that the renowned savant was staying so near, I had to stop before leaving the area."

"Well, I'm glad you took the initiative. I'd heard you were traveling the British Isles, though."

"I was, but I've finished my studies and have produced a book. Humboldt told me all about your own study of the Chamonix glacier near your former home of Savoy. I always felt like a dwarf walking around in the shoes of a giant. You are the master of so many fields, whereas I..."

Agassiz reached into his satchel and slid a book across the table. *Études sur les Glaciers* by Louis Agassiz. Nicollet picked it up and flipped through some of the pages.

This is no chance meeting. He is here not only because of personal jealousy but also because of my big mouth. "Have you come to debate me, Louis?"

"On the contrary, I've come to discuss your findings and remarks on the James River. When you described how the valley had been 'scooped out by some powerful denuding cause,' I knew I had to meet you."

This is not what I expected from Humboldt's apprentice. "I think you have come here to debate me, Louis. You've caught me at a strange time, though. I plan to travel soon and the details of this trip have left me a little distracted."

"I'd like you to keep the book. Wherever you are traveling, let it keep you company and give you food for thought."

"How can I debate with something that exists in black and white, fixed and unchangeable?" Nicollet asked.

"Glaciers are proof that even the most stubborn boulder can be worn away and removed by the progress of time," Agassiz said with a wry smile. "If you don't want to discuss glaciers, perhaps we could discuss other matters. Tell me about this trip you are taking. Tell me about the Indians of the west."

This is going to be a long night. Perhaps it will take my mind off of things for a while. "First, a toast. To Alexander von Humboldt, our mentor."

Nicollet raised his glass and so did Agassiz, who carefully held the glass with a hand deprived of two fingers.

CHAPTER SEVENTY-SIX

BALTIMORE
1843

Sweat trickled down Davey Faribault's face and into the cloth of his soaked collar. The heat was becoming more than he could take.

"We will be reaching your destination in Baltimore in just a few minutes," the train attendant told him, having been with him for most of the sweltering day.

Faribault glanced over at the ogre sleeping beside him in the aisle seat and simply shrugged, choosing to wait silently in the heat of the day rather than wake his gruff traveling companion. Outside the window, Faribault could see the urban sprawl growing denser, making it impossible to picture Nicollet in such a place.

Dressed in a traveling jacket, Faribault let the heat begin to fester in his mind. He tried to rid himself of it by loosening the top buttons of his shirt to allow more airflow.

Beside him, Sargent Jim Taopi slept in a loose cotton shirt, unbuttoned halfway to his navel. Upon his head, he wore an ornate smoking cap with a foxtail that replaced the original tassel and a large eagle feather that added an extra foot to his height. Faribault had insisted on Taopi wearing his old uniform to discourage thieves, but his companion also kept his sheathed knife strapped to his thigh.

"Jim," Faribault elbowed his friend. "Jim, wake up."

Taopi simply grunted. Faribault found himself wincing as he looked at the right side of Taopi's face. Even after living a life out in the frontier, Faribault still felt like a greenhorn compared to Taopi.

"Jim, wake up," Faribault tried again and a white eye opened. "The train is pulling into the station. We need to be ready to disembark."

Taopi again grunted, carefully adjusted his circular smoking cap, and grabbed the seat in front of him for leverage.

As soon as the two stepped out of the train car, the air quality improved and Faribault felt a little less anxious. After crossing the platform of paving stones and steel, he scanned the streets for the hotel Nicollet described to them.

"I don't understand why Nicollet would choose to live in a city. Look at the filth."

Taopi didn't answer, nor did he look.

"Are you having second thoughts?"

"Of course not. I owe Nicollet a life debt."

"No, do you have second thoughts about Red Blanket Woman?"

The trio had traveled by water through the Great Lakes until they reached Niagara Falls, where Father De Smet arranged for food and shelter at a convent. For his part, Davy Faribault spread lies about the stolen bride of Hank Sibley dying of fever. "There is no place for her in

THE ALCHEMIST'S MAP

the West after she betrayed her husband. As long as Sibley thinks she is dead, she will be safe in Buffalo."

"When this is over, are you going to marry her?"

Taopi ignored the question as they walked down the streets of Baltimore. "When the mission is over, I'll return to Minnesota."

"You will?"

"I am a Guardian of the Frontier, and I will watch over Red Blanket Woman's daughter as if she were my own, even if she remains in Sibley's house."

"Then I'd suggest avoiding Hank Sibley for a few years," Faribault teased.

He found Galabrun's Hotel quickly, leading Taopi right to the front doors. Large fans run by a system of pulleys provided a cool breeze for the patrons. At a table along the wall, a group of three soldiers nodded to Taopi, even though Faribault doubted any of them had crossed the Mississippi.

"What can I get for you fellas?" the bartender asked.

"We're here to meet someone," Faribault said.

"It doesn't mean you can't refresh yourself while you wait."

"I'll have a hard apple cider," Faribault nodded and searched for a few coins in his pocket.

"Tennessee whiskey," Taopi said.

Faribault nervously watched as the bartender tried to make sense of his companion's dark features, but dressed in "civilized" clothes, Taopi was quickly served anyway.

"His room is upstairs?" Taopi finally asked after taking a swig of his whiskey.

"Yes, on the second floor," Faribault answered.

Two men burst in through the front door, causing Faribault to spill a little of his cider. Annoyed, he watched a man in a bowtie leading an older man with a medical bag through the inn and to the back.

A few minutes later, the man in the silk bow tie returned from the back room. "Can we get some help? There is a man who is sick. We need to bring him to a carriage." The man's plea fell on deaf ears. "Please!"

Taopi cleared his throat and tossed back the last bit of whiskey before finding his way to the hotel staircase.

From the bar, Faribault could hear excited voices coming from the back room, including more words from Taopi than he had heard in a week of traveling.

"David," Taopi called out from the doorway, suddenly using his first name.

With the eyes of the tavern upon him, Faribault nervously walked to the rear. Three slaves stood in a corner near the entrance to the water closets, watching with wide eyes as the doctor tended to the man lying on the floor. Although the man's pants were down around his ankles, a blanket had been tossed over his legs to give him a little dignity. Puddles of bloody vomit pooled on the wooden floorboards beside him.

The man with the silk bow tie stood with tears in his eyes, holding another heavy blanket that would have been used to transport the man. Still reacting to the smells of illness and death lingering in the air of the narrow hallway, Faribault wrinkled his brow indignantly until he saw Taopi drop to his knees and take hold of the dying man's right hand.

"You know him?" the man in the silk bow tie asked.

Taopi nodded, ripping his ornate smoking cap from his head to wipe away the beaded sweat and trickle of vomit from the dying man's face, Taopi's lone eagle feather falling forgotten to the floor. The act of gentle compassion and the gruesome pink scars of Taopi's exposed scalp made Faribault queasy.

The dying man's bright red vest and white undershirt had been torn open to expose a thin pale chest struggling to take in a full breath.

THE ALCHEMIST'S MAP

"I've contacted his colleagues," the man in the silk bow tie told the older doctor, who was busy listening to the dying man's labored breathing with his stethoscope. "A carriage should be arriving soon to take him to the closest hospital."

"This man would die if we transported him right now," the elderly doctor explained as his focus turned to the man's spotted hands. "His lungs are filling with fluids."

Oh dear God, does the man have smallpox? Faribault wondered, remembering the epidemic that had swept through the frontier. But the dark little dots were relegated only to the man's palms, and did not boil and bubble like smallpox.

"This is an important man, doctor," Taopi said, sniffling a bit.

Taopi is crying? Faribault recoiled. *What is wrong with him?*

"Whatever this man needs, give it to him," Taopi insisted. "Money is no obstacle. Faribault, give him some money."

"Money will not save this poor fellow," the older doctor said. "The only thing we can do for him is find a bed and a priest. I think he has been poisoned."

At that, Taopi grabbed the doctor by his collar and slammed him against the narrow wall of the hallway. "Don't say such things. Save him!"

Then the dying man's eyes fluttered open and looked right at him. Suddenly the narrow hallway spun, and Faribault had to put a hand on the wall to keep his balance.

"Look what they have done to me," Professor Nicollet spoke in a tattered whisper. It was impossible to see the jovial eyes, the gentle smile, and the dark flop of hair that once swept down over the man's brow. Instead, he saw a grey face with hollow eyes.

Faribault dropped his satchel and pushed his way past the doctor, taking the spotted hand in his own, kissing the top of it. "Professor Nicollet, it's Davey. We will watch over you now."

CHAPTER SEVENTY-SEVEN

BALTIMORE
1843

By late evening, after watching Joseph Nicollet drift in and out of consciousness, Jim Taopi positioned his chair a few feet from the bed. In the corner of the room, Davey Faribault sat despondent, while the man in the silk bowtie, Dr. Charles Jackson, paced nervously at the foot of the bed.

"If I had known he was this sick, I would have insisted he see a doctor instead of meeting me over matters of geology. I didn't know. I just didn't know. My wife had heard rumors, but there was no indication in his letters that his condition was this... was this grave."

Poisoning... That had been the initial diagnosis of Nicollet's illness. Taopi could see the symptoms growing worse by the minute as Nicollet's lungs labored for breath.

THE ALCHEMIST'S MAP

"Dr. Jackson, the fault does not fall on you," Faribault said after running his fingers through his hair. "You can leave. We were his traveling companions. We accept responsibility for his care."

The nervous doctor took a few steps towards the door and stopped. "I have something. It is a soil analysis that he asked me to complete." Jackson set the papers on a stack of books that had been earlier found in Nicollet's possession.

"Thank you, Dr. Jackson," Faribault said.

As soon as Dr. Jackson left, Taopi whispered into Nicollet's ear. "Professor Nicollet. It is Taopi. Who did this to you?"

Nicollet's eyes fluttered. "I saw her," Nicollet whispered softly. "She was waiting for me in the waters. She tried to…"

"Who, Professor Nicollet?" Faribault whispered insistently.

Taopi shook his head. "He's hallucinating." Beads of sweat covered Nicollet's brow, and his body randomly convulsed.

"We were there, boys. I was so close but could not see her. Now she has come for me," Nicollet whispered before a fit of coughing shook him terribly. "But I didn't let her steal my soul. I tricked her."

"Rest, Professor," Taopi said. "The other doctor will be back any minute with some better medicine, understand?"

Nicollet managed a slight smile.

Taopi rose and began to inspect the room.

A crime scene, Taopi noted.

Already, he'd spoken to the bartender, who explained that Nicollet had met with a dark-haired man who had brought books and his own bottle of wine. Taopi found both books and an empty bottle of wine in the room. The books were Charles Lyle's *Principles of Geology*, George Fanshaw's *Geological Reports of 1835 and 1836*, Gerard Troost's *Geological Reports of Tennessee,* Alexander Humboldt's *Tableaux de la Nature,* and Louis Agassiz's *Études sur les Glaciers.*

The bartender also explained that shortly before Taopi and Faribault arrived, Dr. Jackson asked about Nicollet and went upstairs to call upon him. Jackson was not the same man as the Saturday visitor.

Nicollet had already put his belongings in storage, and although he was a scientist, the presence of the five books seemed out of place, especially with the bartender mentioning the wine and books brought by the dark-haired man. Taopi flipped through the books for a moment.

At the table by the window, he found an assortment of notebooks written in the hand of Nicollet. He thumbed through them until he found a few drawings that included a turtle, a woman surrounded by lily pads, a man on fire, and some sort of water serpent. He slipped the notebooks into his shirt.

"Are you stealing those?" Faribault asked.

"I am no thief," Taopi snapped. "If Nicollet dies, these can't be found in his possession."

"What are you talking about? Put them back. You can't even read."

"Then I will find someone who can," Taopi added, stuffing the canisters in his leather satchel.

"Those might be important!"

Taopi nodded, snatched Dr. Jackson's analysis, and added it to the satchel. "I will keep them safe until we can find someone who can make sense of it all."

It only took a few minutes to search the rest of the hotel room.

"What are you looking for?" Faribault finally asked.

"The green box. It held a wampum belt and his journal, along with all of his other valuables. I once caught Colton trying to break into it."

"Edgar Colton?"

Taopi nodded. "Another time. Right now, we need to find that box before it is too late."

THE ALCHEMIST'S MAP

He returned to the five books, slipping each of them inside of his satchel also.

A few minutes later, the elderly local doctor returned out of breath with several bottles in a leather bound box. He quickly fed Nicollet a few tablespoons of the concoction while providing comfort for his fever.

Taopi stood with his arms crossed while they watched the doctor before finally whispering into Faribault's ear, "We need to talk in private."

Taopi led Faribault into the quiet stairway and stopped at the top of the stairwell leading down to the tavern. "Did you hear what Nicollet first said to us?"

"Yes, but the man was hallucinating."

Taopi shrugged it off. "Do you remember what the doctor said? He thought Nicollet might be poisoned."

"Or it could just be pneumonia," Faribault added. "Even if it was poisoning, who in God's name would want to poison him?"

"Nicollet knew things," Taopi insisted. "Dangerous things. When we first met him, he was already on a dangerous path. Someone did not want him taking another trip"

"But who?"

Four sharply-dressed men appeared at the bottom of the stairs, drawing their attention. The grim men steadily ascended the stairs.

"Can we help you fellows?" Taopi said, giving them a cold look.

"You must be Hassler," Faribault politely smiled.

"No, we were sent to retrieve Professor Nicollet. Is he up here?"

Faribault nodded, but Taopi stood in the way. "*Who* sent you?"

"We work for the Corps of Topographical Engineers. Colonel Abert sent us as soon as he heard the news."

Taopi held his ground, until all the men were suddenly aware of a presence behind them—the elderly doctor.

"Science has been deprived by too early a death," he declared, and only then did Taopi step away to find support at the railing of the stairs.

Abert's men quickly rushed by, and in a daze, Taopi slowly descended the stairs to the bar below. At the bar, Taopi ordered a shot of whiskey.

A few minutes later, Faribault slid up beside him. "He is dead." Faribault then set down a ten-dollar bill on the counter. "Give us the bottle."

He filled Taopi's cup, then filled his own.

"To Professor Nicollet. May his journey be swift."

Taopi finished half of Faribault's whiskey bottle before he understood what needed to be done. Reaching into his satchel, he found the samples. Two of them belonged to Joseph Nicollet. One canister, which he removed, was slightly different.

"Someone killed Nicollet to keep him from going on another expedition."

"Who?"

Taopi rotated the tin specimen, showing what was written on the white label to Faribault: *"Property of Harvard University."* "We'll start by asking Dr. Jackson a few more questions."

CHAPTER SEVENTY-EIGHT
CAMBRIDGE
1844

Everyone smiled and chuckled, but Karl Geyer knew it was all a show. Inside of Antoine Clément's fur coat, a twelve-inch blade waited to be called upon. Sir William Drummond Stewart wore a brash red military jacket with two small pistols tucked in the pockets.

Will they slaughter this poor man? Geyer wondered.

The chill of a Massachusetts winter did not bother Geyer, having spent the past several years on the frontier. Nor did it bother Clément and Drummond. Professor Asa Gray, however, did not have enough buttons on his winter coat to shield him from the cold, and by the time they crossed the campus of Harvard University, he was visibly shaking.

"I kept the botanical specimens stored in the basement," Gray said.

"Until they could be claimed or their owner could be located. I hope you understand how embarrassing this is for me and my university."

"Karl has more flowers now than he knows what to do with," Stewart playfully rolled his eyes and shrugged. "I'm not sure our ship could hold another case."

Gray glanced over, almost hopeful. Leaving the collection of botanical specimens would strengthen the esteem of Gray's new department, but Geyer had no intention of making such an altruistic gesture.

"Lead on, Professor Gray," Geyer said.

While their genial host continued, Geyer felt his own face harden despite the warmth of the basement they were now in.

Finally, Gray pulled a canvas tarp away to reveal a stack of crates against a wall. When he opened one of the lids, Geyer found himself looking at a collection of specimens he'd found at distant Lake Tewapadan, or "Lura," as had been carved into the tree.

Thoughts of Nicollet flooded his mind, and Geyer leaned against the crates and then slid down onto the floor, covering his head with his hands as he sobbed. When news of Nicollet's death reached him, he was thousands of miles from Galabrun's Hotel, unable to show his respects. Even though Nicollet had died months earlier, seeing the lost collection of specimens hit hard.

"Come, Professor Gray," Stewart said. "Let's give Karl a few moments of privacy. Show me the rest of your department, and we can make arrangements for the transfer of Mr. Geyer's collection."

Antoine Clément stayed, and when Geyer finished mourning, he looked up at the dispassionate face of the giant Métis. "How did this happen? Why did this happen?"

Clément knelt down beside him, and lowered his voice to say, "They thought that your plants hid something of greater value, so arrangements were made to reroute the wagon from St. Louis to Wisconsin.

THE ALCHEMIST'S MAP

It wasn't until they arrived at Detroit that they discovered the crates contained only plants... so they were given to Henry Schoolcraft, who donated them to the University of Michigan's new science department, and later, followed Professor Gray here to Harvard."

"Schoolcraft stole them?"

Clément shook his head. "Yes and no. Don't worry about it. You will take your collection with you back to England."

"You're not coming with?"

"Publicly? Billy and I are both leaving America, but privately, we plan to finish what Professor Nicollet started," Clément patted the crates. "We'll get to the bottom of this."

CHAPTER SEVENTY-NINE

ROME
1846

Rome no longer held any majesty for Peter De Smet. Vatican City still commanded reverence, and the Capitoline Museum still inspired awe, but after standing upon the top of the world, De Smet returned to Europe a changed man.

He sipped his demitasse of kapuziner, glanced over at the white obelisk that looked like a naked pine tree, and watched the crowd passing by on the Piazza Venezia. Even though the Capitoline Museums dominated the horizon, memories of the Canadian Rockies dwarfed the manmade structures of Rome.

A tall, thin man in a wool jacket suddenly slipped out of the crowd and sat down across from him at the little table. *Conrad Simmons.*

THE ALCHEMIST'S MAP

The man across from him had a narrow face but appeared vibrant despite his thinning grey hair. Out of his priestly ropes, Simmons looked like an ordinary commoner instead of one of the more influential men in Rome.

"It is good to see you again, Conrad," De Smet said. "I did not expect to return to Rome so soon."

"Some matters are best discussed in person," Simmons shrugged, and then extended his hand. "So Reverend De Smet, you have traveled the vast continent of North America. Tell me about your latest travels."

"I have a report written up. Would you like it?"

"No, I suppose I already know about your exploits in the upper Missouri, along with the actions of the Order of Eos. So did this Mr. James Sinclair find the fabled Undine at the end of the Long River?"

It startled De Smet to hear Simmons talk so openly about the conspiracies he and Nicollet had investigated. "He certainly found a Continental Divide, but beyond that, I did not find anything to conclude he went beyond guiding settlers to a new home."

"It was an itch that needed scratching," Simmons summarized. "Your efforts will not go unnoticed."

"Thank you," De Smet humbly reflected on three of the hardest years in his life. "Perhaps you are not the man to answer this, but I made inquiries earlier about—"

"Of course," Simmons cut him off. "The Church will certainly help fund any missionary efforts for the evangelizing of all Indian tribes you deem necessary."

"Yes... thank you, but..."

Simmons smiled. "That is not the inquiry you were referencing?"

"No. I wanted to know about the death of Joseph Nicollet."

Simmons' mouth tightened, and the busy streets of Rome returned for a moment while De Smet waited for a response. "I read in the newspapers that Professor Nicollet's death is attributed to pneumonia and a lingering stomach ailment he acquired during his journeys in the West," Simmons coyly answered.

De Smet had been thousands of miles away from Galabrun's Hotel when Nicollet fell ill, unable to help or investigate. Davey Faribault told him the rest, including the list of suspects. "I read similar news, but I also know the symptoms he displayed could also be the result of more nefarious causes."

"Professor Nicollet was a beloved and respected man," Simmons said and his gaze left the table to scan the crowd. "Who would benefit from his death?"

"Surely, you must have your own opinions on the matter."

"Nicollet wanted to return to the frontier in order to finish his studies on the customs of the Chippewa and Sioux. The United States is driven by the belief in Manifest Destiny. If these progressive minds do not value the lives of the indigenous tribes, why would they think twice about removing the son of a watchmaker?"

De Smet nodded in acceptance. "If Nicollet did more than just map—if he actually found what he set out to find, the effect of such a discovery would create confusion and chaos. There are some who would rather kill one man than allow such a discovery to happen so publicly."

"Are you suggesting the Catholic Church was behind Nicollet's death?" Simmons asked, his eyebrow raised.

"Was it?" De Smet asked bluntly and watched the man's steady reaction. "He was an ally of the Jesuits, but I know Nicollet entertained at least three visiting priests during the last two months of his life. If he said the wrong thing to the wrong man—"

"For having been halfway across the continent, you are remarkably well-informed. Perhaps he did say the wrong thing to the wrong man—but neither the Catholic Church nor the Periphery had anything to do

THE ALCHEMIST'S MAP

with Nicollet's death. If anything, we went out of our way to protect him from *himself*. Have you seen copies of his infamous map?"

De Smet nodded. The topographic masterpiece had gone to the printers with hundreds of names written upon the once-blank region now known as the "Minnesota" and "Dakota" territories. Nicollet showed little restraint, blatantly relabeling three rivers as the "Lahontan River," the "Le Sueur River," and the "Blue Earth River." Along with putting an "x" at the location of the fabled Fort L'Huillier, Nicollet labeled a swath of land almost two hundred miles wide the "UNDINE REGION."

"Did you try to protect him?" De Smet asked.

"We've been trying to protect him since the very beginning. A year before he died, we sent an agent to inform him that his own hired chef might have nefarious connections. Instead of accepting our help, he left for Niagara Falls."

The map made sense. "For being such a delicate little man, he was certainly made of steel. Nicollet refused, didn't he?"

"He did," Simmons admitted, "and it seems he had plans to return to the frontier. I wish I had answers, but I do not know what happened to Nicollet any more than I know what happened to Lady Drummond and her map."

"Nicollet deserves justice."

"I understand, but your involvement in these matters must come to an end. Build your missions. Convert the people of the plains. Do not trouble yourself any more over these... theories."

"I will go to my grave trying to sort it out," De Smet admitted, "but I will certainly return to the plains as a servant."

The cup of kapuziner was cold now, but De Smet drank it just to calm the bile churning in his belly.

"Is there anything else, Father De Smet? Despite being retired, I still have found ways to keep myself busy, and duty calls."

"Yes, there is... one more thing." De Smet reached into the pockets of his black cassock, found the leather-bound journal, and set it on the table. "I believe you will be quite interested in what Nicollet truly discovered on his journeys."

Conrad Simmons' forehead wrinkled as he studied it.

"What is this?"

"It is his personal journal. One of his friends brought it to me shortly after his death," De Smet explained. "I know his friends are not affiliated with the Periphery, but I do not believe they will let matters rest. While I promise to not seek vengeance for the death of Nicollet, I cannot speak for his friends."

"Have you read this?" Conrad Simmons asked.

"I have. It begins the day Lady Drummond died, and it ends with him looking forward to another expedition. Nicollet was not withering away with pneumonia; he planned to finish the task you'd given him."

"Do you know where he planned to go?" Simmons asked.

"I have a general idea," De Smet admitted, "but only Nicollet knew the specific location."

CHAPTER EIGHTY

DETROIT

1846

The city of Detroit began as a Stopping Place for the Anishinaabe during their spiritual migration, the Seven Fires. After leaving the shores of the Atlantic, the Anishinaabe had followed prophecy and providence to Montreal Island and Niagara Falls before a young hunter found the sacred Miigis shells that identified the third stopping place, Waawiyegaama, or "Round Lake."

Round Lake later became known as "Lake St. Clair," the village became known as "Detroit," and the island became known as "Belle Island." Fur traders understood the strategic location between two Great Lakes and white civilization took root long after the Anishinaabe had reached Minnesota.

Detroit had quadrupled its population between the time of Nicollet's arrival in America in 1831 and his death in 1843. Much of what Solomon Delhut saw out the window of the carriage had not existed when his estate on Belle Island had been built, but thanks to his investments in the iron ore mines on the Upper Peninsula, the city was on the verge of blossoming into something even greater.

Solomon Delhut hated taking the ferry across the Detroit River, and hoped one day to build a bridge across the river and into the Canadian city of Windsor. After the ferry docked, his carriage driver navigated the rig down the ramp successfully, much to Solomon's relief. It was night, but not seeing the peril somehow made it easier.

It was a short ride to his estate, a two-story block stone structure built among the old oaks at the center of the island. For added security, he had constructed a flagstone wall around his two-hundred-acre home.

A well-lit house welcomed his carriage as it came up the lane. Despite all the lights, he didn't see his family through the windows like he normally would, so he checked his watch.

It was already five minutes past eight.

As soon as the carriage stopped in front of his home, he burst from the carriage to his front door.

No one greeted him.

The scent of baked pork filled the air, leading him to the dining room, where the place settings were prepared and waiting. "Hello?"

No one answered, so he continued to the kitchen.

When he opened the swinging door, a pistol greeted him. "Please remain calm, sir. I don't want my friend to harm any of your family or household."

Delhut looked over to see his wife Esther, his daughter Emily, and his three-year-old son Pierre, all gagged and bound to the chairs at the kitchen table. Little Pierre let out whimpers that sounded like a pig

THE ALCHEMIST'S MAP

being led to slaughter. The cook, butler, and two maids were also gagged and bound. Behind them, a man with a hideous scar on his face held a machete and a pistol.

A third man stepped out from behind the door with a pistol leveled at his belly. "Stick out your hands."

In just a moment, the towering giant had his hands wrapped with rope, which then wrapped around his arms three times.

"Do you see that man over there with the mangled face?" the slender man with the moustache asked. "He saw his entire village butchered in front of him when he was a child. He'll not hesitate to kill each and every last member of your family if you don't cooperate. Their lives hang in the balance. If you give us the right answers, they might be spared. Do you understand what is happening?"

Delhut nodded.

"Good. Let's go to the dining room where we can talk in private," the mustached man said.

The giant joined them as Delhut was led to the prepared table, where they sat him down. "We're here to ask you questions about Joseph Nicollet."

Nicollet?

Delhut felt a convulsion ripple through his body. He'd hoped the three men were only thieves looking to rob him, but the mention of Nicollet meant something far worse, and the thought of the scarred man with the machete filled his mind.

Seeing his hands shaking involuntarily, Delhut tried to control his breathing, forcing himself to take deep breaths and release them slowly.

I am Pater Familias—I must act like it! But Nicollet? It can't be.

"So you know the name 'Nicollet?'"

Delhut nodded again. *Nicollet had powerful friends. Who has come to avenge him?*

The mustached man nodded. "That is a good start. Before we get to the heart of the matter, let's find out if we can agree on a few basic facts. When Nicollet first came to Fort Snelling, he was delayed for months. Who was your man at the fort?"

A Scottish accent? Stewart? Thank God, perhaps I can reason with these men. "Hank Sibley worked for my father, so we knew he could be trusted with basic instructions. He informed us about Nicollet's arrival."

"Us?" Stewart pressed.

At worst, Stewart is now a Periphery agent. He is not my true enemy. "Schoolcraft knew about Nicollet also. Both had orders to keep him from exploring the upper Mississippi."

"Yet Sibley eventually relented once you arranged for a spy to accompany the expedition. Who was your spy?"

"I don't know. Sibley made the arrangements."

Stewart pointed to the big man with him. "You're going to have to do better than that. We are committed men, surely you understand that."

"I think it was a cook."

"Maxwell?" the giant asked.

Delhut gave a quick nod. "That sounds right."

Stewart gestured and the giant walked back to the kitchen to switch places with the scarred man. The scarred Indian returned alone and stood beside him.

"Mr. Solomon just told me that the hired spy on the expedition was a cook by the name of 'Maxwell,'" Stewart explained.

The Indian's mouth tightened and he shook his head. In a flash, a blade flew from its sheath and was leveled at Delhut's scalp. "When they took my scalp, it surprised me how hot the blade felt. The sound was actually the worst part as it sawed off the flesh. Then the hot blood blinded me from seeing anything more."

THE ALCHEMIST'S MAP

With a handful of hair, the crazed Indian tilted Delhut's head back until their noses almost touched. "I know who you hired to kill Nicollet."

"Kill... Nicollet? No! No one was hired to kill Nicollet. The cook was paid to see where Nicollet went, that is all," Delhut repeated.

"Why do you think we're standing in your house right now? We know who your men were."

"Give him time, Jim," Stewart said. "He's just coming around to the idea that it's all over. He just needs to decide if his secrets are worth the lives of his family. If you know who I am, then you know how this whole ordeal began... it began with you, didn't it? So you see, Mr. Delhut, we're going to get the answers we need from you. It all depends on how many of your family members you're willing to see murdered before you give us the answers we want. Should we start with the servants or your family members?"

"Do you have any idea who I am?" Delhut snapped.

"Of course," Stewart smirked. "You're Solomon Delhut, secret member of the Order of Eos, to which my uncle, William Drummond, also belonged. After being denied membership to the Order, I learned more about it and its origins than most of its members probably know. I know you were responsible for the death of my aunt."

"Your aunt?"

"You're easing our conscience with every lie—Lady Margaret Drummond. Her death brought Joseph Nicollet and I together, and Nicollet's death has brought you and I together." Stewart's grin and tone were jovial but his eyes were full of malice.

"I had nothing to do with her death. In fact—"

Stewart backhanded Delhut, bringing a sudden sharp pain and then a dull throb from the cuts his own teeth made against the soft flesh of his mouth. Blood filled his mouth, leaving him no choice but to let it drip down his chin and onto his clean floors.

"We'll get back to my Aunt Maggie in a bit. Now, a wealthy man like yourself, with all of his connections... You certainly understand why we won't be bringing any of this to a court of law. So for the sake of propriety, let me continue with the evidence that has brought us here today."

William Stewart pulled an envelope from his pocket and opened it to reveal a dried plant.

Schoolcraft! That pompous fool has brought these men into my house.

"Thanks to my fierce-looking friend," Stewart continued, "we learned what happened to Geyer's wagon when it left Fort Snelling, but we never understood where it had ended up. Professor Nicollet eventually found out, but his good nature kept him from seeing the worst intentions in others. Nicollet believed Sibley was his friend, but Sibley was the one who arranged for the wagon to be stolen and sent here to Michigan, but instead of standing in Schoolcraft's dining room, we stand in yours. Do you know why?"

Schoolcraft should have burned the contents of the wagon when they proved worthless. Have they already tortured Schoolcraft?

Then Stewart produced a metal container, which he opened and sprinkled its contents onto the pool of blood in front of him.

Blue earth.

Copper vitriol.

Stewart knows about the Philosopher's Stone.

"So? Are we going to get a confession?" Stewart asked.

"I didn't do anything to Joseph Nicollet. I swear. You have to believe me."

"Tell him how we traced the crime here," Stewart said to the man with the facial scars.

"The chemist," the man answered. "He left the three blue earth

THE ALCHEMIST'S MAP

samples, two of which had containers that belonged to Joseph Nicollet and the third was labeled 'Charles T. Jackson.' He was there the day Nicollet died, and even seemed motivated to save him, but he was already your man, wasn't he?"

"Charles Jackson never would have hurt Nicollet. He was a doctor, for Christ's sake!"

"So he was your man."

"Charles... Charles is simply an old friend. We went to Harvard together. I had nothing to do with Nicollet's death, I swear!"

"We'll discover the truth later. Right now, we're just getting to know each other. We're just making introductions. I'm only explaining why we're here. I'm thankful my fierce friend had the foresight to not murder Dr. Jackson right after the funeral," Stewart explained. "Luckily, our patience paid off. We investigated this chemist enlisted by Nicollet, and he led us right back to you, who rewarded his services by appointing him as United States Geologist for the Lake Superior land district. What was Jackson hired to oversee?" Stewart asked, looking at his friend.

"Copper production," the scarred Indian answered.

Delhut found his heart pounding in his chest, finally understanding why the men stood in his dining room. "Yes, I hired Jackson because of his expertise in copper, but you've twisted the facts. I hired Jackson after Nicollet's death."

"You're saying it was a coincidence he happened to show up on the day Nicollet died," Stewart mocked. "I don't think so. When you learned Nicollet had copper samples, you paid him to poison Nicollet."

"Why would I have Jackson kill Nicollet?" Delhut asked. "Tell me!"

The two men didn't have an answer, which further terrified him.

So Delhut continued, "Jackson doesn't know anything about the Philosopher's Stone. I'd never trust that man with the knowledge of what I'm doing. A few years ago, I had him do an analysis of the geology in Nova Scotia, so he knew my interest in copper. It was Joseph Nicollet who approached him at some sort of scientific assembly. It was Nicollet who gave him the vitriol samples."

"But after Nicollet's death, Jackson gets a promotion. We followed him right to you. Why did Jackson go to you after Nicollet was dead?"

"For the same reasons you're here today. He saw Nicollet as a friend, and like you, realized there might be some foul play involved. Two of the samples were unlike any vitriol samples Jackson had ever seen."

"Exactly—which is why you had him killed."

Delhut had heard enough, so he cut right to the heart of the matter. "Don't you buffoons understand? I wanted Nicollet to lead me to the Philosopher's Stone!" A calm came over him as he openly confessed his secrets in front of his enemies. "I realize you are my enemy, but you must believe that I had no interest in killing Joseph Nicollet."

"Then why did Henry Schoolcraft hire someone to kill Nicollet on his return from Lapointe?" the Indian asked.

"Schoolcraft? Schoolcraft didn't hire anyone to kill Nicollet. Once he realized we couldn't keep him away, we decided he could find it for us."

"Do I need to dig up the corpse of the assassin and shove his rotting skull in your face to refresh your memory? Or would you like to visit with him immediately?"

"Taopi, hold on a minute," Stewart said, then asked Delhut, "So who killed Nicollet?"

"My first instinct was that the Church had him killed," Delhut answered. "Yet here you are, threatening the lives of my family. I wish I had an idea, but I do not. It's as much a mystery to me as it is to you."

Stewart did not look convinced. Then an idea flashed in Delhut's mind. It was an absolutely abominable idea—one that would cause his ancestors to roll over in their graves. Yet he had no other choice.

THE ALCHEMIST'S MAP

Tied up with their mother in the kitchen, Delhut's children mattered far more than secrets and relics.

"Before you do anything you'll regret," Solomon Delhut desperately said, "I need to show you something, something that will prove my innocence."

CHAPTER EIGHTY-ONE

DETROIT
1846

Pierre Delhut sat beside his mother, tied to a chair, closely studying the intruder that paced around the kitchen. Unlike the other Indian, who had fierce scars on his face, the tall one seemed more graceful than menacing, and when he flashed a smile, his chipped tooth made him appear more jovial than menacing.

One of the strangers stepped into the frame of the back door to ask, "Everything under control?"

The tall Indian calmly nodded.

From the dining room, he could hear his father talking with the scarred Indian and the mustached man, who seemed to be the leader. Pierre counted four other masked men besides the two Indians and the mustached man. The masked men waited outside in the darkness.

Who are these men? Pierre wondered, wide-eyed. *Why are they here?*

The dining room grew silent.

From the sound of the footsteps, the three had gone into his father's study upstairs.

The sound of boots on stairs echoed through the house, and a moment later, the front doors burst open.

Voices.

Then the scarred Indian returned to the kitchen with one of the masked men beside him. "You need to see this," he said, and the tall Indian with the kind face left to be replaced by one of the men wearing a mask.

CHAPTER EIGHTY-TWO
DETROIT
1846

When Antoine Clément entered the study, Solomon Delhut was under a chair, with a crossbar pinned against his throat. Stewart sat on the chair, allowing just enough space so Delhut could breath.

Jim Taopi ignored the violent scene and pointed out the Alchemist's Map to Clément.

We've found it?

For fifteen years, Clément had heard all about the stolen map and the mysterious treasure it described. It was the reason the Scottish nobleman had wandered into the West. It was the reason he'd abducted Joseph Nicollet at knifepoint from his hotel room in St. Louis.

It had also brought Clément to Terra Sancta, the holy lands of

THE ALCHEMIST'S MAP

multiple faiths, on a journey that caused him to rethink everything he had once believed.

It's smaller than I imagined.

Some sort of transparent film protected the ancient map, but Clément immediately recognized the features. All along the edges were drawings of the sun, moon, stars, and constellations, with notations that only a man such as Joseph Nicollet could have found meaning in. The writing used characters that occasionally looked like modern letters but gave him no clue as to what was written. At the center of the map, Clément saw a series of rivers that all came together.

Clément knew what would soon happen, so he acted. He walked over to Stewart, wrapped his arm around his neck and pulled him off the chair and away from Delhut. For a moment, Stewart attempted to struggle, but with a powerful squeeze, Clément let his will be known.

"Yes, fine. Let go of me, you dumb brute," Stewart said.

Clément obliged, but stood between Stewart and Delhut, who gathered his breath as Clément gently moved the chair off him. Delhut remained on the floor, glancing up at Taopi, who now stood closest.

"Is that what I think it is?" Clément asked. Even though the evidence connecting Solomon Delhut to Nicollet was strong, Clément had felt it was reckless to shake down a prominent millionaire with powerful friends. *Billy was right about his connections.*

Stewart's mouth tightened and he advanced, stopping at the edge of the table. "How does this exonerate you? If anything, it condemns you."

Solomon Delhut touched his neck and then sat up, but did not threaten to move any further. "You are looking at the Abbaron Map. It's been in the possession of my family for countless generations."

"Lies," Stewart said. "You could have stolen it yesterday, for all I know."

"Then look at the book I showed you. Find the passage I have marked. How could I have anticipated your arrival, Mr. Stewart? How can you explain the book?"

Stewart picked up the book, holding it at arm's length like he would a poisonous snake, and with each muttered phrase, his demeanor changed. He shook his head twice as if debating mentally with the old text, and when he finished, he seemed angrier than when he had started.

For a moment, Clément worried he was about to kill Delhut in cold blood. Delhut sensed it too and just sat, wide-eyed, as Stewart loomed over him. Then he threw the old text at him and walked back over to the map.

"How does this prove your innocence?" Stewart asked. "We know you stole Karl Geyer's wagon, and we know your man visited him on the day he died. The day he was poisoned!"

Clément watched Delhut studying each of them. *This man is too dangerous to let live. We murdered him the moment we stepped foot in his house.*

Delhut remained steady. "I confess that I've been seeking answers about the Philosopher's Stone, and my meddling involved your aunt and cousin, as well as dear Professor Nicollet. The man responsible for their deaths is also responsible for the death of my cousin, Gerard Beranger. I fear this man even more than I fear the three of you, for his presence endangers my entire family, and even those who are not yet born."

"Who is he?" Stewart asked.

"I do not know, but he has been hunting for me, that is clear, and my desire to acquire the Drummond map has cost me everything. To understand his motivations, you'll have to ask him yourself. If you find him for me, then this intrusion and assault will be forgiven," Delhut said.

At this, Stewart bristled, and from his jacket, he smoothly pulled out a pistol, aimed it at Delhut's face, and cocked the hammer.

CHAPTER EIGHTY-THREE
DETROIT
1846

For four centuries, King Solomon's First Temple had been the resting place of the Ark of the Covenant, as well as the center of worship for the Hebrew people. Archeologists confirm Biblical accounts of the "First Temple" period with an analysis of abandoned jewelry, burnt stones, and arrowheads dating from the Babylonian period. The only information on the First Temple is the Tanakh, which credits a joint effort from King Solomon of Israel and King Hiram of Tyre with the temple's construction approximately in the year 950 B.C.

According to the Book of Deuteronomy, the original command given by God concerning the Ark of the Covenant is that any altar dedicated to the Lord should be constructed of "unhewn" or "uncut" stone. Although neither the Bible nor the Tanakh explicitly describe any stone-cutting process in the creation of Solomon's Temple, the contradiction birthed a legend found in the Gemara, the Talmud, and the Midrashim about Solomon's Shamir, a substance able to cut through and disintegrate stone, iron, or diamond.

By the time Christian Crusaders had returned to the Holy Land two thousand years later, Jerusalem and Solomon's Temple had been destroyed numerous times, but the legend only grew.

William Drummond Stewart knew most of the legends about King Solomon and the Templar Knights, but his mind swam as he read about the existence of the Abbaron Map. For centuries, his family had possessed the Alchemist's Map, an ancient document believed to show the location of the resting place of the legendary Philosopher's Stone. Having gazed upon the map, Joseph Nicollet followed men like Pierre-Charles Le Sueur and Baron Lahontan on a quest for mystical waters where the earth bled blue, yet the whole time, the Delhut family had a twin copy.

"Nicollet came to investigate a legend, didn't he?" Delhut asked, ignoring the pistol. "Granted, he also came for scientific purposes, but that was all pretense, wasn't it? When he was in France, he saw something he never should have seen—a map."

According to the eccentric Palestinian sage Stewart and Clément had met on their recent journey, King Solomon had organized an expedition of Phoenician sailors led by a Hebrew named "Abbaron," who followed Solomon's star map in search of an ancient treasure—only to vanish on the far side of the earth.

"When I learned your family possessed one of the ancient Phoenician star maps," Delhut continued, "I offered to buy the map from your aunt. My family has obsessed over the Philosopher's Stone and Grail lore for generations, so when I learned Lady Drummond meant to sell her

THE ALCHEMIST'S MAP

most-prized family heirloom, I swept in to buy it from her. Except..."

"Except someone killed her," Stewart finished.

"If you allow me to live, you can investigate everything I say. Yes, I bear the sins of my fathers. Yes, I belong to the Order of Eos. But, I never murdered an old woman, and I never did any harm to Joseph Nicollet. Why would I kill Lady Drummond to acquire what I already possess? The map is proof that I had no reason to harm Lady Drummond and all the reason in the world to keep Nicollet alive."

Stewart looked down at the Abbaron Map, trying to make sense of it all. "How is this second map proof you meant Nicollet no ill will? If you had this map, you obviously would see him as a threat to what you desire."

"My ancestors immigrated to America from Saint-Germain-Laval in 1674. We've spent the better part of two centuries looking for the damned Philosopher's Stone. Honestly, I'd given up all hope that such a thing even existed until Nicollet began poking his nose around. Was he a threat? Of course not! He was a savior. I prayed he would find it."

"If you were the buyer, who killed Lady Drummond?" Stewart asked.

"In this matter, we are allies. My cousin, Gerard Beranger, owned an imported liquor store on the Rue de la Contrescarpe. He was murdered during the July Revolution, but I suspect the same person who killed him killed Drummond, and most likely, recently killed Joseph Nicollet."

Stewart looked down at the map of the Undine, seemingly drawn by the same artist that made the Al Marakk Map. Covered with symbols from alchemy, history, and lore, its centerpiece was the place where rivers flowed in all directions and the earth bled blue.

"What is this?" Stewart asked.

"I can trace my lineage back to the Vikings of old. Before the kings of France and England intruded into our affairs, my kin sailed seas and rivers, all the way to old Babylon, where they learned about the legendary Star of the West. Five hundred years before Columbus discovered America, my ancestors knew the truth: we were only returning."

"So why are there two maps?" Stewart asked, looking for confirmation of his many theories.

"The Alchemist's Map was made to guide men to the lost treasure. The Abbaron Map was made by the men who failed to obtain it—but they nevertheless described a lost continent beyond the edge of the known world. When I failed to acquire the Alchemist's Map, I did everything in my power to spy on the man who'd seen it—Joseph Nicollet. So yes, I hired men to watch his every move, and yes, I paid men to intercept the wagon. Don't you understand, Lord Stewart? Our families are allies in the quest for the Philosopher's Stone. I want it to be found."

Stewart released the hammer and lowered the pistol.

"Take the map," Delhut added. "Let it be a pledge between our two families."

"What kind of pledge?"

"If you let me live, it would be my pleasure to root out Nicollet's killer and deliver him to you. After all, he's a threat to both of us. Nicollet's blood is on my hands. If it hadn't been for my meddling, the Alchemist's Map might still be in your possession. This map is worthless to me now."

"Why is it worthless?" Stewart asked.

"If Joseph Nicollet could not find the Philosopher's Stone, then who can?" Delhut asked honestly.

Stewart stood at the window for a moment. *Perhaps he did find it, but wanted to keep it from men like you.*

CHAPTER EIGHTY-FOUR

CHARLESTON
1850

The Patron's Medal and Founder's Medal are two prestigious awards given out by the Royal Geographical Society for the promotion and encouragement of geographical science and discovery. The awards originated from King William IV of Great Britain in the form of an annual gift of fifty guineas.

In 1850, David Livingston received the Founder's Medal for his journey to the great lake of Ngami in Africa. The other award was granted to Senator John C. Frémont, for his "important geographical labours in the far west of the American Continent."

While all of Charleston celebrated the man they once called a bastard, Frémont still mourned the loss of his mentor. During his speech, he tried to honor Nicollet by crediting him for taking a chance on an eager mathematician and included a couple anecdotes about their expeditions of 1838 and 1839.

Unfortunately, the crowd of vampires only wanted to ask about Frémont The Pathfinder, the man who'd mapped the West and helped win the Mexican-American War. Jessie Frémont managed the flock of bloodthirsty well-wishers, steering him from group to group.

Only Nicollet believed in me. Where were these fine people a decade ago?

Finally, a military officer stood in front of Frémont, vigorously shaking his hand. "Senator Frémont, it is a pleasure to meet you. I also had the opportunity to participate in an expedition with Joseph Nicollet."

"You did?" Frémont asked, now paying even closer attention to the man. In a way, he looked to be almost a mirrored image of himself. He wore a military uniform with the rank of major, and his hair and beard were flecked with grey. His cheeks bore distinctive smallpox scars despite his attempts to cover them with his beard. "How did you know Nicollet?"

"I was hired to bring him to the headwaters of the Mississippi River; we were rescuing a missionary and his wife during an Indian uprising."

"You were stationed at Fort Snelling?"

"I was, under Major Tolliver. I was transferred out to Fort Union by the time you arrived at Fort Snelling in 1838."

"Daniel Lyons?" Frémont asked.

"Nicollet spoke of me?" Lyons asked, looking pleased.

No, not Nicollet. Frémont suddenly felt a knot twisting in his stomach. "You made quite an impression. Are you stationed here in South Carolina?"

"Fort Sumter. After serving for four years out on the frontier, I

THE ALCHEMIST'S MAP

managed to get a comfortable position here in Charleston, my home. I supervise construction of the new fort."

"Fort Sumter?" Frémont repeated. "You know, Nicollet requested you to be part of his later expeditions, but you could not be located."

Lyons put his hands on his hips and shook his head. "Ah, yes, well, I was reassigned to the upper Missouri after Fort Snelling for a year or so and then I spent a winter in Mexico City."

Jessie sensed the conversation went too long and returned to his side, prompting Frémont to follow his wife to the next conversation. "Nicollet meant a lot to me, Major Lyons. Before I leave Charleston, we should meet and discuss our experiences."

"That would be wonderful, and an honor," Lyons said with a smile. "You now know where you can find me."

Yes, and so will Kit Carson.

CHAPTER EIGHTY-FIVE

FORT SUMTER
1850

Fort Sumter is built on an island that sits off a peninsula protecting the port of Charleston. To reach the city, ships must pass between Sullivan's Island and the port, where the channels narrow to less than a mile. With its high sea walls, Fort Sumter acts as a gate for any ship passing by, and the cannons are strategically placed to sink any ship entering or leaving the bay if need be.

Although technically built on an island, Fort Sumter has a narrow land bridge that exists just below the water that connects it to the mainland. The engineers who built the fort knew that the swampy delta that formed the peninsula would act as a natural obstruction during any attempts to take the fort by land.

THE ALCHEMIST'S MAP

While John C. Frémont waited in an anchored boat, he studied Fort Sumter, wondering how he would attack it if given the order. He paced the deck of his boat, anchored in the channel of the Stono River, while he watched the small rowboat cross the shallow swamp from the quiet fort. He could not remember the names of the two men who rowed, but he could recognize the stern, square face of the man at the prow even in the dark—Kit Carson.

It had been a decade since Carson confronted him at Fort Pierre, looking for the man who had brought disease into his life.

When Frémont saw a bound and gagged Major Daniel Lyons in the belly of the rowboat, he wondered, *Am I delivering justice or am I a cold-blooded murderer?*

After two mapping expeditions and serving with Carson during the Mexican War, Frémont would have done anything for his trusted friend, so he stood at a distance as Carson and the other frontiersmen forced a confession out of Captain Lyons.

Lyons told a story that supported Carson's long-held theory. With the mighty Sioux and dozens of smaller tribes standing in the way of Manifest Destiny, the choice was either military invasion or something far more subtle—disease. Having survived the smallpox in his youth, Lyons was chosen by his puppet-masters to deliver infected blankets as trade goods for a dozen local posts on the upper Missouri, resulting in an epidemic that killed far more than any military operation could have done. Frémont listened as Lyons all but confessed to the murder of Carson's precious bride, Sweet Grass.

Then the confession took an unexpected turn, and Frémont rushed over to Lyons, pushing one of the thugs out of the way. "What did you just say? Repeat it!"

"I don't know the man's name," Lyons said. "None of it could be official orders. None of it could be traced up the chain of command."

"The man who gave you the orders! What did you just say about him?"

Lyons looked up, bewildered by the face of the celebrity who held him by the neck. "The Russian? I told you, I never knew his name. That was the whole point. He was just an intermediary, a go-between."

The bloodlust in Carson's eyes turned to astonishment as the knife in Frémont's hand tumbled to the floor and he found himself clinging to the wall in order to keep himself from falling over.

"What is it?" Carson asked.

It all suddenly made sense, however horrific.

Still facing the wall, Frémont asked, "Did he have any physical defects?"

"Yes," Lyons answered, sounding almost hopeful his life would be spared. "The Russian only had three fingers on one of his hands."

At this, Frémont burst from the torture chamber, staggering wildly until he found himself outside, under the starry South Carolina sky of his youth.

In a nearby tree, a Chuck-will's-widow called for its feathery mate, unaware of the turmoil inside the senator from California.

Kit Carson's heavy breathing joined the cry of the nightjar bird for a few moments. "Who is this Russian?"

"Krasdan Krai is not Russian," Frémont clarified. He bent over slightly, putting his hands on his knees so as not to vomit from a spinning mind. "He is originally from Kuban, a wild territory along the Black Sea. I heard the story repeatedly as a young man; how the bold Krasdan snuck into the camp of an international expedition to steal a few horses for his village.

"When the expedition leader found out, he pressured the Khan of Kuban for their return, explaining that Jefferson, the Shah of America, would not be made the fool. With Czar Alexander as an ally of the

THE ALCHEMIST'S MAP

traveling American, the Khan quickly sifted through all the villages until the thief was found.

"The Khan of Kuban offered the head of young Krasdan Krai to the powerful American, but in an act of power and mercy, two fingers were taken for the two horses. In an even more magnanimous act, Krasdan Krai was then adopted and brought all the way back to America to serve the man who spared his life."

"You know the Russian? You know his master?" Carson asked, dejected that his vengeance would not be complete in killing Lyons.

"Yes, we once served the same master, so I know where the Russian lives," Frémont admitted. *And where his master does, too.*

CHAPTER EIGHTY-SIX

MURTHLY CASTLE, SCOTLAND
1851

How much do I tell him about my life? Lord William Drummond Stewart wondered as he looked at his twenty-year-old son, George, tending to the grove of trees.

All over Murthly Estate, he'd installed reminders of his time on the frontier, including the trees, paintings, exhibits, stuffed beasts, fish, and fowl, and the chapel he'd built in memory of Nicollet.

I first left twenty years ago and now George is about to follow in my military footsteps as a Highlander. He must feel dwarfed by my legacy, yet I am dwarfed by that of Nicollet.

Stewart lived alone in the main castle with only his personal valet, Antoine Clément, to keep him company. George and Christina lived in

THE ALCHEMIST'S MAP

the cottage next to the castle, but like the rest of his family, he kept them at arm's length in fear of faceless reprisal.

Antoine Clément brought in the daily mail, which included a package.

Stewart immediately noted the sweet lavender perfume radiating from the box. *Caswell No. 6.* The package had been sent from Columbia, South Carolina.

Stewart took the package to a table, and procuring a small hammer, he pried away at the wooden box until it came apart at the seams. Inside a layer of burlap and felt, he found packing straw, but instead of a broken perfume bottle, he found something far different.

A gasp slipped from his lips, and surrounded by lordly comforts, he stepped back in shock.

Stewart returned to the box a moment later and not only confirmed what he'd seen but also found a note. Although the author of the note was not given, he understood who had sent it.

"What is it?" Clément asked.

Stewart chose his words carefully, "Justice."

The perfume scent had saturated the straw in order to cover the subtle scent of decay. Stewart lifted the severed hand and held it up to study it closely.

The hand had two missing fingers, severed and healed long before the hand had been taken and placed in the box.

The other strange feature was that the palm of the hand was filled with overflowing blue copper vitriol.

They finally found the killer. But how?

Stewart glanced at Clément, who nodded.

A final trip to America to finish it all.

CHAPTER EIGHTY-SEVEN
SANTEE HILLS
1851

When he closed his eyes, Joel Poinsett could not see the ensemble of slave children led by the talented soloist singing "We Three Kings of Orient" to the collection of friends gathered in his home. No, when he closed his eyes, he saw Joseph Nicollet. With Christmas approaching, his wife wanted to rehearse the public program they would provide to friends and family.

Star of wonder
Star of night
Star with royal beauty bright
Westward leading still proceeding...

Poinsett opened his eyes, unable to avoid his guilt.

THE ALCHEMIST'S MAP

His wife, Mary, held his hand as if to restrain his unexpected emotional response. Mary and the small crowd of household staff applauded.

"So lovely," Mary whispered. "So beautiful."

"Yes, quite lovely," Poinsett said and slipped his hand from her grip. "You must excuse me, my dear."

He rose from his cushioned chair and quickly exited the room before the next song began. He heard his plantation manager introducing the tune by the time he reached the back door.

As soon as he breathed the cool December air, he began to violently cough. His hand reached for a fresh napkin in his pocket to hold over his mouth. His left hand held onto the door frame until the coughing ceased.

Instead of going back to the concert, Poinsett walked into the darkness toward the glass cathedral that held his botanical collection from all over the world.

The little flames that kept the ambient temperature stable during the night illuminated the massive greenhouse, even though the condensation on the glass panes diffused the details within.

Stepping inside, Poinsett took another deep breath, and his agitated lungs calmed a little. The humidity from the moist earth soothed his ailments; the hundreds of plants collected on the three tiers of platforms restored his purpose. He opened the shields on a few of the lamps to bring more light to his sanctuary.

His prized Flor de Noche Buena had burst into red blooms, and on the morrow, would be delivered to churches throughout South Carolina.

Most would be dead by January.

Even if his meticulous work did go unappreciated, *he* knew how something wild and ungainly in nature had been shaped and controlled into something beautiful.

The air moved.

"Hello?" Poinsett called out, knowing there were doors on each end of the long rectangular building. He looked up and down the long row of foliage, but no one came to find him. It was then he noticed a fully-opened lamp near the central dome.

Someone had been in his greenhouse.

With two long wings extending forty yards on either side, the central dome reached fifty feet in height, allowing several large tropical trees to grow within. On one of the propagation tables, a burning lamp illuminated a small green chest.

Poinsett glanced back down the row of poinsettias before advancing into the dome for a closer look. His fingers shook as he reached out for the box; it was unlocked.

Opening it, he found the journal of Jean Nicholas Nicollet.

When Poinsett heard footsteps, he didn't even turn, choosing instead to sit down at the table beside the box.

At least Death will have a familiar face.

CHAPTER EIGHTY-EIGHT

SANTEE HILLS
1851

Joel Poinsett understood what was happening when he saw Frémont waiting between two rubber trees with a knife in his hands and a pistol at his side.

He most likely thinks I am a villain, Poinsett decided, and turned to see if others waited in the trap. "What brings the Governor of the California territory to my home?"

"Actually, I'm a senator now, which is why I have traveled all the way back to the east coast—to represent the interests of California."

"Ah yes, I was told you were staying in Washington D.C. with the Bentons," Poinsett said.

"I am. Officially, I am not here right now, am I?"

"Yet the prodigal son has returned," Poinsett forced a smile. "You've grown a beard."

Frémont nodded.

The pistol concerned Poinsett the most. He gave thought to shouting for help, but he doubted his cries would be heard in the mansion from within the greenhouse. If he ran, however, the pistol shot might be heard—assuming Frémont's aim would go astray, which was doubtful.

"I honestly hoped you would feign ignorance," Frémont added from where he now sat. "Part of me wanted to believe you were the kind philanthropist who raised me up from nothing like one of your plants, but this could not be overlooked or ignored."

"I'm not quite sure what conclusions you have reached about the discovery you have in front of you, but I can assure you I continue to be a philanthropist whose concerns are for the future of humanity. You are like the son I never had, and everything I have done is to make the world a better place for the next generation."

"Is that how you justify the murder of Nicollet?"

"Nicollet? This is about Nicollet? He died of pneumonia after years of hardships out on the frontier. How can you blame me for such a thing?"

For the past few years, Poinsett had practiced this argument in anticipation of an accusation that never came. Before he could use logic against his accuser, another man stepped into the light.

Wearing a feathered Tyrolean hat, the second man had also armed himself for the confrontation, cutting off any attempt by Poinsett to run. The high cheekbone of the man melted into a ripple of scarred flesh on the right side of his face, and Poinsett had to steady himself to keep his knees and bladder from giving way.

"This is Jim Taopi," Frémont explained with a smirk. "I asked him to join me here tonight. He is part of the Sioux tribe from Kaposia. Before he kills you, I wanted you to finally meet your enemy face-to-face

THE ALCHEMIST'S MAP

like a man, rather than fighting him with pen and paper like you've done these past few decades."

"I think you've reached the wrong conclusion. My efforts were to civilize the savage, not to—"

Poinsett flinched when Taopi threw something at his feet. At first, he thought the small object to be the pelt of some small animal, but then he realized it was a scalp. "What is this?"

"A witness," Taopi said.

Frémont explained, "When Nicollet died, I was far off in the Rockies, but Taopi immediately suspected foul play. While his path took him on a wild goose chase, vengeance brought us all back together."

Krasdan. Poinsett recognized the scalp of dark hair.

Frémont continued, "It was only by chance that I met Kit Carson out on the prairie and mere luck that Captain Lyons introduced himself to me during a visit to Charleston. But no foul deed goes unpunished."

The thin metal stand failed to support Poinsett's weight this time, and he crashed to the floor as potted plants broke around him. His eyes went to the shard of pot, but Taopi's toe knocked it away before kicking him in the direction of Frémont.

"Show some dignity, Ambassador Poinsett," Frémont said. "Sit with me at the table and die like a man. During the Mexican War, I was forced to execute men who cried like women when they knew their time had come. For the friendship I once shared with you, I offer you a little more dignity."

Poinsett reached out and snatched up the scalp of Krasdan Krai, then stood up and joined Frémont at the table. "Krasdan was born a savage, much like your Indian friend, and the khans wanted to kill him as a sign of friendship, but I refused. To show my resolve, I cut off two of Krasdan's fingers in front of the khans, but then I made it my personal mission to turn the savage into a gentleman. By the time you met him,

Johnny, I had already transformed him into a gentleman."

"And a killer," Frémont said, producing a small glass vial in his hand. "This is the same poison Krasdan Krai used on Nicollet, which produced a fatal illness very similar to pneumonia. Krai told me everything I wanted to know, all while begging for death. You see, Kit Carson is no gentleman, and he wanted answers for why his beautiful wife had to die such a horrible death as smallpox."

Have all my sins come back to haunt me? Poinsett's fingers reached out and touched the dark hair upon the scalp of Krai, as if offering an apology.

Frémont continued, "Krai talked about almost killing Nicollet in Paris, and then again, on the road to Santee Hills—the very same day I first met Nicollet. He arranged for a Cajun to kill Nicollet, who almost killed Stewart instead. He even talked about Nicollet's cook in Georgetown, who was hired to keep him ill so as not to travel. You see, Joel, I needed confirmation of your guilt before I returned here."

Poinsett looked over at Taopi and then back to Frémont. "Please don't let him mutilate my body. What do you want? A confession?"

"I don't think I need a confession; I heard enough from the mouth of Krasdan. Through Hank Sibley, he found two thugs to hire: Edgar Colton and Daniel Lyons. Then he also made a final confession—how you decided to kill Nicollet before he could publish a book on Indians. In exchange for some information, I'm going to allow you the choice of dying in your bed with your wife at your side instead of having your scalp sawed off your head by my friend."

Poinsett looked down to see his hands trembling and tried to compose himself, but his heart and lungs refused to obey. "Honestly, I admired Joseph Nicollet. We were professional friends, and I didn't want anything to happen to him, but he was so…"

"Relentless? He certainly was, wasn't he? All I want from you, Joel, is to tell me why you had him killed."

CHAPTER EIGHTY-NINE

SANTEE HILLS
1851

Antoine Clément snuck into the dark library, and by candlelight, began to investigate while Christmas songs played in the distant dining room. From Frémont's description and Krai's confession, he knew where to find Poinsett's most prized possessions. Behind a wall panel, he found a safe, precious artifacts, and a metal cylinder.

He twisted off the end cap to find a soft velvet interior holding yellowed parchment wrapped in wax paper. Kneeling on the floor of the small room, he carefully unrolled the paper.

The Alchemist's Map—the cause of all this madness.

Sliding it carefully back into the metal tube, he rose, closed the library panel, and extinguished the candle.

Despite his size, his feet were still soft, and he had silently slipped back out of the mansion by the time the slave boys had finished singing "Oh Come All Ye Faithful" to Mrs. Poinsett and the gathered staff.

Once outside, he turned away from the mansion and the greenhouse, and jogged over to the stable, where three men waited in the shadows. He saw the metallic glint of pistols in their hands but walked right up to the man with the hairless lip.

"I believe this belongs to you," Clément said, handing it to Stewart, who not only wore a disguise but had also shaved his uniquely fine mustache for the sake of the mission. The hired thugs had come with them across the Atlantic from Scotland and were only a security measure in case things went wrong.

"Did you look inside?" Stewart asked.

"I did," Clément said. "Have the others returned yet?"

"No, they are in the greenhouse with Poinsett. I have no idea what's taking them so long."

"Let's go pay our respects to a dying man, then," Clément said.

Stewart nodded in affirmation and turned to the thugs, "Prepare the horses. We'll be leaving shortly."

Still holding the Alchemist's Map in his hands, Stewart crossed the dark yard of the Poinsett plantation, Clément close behind.

CHAPTER NINETY

SANTEE HILLS
1851

I *die surrounded by lesser men,* Joel Poinsett fumed internally as he tried to give the barbarians an explanation of his grand plans. "Don't be coy, Johnny. Did you find the Philosopher's Stone? Or was it a dead end?"

"I never expected you to be a man who would chase after legends and lore. Is that why you had him killed?"

"Humph. Nicollet claimed to be a scientist but *he* was the fanatic chasing after phantoms. I could have tolerated the ravings of a lunatic. To most, talk of the Undine or the Philosopher's Stone is as ridiculous as the notion of bats living on the moon. I am a defender of humanity, and if Nicollet had unearthed God or Satan, it would have only strengthened my resolve to defend humanity against the yoke of the Great Oppressor."

"Great Oppressor?" Frémont questioned.

"Do you even know what I've done? I am shaping an America free from the yoke of superstition. To do this, I needed to be rid of three obstacles: the Catholic Church, monarchies, and secret societies built upon lore and lies."

"But you are a Freemason yourself."

"Which was how I investigated legends that made grown men chase after phantoms."

"So that is why you killed Nicollet?" Frémont asked.

"I did not kill Nicollet when he went chasing after the Lapis Elixir, but when he threatened our Manifest Destiny, I could not let him stand in the way."

This silenced Frémont for a few moments. "So you killed him because he was planning to write a book about the Chippewa and Sioux?"

"Disappointed?" Poinsett said. "You always loved romanticized tales of good and evil. Nicollet's popularity grew daily, and the more disciples this pseudoscientist gained, the more dangerous his words and thoughts became. The America of my dreams is a place free of ancient beliefs and mysticism. Nicollet would not only have emboldened the Ancien Régime, but also would have preserved the cultures of other savage races who are an obstacle in our path."

Frémont cocked the pistol.

This is how Mary will find me, with a bullet hole in my head.

Frémont thrust it forward but did not fire. Instead, he aimed it at Taopi, who held a deer-antler knife in his hand.

Poinsett felt hot urine pool in his chair and begin to run down his leg as Frémont's pistol prevented the plunge of the knife. The Indian snarled and reluctantly lowered his knife.

THE ALCHEMIST'S MAP

"I think it is time for you to make your choice before Jim makes it for you," Frémont said and handed him the glass vial of poison. "Do it for your wife, I beg you."

"You do understand that I have leukemia?" Poinsett asked, first looking down at the glass vial and then at the eyes of his former protégé. "I will soon be dead, even without your assistance."

"There must be a reckoning," Taopi said as he sheathed the big blade.

All three men flinched when the air again shifted within the greenhouse. For a moment, Poinsett foolishly thought about running or wrestling the pistol from Frémont, but his captors were far younger and stronger.

Two more men, also dressed in black, cautiously approached. One was a towering Métis, and the other held a three-foot tube.

"You found it," Frémont said.

"Yes," the brute said, "Do you have your answers?"

Frémont shrugged. "Ambassador Poinsett said Nicollet was an old boulder in the river of Manifest Destiny. Where was it?"

"Antoine found it right where Krai said it would be," the thin man said and then boldly walked over to the table. "I'm Baron William Drummond Stewart, you piece of shit." Then the Baron knocked him out of the chair with a punch.

Ah, the death of Lady Drummond. I really am *being made to atone for all my sins this day.*

"Unkce," the scarred Indian said, causing Frémont to smirk.

"Lake Full of Shit," Frémont repeated. "Long after you are dead, Ambassador Poinsett, Nicollet will still have the last laugh with his map."

"The Order of Eos will hardly believe what they see printed, but why did you dirty your hands in all of this?" Stewart asked Poinsett. "Do you even know what the Al Marakk Map is?"

"Just another stone in the river," Poinsett said. "I should have destroyed it when Krasdan brought it to me, but I had too much appreciation for the irony of it."

"Irony?" Frémont mocked bitterly. "How so? It brought the death of the two greatest men I've known in my life? Is that the irony?"

"The irony is that it was all a wild goose chase. Nicollet didn't find anything. George Fanshaw didn't find anything. Henry Schoolcraft didn't find anything. The Jesuits didn't find anything. Pierre-Charles Le Sueur didn't find anything. Baron Lahontan didn't find anything. Do you know why no one found anything? Because the Al Marakk map and the Philosopher's Stone are childish superstitions. There is no place for men like Nicollet in the modern world."

"If you don't believe any of the legends, why did you have an old woman murdered?" Stewart asked. "Don't forget, today you will pay for more than just the death of Nicollet. You'll pay for the tens of thousands who died from smallpox on the prairie, and you'll pay for the death of my aunt and cousin. Death has come for you. What do you have to say for yourself?"

"I had two choices," Poinsett said. "I either had to prove it was all a lie... or to keep lunatics from ever finding their Great Work. I joined the Freemasons hoping to find a brotherhood beyond the superstitions of the church, but even in their ranks, ritual and superstition clouds their judgment. America has a chance to be the light of reason for the rest of the world, but not in the shadow of superstition. I tried to welcome the savages to this new world but they are as stubborn in their beliefs as Christians and Freemasons. Sometimes, when propagating new plants, you just have to cut away the old growth so new growth can appear."

"I've heard enough," Stewart said.

"So have I," the scarred Indian added.

Even Frémont nodded.

THE ALCHEMIST'S MAP

This is the end. Poinsett reached out his shaking hand and grasped the poison with his fingers. "You might kill me, but you will not stop the world I've planted from coming to fruition." Poinsett lifted the glass vial. "Shall we make a toast?"

Frémont nodded slowly. "To Nicollet."

"To Nicollet," Poinsett repeated and drank down the cold liquid. *And to Manifest Destiny.*

EPILOGUE

LAKE MANITO
1852

High above Lake Manito, an epic battle continued in the stars. Ojiig the Fisher Cat stood watch in the northern sky while the rest of the cosmos spun around it.

Along the horizon, the Wintermaker rose in the night sky. The human-shaped constellation, with its distinctive hunting belt, marked the arrival of winter, although the Leaves Falling Moon had just ended and the Freezing Over Moon had just begun.

And somewhere in the River of Souls, my father Chagobay floats also.

Nanakonan felt the warmth of his small fire as he gazed up at the stars.

He found Kiou-hatten-nanank, the star that does not move, and remembered how his father and Nicollet had talked about Maang the

THE ALCHEMIST'S MAP

Loon, which held the North Star. Nowhere in the sky, however, could he see the Serpent Star, the comet that had brought Nicollet.

Did we fail? Or was Nicollet not the one from prophecy?

The Serpent Star had come when Nanakonan was just a boy, and now he was a man, already past the age when he should have taken a wife and started his own family. According to his father and Nicollet, the Serpent Star arrived once a generation, which meant he had to prepare himself to pass his stories and knowledge to the next generation.

Long before Chief Bad Earth of the Pillagers had abducted his father and Nicollet on the Blue Knife River, the lake was known for being cursed, which allowed Nanakonan to live alone in physical beauty and spiritual darkness.

I will build a home along this bluff and find a wife at Leech Lake next spring, he decided and stood from the fire to retire to his flimsy shelter of birch bark and deer hide.

But something caused him to pause.

Staring out over the lake, he spotted the slightest motion far off in the distance, where the wild rice fields skirted the outlet leading to the Crow Wing River. In the darkness, a single canoe crossed Lake Manito.

Nanakonan ran into his shelter to arm himself.

By the time he returned, the men were halfway across the width of the lake, angling directly toward his bluff overlooking the Blue Knife River. He took out one of the arrows from his quiver, quickly tore off a piece of his sleeve, and wrapped it around the tip of the arrow, which he set upon the dying coals of the fire. When it lit, he notched it and fired it in the distant lake.

The paddlers stopped, seeing both the streak of fire and the sound of the arrow striking the cold water.

Nanakonan steadied himself behind a tree, his rifle now at his shoulder as he leaned against the tree for support.

Put a hole in the canoe and Lake Manito can do the killing for me.

"We seek Nanakonan, son of Chagobay the Midē´."

It was an American voice that called out.

"Chagobay is dead, and his son has fled into Canada. Who are you?"

There were three figures in the canoe, enough to overwhelm him if he did not deal with them properly.

"We are friends of Nicollet," the American voice answered.

"If you are truly friends of Nicollet, then you will understand why I would rather shoot you than trust the voice of a stranger."

"I am Taopi," a deeper, gruff voice answered. "Adoptive father of Little Bird, daughter of Red Blanket Woman."

The name was enough, but he remained cautious. "Who are the others with you?"

The American answered, "I am David Faribault, son of Jean-Baptiste Faribault, friend of the Eastern Dakota."

"And the other?" Nanakonan asked.

"I am Iron Walker, Manza-Ostag Mani, son of Chief Sleepy Eyes of the Sisseton."

"May we proceed?" Faribault called out.

"Know that I hold your lives at the end of my rifle. You may proceed to the mouth of the Blue Knife River but stay in your canoe until I give you word."

Fifteen years had passed since Nanakonan stood at the prow of the canoe to lead Nicollet and the rest of his expedition into the sacred waters of Lake Manito, but only Nicollet had traveled across the lake to the place where the earth bled blue. Nanakonan picked up his weapons, and in the dim starlight, followed the trail that led to the wide mouth of the river. He stopped before stepping into the open, picking a thick walnut tree as protection.

The canoe approached cautiously, and upon hitting a shallow sand

THE ALCHEMIST'S MAP

bar, waited. "Why do you seek the son of a heretic and traitor?"

"Chagobay knew the truth about Nicollet, and trusted him with secrets. Nicollet died protecting the secrets told by Chagobay, and now we have come to offer ourselves to protect these same secrets."

How do they know?

"Nicollet is dead," Taopi said. "Killed by men who seek your Water Drum."

"Mighty Chief Wahanantan is dead of old age," Iron Walker said, "and his son Waneta was killed by cowards because of his blindness. When my father Sleepy Eyes dies, we will be the last of the Guardians of the Frontier."

"What would the Sioux know of the Water Drum?" Nanakonan asked bitterly.

"The fate of all nations are tied to the Water Drum," Faribault said. "My mother, a Dakota, knew it as the 'White Egg,' which will be used to fight the one known as 'No Soul.' My French father called it the 'Philosopher's Stone.' Nicollet came to these lands seeking the truth about the legends, and died because of it. If you have become its caretaker, we have come to give you our aid and assistance. This wampum belt given to Nicollet is proof of our intentions. Let us show you our faces so that we might speak plainly."

Upon their faces, caked blue earth showed their connection to Nicollet, and Nanakonan invited them to sit at his fire to learn more.

Taopi told him what had happened to Nicollet after their paths diverged at the Blue Knife, including the harrowing tale of murder on the trip to Madeline Island.

Next, Iron Walker told him about Nicollet's trip to Lake Shetek and the Pipestone quarry on the advice of the mystical shaman Nicollet met in St. Louis.

Finally, Faribault told him about Nicollet's journey to the Haunted

Valley, where they found remnants of the same blue vitriol Nicollet had collected along the Blue Knife. "Nicollet returned to Washington to try to protect both our nations, but not even a great man like Nicollet can stop the inevitable."

"When Nicollet did not return as he promised, I feared the worst," Nanakonan said. "My father thought the Serpent Star was a sign that the Seventh Fire had come to an end. He believed Nicollet was the boy with a strange light in his eyes."

"If not for Nicollet, our nations would have gone to war again, leaving the tattered land to be taken that much sooner by the Americans," Taopi said. "Wise chief Wahanantan spoke of the same Serpent Star bringing others like Nicollet in previous generations. He might not have been the one to wield the stone, but he did his part."

"The Serpent Star," Faribault said, "comes every seventy-five years, and perhaps the next one will bring another great man like Nicollet to guide the way. We will be old men by that time, but we must decide what to do today."

"What is there to decide?" Nanakonan asked.

The three men looked at each other indecisively.

Faribault started, "We have powerful allies. The strength of the Black Robes has been restored, and all I need to do is speak the word to Father De Smet and he would send Jesuit priests to our aid."

Taopi added, "Brunia, who you knew as an honorable man, has a wealthy, powerful friend who understands what your father Chagobay protected, but the secret of the Water Drum only passed into the possession of the Chippewa when the Serpent Star came in 1759. Before that, it was guarded by the Dakota, until a Frenchman found it in 1682."

"The four of us must make a decision," Faribault said. "Do we fight against the future like the Tizaptanons, or do we make peace with it like Sleepy Eyes suggests? Do we choose Free Will or Fate?"

THE ALCHEMIST'S MAP

"It seems your decision has already been made," Nanakonan said. "You've come to steal it from me, with or without my permission."

The men did not respond for a few moments, and Nanakonan felt the weight of his knife at his side.

"Nicollet went to the grave wondering if he'd found the legendary Philosopher's Stone," Taopi said. "He is the reason we are here today. Tomorrow, with your permission, we want to search the place where he was abducted by the Pillagers."

"And if I do not grant permission?"

Taopi smirked. "It does not matter now, does it? Your return to this place has confirmed everything, even without holding the proof in our hands."

Nanakonan looked back into the stars, to the River of Souls, the Wintermaker, and Ojiig the Fisher Cat. "Then tomorrow I will show you the truth, and you will depart in peace, and leave me to the destiny fate has chosen."

Even though the bleeding star was no longer visible, it followed an inevitable path, already beyond the rings of Saturn and the frozen blue of Neptune, where it would slowly turn for another glimpse into the world of men.

THE END

AUTHOR'S NOTE

I WAS BORN in the modern world at a place once home to the Oceti Sakowin. Raised in the city of Sioux Falls and later rural Minnehaha county, I had to look beyond shopping malls and gas stations to discover the history of my childhood home. Surrounded by folks who looked like me, I developed a curiosity for the places and faces of indigenous South Dakota. Visits to the Black Hills, Sicha Hollow, Fort Sisseton, Pipestone, and the Falls, as well as my limited encounters with modern Sioux acquaintances (collectively the Seven Council Fires and specifically the Dakota), quickly separated the fantasy of Longfellow's love story of Hiawatha and Minnehaha from the reality of life in reservations such as Pine Ridge and Rosebud.

As an adult, I moved to Minnesota, where intriguing names like Mankato, Blue Earth, Sleepy Eye, Le Sueur, Sibley, and Nicollet sparked new obsessions, and ultimately, led me to write *The Alchemist's Map*. Recently, I spent three years walking in the footsteps of the "Pilgrim of Science," Joseph Nicollet, in an attempt to understand, once again, where reality and fantasy converged.

Just as Nicollet tried to understand his mysterious predecessor, I also tried to understand the enigmatic man who mapped the upper midwest, leaving behind clues to an audacious assertion. *The Alchemist's Map* is a work of fiction (the Philosopher's Stone *can't* be real, right?), and the characters, places, and incidents are products of my imagination. Any resemblance to actual events or locales or persons, now long dead, is entirely coincidental. However, I faithfully followed Nicollet's expeditions, where he met the Chippewa (Anishinaabe), Sioux (Oceti Sakowin), and dozens of fascinating historical figures.

My goal for writing *The Alchemist's Map* was to write an adventure that merged the fantasy of *Song of Hiawatha* with the realism of true history, one that would earn me an approving wink from Professor Nicollet.

Thank you for joining Nicollet on his secret quest to find the Philosopher's Stone.

Sincerely,
Jason Lee Willis

ACKNOWLEDGEMENTS

FIRST AND FOREMOST, I wish to thank my wife and cheerleader, Julie, who indulged my road trips ranging from Nova Scotia to Minnesota and endured countless mornings of me crashing around the house at 4:50am to get my thousand words written before the day began.

Next, I'd like to thank the team at Fox Pointe Publishing for believing in this unique tale. Thank you especially to Kiersten Hall, who trusted in me and the premise of a Bilbo Baggins character going on an Indiana Jones adventure set in 19th century Minnesota. I tip my hat to Chelsea Farr, my editor, who had the job of untangling all the knotted plotlines that can only make sense to the writer; her discerning mind and probing curiosity added that spritz of Caswell No. 6 to an already garish ensemble. A special thanks to Becca Hudson for giving the cover a stunning jacket that Nicollet hopefully would have worn with pride.

The challenge of sorting through history and storytelling fell upon my team of friends and colleagues, who endured reading beta copies of the tale, helping me determine what aspects of Nicollet's amazing life worked for a reader. The earliest readers, Ron Willis and John Pfeffer, read it daily on the first Google Docs. Then the early drafts were read by Sandi Garlow, Nan Dashwood, Baylee Pawsey, Tony Amundson, Jim Swanson, Sarah Karels, Clara Hughes, Roxy Janke, Christie Jones, Kathy Gjerde, and Collette Willis, who helped me find focus. My later drafts were read by Dave Guertin, Jerry Thul, Melanie Urban, Caleb and Curtis at North Star, Chandler See, and Annie Schmitz, all of whom helped guide the story back home.

Special thanks to my "Footsteps of Nicollet" team, who came with me over three summers as we traveled by wagon (Toyota minivan), kayak, and canoe on the same expedition routes that Nicollet took in 1836, 1838, and 1839. John Pfeffer, Jonah Willis, Chandler See, Jordan Christensen, Julie Willis, Dave Guertin, Grace Carleton, Mary Pfeffer, and Nell Gehrke all had a part in my crazy road trips and wild canoe adventures.

My gratitude to the research of Martha Bray for her invaluable biographical work on the life of Joseph Nicollet; William Warren's *History of the Ojibwe People;* Frederic Baraga's *A Dictionary of the Ojibwe Language;* Warren Upham's *Minnesota Geographic Names;* Thomas Hughes' *History of Blue Earth County;* and Aleck Paul's "Origin of the Constellation Fisher."

CAST OF CHARACTERS

THOSE FROM EUROPE

Agassiz, Louis: A Swiss-born biologist and geologist and pioneer in Ice Age theory.*

Arago, François: A renowned French astronomer, mathematician, and physicist. Director of the Paris Observatory, freemason, and supporter of the Carbonari.*

Battersby, Christina: William Drummond Stewart's servant and the mother of his child, George.*

Beranger, Gerard: A French merchant in Paris.

Cairns, Sgt. Lewis: A friend of William Drummond Stewart's who served with him in the Napoleonic Wars. Stewart charged him with investigating the murder of his Aunt Maggie.

Champollion, Jean-François: A French scholar, linguist, and Egyptologist famous for deciphering the Rosetta Stone.*

Croÿ-Solre, Gustave-Max: A French cardinal and member of the House of Croÿ.*

Charles X: The King of France and member of the Bourbon Restoration.*

De Beligny, Capt. Gaspard: A French tourist and member of Nicollet's 1838 expedition.

De Montmort, Viscount: A French attaché and member of Nicollet's 1838 expedition.*

De Smet, Father Pierre-Jean: A Jesuit missionary sent to care for Native American tribes.*

Drummond, Lady Margaret: A Scottish noblewoman and the aunt of William Drummond Stewart.

Drummond, Lord William: A Scottish diplomat, poet, and philosopher from Logiealmond. Margaret Drummond's brother and William Drummond Stewart's uncle.*

Drummond, Susan: Margaret Drummond's teenage niece and the cousin of William Drummond Stewart.

Flandin, Eugene: The son of a wealthy French merchant and a member of Nicollet's 1838 expedition.*

Forsberg: A Swedish-born voyageur and part of Nicollet's 1838 expedition.

Geyer, Karl Andreas: A German botanist. Member of Nicollet and Stewart expeditions.*

Herschel, John: An English astronomer, chemist, mathematician, and inventor.*

Krai, Krasdan: A Kubanian spy subordinate to the "benefactor."

LaPlace, Pierre-Simon: A French scholar and mentor to Napoleon Bonaparte and Joseph Nicollet.*

Lavoisier, Cosette: A French woman who worked as a housekeeper for Nicollet in Paris.

Leeves, Julianna: The daughter of William Leeves of Sussex, later known as Elizabeth Sabine.*

Lupo, Father Blanco: An investigator from a covert Christian organization, the Periphery.

Nicollet, Joseph: Renowned astronomer, mathematician, and explorer.*

Palissy, Jacques: A French spy subordinate to Krasdan Krai.

Sabine, Sir Edward: An Irish astronomer, geophysicist, and explorer.*
Simmons, Conrad: An investigative agent for the Catholic Church.
Stewart, Sir William Drummond: A Scottish nobleman, the Hero of Waterloo, and an American frontiersman.*
Von Humboldt, Alexander: A Prussian geographer, explorer, meteorologist, and naturalist.*
Whitmore: Margaret Drummond's manservant.

THOSE FROM THE EAST

Abert, Col. John Jacob: The founder of the Corps of Topographical Engineers.*
Astor, John Jacob: America's first multi-millionaire and the founder of the American Fur Company.*
Benton, Jessie: The daughter of Senator Thomas Hart Benton.*
Benton, Thomas Hart: A Missouri Senator and an architect of Manifest Destiny.*
Crooks, Ramsay: A Scottish-Canadian fur trader who later managed the American Fur Company during its expansion into the Oregon Territory.*
Delhut, Solomon: A former American Fur Company agent turned Detroit businessman and a member of the Order of Eos.*
Eastin, Mary Ann: The niece of President Andrew Jackson. Served as "First Lady" following the death of Jackson's wife.*

Fanshaw, George: A British-American geologist, responsible for the Albany and Schenectady Railroad, a survey of the Louisiana Purchase, the removal of the Cherokee from Georgia, and negotiating the border between the United States and Canada.*

Frémont, John C.: A mathematician and novice explorer on Nicollet's 1838 and 1839 expeditions.*

Gray, Prof. Asa: A professor of botany at Harvard University.*

Gunn, Malcolm: An associate of Solomon Delhut's and fellow member of the Order of Eos.

Hassler, Ferdinand: A Swiss surveyor responsible for mapping the east coast of the United States.*

Jackson, Dr. Charles T.: An American physician, chemist, and geologist who made geological exploration of Nova Scotia, New England, and later served as copper consultant in Michigan.*

Poinsett, Joel: A South Carolina diplomat, physician, and explorer known for developing the Poinsettia and establishing the Smithsonian Museum.*

THOSE FROM THE UPPER MISSISSIPPI

Bad Earth: A Pillager chief near Leech Lake.*

Bottineau, Pierre: A Métis trader at Fort Snelling.*

Boutwell, Hester Crooks: The daughter of Ramsay Crooks and the wife of William.*

Boutwell, William: A protestant missionary and explorer, husband of Hester.*

Brunia: A Métis guide from northern Minnesota.*

Chagobay: An Ojibwe Midē′ and guide for the 1836 Nicollet Expedition.*

Clément, Antoine: A Métis and a friend/associate of William Drummond Stewart.*

Colton, Lt. Edgar: A sharp-shooter stationed at Fort Snelling and veteran of the Black Hawk War.

Emerson, Dr. John: Fort Snelling's surgeon.*

Faribault, Jean Baptiste: A French-Canadian fur trader who settled near Fort Snelling. Father of David, George, and Alexander, the founder of the city of Faribault. Married to Elizabeth Pelagie Ainse, half-Dakota daughter of a British superintendent.*

Faribault, David: A Sioux translator hired for the 1838 Nicollet Expedition.*

Flat Mouth: The elder Ojibwe chieftain in northern Minnesota.*

Lyons, Capt. Daniel: A southern officer noted for his small pox scars.*

Maxwell, Big Moe: An American Fur Company cook hired for Nicollet's expeditions.*

Nanakonan: The son of Chippewa Midē′ Chagobay.*

Robinson, Harriet: An African-American kept in slavery by the Tolliver (Taliaferro) family. Future wife of Dred Scott.*

Schoolcraft, Henry: An Indian Agent, explorer, and writer stationed at Madeline Island on Lake Superior. Credited with discovering the source of the Mississippi River.*

Scott, Dred: An African-American kept in slavery by Dr. John Emerson. Future husband of Harriet Robinson Scott.*

Sha-Koo-Zoo-Shetek: A member of the fictional Glusta tribe and a traveling shaman in search of the Wishwee.*

Sibley, Hank: An American Fur Trade manager from Michigan stationed near Fort Snelling.*

Tolliver, Elizabeth: The wife of Lawrence Tolliver.*

Tolliver, Major Lawrence: An Indian Agent and commanding officer at Fort Snelling.*

THOSE FROM THE PRAIRIE

Black Eagle: A Wahpekute chief near Spirit Lake, Iowa.*

Carson, Kit: An American fur-trapper and wilderness guide.*

Clewett: A voyageur and member of Nicollet's 1838 expedition.*

Grey Heron: A Tizaptonan chief in southern Minnesota.

Iron Walker (or **Manza Ostag Mani**): The oldest son of Chief Sleepy Eyes.*

Laframboise, Joseph: A Métis fur-trader stationed at the Grand Oasis.*

Little Bird: Red Blanket Woman and Hank Sibley's infant daughter.*

Ohanzee: A renegade member of the exiled Tizaptanon band of Dakota.

Old Bets: An elderly Sioux woman working as a ferrywoman at Fort Snelling.*

Sleepy Eyes (or **Ishtakaba**): A chief of the Sisseton band of Dakota.*

Stands on Clouds (later known as **Cut Nose**): A guide for the 1838 Undine Expedition.*

Taopi, Sgt. Jim (or **Sugmanitu Tonka, or Wounded Man**): A survivor of a Chippewa attack on Kaposia.*

Red Blanket Woman: The daughter of Chief Bad Hail and wife to Hank Sibley.*

Renville, Joseph: A French-Canadian soldier who settled at Lac Qui Parle to act as a translator, fur trader, and missionary. Father of Joseph Renville Jr.*

Renville Jr., Joseph: A guide, translator, and member of Nicollet's 1838 expedition.*

Thunder Face: The chief of the renegade Tizaptonans at Two Lakes.*

Wanata: The adult son of Chief Wahanantan of the Yanktonai.*

Wahanantan (or **He Who Charges**): The chief of the Yanktonai Sioux at Devil's Lake.*

*= *denotes a character based on a real-life historical figure*

INDIGENOUS NAMES AND TERMS

ANISHINAABEG: A large ethnic group of tribes (including the Potawatomi) ranging from Nova Scotia to Minnesota, where they are also known as the Ojibwe or Chippewa. Originally brothers to the Micmac Tribe of Nova Scotia, the *Being Made Out of Nothing* traveled from the east along the **SEVEN FIRES** migration until settling in Minnesota.

FISHER CAT, or **OJIIG:** An Anishinaabe legend for the Big Dipper, describing a battle between the heroic Ojiig and evil forces trying to bring continual winter. After freeing the summer birds from their captors, Ojiig fled into the stars.

GREAT THUNDERBIRD, or **GITCHI-ANIMIKII:** A fictionalized myth based upon the legend of "Iyash and the Horned Serpent." In Anishinaabe culture, the thunderbirds were spiritual beings and the nemesis of water serpents. The Dakota also have a Great Thunderbird, the mortal enemy of the Horned Serpent, who is called "Wakinyan."

KEY OF DEATH: A fictional myth based on Nicollet's encounter with Sha-Koo-Zoo-Shetec-Warrett at Council Bluffs, who Nicollet described as "a fine young man with large, blue eyes, full of gentleness." Please note: **GLUSTA** is a Dakota word for "peacemaker" but is not a real tribe.

MANABOZHO: An Anishinaabe deity who took on a human form to guide the people. He is also referred to as Hiawatha, Nanabozho, Nanabush, and Glooscap in other cultures.

MANITO, or **MANITOU:** An Anishinaabe word for spirit. In some traditions, Gitche Manitou can refer to "great spirit" or supreme being. In other traditions, manito refers to a water spirit. **MISHI-GINEBIG** is another term for a water spirit, a horned serpent prevalent in numerous cultures, including the Dakota's **UNKTEHI**.

MIIGIS, or **MEGIS:** Belonging to the Seven Fires Prophecy, sacred shells (cowrie) believed to have led the Anishinaabe on their migration along the Seven Stopping Places.

OCETI SAKOWIN: The Seven Council Fires. Also known as the Sioux. Seven tribes ranging from Minnesota to the Black Hills.
   The Eastern Sioux: also known as **Dakota** and **Santee,** or the *Guardians of the Frontier* in Nicollet's time:
      Mdewakanton, or **Dwellers of Spirit Lake,** located south of Mille Lacs
      Warpekutey, or **Leaf Shooters,** located south of the lower Minnesota River
      Warpeton, or **People of the Leaves,** located along the upper Minnesota River.
      Sisseton, or Fish Scale Village, located in southwestern Minnesota.
   Middle Sioux:
      Yankton, or **End Village,** located in eastern North/South Dakota.
      Yanktonnan, or **Little End Village,** located in central South Dakota
   Teton Sioux:
      Lakota, or **People of the Prairies,** located west of the Missouri River.

SERPENT STAR: A fictional term for the appearance of Halley's Comet.

SEVEN FIRES: An Anishinabeg prophecy that marks time periods, or fires, as well as key spiritual teachings. It describes historical events as well as unfulfilled future events.

SEVEN STOPPING PLACES of the Anishinaabeg's Seven Fires migration, which began amongst the Abenaki of Nova Scotia:

Mooniyaang, or "turtle-shaped island," or Montreal Island

Wayaanag-gakaabikaa, or "concave-waterfalls," now known as Niagara Falls.

Waawiyegamaa, the "round lake," Lake St. Clair near modern Detroit.

Manido Minising, or Manitoulin Island.

Baawiting, or "The Rapids," of Sault. Ste. Marie, where they first made contact with the Sioux. Also the first place recorded by explorers.

Mooningwanekaaning, later known as Madeline Island of the Apostle Islands in Shaugawaumikong Bay.

Land Where Food Grows Upon the Waters. The exact location of the 7th Stopping place is disputed. Some believed it to be Fond Du Lac, Mille Lacs, or even Turtle Mountain in North Dakota.

SPIRIT LAKE: A prevalent concept in Dakota culture, often referring to a sacred island of creation. Nicollet noted several locations denoting a Spirit Lake.

TURTLE ISLAND: A common metaphor found in many Native tribes in North American to refer to the continent. It also is found in many creation and flood myths, where the turtle's shell becomes a rebirth of the world. In the Anishinaabe tradition, Turtle Island represents the location of the Seventh Stopping Place, whose location west of Lake Superior is widely debated.

WABENO, or **FIRE HANDLER:** Part of the Midewiwin religious system, which includes priestly **MIDĒ′** and **JESSAKKID**. Please note: the Wijigan (skull) Clan is a fictional invention.

WATER DRUM: A key part of the Seventh Fire prophecy. Its discovery will bring healing and a rekindling of the Sacred Fire.

WINTERMAKER, or **BIBOONIKE:** An Anishinaabe legend whose name varies from community to community, but is collectively represented by the constellation Orion, the hunter.

WISHWEE: A Dakota legend chronicling the journey of a warrior who ultimately battles an evil monster known as **NO SOUL**, who is defeated by an object described as a **WHITE EGG**.

DISCUSSION QUESTIONS

1.) If you could ask the author any question, what would it be?

2.) What scene stuck with you the most?

3.) If you were to make a movie of this book, who would you cast?

4.) What character in the book would you like to meet?

5.) If you were to embark on an expedition, whose role would you fill in the party?

6.) Evaluate the scientific "hats" that Nicollet wore. Where was his greatest talent? Mathematics? Astronomy? Meteorology? Cartography? Anthropology? Geology?

7.) Let's talk about Nicollet's midlife crisis! What was he searching for in America? How does the novel incorporate the loss of time?

8.) Both the scientific and religious communities distrusted Nicollet for his affiliation with the other, yet Nicollet boldly walked the line between the two. What were some of his achievements of faith and science? How did this struggle define Nicollet?

9.) Nicollet's expeditions defined a new territory. What did you learn about the places and faces described by Nicollet? How do they compare to your own travels?

10.) During Nicollet's time in America, he visited several Native American cultures? What did you learn from his brief encounters? How does it compare to your prior understanding?

11.) How do Nicollet's experiences as a young man in Cluses during the French Revolution shape his character? How do they affect his treatment of others?

12.) Is Nicollet more alchemist or scientist?

13.) Although the U.S. government funded a scientific expedition, Nicollet left the term "UNDINE" on his map. What does the Undine represent?

14.) What attracted people (both male and female) to Nicollet? Discuss the many loves of his life. Did Nicollet have a true love?

15.) Discuss the relationship between Stewart and Brunia/Clément. How was Stewart's relationship with Nicollet similar/different?

16.) What prompted Stewart to travel to the Holy Land instead of returning to North America?

17.) Although Nicollet's expeditions did not include women, women like Mary Ann Estin and Old Bets still had a role in the events. Which female character stood out to you the most and why?

18.) Discuss the metaphor of puppet-masters in the context of the story. Which puppet-master had the greatest impact?

19.) What was it about Nicollet that inspired loyalty and friendship in so many different people? What was it about him that earned him his enemies?

20.) What would Nicollet have thought about his friends teaming up after his death to avenge him? Or about how they became Guardians of the Frontier together?

21.) If Nicollet had lived, how might the ending of the book have been different?

22.) Here be dragons! The renowned astronomer visited sacred locations, explored legends, and referenced alchemy on his map. What are your views on the fantasy elements in the story? Is it possible the real-life Nicollet was also searching for the Philosopher's Stone?

23.) How do the mythologies, folktales, and prophecies of the different North American and European cultures mentioned in the book overlap? Do you know of any other cultures that have something like a Philosopher's Stone in their mythos? Are they guarded by "evil" creatures or wielded by "good" warriors?

24.) In real life, Chief Sleepy Eyes advocated for his people to integrate with American culture, and Jesuit missionary Father De Smet helped provide a bridge of cultures, as well. However, by 1862, Minnesota erupted into war between settlers and the Dakota. What went wrong? What problems were rooted in the time of Nicollet?

25.) How does Sergeant Jim Taopi represent different facets of Dakota culture? How does the fictional character compare to the real historical figure?

26.) Was there anything else Nicollet could have done to slow down Manifest Destiny? How much did his accomplishments and actions contribute to the progress of Manifest Destiny?

27.) During his expeditions, Nicollet would have witnessed slavery in the deep south as well in Minnesota, where he met Dred Scott. How were the events of Nicollet's time a precursor to the Civil War?

28.) Which villains in this story can be defended? Which "good guys" can be criticized or condemned?

29.) In what ways did you notice the story diverge from history?

30.) Halley's Comet is a once-in-a-generation event. Two generations removed from Nicollet's era, what are some issues we still share with the folks of 1835?

ABOUT THE AUTHOR

JASON LEE WILLIS is a professional storyteller who both writes and teaches. As a high school English teacher, he specializes in indigenous studies, creative writing, and mythology. When he wears the hat of a writer, he wakes every morning at five a.m. to write a thousand words prior to beginning his day job. Jason grew up in South Dakota and currently lives in Minnesota, where he lives the life of a hobbit by gardening, writing, walking around barefoot, wearing vests, fishing, and going on adventures with his wife Julie.